PRAISE FOR IAN HAMILTON

PRAISE FOR *THE WATER RAT OF WANCHAI*

WINNER OF THE ARTHUR ELLIS AWARD FOR BEST FIRST NOVEL

"Ian Hamilton's *The Water Rat of Wanchai* is a smart, action-packed thriller of the first order, and Ava Lee, a gay Asian-Canadian forensics accountant with a razor-sharp mind and highly developed martial arts skills, is a protagonist to be reckoned with. We were impressed by Hamilton's tight plotting; his well-rendered settings, from the glitz of Bangkok to the grit of Guyana; and his ability to portray a wide range of sharply individualized characters in clean but sophisticated prose." — Judges' Citation, Arthur Ellis Award for Best First Novel

"Ava Lee is tough, fearless, quirky, and resourceful, and she has more — well, you know — than a dozen male detectives I can think of… Hamilton has created a true original in Ava Lee." — Linwood Barclay, author of *No Time for Goodbye*

"If the other novels [in the series] are half as good as this debut by Ian Hamilton, then readers are going to celebrate. Hamilton has created a marvellous character in Ava Lee… This is a terrific story that's certain to be on the Arthur Ellis Best First Novel list." — *Globe and Mail*

"[Ava Lee's] lethal knowledge… torques up her sex appeal to the approximate level of a female lead in a Quentin Tarantino film." — *National Post*

"The heroine in *The Water Rat of Wanchai* by Ian Hamilton sounds too good to be true, but the heroics work better that way… formidable… The story breezes along with something close to total clarity… Ava is unbeatable at just about everything. Just wait for her to roll out her bak mei against the bad guys. She's perfect. She's fast." — *Toronto Star*

"Imagine a book about a forensic accountant that has tension, suspense, and action... When the central character looks like Lucy Liu, kicks like Jackie Chan, and has a travel budget like Donald Trump, the story is anything but boring. *The Water Rat of Wanchai* is such a beast... I look forward to the next one, *The Disciple of Las Vegas*."
— *Montreal Gazette*

"[A] tomb-raiding Dragon Lady Lisbeth, *sans* tattoo and face metal."
— *Winnipeg Free Press*

"An enjoyable romp with a feisty, ingenious heroine whose lethal martial arts skills are as formidable as her keen mind." — *Publishers Weekly*

"Readers will discern in Ava undertones of Lisbeth Salander, the ferocious protagonist of the late Stieg Larsson's crime novels... She, too, is essentially a loner, and small, and physically brutal... There are suggestions in *The Water Rat of Wanchai* of deeper complexities waiting to be more fully revealed. Plus there's pleasure, both for Ava and readers, in the puzzle itself: in figuring out where money has gone, how to get it back, and which humans, helpful or malevolent, are to be dealt with where, and in what ways, in the process... Irresistible."
— Joan Barfoot, *London Free Press*

"*The Water Rat of Wanchai* delivers on all fronts... feels like the beginning of a crime-fighting saga... A great story told with colour, energy, and unexpected punch." — *Hamilton Spectator*

"The best series fiction leaves readers immersed in a world that is both familiar and fresh. Seeds planted early bear fruit later on, creating a rich forest that blooms across a number of books... [Hamilton] creates a terrific atmosphere of suspense..." — *Quill & Quire*

"The book is an absolute page-turner... Hamilton's knack for writing snappy dialogue is evident... I recommend getting in on the ground floor with this character, because for Ava Lee, the sky's the limit."
— *Inside Halton*

"A fascinating story of a hunt for stolen millions. And the hunter, Ava Lee, is a compelling heroine: tough, smart, and resourceful."
— Meg Gardiner, author of *The Nightmare Thief*

"Few heroines are as feisty as *The Girl with the Dragon Tattoo*'s Lisbeth Salander, but Ian Hamilton's Ava Lee could give her a run for her money... Gripping... [Ava is] smart, gutsy, and resourceful."
— *Stylist UK*

"With Ava Lee comes a new star in the world of crime-thrillers... Hamilton has produced a suspenseful and gripping novel featuring a woman who is not afraid of anything... Captivating and hard to put down." — *dapd/sda*

"Thrillers don't always have to be Scandinavian to work. Ava Lee is a wonderful Chinese Canadian investigator who uses unconventional methods of investigation in a mysterious Eastern setting." — *Elle* (Germany)

"Ava has flair, charm, and sex appeal... *The Water Rat of Wanchai* is a successful first book in a series, which will definitely have you longing for more." — *Sonntag-Express*

"Hamilton is in the process of writing six books and film rights have already been sold. If the other cases are similar to this first one, Ava Lee is sure to quickly shake up Germany's thriller business."
— *Handelsblatt*

"Brilliantly researched and incredibly exciting!" — *Bücher*

"Page-turning till the end of the book!... Ava Lee is the upcoming crime star." — *dpa*

"Exciting thriller debut with an astonishing end." — *Westdeutsche Zeitung*

"Seldom does one get a thriller about white-collar crime, with an intelligent, independent lesbian and Asian protagonist. It's also rare to find a book with such interesting and exotic settings... Readers will find great amusement in Ava's unconventional ways and will certainly enjoy accompanying her on her travels." — *Literaturkurier*

PRAISE FOR *THE DISCIPLE OF LAS VEGAS*

FINALIST, BARRY AWARD FOR BEST ORIGINAL TRADE PAPERBACK

"I started to read *The Disciple of Las Vegas* at around ten at night. And I did something I have only done with two other books (Cormac McCarthy's *The Road* and Douglas Coupland's *Player One*): I read the novel in one sitting. Ava Lee is too cool. She wonderfully straddles two worlds and two identities. She does some dastardly things and still remains our hero thanks to the charm Ian Hamilton has given her on the printed page. It would take a female George Clooney to portray her in a film. The action and plot move quickly and with power. Wow. A punch to the ear, indeed." — J. J. Lee, author of *The Measure of a Man*

"I loved *The Water Rat of Wanchai,* the first novel featuring Ava Lee. Now, Ava and Uncle make a return that's even better... Simply irresistible." — Margaret Cannon, *Globe and Mail*

"This is slick, fast-moving escapism reminiscent of Ian Fleming, with more to come in what shapes up as a high-energy, high-concept series." — *Booklist*

"Fast paced... Enough personal depth to lift this thriller above solely action-oriented fare." — *Publishers Weekly*

"Lee is a hugely original creation, and Hamilton packs his adventure with interesting facts and plenty of action." — *Irish Independent*

"Hamilton makes each page crackle with the kind of energy that could easily jump to the movie screen... This riveting read will keep you up late at night." — *Penthouse*

"Hamilton gives his reader plenty to think about... Entertaining." — *Kitchener-Waterloo Record*

PRAISE FOR *THE WILD BEASTS OF WUHAN*

LAMBDA LITERARY AWARD FINALIST: LESBIAN MYSTERY

"Smart and savvy Ava Lee returns in this slick mystery set in the rarefied world of high art... [A] great caper tale. Hamilton has great fun chasing villains and tossing clues about. *The Wild Beasts of Wuhan* is the best Ava Lee novel yet, and promises more and better to come." — Margaret Cannon, *Globe and Mail*

"One of my favourite new mystery series, perfect escapism." — *National Post*

"As a mystery lover, I'm devouring each book as it comes out... What I love in the novels: The constant travel, the high-stakes negotiation, and Ava's willingness to go into battle against formidable opponents, using only her martial arts skills to defend herself... If you want a great read and an education in high-level business dealings, Ian Hamilton is an author to watch." — *Toronto Star*

"Fast-paced and very entertaining." — *Montreal Gazette*

"Ava Lee is definitely a winner." — *Saskatoon Star Phoenix*

"*The Wild Beasts of Wuhan* is an entertaining dip into potentially fatal worlds of artistic skulduggery." — *Sudbury Star*

"Hamilton uses Ava's investigations as comprehensive and intriguing mechanisms for plot and character development." — *Quill & Quire*

"You haven't seen cold and calculating until you've double-crossed this number cruncher. Another strong entry from Arthur Ellis Award–winner Hamilton." — *Booklist*

"An intelligent kick-ass heroine anchors Canadian author Hamilton's excellent third novel featuring forensic accountant Ava Lee... Clearly conversant with the art world, Hamilton makes the intricacies of forgery as interesting as a Ponzi scheme." — *Publishers Weekly*, *Starred Review*

"A lively series about Ava Lee, a sexy forensic financial investigator." — *Tampa Bay Times*

"This book is miles from the ordinary. The main character, Ava Lee is 'the whole package.'" — *Minneapolis Star Tribune*

"A strong heroine is challenged to discover the details of an intercontinental art scheme. Although Hamilton's star Ava Lee is technically a forensic accountant, she's more badass private investigator than desk jockey." — *Kirkus Reviews*

PRAISE FOR *THE RED POLE OF MACAU*

"Ava Lee returns as one of crime fiction's most intriguing characters. *The Red Pole of Macau* is the best page-turner of the season from the hottest writer in the business!" — John Lawrence Reynolds, author of *Beach Strip*

"Ava Lee, that wily, wonderful hunter of nasty business brutes, is back in her best adventure ever... If you haven't yet discovered Ava Lee, start here." — *Globe and Mail*

"The best in the series so far." — *London Free Press*

"Ava [Lee] is a character we all could use at one time or another. Failing that, we follow her in her best adventure yet." — *Hamilton Spectator*

"A romp of a story with a terrific heroine." — *Saskatoon Star Phoenix*

"Fast-paced... The action unfolds like a well-oiled action-flick."
—*Kitchener-Waterloo Record*

"A change of pace for our girl [Ava Lee]... Suspenseful." —*Toronto Star*

"Hamilton packs tremendous potential in his heroine... A refreshingly relevant series. This reader will happily pay House of Anansi for the fifth installment." —*Canadian Literature*

PRAISE FOR *THE SCOTTISH BANKER OF SURABAYA*

"Hamilton deepens Ava's character, and imbues her with greater mettle and emotional fire, to the extent that book five is his best, most memorable, to date." —*National Post*

"In today's crowded mystery market, it's no easy feat coming up with a protagonist who stands out from the pack. But Ian Hamilton has made a great job of it with his Ava Lee books. Young, stylish, Chinese Canadian, lesbian, and a brilliant forensic accountant, Ava is as complex a character as you could want... [A] highly addictive series... Hamilton knows how to keep the pages turning. He eases us into the seemingly tame world of white-collar crime, then raises the stakes, bringing the action to its peak with an intensity and violence that's stomach-churning. His Ava Lee is a winner and a welcome addition to the world of strong female avengers." —*NOW Magazine*

"Most of the series' success rests in Hamilton's tight plotting, attention to detail, and complex powerhouse of a heroine: strong but vulnerable, capable but not impervious... With their tight plotting and crackerjack heroine, Hamilton's novels are the sort of crowd-pleasing, narrative-focused fiction we find all too rarely in this country." —*Quill & Quire*

"Ava is such a cool character, intelligent, Chinese Canadian, unconventional, and original... Irresistible." —*Owen Sound Sun Times*

PRAISE FOR *THE TWO SISTERS OF BORNEO*

NATIONAL BESTSELLER

"There are plenty of surprises waiting for Ava, and for the reader, all uncovered with great satisfaction." — *National Post*

"Ian Hamilton's great new Ava Lee mystery has the same wow factor as its five predecessors. The plot is complex and fast-paced, the writing tight, and its protagonist is one of the most interesting female avengers to come along in a while." — *NOW Magazine* (NNNN)

"The appeal of the Ava Lee series owes much to her brand name lifestyle; it stirs pleasantly giddy emotions to encounter such a devotedly elegant heroine. But, better still, the detailing of financial shenanigans is done in such clear language that even readers who have trouble balancing their bank books can appreciate the way conmen set out to fleece unsuspecting victims." — *Toronto Star*

"Hamilton has a unique gift for concocting sizzling thrillers." — *Edmonton Journal*

"Hamilton has this formula down to an art, but he manages to avoid cliché and his ability to evoke a place keeps the series fresh." — *Globe and Mail*

"From her introduction in *The Water Rat of Wanchai*, Ava Lee has stood as a stylish, street-smart leading lady whose resourcefulness and creativity have helped her to uncover criminal activity in everything from illegal online gambling rings to international art heists. In Hamilton's newest installment to the series, readers accompany Ava on great adventures and to interesting locales, roaming from Hong Kong to the Netherlands to Borneo. The pulse-pounding, fast-paced narrative is chocked full of divergent plot twists and intriguing personalities that make it a popular escapist summer read. The captivating female sleuth does not disappoint as she circles the globe on a quest to uncover an unusually intriguing investment fiasco involving fraud, deception and violence." — *ExpressMilwaukee.com*

"Ava may be the most chic figure in crime fiction." — *Hamilton Spectator*

"The series as a whole is as good as the modern thriller genre gets." — *The Cord*

PRAISE FOR *THE KING OF SHANGHAI*

"The only thing scarier than being ripped off for a few million bucks is being the guy who took it and having Ava Lee on your tail. If Hamilton's kick-ass forensic accountant has your number, it's up." — Linwood Barclay

"One of Ian Hamilton's best." — *Globe and Mail*

"Brilliant, sexy, and formidably martial arts-trained forensic accountant Ava Lee is back in her seventh adventure (after *The Two Sisters of Borneo*)... Ever since his dazzling surprise debut with *The Water Rat of Wanchai*, Hamilton has propelled Ava along through the series with expanded storytelling and nuanced character development: there's always something new to discover about Ava. Fast-paced suspense, exotic locales, and a rich cast of characters (some, like Ava's driver, Sonny, are both dangerous and lovable) make for yet another hugely entertaining hit." — *Publishers Weekly*, *Starred review*

"A luxurious sense of place... Hamilton's knack for creating fascinating detail will keep readers hooked... Good fun for those who like to combine crime fiction with armchair travelling." — *Booklist*

"Ava would be a sure thing to whip everybody, Putin included, at the negotiating table." — *Toronto Star*

"After six novels starring Chinese Canadian Ava Lee and her perilously thrilling exploits, best-selling Canadian author Ian Hamilton has jolted his creation out of what wasn't even yet a rut and hurled her abruptly into a new circumstance, with fresh ambitions." — *London Free Press*

"It's a measure of Hamilton's quality as a thriller writer that he compels your attention even before he starts ratcheting up the suspense." — *Regina Leader Post*

"An unputdownable book that I would highly recommend for all." — *Words of Mystery*

"Ava is as powerful and brilliant as ever." — *Literary Treats*

PRAISE FOR *THE PRINCELING OF NANJING*

NATIONAL BESTSELLER

A KOBO BEST BOOK OF THE YEAR

"The reader is offered plenty of Ava in full flower as the Chinese Canadian glamour puss who happens to be gay, whip smart, and unafraid of whatever dangers come her way." — *Toronto Star*

"Hamilton's Chinese Canadian heroine is one of a kind... [An] exotic thriller that also offers a fascinating inside look at fiscal misconduct in China... As a unique series character, Ava Lee's become indispensable." — *Calgary Herald*

"Ava Lee has a new business, a new look, and, most important, a new triad boss to appreciate her particular financial talents... We know that Ava will come up with a plan and Hamilton will come up with a twist." — *Globe and Mail*

"Like the best series writers — Ian Rankin and Peter Robinson come to mind — Hamilton manages to... keep the Ava Lee books fresh... A compulsive read, a page-turner of the old school... *The Princeling of Nanjing* is a welcome return of an old favourite, and bodes well for future books." — *Quill & Quire*

"Hamilton uses his people and plot to examine Chinese class and power structures that open opportunities for massive depravities and corruptions." — *London Free Press*

"As usual with a Hamilton-Lee novel, matters take a decided twist as the plot unrolls." — *Owen Sound Times*

"One of those grip-tight novels that makes one read 'just one more chapter' and you discover it's 3 a.m. The novel is built on complicated webs artfully woven into clear, magnetic storytelling. Author Ian Hamilton delivers the intrigue within complex and relentless webs in high style and once again proves that everyone, once in their lives, needs an Ava Lee at their backs." — *Canadian Mystery Reviews*

"The best of the Ava Lee series to date... *Princeling* features several chapters of pure, unadulterated financial sleuthing, which both gave me some nerdy feels and tickled my puzzle-loving mind." — *Literary Treats*

"*The Princeling of Nanjing* was another addition to the Ava Lee series that did not disappoint." — *Words of Mystery*

PRAISE FOR *THE COUTURIER OF MILAN*

NATIONAL BESTSELLER

"The latest in the excellent series starring Ava Lee, businesswoman extraordinaire, *The Couturier of Milan* is another winner for Ian Hamilton... The novel is a hoot. At a point where most crime series start to run out of steam, Ava Lee just keeps rolling on." — *Globe and Mail*

"In Ava Lee, Ian Hamilton has created a crime fighter who breaks the mould with every new book (and, frankly, with every new chapter)." — CBC Books

"The pleasure in following Ava's clever plans for countering the bad guys remains as ever a persuasive attraction." — *Toronto Star*

"Fashionably fierce forensics... But Hamilton has built around Ava Lee an award-winning series that absorbs intriguing aspects of both Asian and Canadian cultures." — *London Free Press*

PRAISE FOR *THE IMAM OF TAWI-TAWI*

"The best of the series so far." — *Globe and Mail*

"One of his best... Tightly plotted and quick-moving, this is a spare yet terrifically suspenseful novel." — *Publishers Weekly*

"Combines lots of action with Ava's acute intelligence and ability to solve even the most complex problems." — *Literary Hub*

"Fast-paced, smoothly written, and fun." — *London Free Press*

"An engrossing novel." — *Reviewing the Evidence*

"Hamilton's rapid-fire storytelling moves the tale along at breakneck speed, as Ava globe-trots to put clues together. Hamilton has always had a knack for combing Fleming-style descriptors with modern storytelling devices and character beats, and this book is no different." — *The Mind Reels*

"An engaging and compelling mystery." — *Literary Treats*

PRAISE FOR *THE GODDESS OF YANTAI*
NATIONAL BESTSELLER

"Ava at her most intimate and vulnerable." — *Toronto Star*

"This time, [Ava's] crusade is personal, and so is her outrage." — *London Free Press*

"In *The Goddess of Yantai*... Ava's personal and professional lives collide in a manner that shakes the usually unflappable character." — *Quill & Quire*

"Told in his typical punchy and forthright style, Hamilton's latest thriller is a rapid-fire read that leaves the reader breathless and eagerly anticipating the next installment... This is a series of books that just seems to get better and better."— *The Mind Reels*

"I wanted to just rip through this book... If you love great writing, an intense pace, and a bit of a thrill, then [the Ava Lee novels] are perfect for you."— *Reading on the Run*

"Action packed and thrilling."— *Words of Mystery*

PRAISE FOR *THE MOUNTAIN MASTER OF SHA TIN*

"Whether it's the triad plot lines or the elegant detective skills of Lee, Ian Hamilton has managed to maintain a freshness to his stories. *The Mountain Master of Sha Tin* is as slick and smart as *The Water Rat of Wanchai*, the first Ava Lee novel . . . This is one of Canada's best series by one of our best writers."— *Globe and Mail*

"Propulsive."— *London Free Press*

"Hamilton's punchy, fast-paced style has woven a tapestry in over a dozen novels that have introduced us to a variety of characters . . . This novel, like the previous tales, rockets along."— *The Mind Reels*

"Hamilton provides a fascinating peek into a disturbingly glamorous world."— *Publishers Weekly*

"Another action-packed entry in a solid series."— *Booklist*

THE DIAMOND QUEEN OF SINGAPORE

The Ava Lee Series

The Dragon Head of Hong Kong: The Ava Lee Prequel (e-book)

The Water Rat of Wanchai

The Disciple of Las Vegas

The Wild Beasts of Wuhan

The Red Pole of Macau

The Scottish Banker of Surabaya

The Two Sisters of Borneo

The King of Shanghai

The Princeling of Nanjing

The Couturier of Milan

The Imam of Tawi-Tawi

The Goddess of Yantai

The Mountain Master of Sha Tin

The Lost Decades of Uncle Chow Tung

Fate

Foresight

THE DIAMOND QUEEN OF SINGAPORE

AN AVA LEE NOVEL

THE TRIAD YEARS

IAN HAMILTON

SPIDERLINE

Published in Canada in 2020 and the USA in 2020 by House of Anansi Press Inc.
www.houseofanansi.com

House of Anansi Press is committed to protecting our natural environment. This book is made of material from well-managed FSC®-certified forests, recycled materials, and other controlled sources.

24 23 22 21 20   1 2 3 4 5

Library and Archives Canada Cataloguing in Publication

Title: The diamond queen of Singapore / Ian Hamilton.
Names: Hamilton, Ian, 1946– author.
Series: Hamilton, Ian, 1946– Ava Lee series.
Description: Series statement: An Ava Lee novel: the Triad years
Identifiers: Canadiana (print) 2019019118X | Canadiana (ebook) 20190191228 |
ISBN 9781487002060 (softcover) | ISBN 9781487002077 (EPUB) |
ISBN 9781487002084 (Kindle)
Classification: LCC PS8615.A4423 D52 2020 | DDC C813/.6—dc23

Book design: Alysia Shewchuk

Canada Council for the Arts · Conseil des Arts du Canada
ONTARIO ARTS COUNCIL · CONSEIL DES ARTS DE L'ONTARIO
an Ontario government agency · un organisme du gouvernement de l'Ontario

We acknowledge for their financial support of our publishing program the Canada Council for the Arts, the Ontario Arts Council, and the Government of Canada.

Printed and bound in Canada

MIX
Paper from responsible sources
FSC www.fsc.org
FSC® C103567

This book is dedicated to Sarah MacLachlan,
my publisher. She took a chance on me, and
sixteen books later, I hope I've justified it.

(1)

AVA LEE WAS NERVOUS, WHICH WASN'T A USUAL STATE for her. She was in her car, an Audi A6, driving up the Don Valley Parkway in the centre of Toronto towards the northern suburb of Richmond Hill, where her mother lived. Normally, visiting her mother, Jennie Lee, wouldn't be a cause for concern, but sitting next to Ava was Pang Fai, arguably China's finest film actress, and Ava's lover. Fai was going to meet Jennie for the first time, and that was the cause of some of Ava's anxiety. The remainder was because Jennie had invited a group of friends to meet Fai, and Ava had no idea how they would behave.

Ava and Fai had been lovers for almost a year. It was a monogamous relationship, despite the fact they had to struggle to find time together. Their work commitments had been one impediment; another was that Fai's home was in Beijing and Ava's in Toronto. But now Fai had no film work scheduled and Ava had no business issues that required her physical presence. They had spent the previous month together, virtually inseparable, in Beijing, Shanghai, and Fai's home city of Yantai.

The trip to Yantai had been especially memorable. Fai's sexuality was something she'd kept secret, certain it would ruin her career if it became public. Until she'd met Ava, her sex life had consisted of clandestine one-night stands. That secrecy had extended to her immediate family, until Fai and Ava went to Yantai. Before they arrived, Fai had dropped some hints to her mother about the nature of their relationship, but her mother obviously hadn't picked up on them; she spent their first hour together trying to establish separate sleeping arrangements for Fai and Ava. Finally Fai had said, "Mum, Ava and I are going to sleep together. We're in love. I know you would have preferred me to bring home a man, but that's not how it is, and that's not how it's going to be."

It had been awkward for a few days, but eventually everyone began to relax. At one point Fai's father had said to her, "I never liked your taste in men. None of them were worthy of you, especially that Lau Lau. It's nice to see you so happy with someone." That caused Ava and Fai to exchange amused glances. Lau Lau and Fai's marriage had been one of convenience rather than love. He had been one of China's finest film directors until liquor, drugs, and the pressure of concealing his homosexuality destroyed his career. Ava, a huge fan of his work, had met Lau Lau while she was in Beijing to see Fai, decided to pay for him to go into rehab, and, over Fai's objections, financed him to write a script. Fai thought nothing good would come of it. Ava agreed that was possible but was willing to take the chance.

After Yantai, Ava and Fai went back to Beijing for a few days and then decided to go to Toronto so Fai could meet Ava's family and friends. Ava's sexuality wasn't a secret to her closest friends and immediate family, but it wasn't something she saw any need to discuss. Her mother knew Ava was gay, loved her daughter, and was accepting of whatever Ava wanted to do, but that didn't mean she wanted to know the details of her sex life. That suited Ava; she and her mother had co-existed happily without ever talking about it.

Ava and Fai had quietly arrived in Toronto the week before and had spent the days since getting adjusted to the time change. Ava had a condo apartment in Yorkville, a trendy district in the heart of the city, within walking distance of a myriad of high-end shops, first-class restaurants, various museums, and Queen's Park, the seat of the provincial government. If she wanted to take Fai further afield, the subway line was almost at Ava's front door and sights like Niagara Falls were just a few hours' drive away. But the trip to Richmond Hill was the first time they had gotten into a car.

On her second day in Toronto, Ava had contacted her mother to tell her they'd arrived. Ava had told Jennie weeks before that Fai was a special friend and they were coming to Toronto together. Jennie's first reaction was to want to organize a party for them. Her mother was a knowledgeable fan of Chinese films and an admirer of Fai's work, so her wanting to meet the actress was expected, but Ava thought a party was too much. "How about you just invite a few of your female friends and perhaps some of my friends, such as Mimi, for a few drinks and appetizers?" she had responded.

"What if some of the husbands want to come?" Jennie asked. "Fai is just as popular with them."

"No men," Ava said fiercely. "Now, when do you want to do this?"

"Friday afternoon would work. Some of my friends from

Niagara-on-the-Lake are coming into town Thursday for our regular mah-jong game. They can stay over," Jennie said.

"Not too many people, please."

"Just the mah-jong girls and a few others who are film fans," Jennie said. "I'll tell them to be here at two o'clock. That way you'll miss the worst of the Don Valley traffic."

"I can't believe how green everything is," Fai said, interrupting Ava's train of thought.

Ava smiled. Their drive took them through the Don Valley, a long strip of inner-city wilderness, but Fai had voiced the same sentiment several times during their walks through the city, because even the urban areas were interlaced with parks and trees. She had also marvelled at the city's air quality and the bright blue sky, which wasn't a surprising reaction from someone who lived in Beijing. There the smog-laden sky was usually greyish black, and the air on many days was so foul that residents wore masks over their noses and mouths. "When you live here, you rather take it for granted," Ava said.

They approached Highway 7, the southern boundary of Richmond Hill. Ava exited the Parkway and drove west, past a nearly continuous line of malls occupied by stores and restaurants all signed in Chinese. Ava saw they'd caught Fai's interest and said, "There are more than half a million Chinese living in and around Toronto. This is one of the most popular neighbourhoods for them."

"And this is where you were raised?"

"Yes, but I went to school in the city, at Havergal College, which is not that far from my condo," Ava said. "You'll meet my Canadian best friend, Mimi, today. We met at Havergal, so you can grill her about what I was like as a teenager."

"When you say 'best friend,' do you mean she was a girlfriend — a gay girlfriend?"

"Not at all," Ava said. "She's straight. In fact she married my friend Derek Liang. I wasn't crazy about the idea at the time, but it's worked out very well. I'm godmother to their daughter."

Ava turned right onto Leslie Street and started north. After three kilometres the landscape began to change from office and retail buildings to houses. After Ava turned left onto 16th Avenue and then took the next right, they were in a completely residential community, two-storey brick homes of only slightly varying design. When Ava's father, Marcus, bought the house for Jennie, it had just been built; the driveway had been gravel and the front yard a sea of mud. Ava had never liked the sameness of the neighbourhood, but her mother loved the house, the front yard that she kept neatly trimmed, and the backyard where she maintained a herb garden. The house was now worth more than a million dollars and was her mother's biggest asset.

"The houses are so large," Fai said. In Beijing Fai lived in a tiny row house that shared a courtyard with about ten others, in a compound located in a hutong that was several hundred years old. Her entire living space was no more than a hundred square metres, and her parents' home in Yantai was only marginally bigger.

"They are larger than most people need. It was the style then — the land was cheap."

Ava turned onto her mother's street. Jennie's house was third on the left, and the first thing Ava noticed was how many cars were parked on the driveway and along the street. Hoping they didn't all belong to people her mother had invited, she had a sinking feeling that they did.

She found a parking spot three houses down from her mother's. She and Fai stepped out of the car into the bright sunshine of an early summer day, the heat moderated by a slight breeze. Wearing black linen slacks and a long-sleeved coral Brooks Brothers button-down shirt, Ava was dressed more formally than usual for a visit to her mother's, but she knew that on this occasion Jennie would have been disappointed by anything less. Fai wore a loose-fitting light-blue sleeveless cotton dress that came to just above her knees. Even dressed so plainly—flat shoes, no makeup, and her hair hanging loosely around her face—Ava thought she looked incredible, and said so.

"I was trying for a low-key professional look," Fai said.

"You're a movie star. No one expects you to look professional," Ava said, and then caught herself. "That didn't come out the way I intended."

Fai laughed. "Is your mother as direct as you?"

"With me and my sister, Marian, but usually not with anyone else," Ava said as they reached the house and started walking up the driveway.

The front door opened before they reached it and Jennie Lee stepped into view. Ava guessed her mother had been on the lookout for them.

"Welcome, girls," Jennie said, her voice filled with excitement.

Ava knew her mother was sixty or maybe a bit older, but Jennie was evasive when it came to the exact number. At five feet four inches she was an inch taller than Ava, and just as slim and fine-boned. She parted her hair—still jet black from expert colouring—in the middle and wore it stylishly curved to mid-ear. She spent several thousands of dollars a year on face creams; although Ava wasn't convinced that the creams were the reason for her mother's still unlined, wrinkle-free skin, Jennie was convinced they were.

"Hi, Mummy," Ava said.

Jennie came down the front steps and walked towards them. Normally she and Ava hugged when they met, but this time Jennie's attention was fixed on Fai. She held out her right hand, palm down, inviting Fai to take it. "It's such an honour to have you here. And, my goodness, you are even more beautiful in person than on the screen. How is it possible?"

"And now I can see where Ava gets her looks," Fai said. "Are you sure you're her mother and not her sister?"

Unlike Ava, Jennie was never bashful about accepting compliments. "Thank you. I actually hear that quite often," she said. "Let's go inside — everyone is so eager to meet you."

Ava was hoping her mother had restricted the guest list to her mah-jong and casino-trip friends, but when they entered the house, they found themselves facing several clusters of women, maybe twenty in total, all of them Chinese.

"Most of you know my daughter Ava. And this, of course, is her friend Pang Fai."

"I think I'm going to faint," one of the women said, which generated a wave of nervous laughter.

"Ava, when your mother said you were bringing Pang Fai to visit, I didn't really believe her," said a woman whom Ava recognized as one of Jennie's long-time mah-jong partners.

"Why didn't you believe me?"

"Because it was too fantastic to be true," the woman said. "I apologize, Jennie."

"How are you enjoying Canada?" another woman asked Fai.

"Well, I've only been here a few days, but so far I really like it. Everything is so clean here — especially the air."

Someone else started to say something, but Jennie cut her off. "Ladies, that's enough questions for now. Let me get Ava and Fai a drink and maybe something to eat. They're not rushing off, so you'll have plenty of time to talk to them."

"Ava!" a voice said from the entrance to the kitchen.

Ava turned and saw her sister, Marian. She rushed towards her and they hugged. "When did you get here?" Ava asked.

"I flew down this morning."

"And when do you go back?"

"Early tomorrow morning."

"Can't you stay a big longer?"

"None of my regular sitters were available, and Bruce is in the middle of a federal-provincial government negotiation. Getting him to stay home with the girls today was enough of a feat."

Bruce was Marian's husband. He was a *gweilo* — a Westerner — and a senior public servant in Ottawa. Marian was trained as a lawyer, but after the birth of their first daughter she had become a stay-at-home mother. It wasn't a life that Ava would have chosen, and although Jennie had stayed home with Ava and Marian, she still complained from time to time about Marian wasting her education.

"How are Bruce and Mummy getting along these days?" Ava asked.

"Same as usual — they're not," Marian said with a tight smile. "I've given up hoping they ever will."

"Well, they couldn't be more different, and neither of them is particularly flexible," Ava said. "Even you have to admit that Bruce is a bit anal, and Mummy, with no sense of time and her slap-happy attitude, is the kind of person who can't help but get under his skin."

"What are you two talking about?" Jennie asked as she guided Fai towards the kitchen.

"Bruce," Ava said.

"My daughter married a *gweilo*," Jennie said to Fai. "He's a nice person, but we don't get along all the time. Although he is very kind to my daughter and gave me two beautiful granddaughters, so I can't think badly of him."

Ava started to say something and then stopped. There was no point in talking to her mother about Bruce. "What do you have to drink?" she asked.

"Just about anything you can name, but most of the women are drinking wine," Jennie said.

"There's also lots to eat — dumplings, spring rolls, cha siu bao," Marian said.

"I'll eat later. For now I'll have a glass of Chardonnay," Ava said.

"That will suit me as well," Fai said.

"I'll get them for you," Jennie said.

When Jennie had left, Marian said to Fai, "You've caused quite a sensation. Mummy's friends were here early with their smartphones fully charged. Fair warning — they'll want to take selfies and film themselves with you. I'm surprised how tech-savvy they all are."

"Fai is accustomed to dealing with fans," Ava said.

"Of course, she must be. It is just that I find this particular group rather overwhelming at times. Some of them are really smart but, given their situations, don't have many ways of expressing it."

"What do you mean by 'their situations'?" Fai asked.

Ava turned to Fai. "Marian means that many of them are second or third wives, like my mother. Their husbands support them but are normally in Hong Kong with their first wives, so these women are left with time on their hands and in need of something to fill it."

"Like mah-jong and casino outings," Marian said.

"That's true to a point, if perhaps a little unfair," Ava said. "I know most of them like to gamble, but I think the socializing is a large part of the experience for them."

"Bruce doesn't see it that way."

"He's also not Chinese, and he's not dependent on the kind of circle of friends Mummy has."

Marian lowered her head. "Sorry. You're right, I shouldn't be so judgmental. It's just that when you live far away, as I do, and have such a different life, it's easy to forget what Mummy went through."

Ava reached for her sister and pulled her close. Disagreements about their mother and her behaviour had characterized their relationship for years, and Bruce's attitude towards Jennie had only intensified them. Ava had resolved several years ago not to engage, and she felt bad every time she did. "I'm sorry too. I know she can be difficult sometimes."

"Ah, how nice to see my daughters so close," Jennie said as she returned with two glasses of wine. She watched Fai take a sip and then added, "Can we leave the kitchen and mingle a bit?"

Fai took another sip and smiled at Jennie. "Mrs. Lee, I'll be happy to mingle, and I don't mind people taking a few pictures. But I'm really here to meet you and Marian, and Ava mentioned her friend Mimi."

"Yes, keep everything in moderation," Ava said to her mother. "And speaking of Mimi, where is she? Did you invite her?"

"Of course. She called last night to confirm my address and said she'd be here," Jennie said. "I'm surprised she isn't. She was always very punctual."

Ava took out her phone and called Mimi's number. When it went directly to voicemail, she ended the call and sent a text that read, Where are you? Anxious to see you.

"Shall we go into the living room now?" Jennie asked.

"Sure," Ava said, and then looped her arm through Fai's. "I'll stay close."

For the next hour Fai circulated, chatting with everyone there, with Ava by her side and Jennie hovering nearby. Twice Jennie left to refill Fai's wineglass, and Ava and Fai took five minutes to sit down and eat a small plate of food brought to them by Marian. "When everyone leaves we can have a proper meal, just the four of us," Jennie said.

By four o'clock there was still no sign of Mimi. Ava checked her phone several times to see if she had replied to the text. She hadn't, and Ava began to worry. Mimi was conscientious as well as punctual. It was unusual of her not to let them know if she was going to be late. Ava tried her phone again with no success, and then sent another text.

As the guests began to leave and things calmed down, Ava found a quiet corner and phoned Derek. His phone rang four times and Ava was readying herself to leave a message when he answered. "Yes."

Even in that one word Ava could sense distress. "Derek, it's Ava. Has something happened to Mimi? I'm at my mother's. She was supposed to join us."

"She's okay. I mean, nothing has happened to her," he said, his distress becoming more evident.

"Then why isn't she here?"

"It's her father," Derek said.

"Is he ill?"

"Ava, the man is dead."

"Oh no," Ava said. She struggled for words before saying, "When? How?"

"This morning . . ." he began, and then went strangely silent.

"What about this morning? Was there an accident?" she asked, and then added, almost impatiently, "Derek, please don't make me guess."

"Mrs. Gregory found him in the garden shed around lunchtime. He had spent the morning trimming bushes and cutting the grass," he said. "She watched him go into the shed with his tools when he was finished, and then a minute later she heard a gunshot."

Ava felt a bone-numbing chill. "I can't believe that," she said. "I've known him for so many years."

"I guess none of us knew him as well as we thought. Mimi has been crying for hours, and Mrs. Gregory is in a state of shock."

"Derek, is there anything I can do? Where are you?"

"We're at the Gregory house."

"I know where it is. I'm at my mother's, and I can be there in half an hour."

"I think Mimi would appreciate it."

"Then tell her I'm on my way."

(2)

THE NEXT WEEK WAS EMOTIONALLY CHARGED AND CHAotic. Ava shuttled back and forth between her condo and the Gregory family home in Leaside, a neighbourhood a few kilometres northeast of Yorkville. Mimi had moved in with her mother, leaving Derek and their daughter, Amber, in their own home a few blocks away.

June Gregory was distraught to a point where she was barely able to communicate. That threw all the responsibility for decision making onto Mimi, who was almost as upset. Derek did what he could, but he was so overwhelmed by looking after Amber and trying to cope with his wife's grief that he wasn't thinking that clearly either.

Mimi was an only child, as were both her parents, so at Mimi's request and with her mother's muted approval, Ava stepped in to help. She dealt with the police, the family doctor, and the crematorium. There was some talk about a funeral, which finally prompted Mrs. Gregory to speak. "There will be no funeral and no celebration of life, or whatever the current fashion is. I want him cremated and that will be the end of it." Mimi started to protest but was cut off by her mother. "I won't talk about this anymore. I've made up my mind."

The police quickly ruled Phillip Gregory's death a suicide, the family doctor prescribed sedatives for both June and Mimi, and the crematorium delivered Phil Gregory's ashes to the house eight days after his death. June asked Ava to take the urn to the basement and put it somewhere where it couldn't be seen.

June Gregory's decision to put her husband's ashes in the basement and her reaction to the idea of a memorial service weren't the only things Ava found strange. Although she had never experienced the death by suicide of someone close to her, she was surprised by what she perceived to be a festering rage in Mrs. Gregory. June's mood wasn't constant. She could be quiet for periods of time or start sobbing in others, but she rejected any kind of comfort that Mimi and Derek offered and then would unleash an anger that was biting and bitter, with her husband the object of her outpourings.

Odder still was when, on one occasion after such an outburst, Mrs. Gregory turned to Ava and Mimi and said, "I killed him. I know I did. I should have kept my mouth shut and just gotten on with things." Mimi asked what she meant, but her mother shook her head and relapsed into silence.

When Ava related this incident to Derek, he told her June had said the same thing to him and had also refused to explain when he pressed her on it. "I think she's just feeling guilty," he said. "I've read that those closest to people who commit suicide quite often blame themselves for not noticing any signs that might have helped them prevent it."

"I hope Mimi isn't feeling that way," Ava said.

"She has a little bit of guilt, but there's more sadness. She keeps thinking about what a good father he was when she was young. There was nothing he wouldn't do for her, and she regrets that she didn't do more for him when she got older."

Fai stuck close to Ava, offering any help she could. Despite being a celebrity — or maybe because of it — there was a vulnerability to Fai that Ava had been thoroughly exposed to, but now Ava saw another side to her, and that was her unstinting kindness. She sat for hours with Mimi and her mother, holding their hands and communicating as best as she could in English.

The second week after Phil Gregory's death was less demanding on Ava. Mrs. Gregory and Mimi began to resume parts of their normal lives, and Derek was there doing the best he could. When Mimi had moved back to her own house, Ava called her every day and visited every second day. In between she managed to take Fai to Niagara Falls and to a play at the Shaw Festival in Niagara-on-the-Lake, the beautiful tourist town twenty-five kilometres north of the Falls on the Niagara River. Fai was quite taken with Niagara-on-the-Lake, and even more so when Ava told her how just about every hotel in the town had been purchased and upgraded by Si Wai Lai, a Chinese businesswoman originally from Guangzhou.

Twice during the second week, Ava and Fai had dinner with Jennie. They had left Jennie's house immediately after getting the news about Phil Gregory, and they hadn't seen her for the rest of that week. Jennie said she understood, but Ava knew that it was one thing for her mother to say that and another for her to really mean it. The two dinners were an attempt to make up, and Ava told her that she was paying for both. The first night, the three of them ate together at Lai Wah Heen, an upscale downtown restaurant. The evening started a bit awkwardly, but the wine flowed and Fai readily answered Jennie's gossipy questions about various Chinese television and movie stars. It ended with Jennie tightly hugging the two of them as they said goodbye.

"We'll get together again later in the week, and you can invite a couple of your friends to join us if you want. What restaurant in Richmond Hill is your favourite these days?" Ava asked.

"I'm really fond of Johnny's on Bayview Avenue. His barbecued pork is terrific, and his roast duck might be the best in the city. But you have to let me know what night is good for you, because you have to order both dishes twenty-four hours in advance," Jennie said. "And I don't want to invite any friends. I like having the two of you to myself."

As usual, Jennie's choice of restaurant was excellent. Ava's love of food was a trait she'd inherited from her mother, who ate out four or five nights a week and was always willing to give a new Chinese restaurant a chance to impress.

Towards the end of dinner, they were interrupted by two women seated nearby who had been staring at their table off and on all night. Finally the women approached. "Excuse me, but my friend and I made a bet that we need you to settle," one of them said to Fai. "My friend says that you're Pang Fai, the Chinese movie actress. I say you aren't. I mean, what would Pang Fai be doing in Richmond Hill?"

"She'd be eating dinner, which is what I'm doing. How much was the bet?" Fai asked.

"One hundred dollars."

"Then that is what you owe your friend," Fai said with a smile.

The women's mouths gaped, but before they could say anything, Fai added, "You can take a picture with me and I'll give you an autograph, but please don't make any more of a fuss by telling someone else. I'm trying to enjoy a quiet evening with my friends."

When the women had left, Jennie said, "You handled that so well."

"I've had practice," Fai replied.

"Has anyone recognized you in the city?"

"Not yet, and I rather like the anonymity."

"Maybe that will encourage you to stay a bit longer," Jennie said hopefully.

"I have no plans to leave. As long as Ava can put up with me, I'll be here."

"And Ava, how about you? Any trips planned?" Jennie asked.

"No, Mummy," Ava said, and then heard her phone ring. She glanced at the screen and saw it was Derek. "I have to take this," she said to her mother as she answered the call. "Derek, is everything okay?"

"Not quite. Mimi and I are at Mrs. Gregory's house. Is there any way you can come over tonight?"

"Has something happened?"

"You could say that," Derek said. "We've just found out why she keeps saying she killed her husband."

(3)

IT WAS PAST NINE IN THE EVENING WHEN AVA AND FAI reached the house to find Derek sitting on the front steps. Ava parked the car, and the two women walked over to meet him. As they drew near, Ava saw his face, illuminated by a porch light. His brow was furrowed, and there was dried spit in the corners of his mouth.

"Thanks for coming," he said to Ava, stepping down onto the sidewalk to hug her and then Fai.

"What's going on?" she asked.

"June went kind of crazy."

"That isn't telling me much."

"Let's sit on the porch," he said. "Mimi gave her mother a couple of sedatives to quiet her down, and now she's trying to get Amber to go back to sleep."

There were four wooden Muskoka chairs in a line on the porch. Derek sat in the one farthest from the front door, and Ava sat next to him. "So, what happened?"

"Before I start, do you want a drink or anything?" he asked.

"No. Just tell me what happened."

He sighed, scrunching his shoulders together. "We came

here for dinner. June was quiet. Mimi and I made small talk with each other and directed some at her, but she wasn't very responsive. Then Mimi asked her if she had talked to the lawyer about Phillip's will. June stared across the table at her and said, 'If only you knew.' Naturally Mimi said, 'If only I knew what?' At that point, things got weird."

"How so?"

"June started to scream. She said there was no need to see a lawyer about the will because Phil hadn't left her anything," Derek said.

"But even if he didn't in the will, by law in this province she is entitled to half of his assets," Ava said, surprised at the suggestion that Phil Gregory hadn't provided for his wife.

Derek shook his head. "You misunderstand. According to June, he didn't have any assets to leave."

"How can that be? He was a vice-president of a major food company. I'm sure he had a pension plan, life insurance, savings of some type, equity in this house."

"Mimi said the same thing, and then June stood up and left the room. She came back a few minutes later with her arms filled with papers. She threw them on the table and shouted that that was all he had left her."

The front door of the house opened, and Mimi stepped onto the porch. "Mum and Amber are both sleeping now," she said, and walked towards Ava. "Thank you for coming, although I can't help feeling we're abusing your friendship."

Ava got to her feet and walked over to her friend with arms extended. They hugged, Ava's head barely reaching Mimi's shoulder.

"Why is your mother so angry at your father?" Ava asked.

"According to her, he lost all their money. There's nothing

left. Even this house, which she thought was paid for, has been remortgaged and is subject to a line of credit that's maxed out."

"Let's sit down," Ava said, taking Mimi's hand and guiding her to a chair. When they were settled, she said, "How does your mother know about the money and the house?"

"My father told her, but only after she had found evidence of it."

"When?"

Mimi shook her head. "My father was depressed for months. We asked him if something was wrong, but he always denied it. His spirits would pick up for a few days, and then he'd fall back into a depression. I think the 'good' moods were his attempt to fool us about how he really felt," she said. She looked at Derek with tears in her eyes. "I should have been more attentive."

"Mimi, you did what you could," he said, reaching out to rest his hand on his wife's knee. "Your father didn't want us to know, and there was nothing you could have done to change that. Now tell Ava what your mother found out."

"Sorry, I got sidetracked," Mimi said to Ava.

"Take your time."

"Well, several weeks ago my mother asked him again why he seemed so depressed. When he told her he wasn't, she kept pressing him until — she says — he lost his temper and began to yell at her," Mimi said. "In all the years of their marriage, he'd never done anything like that. He was always so mild-mannered with her."

"Did she talk to you about any of this at the time?"

"She didn't say a word to me, but that isn't unusual. My

parents are private people. Neither of them ever discussed their problems or — God forbid — their feelings with me," Mimi said, her voice trembling. "They also didn't have friends — at least not anyone I know about — they could confide in. It was always June and Phil united against the world, or so I thought. And I guess my mother did as well, until she found out about the money."

"You said he told her about the money?"

"Yes, but only under duress, and only after she found a stack of papers hidden at the bottom of his dresser drawer. She pretends she found them by accident, but I don't believe that. I think she suspected he was hiding something and went looking for it," said Mimi.

"What kind of papers?"

"Financial statements and the like. But what really caused her alarm were the letters at the top of the stack, from the Harvest Investment Fund and a law firm in the city. After she read them, she confronted my father. According to her, when he saw she had them, he turned white as a ghost, and then he said things weren't as bad as they appeared."

"We've read the letters," Derek said.

"The oldest goes back a year," Mimi said. "It's a notice from the Harvest Fund to investors telling them that the fund's annual profit-sharing payment would be delayed until the fund finalized its tax filing for the year. Then there are another five or six letters, coming every few weeks or so, all of them making excuses and apologizing for the continued delay in payment. The final letter says the fund had to end its operations, that it had incurred some serious losses. What was particularly cruel was that the fund's manager claimed they were converting all the remaining assets into cash and investors could expect their accounts to be settled in the near future."

"How long ago was that last letter?"

"About ten months."

"And there has been no settlement?"

"He received nothing and didn't hear another word from the fund."

"How much of your parents' money had he invested in the fund?"

"All of it."

Ava paused. "You mentioned some letters from a law firm."

"My father and a group of other investors hired them to go after the fund. From what we read — the last letter from the firm was a month ago — they haven't had any success in getting the money back."

"Do you think he could have been caught up in a Ponzi scheme?" Derek asked tentatively, as if hoping for a negative answer.

"That's possible, but it isn't the only possible explanation," Ava said. "Though I'm sure there's no explanation that would have made it easier for Mr. Gregory. I can imagine that most of the past year was absolute torture for him."

"Well, whatever torture he was enduring, my mother said she made it even worse. She said that when she found out about the money, she nagged and harangued him constantly. She accused him of every failing a human being could have, and she didn't let up. She said she would go on at him for days on end, and that he took it without any real reaction, which made her even angrier," Mimi said, starting to cry. "But then he went into the garden shed —" Mimi forced back a sob. "She blames herself for his death. She says she drove him to it."

Derek stood up and wrapped his arms around his wife, kissing the top of her head. "No one knows what he was thinking. He might have done what he did regardless of how your mother reacted," he said.

"I know, but it's going to be difficult to convince her of that," Mimi said, sobbing.

"Was all their money in this fund?" Ava asked, trying to change an uncomfortable subject.

Mimi wiped her eyes and gathered herself. "My mother says she's been left with virtually nothing."

"Did she try to contact the fund to get some kind of explanation?"

"I don't know, but I doubt it. It sounds to me that she just went after my father."

"And you said the lawyers haven't had any success."

"They haven't been able to get any of the money back, but from their letters it appears they did manage to track down the guy who ran the fund. His name is Malcolm Muir. They met with him, but nothing came of it," Mimi said.

"Did the lawyers make any suggestions for further action?"

"In their last letter they say that suing Muir and the fund is the only real option available, but they aren't optimistic that a lawsuit would succeed. Evidently Muir has made clever use of our bankruptcy laws. The law firm also asked for a large retainer before proceeding, so I doubt that my father signed on."

"How about the other people who hired the firm?"

"I don't know."

"Do you know who they are?"

"None of the names are familiar to me."

Ava hesitated as other questions began to enter her mind. "Tell me again the name of this fund."

"The Harvest Investment Fund."

"That's an unusual name."

"It seems to be connected to Harvest Table Bible Chapel. My father started going there four or five years ago," Mimi said. "After being a rather lukewarm Anglican for most of his life, he became a very enthusiastic evangelical Christian after hearing Pastor Sammy Rogers preach."

"Rogers is connected to the chapel?"

"Rogers *is* the chapel, and calling it a chapel is a bit of a joke. It's a monster structure north of the city, about halfway between here and Barrie," Derek interjected. "It must have cost millions to build."

"Your father went there?" Ava asked Mimi.

"He went twice a week, on Wednesday evenings for Bible study and every Sunday for the service."

"Did your mother go with him?"

"Everything about Harvest Table embarrassed her. It became a source of friction between them. That could be another reason why she went off on him when she found out about the money."

"Did the lawyers contact the chapel to ask about this fund?"

"I don't know, but my mother says my father insisted that the chapel had nothing to do with the fund. And on the bottom of the statements from the fund it says very clearly that it's not part of the Harvest Table Bible Chapel organization."

"Then why use a similar name? That doesn't make much sense."

"Let me get one of the statements for you," Mimi said,

getting to her feet before Ava could respond.

Derek waited until his wife had gone inside before he leaned towards Ava. "Can you help with this? I know you don't do this kind of work anymore, but no one was better than you at finding money and getting it back. Mimi is too embarrassed to ask you, but we would appreciate it all the same."

"Of course I'll help," Ava said. "But I can't promise I'll accomplish anything until I see what I'm dealing with."

"Even if the money is truly gone, it would be good to know what happened to it and what happened to the people who took it."

"Here's one of the statements," Mimi said as she came back onto the porch. "They all have the same disclaimer at the bottom."

Ava took the page from Mimi and read aloud: "The Harvest Investment Fund is not affiliated in any way with Harvest Table Bible Chapel. The Fund is completely independent and has no formal or informal ties to the Chapel or any of the Chapel's organizations."

"What I don't get is, if it wasn't tied to the chapel, why would the chapel let them use their name?" Derek said.

"It's a common name, so I doubt you could trademark it," Ava said. "But that still raises the question of why there needed to be a disclaimer in the first place."

"Maybe because the only people allowed to invest in the fund were chapel members," Derek said.

"Why do you say that?"

"There's a document among Phil's papers that lays out the terms and conditions for joining the fund. I read it quickly while we were waiting for you."

"How many other papers does Mrs. Gregory have?" Ava asked.

"The fund reported to the investors every month with what looks like a combination of statement and newsletter. I think Phil kept them all."

"Could I take them with me?"

Mimi looked at Ava and then turned to Derek. "You didn't ask Ava to help, did you?"

"No, he didn't. I offered, and I won't take no for an answer," Ava said.

"I asked you to come here so I could get your advice on what we might do. I don't expect you to get involved directly. You have enough going on in your life without taking on my family's problems," Mimi said. "Derek and I have already decided to contact the legal firm to see if a lawsuit is going ahead. If it is, we'll try to attach my mother's name to it, as long as the cost is reasonable."

"Well, while you're doing that, why don't I take a look at the paperwork," Ava said. "Mimi, it *is* what I'm trained to do."

"I know you are. I also know that you've moved on from debt collection."

"But I haven't stopped using my accounting skills," Ava said.

Mimi sighed. "Okay. And thank you."

"Good, Now why don't you get me the paperwork."

"I'll go inside and get it," Derek said. "It isn't in any particular order."

"I don't care about that. I'll organize it," Ava said.

"Thank you for doing this," Mimi said again as Derek left.

"I'm pleased to get a chance to give something back after all the things you and Derek have done for me over the years."

Mimi squeezed Ava's hand. "We could look after my mother financially if we have to, but I know she wouldn't want us to. She's an incredibly proud and independent woman. "

"I can't promise I'll find out what happened to the money," Ava said, "but I'll do what I can."

"I know you will."

(4)

IT WAS ALMOST MIDNIGHT WHEN AVA AND FAI GOT back to the Yorkville condo.

"Do you want to share a shower?" Fai asked as Ava turned on the lights.

"I'd love to, but can you wait a little? I could use a glass of wine, and I wouldn't mind putting these papers into some kind of order before going to bed."

Fai smiled. "I'll get the wine."

Ava sat at the kitchen table and opened the file folder. Her plan was to simply group the documents by type and then by date. At first glance she saw a terms sheet, newsletter/statements, the lawyer's letters, and the letters from the fund that, one by one, told Phil Gregory his life was ruined.

"Where shall I put your wine?" Fai asked, holding up two glasses.

"Here," Ava said, pushing some of the papers aside to make room.

"I'm going into the bedroom to check my emails. Come and get me when you're finished."

Ava took a sip of wine, picked up a stack of paper, and

began to sort the pages into piles. Everything was dated, which pleased her because it would make it easier to form an idea of how the Harvest Fund had operated. She worked quickly, the growing stack of statements dwarfing the terms document and letters. When that was finished, she began to organize each stack by date. The terms sheet was dated July five years before, and the first statement was from the following September. Mimi had said her father had been going to the chapel for four or five years. It seemed to Ava he had joined the fund around the same time he started attending the church. She wondered if that was a coincidence.

The sorting went quickly. Mr. Gregory seemed to have kept everything he'd been sent; there wasn't a single statement missing, from the first date to the last. She was tempted to start reading the statements, but knowing that Fai was waiting for her, she decided just to scan the terms sheet. Its heading was certainly different from any she'd seen before. It read: "Putting Your Money to Work for God, Your Community, and Your Family." And the first paragraph continued along a similar vein: "The Harvest Investment Fund has been created as a vehicle for Christians to put their money to work in ways that reflect their beliefs and values. The Fund will invest only in businesses that benefit the community and will direct half of its profits to charitable Christian causes at home and around the world."

"Ava," Fai said, walking into the kitchen with her phone in one hand and her glass of wine in the other, "Chen's on the line and wants to speak to you."

Ava put down the terms sheet. "What does he want?"

"He has news about Lau Lau," Fai said.

Chen was Fai's agent in Beijing and had also represented Lau

Lau in the past. Ava had convinced him to find a rehabilitation centre for his former client. She took the phone. "Hello, Chen. Are things going alright at rehab, or has Lau Lau relapsed?"

"I haven't spoken to him, but he must be doing okay. He sent me an email last night with a script."

"He finished it that quickly?"

"He has been in rehab for over a month. I'm sure he started writing as soon as he could, and a script is only about a third as long as an average novel," Chen said. "Besides, Lau Lau always did work fast. He'd get an idea and rework it in his head over and over again before he put it down on paper."

"Have you read it?"

"I have."

"What do you think?"

"I don't want to give you an opinion just yet. I'd like to think about it a bit more, maybe reread it, and I want Fai to read it as well. After we've talked, I'll tell you what I think."

"Okay."

"And Fai has something else to talk to you about," he said, almost conspiratorially. "Listen, Ava, I've just offered her an opportunity of the kind that doesn't come along very often. My fear is that she won't accept it unless you give her your blessing. Truthfully, I've never known her to be as happy as she is now, and you're the largest part of that, but it shouldn't mean she gives up her career. She's an actress — she needs to act."

"I've never suggested that she shouldn't," Ava said, catching Fai's eye.

"Good. Then you two talk. Tell her to call me back when she makes up her mind," Chen said.

Ava ended the call. "That was an interesting conversation," she said to Fai.

Fai sat down next to her. "It is good news about Lau Lau. Even if the script is terrible, he's working again."

"That was of less interest to me than whatever Chen was not so subtly hinting at about you."

"Just a moment," Fai said. She went to the fridge, took out the bottle of wine, and brought it to the table. She refilled their glasses, took a sip, and then sat down again. "I've been offered a film role in Taiwan that he wants me to accept."

"Does it sound like a good part?"

"Maybe better than good. The director is Andy Gao. He's been one of my favourites for years, even though I haven't had a chance to work with him."

"He has made some great films," Ava said.

"I agree, and the one he's working on now sounds wonderful. It's a love story between a middle-aged woman and an older man. Chen says the script is fantastic and that the role of the woman is perfect for me," Fai said, and then smiled. "The story even has a happy ending, which would be a welcome change."

"Then you should do it," Ava said.

"I'd like to, but there's a complication."

"What do you mean?"

"Andy told Chen that he needs me on set immediately."

"Why?"

"They were ready to start shooting yesterday when the lead actress suddenly became ill."

"How ill?"

"Actually, she overdosed on drugs. Even if she could return to the set in a week or two, the insurance company won't cover her or the film," Fai said. "Andy is stuck."

"He's hardly stuck if you're his backup plan," Ava said,

smiling. "It sounds like a great role for you. How long will you need to be in Taiwan?"

"Six weeks, give or take. Andy has a reputation for being super organized and efficient."

"That's not so bad. *Mao's Daughter* took longer than that."

"If I accept the part, you do understand that I'd be getting on a plane as soon as tomorrow?"

"Of course I understand, but it sounds like a great opportunity."

"I think it is."

"Fai, I'll miss you, but I'm happy for you," Ava said, and then waved her hands over the stacks of paper. "Besides, I've got this mess to sort through, and it will likely occupy quite a bit of my time."

"Then I'll call Chen and tell him to book my flight," Fai said, leaning towards Ava with her lips puckered. They kissed with more than a hint of passion.

"You're my lucky charm," Fai said when finally pulled apart. "I've always wanted to work with Andy Gao, *and* do a love story with a happy ending, *and* work in Taiwan. Now I get to do all three at one time."

"Go and call Chen," Ava said. "But do me a favour, will you? Read Lau Lau's script while you're in the air and talk to Chen about it when you're done. I'm keen to know what the two of you think about it."

"I will, I promise," Fai said.

"And don't talk to Chen for too long," Ava said. She smiled. "This will be our last chance to be alone together for a while. Let's make it a shower to remember."

(5)

CHEN BOOKED FAI ON AN EVA AIRWAYS EVENING flight that flew from Toronto direct to Taipei. That gave Fai and Ava the day together, but it was hardly relaxing. Fai needed a visa, which meant filling out numerous forms and then driving to the Taipei Economic and Cultural Office on Yonge Street with the application and Fai's passport. When they got there, they were initially told it might take up to three days to get the visa approved, but when Fai explained the reason for her trip and the official realized who she was, they were fast-tracked. Still, it was mid-afternoon by the time Ava pointed the Audi in the direction of Pearson International Airport, in the city's northwest corner.

They had spent close to six weeks together, minus a few days when Ava had been in Hong Kong. It was the longest continuous time Ava had ever spent with someone who wasn't her mother or sister. In previous relationships, the most had been a two-week holiday, and by the end of that Ava had begun to feel suffocated. This was different. She was actually sad to see Fai leave, and she was quietly pleased when Fai packed only half of the clothes she'd brought with her. The other half remained hanging in the closet or nestled in Ava's drawers.

It was early rush hour in a city where rush hour was getting perpetually earlier, and it was stop-and-go along the Gardiner Expressway and for part of the way up Highway 427. But by four-thirty Ava had reached the airport and was walking with Fai into Terminal 1.

Chen had booked Fai a first-class ticket, so check-in was quick and smooth. Security was another matter — even the priority lanes were jammed.

"You don't have to hang around until I clear security," Fai said.

"And I won't. It's hard enough watching you leave without having to do it inch by inch."

Fai threw her arms around Ava's shoulders and pulled her close. "I'll stay in touch," she said.

"Make sure you do."

"Good luck with Mimi's family problem."

"I suspect I'll need more than luck," Ava said, and then hugged Fai so hard she could almost count her ribs.

The line in front of Fai shuffled forward. "I have to go," Fai said. "I love you."

"Love you too. See you in six weeks," Ava said.

Highway 427 was lighter going south and the Gardiner wasn't bad going east, so Ava made it home by six-thirty. She parked the car, thought about going to a restaurant in the neighbourhood for dinner, and then decided she'd eat at home and start working through the Harvest documents.

The condo was eerily quiet when she entered it, and Ava felt Fai's absence immediately. This was a new experience for her. Her home had always been her refuge, a place where she could be gloriously alone. Now it felt cold, as if something was missing—and it was, of course. Ava went to the fridge, took out the leftover wine, and emptied the remains into a glass. Then she walked over to an oak credenza to get a couple of pens and a Moleskine notebook. She carried them back to the table, opened the notebook, and wrote across the top of the first page: *Gregory / Harvest Investment Fund.*

She looked at the stack of statements. Where to begin? She flipped to the last one Phil Gregory had been sent. It consisted of two pages; the first was titled "HARVEST FUND ASSETS," and under that was the amount $31,554,629. Down the left side of the page was a list of common investment sectors, including automotive, banking, oil and gas, and agriculture. Beside each sector was a dollar figure that Ava assumed was supposed to represent the value of the fund's holdings in it. Near the bottom of the page, in a different font, it read: "Phillip Gregory's Account Balance: $2,743,489." Directly beneath was the now familiar disclaimer that the fund wasn't affiliated with the Chapel.

Ava turned the page, expecting to find more details about the fund's holdings. There was only text: six paragraphs, each describing the good work the fund's investments had achieved in various African and Asian countries, by installing water purification systems, supporting missionaries, and donating to the construction of schools and health facilities. At the bottom of that page was the name Malcolm Muir and the words "Together in Christ."

That can't be all there is, she thought. *Surely there have to be other numbers, some reasonable level of detail.* She picked up another statement and found it was identical to the one she'd just read. She looked at the one with the earliest date.

It followed the same pattern. The fund's assets were listed as $6,321,623, and Phil Gregory's account contained $250,000, which she assumed was his first contribution. She made a note: *How many people invested in the fund?* and then thought, *How on earth could people put their money into something like this?*

She turned her attention to the terms sheet, hoping it would shed some light. It did, but in a way that made Ava shake her head. Its introduction read: THE FUND PROVIDES MEMBERS OF HARVEST TABLE BIBLE CHAPEL AN OPPORTUNITY TO INVEST AS PART OF OUR CHRISTIAN COMMUNITY IN COMPANIES THAT REFLECT CHRISTIAN VALUES OR ARE OWNED AND/OR MANAGED BY PEOPLE OF AVOWED CHRISTIAN FAITH. MOREOVER, THE FUND IS COMMITTED TO INVESTING HALF OF ANY PROFITS IT GENERATES TO PROMOTE CHRISTIANITY IN THE DEVELOPING WORLD AND TO PROVIDE MATERIAL SUPPORT TO CHRISTIAN COMMUNITIES IN NEED.

The terms sheet was quite specific that membership in the fund was restricted to members of the Chapel, but immediately added in bold lettering: THE FUND IS NOT FORMALLY OR INFORMALLY PART OF THE HARVEST TABLE BIBLE CHAPEL ORGANIZATION, ALTHOUGH ITS OBJECTIVES ARE ENDORSED BY CHAPEL LEADERSHIP. It went on to say that in line with those objectives, the fund would be managed by Chapel members who were experienced and skilled in financial management. That team would be led by Malcolm Muir, who was also a member of Harvest Table Bible Chapel's finance committee. Then, again emphasized, it read: MR. MUIR AND THE OTHER TEAM MEMBERS WILL NOT BE PAID MANAGEMENT FEES. THIS WORK IS VOLUNTARY ON THEIR

PART. ANY COMPENSATION THEY RECEIVE WILL BE IN THE FORM OF THE PROFITS THEY MAKE FROM THEIR OWN INVESTMENTS IN THE FUND, AND THOSE PROFITS WILL BE AT THE SAME LEVEL AS FOR ANY OTHER INVESTOR.

The terms sheet went on to specify that membership in the fund required an initial investment of $100,000. All of an investor's money could be withdrawn, in whole or in part, on the anniversary of their joining, but the fund reserved the right to take sixty days to return the money after such a request was made. There would be monthly financial statements, regular reports on how the profits were being invested, and an annual meeting that would be open for investors to attend. It all sounded entirely reasonable, Ava thought, especially to someone who might not question the fund's motives.

Aside from Muir's name, there were no other names, phone numbers, or email addresses on the statements. Ava made a note of it, picked up her cell, and called Derek.

"I was wondering when I was going to hear from you," he said.

"Sorry, I've been running around all day with Fai. She needed a visa to go to Taiwan. She's leaving tonight. In fact, she's probably in the air now," Ava said. "I got back here only a few hours ago, but I've managed to get started on the Harvest Fund paperwork."

"You didn't mention she was leaving. Is everything okay between you two?"

"Everything is fine. She was offered a role in a film by a director she likes and decided to take it," Ava said. "It was a last-minute thing."

"I'm glad it's that and nothing else. We really like her,"

Derek said. "I'm also glad you found the time to look at the paperwork. What do you think of it so far?"

"There's a complete lack of detail that looks very suspect," she said. "Mr. Gregory and the other investors were operating on blind faith."

"I'm not surprised to hear that."

"What is surprising is that anyone would put their money into something this half-baked," Ava said. "I can understand the desire to do good works, but there should still be some level of proper accounting."

"How much accounting was done?"

"None that I can see," Ava said. "Whoever put these statements together — it was probably this Malcolm Muir — was most likely just making up stuff."

"From what we learned from the lawyers today, that's not surprising."

"You talked with the lawyers?"

"We met with them. We phoned this morning, not sure that they'd take our call, since we're not technically clients, but when Mimi told them what had happened to her father, they invited us in to talk," Derek said.

"That was considerate of them. Did they want you to join the lawsuit?"

"There is no lawsuit. None of the people from the fund were willing to pay the firm's retainer."

"So why did the lawyers ask you to go to their offices?"

"Perhaps they felt remorse about Phil," Derek said. "In any event, they spent close to an hour telling us what they'd found out."

"Which was?"

"They told us that Malcolm Muir, almost right from the

time the fund started, was moving money overseas to a bank in the Netherlands."

"When was the last of the money sent?"

"A year ago."

"That's when Mr. Gregory got the first letter telling him there would be a delay in his profit sharing."

"Exactly. According to the lawyers, about a month before that letter was sent, two of the investors advised the fund that they wanted to cash out. Each of them had about two million in it," Derek said. "There's a sixty-day wait provision in the fund's terms. On the fortieth day after their requests, Muir put the fund into bankruptcy. He listed its assets as just over ten thousand dollars, which was just enough to pay the bankruptcy trustee."

"So much for Christian values," Ava said, looking down at the notes she'd been making as Derek spoke. "How did the lawyers find out about the bank in the Netherlands?"

"I think it would be better if they explained it to you directly," Derek said, and then paused. "I asked them if they would meet with you and share their information. I said you're a friend of the family who we asked to help, and then I told them a little about what you did with Uncle . . . I hope you don't mind me volunteering your time and talking about your past."

"I don't mind you volunteering my time. Do you have a contact for me?"

"I'll text it to you in a few minutes."

Ava sighed as she put down the phone. If the lawyers knew what had happened and still hadn't been able to recover any of the money, she had doubts she could do any better. Her phone pinged and she opened it to find a text from Derek; it contained the name Todd Howell, a phone number, and an email address. She quickly composed a message to Howell. My name is Ava Lee. You met today with my friend Mimi, the daughter of Phil Gregory. I'm advised that you are prepared to meet with me as well. How is your schedule tomorrow? She sent it, rose from her chair, and went into the bathroom.

When she returned, she was surprised to see that Todd Howell had already replied, and she was even more surprised when she read what he'd written. Our company name is Howell, Barker, and Mason. We are on the 10th floor of the Toronto Commonwealth Bank building at King and Bay. Any time is good for me after ten a.m. Let me know when you think you'll be here. Can't tell you how much I'm looking forward to meeting you. Todd.

What an odd way to end an email. What did Derek actually tell him about me? Ava thought. She had no plans for the following day except going for a run, and her favourite time for that was early morning. I'll be at your office around 11 a.m. she wrote and hit send.

She yawned, then felt hunger pangs and realized she hadn't eaten. She still didn't feel like going out, and while she had leftover noodles in the fridge, they had no appeal. "Screw it, I won't eat," she said out loud. "I'll take a glass of cognac to bed with me."

The glass turned into two as Ava sat on her bed, propped up by pillows, and idly channel-surfed. When she couldn't find anything that caught her attention, she turned to Netflix. She had subscribed to the service during her previous prolonged stay in Toronto but hadn't used it — or watched much other television — during Fai's visit. Now she found the series *Peaky Blinders*. She had seen season one and part of season two, and she was quickly drawn back into the story of the gangster family from Birmingham.

Ava watched two episodes before her eyes began to close. She finished the cognac, turned off the television, and slid under the covers. She turned her head towards the side where Fai slept, pushed her own pillow to one side, and replaced it with Fai's. She inhaled and instantly smelled Fai. Ava felt a tingle between her legs and groaned. Being so much in love could be hell.

(6)

AVA WOKE AT SEVEN WITH THE SUN POURING IN through her bedroom window. The summer hadn't been particularly hot or humid, and on most mornings the air was crisp — perfect weather for joggers and walkers.

She roused herself from bed, made a bathroom dash, and then headed for the kitchen. Two cups of instant coffee later, Ava left the condo in Adidas shorts and a black Giordano T-shirt, made a right turn onto Yorkville Avenue and ran over to Avenue Road. Traffic was heavy going south towards downtown, but it was Toronto-heavy and not Bangkok-heavy, so at least it was moving. She stopped at the corner for a few seconds, deciding whether to go north or south. Then she thought about Mimi and turned right.

There weren't many pedestrians on Avenue Road, so Ava ran unimpeded except for a few stoplights. The route was uphill for the first part but flattened out around St. Clair Avenue. She had to wait for a stoplight at that intersection but then ran around Upper Canada College — the country's most exclusive private boys' school — towards Eglinton Avenue. She normally turned around and ran back from there, but this time she kept going north until she came to a complete stop in front of what looked like an ivy-covered brick-and-stone English mansion, complete with turret. She was at Havergal College, and the building was its most public face. She had driven by the school many times in recent years without really taking it in, but Mimi's troubles had inspired memories of their days there, and Ava had felt an unconscious need to reconnect.

The school went from kindergarten to Grade 12 and welcomed boarders as well as day students. Mimi and Ava had been day students and didn't start attending until Grade 9, which made it difficult to make friends. Ava wasn't sure that her father's money had been well spent on sending her to the school. She believed she would have received as good an education in a public high school, and she wasn't into networking, so the benefits of contacts with the daughters of the wealthy and famous who attended the school were lost on her. Meeting Mimi, though, had justified the years she spent there.

It seemed like several lifetimes ago, Ava thought as she stood looking at the main building and the courtyard that separated it from the street. She knew she was fortunate to have such wonderful friends, people who would support her without question or hesitation. And when it came to Mimi and Derek, they were friends from whom she'd taken more support than she'd ever given. *Now perhaps I have a chance to give back*, she thought, as she turned and started running the seven kilometres home.

Ava reached her condo at ten. Half an hour later she re-emerged freshly showered and in black linen slacks, black pumps, and a powder-blue cotton button-down Brooks

Brothers shirt. Her hair was pulled back and fixed with an ivory chignon pin, and she had put on a trace of red lipstick and black mascara. She carried a Louis Vuitton bag in which she'd placed the Moleskine notebook. The bag might seem slightly ostentatious, as did the Cartier Tank Française watch on her wrist. Her clothes were a reflection of her image of herself as a serious businesswoman, but the bag and the watch sent the additional message that she was also a successful one.

She walked to Avenue Road, turned right, and went past Bloor Street to the subway station at the Royal Ontario Museum. She caught a train going south and four stops later got out at St. Andrew station. Todd Howell's office was in a building that was a five-minute walk along King Street, in the downtown area that headquartered all of Canada's national banks. Ava walked in the shadow of a multitude of skyscrapers that were distinguished architecturally mainly by colour and the materials used on their exteriors. The Toronto Commonwealth Bank was sheathed in black metal and its windows were tinted dark. It looked forbidding from any distance, which Ava was sure was the intent.

Like the other banks, Toronto Commonwealth leased office space to other businesses. When Ava reached the tenth floor, she followed the signs to Howell, Barker, and Mason, which took her past an accountant's office and another law firm until she got to a double set of glass doors. She looked through them at an open space dotted with desks and workstations and surrounded by offices.

Ava opened the doors and was starting to walk towards the reception desk when she heard her name called. She stopped, looked in the direction of the voice, and saw a tall, lean man standing next to one of the workstations and waving at her. When she nodded at him, he approached her with his right hand extended.

"I'm Todd Howell. I'm glad to meet you," he said.

"And I'm Ava Lee."

"I know who you are."

She had no idea how he did, but she saw no reason to ask. He smiled, showing teeth that were yellowish. She looked at his fingers and saw nicotine stains. "Thank you for taking the time to see me," she said.

Most of the people in the open workspace were dressed casually, but not Howell. He wore a navy-blue suit, a white shirt, and a tie that was knotted tightly. Ava guessed he was in his mid-forties. He had a full head of grey hair that stuck out in various directions and made him look boyish, although that impression was somewhat nullified by the deep lines etched across his forehead and down his cheeks.

"The pleasure is mine," he said, and then turned and looked towards the row of offices. "I thought we'd meet in one of the small boardrooms, but they all seem to be occupied. We'll sit in my office instead."

She followed him as he wound his way around the workstations. There were about twenty private offices, she figured, and maybe double that number of desks in the open space. Most of the office doors were open, and Ava glanced into them as they passed. The offices were small and plainly furnished, with a desk, a credenza, a couple of filing cabinets, and a chair or two for visitors. Given that Howell was a partner, she expected his office would be a bit grander, but it wasn't. It was the same size as the others and as sparsely furnished. What made it different was the clutter that covered his desk, the credenza, the top of the filing cabinets, and even the window ledge. Most of the clutter was files, but the credenza was a forest of computer towers.

"Pardon the mess, but I do know where everything is," he said as he sat down at his desk. "I'd love to get rid of those towers, but we have to hang on to the hard drives until we close the cases they're tied to. Many of them are bankruptcies or connected to fraud in its various forms."

"You obviously handle quite a number of them."

"I do. We're a generalist firm, except for me. For some reason I fell into financial law about ten years ago and I haven't been able to get away from it," he said, and smiled. "Mind you, I'm not complaining. Business never lets up, and it seems I'm doing more every year."

"How did the Harvest Investment Fund case find its way to you?"

"One of my neighbours was a victim. Like some of the others, he was embarrassed about being swindled, but his wife spoke to my wife and I was persuaded to raise the subject with him," Howell said. "When I heard what had happened, I offered to help. Although to be truthful, if I'd known what a pain in the ass the case would turn out to be, I would have minded my own business."

"Derek told me you aren't pursuing it any further."

"Not because I don't want to. If I had my way I'd sue Malcolm Muir in every jurisdiction I could. You know who he is, yes?"

"I do."

Howell nodded. "But there's no point in starting any legal action unless we know where the money eventually landed and how much of it is left. And even if we did locate it, there's absolutely no guarantee we'd be able to recover any of it," he said. "My neighbour and the other victims won't put up the money to pursue it any further, and my partners won't finance anything that has so much uncertainty attached to the outcome. I can't say I blame them. In all probability it would just be throwing good money after bad. I haven't officially dropped the case, though. Rather optimistically, I think of it as just being in limbo."

"But Derek told me you know where the money has gone," Ava said. "Was he misinterpreting what you said?"

Howell leaned back in his chair and clasped his hands behind his neck. He stared at Ava, pursing his lips as if he calculating what he wanted to say. "Before I answer any more of your questions, I have to tell you that you have quite the reputation," he said finally.

"I have no idea what you mean by that," she said.

"Derek told me that you're a forensic accountant who was in the debt-collection business in Hong Kong. He said you and your partner specialized in collecting money that was otherwise uncollectable."

"I was in that business, but unfortunately my partner passed away and the business no longer exists."

"You didn't want to go it alone or find another partner? You seem to be quite young to pack it in."

"I went into a less stressful business."

"Maybe so, but you still have knowledge and experience, and I can't believe you've lost any of your skill."

"I'm probably no more capable than you or your staff. As you know, it's very difficult to hide money these days."

"Except that fucker Malcolm Muir seems to have done exactly that and is thumbing his nose at us," Howell snarled.

He suddenly leaned forward, his hands clasped in front on him on top of the desk. "But I'm leaping all over the place. Why don't I tell you what I know, and then maybe we can put our heads together and see if there's a path forward."

"You do understand that the reason I'm here is because of Mimi and Mrs. Gregory? My only interest is in seeing if there's a way to salvage some of the money Mr. Gregory lost."

"I know that, but you're not going to achieve that without taking on Muir."

Ava frowned. "You'll have to excuse me, Mr. Howell, but it seems that you're making a lot of assumptions and putting a lot of trust in someone you don't really know. I'm not sure what Derek told you about me that would cause you to be this forthcoming."

"Oh, I'm prepared to be completely forthcoming, and not just because of Derek," Howell said. "He told me enough that I agreed to meet with you as a friend of the family, but not much more than that. Later, after he and his wife left, I mentioned your name to Eddie Ng—one of the juniors who's been assisting me with the case—and his face lit up. Eddie is Vietnamese Chinese, with family in Hong Kong. He told me you recovered more than twenty million dollars for some Vietnamese people in Toronto who got caught up in a bank scam. He told me that you're a real heroine in that community. He's also heard stories about some of your other exploits. Eddie is a fan."

"People exaggerate. The people we worked for were typically so desperate to get anything back that, when we did manage it, their appreciation was often disproportionate to our actual success."

"But you did retrieve the twenty million?"

"We did."

"And from what I've been told, that was hardly the first time you were successful."

"My partner and I had a decent success rate."

"Your main base of operations was Asia, though, wasn't it?"

"Yes, we had very strong contacts there," Ava said. "That's not to say we didn't have clients outside of Asia."

"How are your contacts in Europe?"

"I know some people here and there."

"That's good enough."

"Good enough for what?"

"Good enough for now. So, can I tell you what I know about Muir and his fund?"

"Go ahead."

"Well, I think it was a scam from the very start. The fund was never registered as an investment vehicle, as a charity, as anything. Muir created a series of numbered companies and used the Harvest Investment name as a doing-business-as entity. All the money that went into the fund was immediately redirected to the numbered companies, and then it was most often transferred between the numbered companies. The companies were established in five different provinces."

"Which means five different provincial jurisdictions and applicable laws," Ava said.

"Exactly. You've encountered this before?"

"No, but I've heard about it."

"So you know what the game is. He establishes the companies and then moves money between them like in a shell game. Except when the shells finally stopped moving, the money was in Europe and he had put every one of the numbered companies in Canada into bankruptcy."

"Who owned the numbered companies?"

"Muir."

"No one else was listed?"

"He used someone from his law firm to stand in as secretary and vice-president."

"And no one associated with Harvest Table Bible Chapel was listed anywhere?"

"Why do you ask that?"

"I read the terms sheet and the monthly statements Mr. Gregory received. I thought the disclaimers separating the chapel from the fund were a bit over-the-top," Ava said. "In fact, they were so oddly excessive that you could think the person who wrote them knew what was going to happen with the fund and was laying the groundwork for the chapel to be able to plead ignorance."

"I thought the same thing, and I made that point quite forcefully when I met with Pastor Sammy Rogers and Patrick Cunningham, the COO and CFO of the organization, along with their lawyers. They were highly insulted, and I was told that if I repeated my opinions in public they wouldn't hesitate to take legal action against me," Howell said. "But I have to admit that our conversation was more cordial after that. Rogers said he was prepared to swear on the Bible he knew nothing about what Muir was up to, and that he would instruct his CFO to cooperate fully with us."

"You believed Rogers?"

Howell paused, then said, "Not at that moment, but Cunningham, the CFO, was co-operative and I found absolutely nothing that connected the chapel to the fund. So in the end I didn't have much choice."

"So it all came down to Muir?"

"Yes."

"What did you decide to do about him?"

"I tried to sue him. By then he had bankrupted all the numbered companies, so the only option I had left was to go after him personally. He lives in Ontario, so I initiated an action here. I thought I was making a little headway, but as soon as I got a judge willing to listen to the case, Muir declared personal bankruptcy."

"He has no assets?"

"He lives in a multi-million-dollar house in the Annex owned by his wife. He drives a Mercedes-Benz Roadster that she owns as well. They eat out several times a week at some of the most expensive restaurants in the city, paid for with her credit cards."

"What does she do for a living?"

"Nothing. Her name is Marla Swift and she is the only child of Frank Swift, who owned a car dealership in Oakville. When he died, she inherited the business and then sold it for millions."

"How convenient for Muir," Ava said.

"Yes, but evidently he wanted a lot more than his wife could provide," Howell said.

"So it seems. How much money did he actually move overseas?"

"About thirty million."

Ava blinked in surprise. "That's about the declared value of the fund in the last statement I saw. I thought this was a Ponzi scheme and that he was making a run for it before he ran out of cash."

"No, I think it was out-and-out theft, because I know of one person who wanted to cash out more than a million dollars and was paid. Muir also didn't miss a single annual profit-sharing payment until the last one was due."

"How large were those payments?"

"On average, I'd say three to four percent," Howell said. "But not everyone took them. In fact, most people just reinvested in the fund, Phillip Gregory included."

"But that still means the fund — theoretically, anyway — was making about an eight percent annual return."

"That's what Muir claimed."

"With half of it supposedly going to good works in Africa and Asia."

"That part of it was pure bullshit. We couldn't locate anyone overseas who received money from the fund," Howell said. "But when you consider that one person who cashed out and the profit sharing to investors, Muir never actually shortchanged anyone until two investors decided to take out four million at once."

"You're making it sound like the fund was actually turning a profit."

"That's what the numbers indicate. Apparently Muir is a smart investment fund manager."

"You just said he's a thief."

"The two descriptions aren't incompatible."

"I guess not," Ava said, processing what she'd been told. Then she asked, "Have you gone to the authorities? Surely there's a case to be made for fraud."

"I went to the Ontario Provincial Police financial crimes unit. They heard me out, but the moment they saw that the fund had never been registered provincially, the stream of bankruptcies, and the involvement of other provincial jurisdictions, they told me the case should be handled by the RCMP. When I went to the Mounties, they told me that, because of the lack of registrations, the fund had been run in effect like a private investment club. They said taking civil action was the most appropriate thing for us to do. The truth is, Muir created a very clever and complicated trail, and I think neither force wanted to invest the manpower in trying to unravel it. Especially when, as I said earlier, the outcome is doubtful."

"But how can they not even attempt to prosecute him?"

"I don't blame the police," Howell said. "Our securities regulations are a joke, and jurisdictional confusion makes us an easy target for fraudsters. When the cops do catch one and get a conviction, the penalties are so minor they wonder why they even bothered."

"Well, at the end of the day, money doesn't have a jurisdiction. You said it was sent to Europe. Derek said it went to the Netherlands. Is that correct?"

"Yes, to the BNSA Bank in Amsterdam. Money was wired there from Muir's various accounts. I have copies of the wires."

"So obviously you also have the Dutch account number."

"We do, but there isn't a name we can attach to it. It's yet another numbered company that was registered through a law firm."

"Is that where the trail ends?"

"For us it did. We hired our own lawyer in Amsterdam and through him went to the bank and the law firm that was used to register the company. It was a waste of time. They both said we had no legal justification to require them to give us information about the account holder or the account's contents," Howell said.

"So you don't know if the money is still in the account."

"That's correct. It could be on Mars by now," Howell said. He paused to lean towards Ava. "Do you have a way of finding out if it's still there?"

"I do know a man in the Netherlands who has excellent bank connections."

"Will you contact him?"

"If I do, I'll need to provide him with specific information."

Howell touched a trio of files that sat in front of him. "Most of what you need is in here. You can take them if you want. I'm not giving you everything I have, but I went through my information and separated what I think is most important."

Ava eyed the files. "That was thoughtful of you. I'll take them to read, but that isn't a commitment to do anything else."

"That's fine."

"Do the files explain how people were persuaded to invest in the fund?"

"You'll find an explanation in my notes," Howell said. "Basically they were all members of the chapel's finance committee. Muir was chairman. That's how they got to know and trust him."

"If they were on this finance committee, how valid is the disclaimer that the chapel and the fund operated independently of each other?"

"The finance committee had no power. Pastor Rogers pretends to believe in democratizing the chapel, so he set up any number of committees to give the members a voice in its various activities. He refers to them as advisory committees, but at the end of the day they have zero power. He makes every decision himself."

"What kind of advice would the finance committee have given him?"

Howell smiled. "Their focus was entirely on ways to expand the chapel's income. How money was spent, according to Rogers, was not part of their advisory mandate."

"Still, Muir must have told him about the fund. Surely he wouldn't have set it up without his approval."

"According to Rogers, Muir did approach him, through Patrick Cunningham. Rogers thought the fund's objectives were admirable and gave it his unofficial blessing, but he insists that neither he nor anyone else in a senior position endorsed it, recommended it to chapel members, or had anything to do with its operation. And, like I told you, I couldn't find a shred of evidence that said otherwise."

Ava glanced at the files again. "Tell me, if I decide to pursue this further, what will you want from me?"

"Nothing."

"Are you saying that if I get some money out of Muir, you won't want a piece of it?"

"I am."

"But you've invested a lot in this."

"I've written it off. What I haven't written off, though, is the possibility that Muir can be brought down. Hell, I'd pay to see that," Howell said.

"Derek mentioned that you met him."

"I did, and so can you. His home address is in one of the files," Howell said. "I went to the house to serve him with papers. He took the papers, laughed, and then slammed the door in my face."

"He knew who you were?" Ava said.

"It wasn't our first meeting. That was when he came here to my office with his lawyer and sat where you're sitting. I told him we were prepared to take him to court to recoup the money he'd stolen. Within five minutes I understood how he was able to con everyone at the chapel," Howell said. "He's a good-looking guy, perfectly groomed, well-dressed, soft-spoken, and carries himself in a dignified manner — until he opens his mouth."

"He was profane?"

"No, he's a specialist in avoiding direct questions. He talks and talks, but by the time you strip away his clichés and stupid anecdotes, there's nothing left of any substance." Howell grimaced. "The longer he talked to me, going around and around in pointless circles, the angrier I got. After all these years dealing with people like him, I thought I was past getting upset, but he was so smug and artificial that I wanted to punch him in the face just to crack that veneer."

"But you didn't."

"Of course not. But Eddie told me Hong Kong debt collectors sometimes do more than punch."

"I hope you aren't being serious," Ava said as she stood up and gathered the files.

"I apologize if that was an inappropriate remark," Howell said quickly. "It is just that this guy has done a lot of damage to a great many nice people. Phil Gregory may be the only suicide, but I can tell you more than a few of the others have contemplated it."

"I'll go through the files. I may even drop in on Malcolm Muir. Either way, my focus will be on the bank in Amsterdam, not figuring out how best to assault him," she said.

"Hey, I did apologize for that crack."

Ava looked across the desk at Howell. "Well, truthfully, Eddie is not entirely wrong. Sometimes it does become necessary to get a little physical — but only as a last resort."

(7)

IT WAS LUNCHTIME WHEN AVA GOT BACK TO YORKVILLE. She dropped off Howell's files at her condo and then went back down to Yorkville Avenue to walk a couple of blocks east to the Dynasty Restaurant. The Dynasty was one of Yorkville's few Chinese restaurants, and fortunately it was a good one. Ava ordered hot and sour soup, fried octopus, and the rainbow fold — fried minced duck with diced vegetables to be wrapped in lettuce and coated with hoisin sauce.

As she waited for the food, Ava reviewed the meeting with Howell. Despite her outwardly less-than-enthusiastic reaction, he had captured her interest when he mentioned how much had been sent overseas to the Dutch bank. Howell's failure to recover any of the money didn't cause her concern. It was enough that he had confirmed Muir hadn't lost it, because as long as the money existed, there was always a chance it could be retrieved. She thought about Jacob Smits, her connection in Amsterdam, then checked her watch to calculate the time difference. She wanted to read the files before calling him but didn't want to leave it too late. Before she could set herself a deadline, the food began to arrive, and she turned her attention to it.

Half an hour later Ava left the Dynasty and walked down to Bloor Street. She went into the bank where she kept her old Moleskine notebooks and provided identification to give her access to her safety deposit box. A few minutes later she was leafing through a notebook with the heading *Borneo: Two Sisters.* She found Jacob's contact information, copied it into the notebook she'd started for Phil Gregory, and then headed back to the condo.

She changed into Adidas training pants and a T-shirt as soon as she arrived, then sat with the files and her Moleskine notebook at the kitchen table. The files were labelled "Malcolm Muir," "Harvest Investment Fund," "Investors and Pastor Sammy Rogers," and "Banking." She reached for the Muir file and then stopped and instead picked up her cell. Derek and Mimi would be anxious to know how the meeting with Howell had gone.

"Hey, I was wondering when I'd hear from you. How was the meeting?" Derek answered.

"It went well enough. Howell is obviously frustrated by his inability to nail Malcolm Muir," she said. "He explained what he tried but also made it clear he's through trying. He's at a dead end both financially and legally."

"Where does that leave us? Did he ask you to help?"

"He asked me to take over the case," Ava said. "I told him my only interest is in helping Mimi and her mother. He said I won't be able to do that unless I go after Muir."

"There is some logic in that."

"Yes, but it's logic that would be much more compelling if I was still in the debt-recovery business. I don't want to go down that hole again, but at the same time I do want to help Mimi. It's a bit of a conundrum," she said. "At the end of our meeting, Howell gave me some files he'd compiled. I promised to read them but I didn't make any commitments beyond that."

"How long do you think it will take?"

Shit, Ava thought as Derek gently applied the pressure. *Well, if I'm going to have this conversation with him, I might as well have it now.*

"Derek, do you remember how I operated when I was on a job with Uncle?"

"Yes. You were a bit of a loner."

"Well, the fact that I'm no longer with Uncle doesn't mean I've changed my approach," she said. "Here's the way I'm going to handle this. First I'm going to read the files. If there's information in them that I think is worth pursuing, I'll pursue it. If there isn't, I'm going to return the files to Howell and you'll have to tell Mrs. Gregory there's nothing else that can be done. If there *is* something of value, then I will chase it down to the very best of my ability. But Derek, I have to be left alone to do that. I won't be issuing daily reports."

"I understand."

"Then let's leave it at that," Ava said, feeling slightly guilty about being so abrupt with Derek. "Listen, I'll read the files today and I'll call you when I'm finished, to let you know — one way or another — what I'm going to do."

"That would be great. And, Ava, I promise that if you decide to keep going after Muir, we'll stay out of your hair."

"We'll talk later," Ava said, and ended the call.

She looked at the files and then reached for the one on top, labelled "Malcolm Muir." When she opened it, the first thing she saw was an 8 × 10-inch glossy colour photo of a man's head with "Muir" written under it. In the photo he was staring straight at the camera. His mouth was tightly drawn and his hooded brown eyes conveyed . . . nothing. There was no surprise, no curiosity, no anger, no pleasure, just a dark blankness. Equally bland were his features; his nose, lips, and ears were neither large nor small, with no distinctive bumps or irregularities. He had a bald spot, and the hair around it was clipped close. He did not look like a man who would inspire trust. Maybe in person he presented a different image, Ava thought, or maybe her opinion of him had been coloured by Howell's.

She returned to the file and leafed through it. There were several documents she had already seen when going through Phil Gregory's papers. She flipped past them until she came to a promotional brochure that appeared to be part of the launch program for the fund. Ava scanned through it, admiring its emphasis on the good works the fund would finance while underplaying the financial returns the investors could expect. Muir had obviously known what would appeal to his target market.

At the back of the file was a thick sheaf of papers held together by large paper clip. The front sheet was headed "Malcolm Muir bio." Behind it were Todd Howell's records of his meetings with Muir, Pastor Rogers, and Patrick Cunningham, the Harvest Table CFO. The bio ran to a loosely organized two pages and looked like it had been written by Howell or someone on his staff. Ava read it, absorbing the bare bones of Muir's life.

Muir was fifty-six. He'd been born in Winnipeg, Manitoba, attended high school there, and went to the University of

Manitoba to study law. He didn't graduate, leaving the university when he was twenty. He took a job with a finance company in Winnipeg that specialized in high-interest loans to people whom the banks wouldn't lend to. There was mention of various night-school courses towards a degree in accounting, but no evidence that a degree had been obtained. He became a district manager for the finance company about ten years later and was transferred to the city of Timmins in northern Ontario. Three years after that he was transferred to Toronto, and at the age of thirty-nine he became a vice-president. In the margin next to this information, someone (probably Howell, Ava thought) had written, *He was in charge of collecting overdue loans. He was evidently very good at it and was known to have hired goons to intimidate customers*

When Muir turned forty-five, his employment with the finance company ended. *Did he resign voluntarily, was he forced to resign, or was he terminated?* someone had written in the margin. The same person had later added, with a different pen, *He was terminated. Evidently he was pocketing a portion of any cash his goons collected.* According to the bio, for the next five years Muir worked with various other finance companies in jobs that all seemed to relate to collections. He didn't last long anywhere, and six years later the only jobs he appeared to have were as chairman of the finance committee and CEO of the Harvest Investment Fund, both supposedly non-paying positions.

Ava started to write some questions in her notebook and then stopped. Perhaps Howell's notes of his meeting with Rogers and Cunningham might provide the answers, so she turned to them. Within a few seconds she was smiling.

Howell had asked the same questions that were on her mind: when did Muir join the congregation, and how did he come to be named chairman of the finance committee?

Cunningham seemed to have done most of the talking in the meeting. His story was that he had been approached by Muir, a new and eager chapel member, who wanted to know if there was something he could do to help raise funds. At that time fundraising was a tightly controlled activity spearheaded by the pastor and a few trusted members of the executive. Muir offered to head up an ex-officio committee and volunteered to contribute twenty thousand dollars to kickstart it. There hadn't been a finance-related committee at the chapel until then. Cunningham had spoken to Pastor Rogers about Muir's approach, and the pastor said he'd go along with it as long as its mandate was restricted to fund-raising. Cunningham went to Muir with the proposal; he accepted the terms and agreed to be the finance committee's first chairman.

The creation of the finance committee and its objectives were announced at a Sunday service, and members of the congregation were invited to join. Ten parishioners immediately applied. Howell wrote in the margin: *Because the committees had no real power, but inclusion in them provided chapel members with a sense of being in the inner circle and tied them more tightly to the organization, there was no limit on committee memberships. Before the implosion of the fund the finance committee had grown to twenty-two members, nearly all of whom had invested in it.*

Ava sat back in her chair. How many people attended the chapel? She had been using Howell's files as a shortcut to information, but she was starting to feel that she was lacking details. She put the files to one side, turned to her computer, and typed "Harvest Table Bible Chapel" into the search engine. There were several pages of results. She scanned them and then opened a link to a photo catalogue.

Ava looked at the first photo and blinked. When Derek had referred to it as a "monster structure," Ava had assumed he was exaggerating. He wasn't. The photo was an aerial view of the chapel and its property. The building sat in the middle of an enormous swath of land, completely surrounded by parking lots that were in turn surrounded by vast rolling lawns. It looked nothing like any church Ava had ever seen. In fact, if she hadn't known what it was, she would have assumed at first glance that it was the corporate headquarters of a major high-tech or finance company.

The next picture showed the front of the building at ground level. It seemed to be about four storeys high, although she couldn't be certain because the floors weren't differentiated. Its red-brick walls ran in straight unbroken panels several metres wide from the ground to the brown tiled roof, the panels separated by sheets of tinted glass. White crosses had been etched into the glass in random fashion. The chapel's front entrance was two immense metal doors that had various biblical scenes etched on them. On either side of the doors, white marble crosses soared towards the sky.

The following shots were of inside the chapel. The cavernous lobby had white tiled floors flecked with gold, walls covered in murals depicting more biblical scenes, and a ceiling that was a huge glass dome. In the lobby were three sets of double wooden doors with WORSHIP CENTRE stencilled in gold above them, and to their left and right were spiral staircases leading to balconies.

The last photos Ava looked at were of what could have been the interior of a large upscale theatre, with upholstered seating, chandeliers, and a deep, wide stage. This was the worship centre. A massive cross towered behind a large granite pulpit at centre stage, flanked by two immense video screens.

Ava opened another website. There were more pictures of the chapel, a short history, and some statistics. She read the numbers: the chapel and its grounds occupied two hundred acres and had more than four thousand parking spots and its own fleet of buses; the worship centre could accommodate seven thousand people.

Pastor Rogers has built an empire, she thought as she entered his name in the search field. Again there were pages of results. One, titled "Canada's Religious Superstar," caught her attention. It was an article published the year before by a U.S. magazine called the *Evangelical*, and while it was primarily fawning, Ava assumed that the facts about Rogers's life would be accurate.

Sammy Rogers had been born in Smiths Falls, near Ottawa, and was the son of a Baptist minister. He graduated from the University of Ottawa with a BA and then attended a Bible college in Alberta. After graduation he went south to Oklahoma for another year of education at a religious university, where he befriended Randy Simmons, the son of Blackstone Simmons, an internationally known evangelist. After leaving university, Rogers joined the Simmons organization. He worked on several crusades, initially as a front man drumming up attendance, but his oratory skills and charisma soon became apparent and he was put on stage as a warm-up for Simmons.

Rogers left Simmons three years later to become pastor of the Warehouse Church in the east end of Toronto. The article said he had been motivated by a wish to return to Canada and the realization that there was no possibility of further advancement with the Simmons organization. The Warehouse Church — which actually operated out of a warehouse — was already well-known in evangelical circles. Its services featured faith healing and speaking in tongues, both of which were familiar to Rogers from his time with Simmons. As successful as the church was before he got there, Rogers doubled and then tripled its attendance. The warehouse could accommodate close to a thousand people, and Rogers drew at least that number twice every Sunday. But with no room to expand, he urged the church executive to find a larger venue. Harvest Table Bible Chapel was the result.

Ava thought briefly about looking at a clip of Rogers in preacher mode but decided she'd gone far enough off track. Instead she reached for the file with the banking information.

Despite the messy appearance of his office, the files Todd Howell had given her were well organized. The top two sheets of paper in the banking file listed every account Muir had opened, along with the dates, deposit amounts, and bank branch information. In the right margin were the dates when he'd either closed the accounts or bankrupted the company aligned with the account. The third sheet was devoted to the bank in the Netherlands, with its contact information, Muir's account number, and a long list of the transfers sent to it, organized by date. The total was just over thirty million. *Time to call Jacob,* she thought, looking in the notebook for his phone number. *I hope he hasn't changed his number.*

A woman's voice answered loudly. "Hallo."

"May I speak to Jacob Smits, please," Ava said.

"*Spreek je Nederlands*?"

"I'm sorry, I don't speak Dutch," Ava said, guessing at the woman's question.

The woman paused and then seemed to cover the mouthpiece, because her voice became muffled. Then she said loudly, "*Slechts een minuut*."

A few seconds later Jacob Smits said, "Hello, can I help you?"

"This is Ava Lee calling from Toronto. I hope I'm not disturbing your dinner."

"We've already eaten," he said, laughing. "I'm happy you called. Can I assume this is about business?"

"It is, though I'm equally pleased to hear your voice. We did good work together, and now I need your help again."

"Yes, we did do good work," Smits said. "What kind of help do you need?"

Ava smiled. Smits was short and stocky, wore suits that were perpetually rumpled, and as a point of national pride usually sported an orange tie. At first glance he looked completely undistinguished, but Ava had learned quickly that he had a razor-sharp mind and a myriad of contacts from his days working with the National Police Corps fraud division and the Dutch Tax and Customs Administration. He worked as a private detective but was also an accountant, and like Ava he got directly to the point. She never had to guess what he was thinking.

"I'm trying to help a friend whose father was caught up in a large fraud scheme based in Canada, but the money found its way to a Dutch bank. Where it went from there, I have no idea."

"How much money are you talking about?"

"The father lost close to three million Canadian dollars, but the entire fraud was more than thirty-two million — about twenty-one million euros," Ava said. "All I really care about is the three million. It's all the money the family had."

"The father must be distraught."

"The father is dead. He committed suicide. The rest of the family is beyond distraught."

"I'm sorry for my assumption," Smits said. "What's the name of the bank?"

"BNSA. I have an address on De Boelelaan street."

"That's in the Zuidas, Amsterdam's financial district. BNSA has its main branch and corporate headquarters there."

"Do you have any contacts at the bank?"

"That depends on what you need to know."

"Over the past five years our Canadian fraudster was transferring money on a regular basis to an account in that bank. I have the account number but not the name or any contact information attached to it. I'd like to know whose name the account is in and how to contact them," Ava said. "I'd also like to know how much money is still in the account and, if money was moved, where it went. A Canadian lawyer hired by the victims traced the money to the bank but that's as far as he got."

"Did he approach the bank?"

"Yes, he hired an Amsterdam law firm, but they couldn't get anything out of BNSA."

"But if a crime was committed — "

"No criminal charges have been laid in Canada or anywhere else," Ava interrupted. "This was a carefully planned and executed fraud that exploited weaknesses in the

Canadian laws. In fact, the main perpetrator continues to live in the open, and in very comfortable circumstances, in Toronto. He is officially bankrupt, of course, as are all the companies he used to mask his activities."

"And you haven't gone after him yet? That isn't like you, Ava, at least not as I remember you."

"I can't operate in Canada the way I did in Asia," Ava said. "Besides, I don't have any real interest in talking to him until I know where the money is or isn't. Help me do that and I'll figure out the next step from there."

"I understand. And as it happens, I have a few contacts at BNSA."

"That's wonderful," Ava said quickly.

"But they won't come cheaply."

"Pay whatever you have to."

"It could be as much ten thousand euros, and it could be double that if I have to go to more than one person."

"I'll wire you thirty thousand euros today, twenty thousand for the possible bank contacts and ten thousand for you as a retainer."

"Do you have my banking information?"

"Are you still with ING?" Ava asked, looking at her notebook.

"Yes."

"Then I have the information I need," Ava said. "I'd also like to send you data I have on the wires sent to BNSA. I have the account number and the date and amount of each transfer."

"Scan it and send it to me," Smits said. "My email address hasn't changed either."

"I'll do it right away."

"And I'll start making calls first thing in the morning."

"Thank you, Jacob."

"Ava, you're paying me. You don't have to thank me."

"I like to think of you as a friend, not just someone I'm paying to do a job."

"That's a real compliment. I'll try not to disappoint you."

Ava ended the call, then sat back in her chair. There were times, despite what she had said to Derek, when she'd missed some aspects of her old job. Working with people like Jacob Smits was one of them.

(8)

AVA SENT THE INFORMATION SHE'D PROMISED TO SMITS, grabbed her notebook, and left the condo to walk to her bank to make the wire transfer. She was halfway there when her phone rang. She looked at the incoming number and smiled.

"You've landed safely," she said.

"I have, and now I have one full day to recover before starting work," Fai said.

"I've spent the day trying to locate Mr. Gregory's money."

"How is that going?"

"I'll know more tomorrow when I hear from my contact in the Netherlands," Ava said. "How was your flight?"

"Long. We ran into headwinds that added an hour to the trip, so we were close to seventeen hours in the air. I don't know how the people flying in economy survived it."

"Did you get any sleep?"

"Some, but I was awake for most of the trip. I watched a couple of films and I read Lau Lau's script. Actually, I read it twice and made some notes," Fai said matter-of-factly.

"I'm glad you read it, but I don't detect any enthusiasm."

"Ava," Fai said, and then hesitated. "It's brilliant, but I have to tell you that I think it would be a dangerous film to make. It would never be approved by the China Movie Syndicate and it would never be distributed in China."

"Lau Lau told me the same thing, but China isn't the only market for good Chinese films."

"Even if you finance it, how will Lau Lau ever get permission to shoot in Beijing and around Tiananmen Square?"

"I'm sure Lau Lau has considered the logistical problems he'd face. Let's not pass judgement on how difficult shooting will be until we hear from him."

"I don't mean to sound so negative," Fai said. "I really do think it's the best thing he's ever written, and I would be honoured to play the role of the mother, even if there were repercussions. But I'm less worried about what would happen to me and Lau Lau and more concerned about what it could mean for you and May Ling and Amanda, and maybe even your father and his family."

Ava went quiet. May Ling Wong and Amanda Yee were her partners in Three Sisters, an investment company with money in Hong Kong, Shanghai, and Beijing. Ava's father, Marcus, and her four half-brothers were in business in Hong Kong. "Is that what you meant by 'dangerous'?" she asked.

"Yes. I spent hours thinking about it on the plane. Lau Lau has no career and no prospects right now, and a film like this, even if it's banned in China, could resurrect his career in places like Taiwan and Europe. As for me, realistically — and despite everything they said to us — I don't believe the Syndicate will finance any film I'm in. So, like Lau Lau, I don't have much to lose," Fai said. "It is different for you and your friends. If the authorities learned that you'd financed this film, they might go after your businesses in Hong Kong, Shanghai, and elsewhere in China. It could be particularly hard on May Ling, the Pos, and Suki Chan, because they live in China."

Ava thought back to how Lau Lau had described the film to her. "He told me the story is about a mother looking for her son who disappeared during the Tiananmen protests. It didn't sound that controversial."

"Anything that touches on what happened in Tiananmen is controversial, and he's embellished the storyline he gave you," Fai said. "Now there's a parallel plot that focuses on a female army officer who has a part in deciding what action to take against the protesters. She's completely opposed to sending troops into Tiananmen to disperse them, and when the troops do go in, she becomes an eyewitness to what occurs. The mother eventually meets her and hears her story."

"I see," Ava said, immediately realizing that could generate a negative reaction. "Well, we're not going to do anything rash. Why don't you speak to Chen and compare notes. I'll read the script myself and then we can set up a conference call when you're settled and over your jet lag. I promise you I'm not going to make any decisions without involving the two of you and all my business partners."

"That makes me feel a bit less anxious," Fai said.

"But, anxious or not, you do think the script is brilliant?"

"I do."

"Well, that's a good start," Ava said.

Fai yawned.

"You must be exhausted," Ava said.

"As soon as we finish speaking I'm going to crawl into bed and sleep until noon," Fai said. "I just wish you were here with me. I miss you already, and I'm sure it's only going to get worse."

"If things move quickly here, maybe I'll join you for a while. I've never been to Taiwan."

Fai yawned again.

"Hey, go to bed," Ava said. "I'm going to crash early tonight, so I'll call you when I get up."

"Okay. Love you."

"Love you too."

Ava put the phone into the pocket of her lightweight Adidas jacket and walked the rest of the way to the bank. Twenty minutes later she left, with her account forty-five thousand dollars lighter. The late afternoon weather was lovely, about twenty degrees with a light breeze, so rather than going back to her condo, Ava decided to take a longer walk.

Howell had mentioned that Muir lived in the Annex, a quiet old neighbourhood within walking distance of the condo. Ava had copied the address into her notebook. Despite its central location, the Annex hadn't been taken over by developers because of a government freeze on construction and because at least five hundred buildings were protected by Heritage Toronto. Large Victorian and Edwardian mansions occupied its tree-lined streets, some of them — given their proximity to the university — used for student residences and frat and sorority houses, but the majority were still single-family dwellings. Ava's bak mei teacher, Grandmaster Tang, lived in such a house in the Annex, using what was once the living room as his studio.

Muir's house was on Elgin Street, a block north of the grandmaster's on Lowther. Ava wasn't sure why she wanted to see it, except that it might help make Muir seem more real. When she reached Elgin, she saw that the houses were an interesting mix of old and new; she was pleased that the newer homes suited, rather than overwhelmed, the street. In Mimi's neighbourhood, tear downs and rebuilds had resulted in faux French chateaus sitting between two bungalows. On Elgin the newer homes were more modest in size and low-key in their use of wood, stone, and windows.

At Muir's home, modesty was absent where windows were concerned. The entire left front side was glass, stretching from a few feet above the foundation to a few feet short of the roof. There were no curtains or blinds, so Ava had a clear view of an office with a desk and chair and an enormous painting on the wall behind them. Muir was sitting at the desk, working on a laptop.

Ava stood on the sidewalk staring at him. She was close enough to see that he was older than he looked in the photo. There were bags under his eyes and deep wrinkles across his forehead, and he had a light stubble on his chin. He was wearing black jeans and a navy-blue Nike golf shirt that fitted snugly over a taut torso. To Ava he didn't look particularly sinister. If she had passed him on the street he wouldn't have been worth a second glance.

Muir raised his head, glanced in Ava's direction, and then refocused on the laptop. She didn't move or avert her gaze. A few seconds later he raised his head again, and this time she seemed to catch his attention. He pursed his lips and furrowed his brow as if trying to remember who she was.

Ava thought about leaving but put one foot on his driveway. Before she knew it she was walking towards the house. She saw Muir rise from his chair and knew he'd seen her approaching. There was no knocker and no window on the solid wood front door. Ava looked up and saw a CCTV camera. She pushed the doorbell and took a step back.

"Who's there?" said a man's voice over the intercom.

"Mr. Muir, my name is Ava Lee," she said.

"I don't think I know you, young lady," he said.

"That's true sir, but we have mutual friends."

"Go on."

"Pastor Sammy Rogers and Harvest Table Bible Chapel," Ava said. "I went to visit a friend on Lowther, but he wasn't in. And then I remembered someone at the chapel telling me about your home. They said the design is unique, and since I'm thinking of doing renovations to my own, I came by to see it. I didn't mean to inconvenience you, and I'm sorry if I've interrupted something."

The door opened partially and Ava found herself looking up at Muir, who was taller than she expected. He examined her, not pretending to be doing otherwise. "I don't believe I've seen you at the chapel," he said.

"That isn't surprising when you consider how many people attend."

"No, you I would have remembered," he said. "You're Chinese, yes?"

"Yes. How did you know?"

"I've spent enough time in Asia to tell Chinese from Korean from Japanese. We have a few Koreans, but not so many Chinese attend the chapel, especially not young and attractive women," he said in a way that made Ava uncomfortable. "So, who is this friend who suggested you come to my house? I have to say I find it very strange."

"I can't blame you for being suspicious," she said.

"That's not much of an answer." He stared at her around the edge of the door. "If you have something to say, I'm listening," he said.

She drew a deep breath. "I was a friend of Phillip Gregory. He was on your finance committee and put money into your investment fund," she said quickly. "He's dead. He committed — "

"Oh, goodness me," Muir interrupted. "Why don't you people leave me alone? What's done is done, the money is lost, and all this moaning and trying to lay blame won't change that."

"Did you hear what I said? The man is dead."

"I didn't know. And now that I do, I don't care," he said calmly. "I have my own problems. I've had to declare bankruptcy and I'm still being hounded by people like you. Is there no decency, no respect for privacy left in this city?"

Before Ava could reply, the door closed in her face.

(9)

AVA FELT ANNOYED AS SHE WALKED BACK TOWARDS Yorkville, but more annoyed with herself than with Muir. There had been no strategy behind her confronting the man, and it had been foolish to mention Phillip Gregory and give Muir her name. "What the hell was I thinking?" she muttered.

Ava had been in her mid-twenties when she started working with Uncle, and she brought with her the natural exuberance of youth. He had never faulted her for being eager but always counselled caution, and in his calm, controlled, understated way he helped educate her in how to deal with difficult people and circumstances. She'd adapted to his style, which was easy enough because it was her basic nature to be thoughtful. Her mantra became, *Take one step at a time and take nothing for granted.* It had served Ava well during her years in the collection business, and if she was going to help the Gregory family, she knew she'd be wise to keep following it. Calling Jacob Smits had been the correct first step, and waiting for him to get back to her with information was the second; dropping in on Malcolm Muir wasn't on the list.

When she returned home, Ava again noticed how quiet it was in the condo. She thought about Fai and their conversation about Lau Lau's script.

Ava looked at the files on her table. There wasn't much point in continuing to burrow into them until she heard back from Jacob. She opened her laptop and clicked on the email from Chen that contained the script. Ava had never read a script before, and at first its format was awkward to her eye, but the story soon had her in its grip. What she found particularly clever was that the actual events at Tiananmen — both the protests and the eventual massacre — were never shown, only alluded to through the mother's conversations with people who had known her son and through the memories of the army officer. If anything, in Ava's opinion, leaving to the imagination the reality of what had happened made it all the more terrifying.

When Ava finished reading it was dark outside. She went into the bathroom and washed her face with cold water. She had cried several times when the power of Lau Lau's words had overwhelmed her, but she hadn't stopped reading. Now she felt a need to gather herself. She thought about calling Fai but decided to let her sleep. Instead she phoned Chen's office in Beijing, where it was late morning.

"Ava, is there a problem?" Chen asked as soon as he came on the line.

"No, I'm calling about Lau Lau's script," she said. "Fai and I have both read it."

"What do you think?"

"I'd like to hear your thoughts first."

Chen paused and then said carefully, "It is powerful, moving. It might be the best thing he's ever written."

"That's what Fai thinks as well, but she has reservations. She's concerned about blowback from the China Movie Syndicate — or worse."

"I share those reservations," Chen said. "If the film were true to the script, it could easily upset the government. Who knows what they'd do to Lau Lau, and to anyone else associated with the film."

"Do you think Lau Lau is concerned?"

"No. He has absolutely nothing to lose."

"Fai said the same thing. And she added herself as someone without much to lose, particularly where working in China is concerned," Ava said. "Is that true?"

"I hate to say it, but she's probably right."

"What about you? We discussed the possibility of your producing it. Would you still want to do that with this script?"

"If I did, I'd also start making retirement plans and looking for a new home in Thailand or Indonesia."

"That doesn't answer my question."

Chen hesitated, then said, "I've been in this business for a long time, and frankly I'm tired of it. I have enough money for a comfortable retirement, and there are capable people working for me who can take over the agency. My happiest days were working with Lau Lau and Fai when they were making great films together. I was part of their team, but I was always on the outside looking in and never felt I made a meaningful contribution. When you first asked if I would consider producing whatever Lau Lau came up with, I know my initial response was slightly negative, but the more I thought about it, the more I realized that I would really like to do it. Helping to create a Chinese film that actually means something could be my swan song, my legacy to a business I've spent my life in."

"I'm happy to hear you say that."

"But the bigger question is what kind of risk you and your friends are prepared to take," Chen said quickly. "I know you all have substantial business interests in China. Are you prepared to put those interests in jeopardy?"

"I'm sure we could find a way to shield our involvement if it came to that," Ava said. "Chen, I'll do whatever you and Fai think is best, but I need you to make your decision based on artistic merit, not on speculation about how the Chinese government will respond to the film. Who knows, they might just ban it in China and otherwise ignore it."

"That's optimistic," Chen said. "Ava, as much as I'd like to see a film like this made, I have to repeat that it isn't too late for you to back out. You managed to get Lau Lau into rehab, which was a minor miracle by itself, and you got him writing again, which was a major miracle. No one will think badly of you if you don't want to finance this film."

"Lau Lau would. And I know someone else who would as well."

"Who?"

"Me."

(10)

AVA HAD TROUBLE SLEEPING. AT FIRST SHE COULDN'T get Lau Lau's script out of her mind, and when she had finally wrestled that into submission, she found herself thinking about Malcolm Muir. Her afternoon encounter with him hadn't bothered her much at the time, or so she thought, but now, as she replayed his dismissive reaction to Phillip Gregory's death, she felt a mixture of anger and disgust.

At two o'clock she got out of bed, drank a glass of water, and phoned Fai.

"You're still up?" Fai answered.

"I can't sleep. I have too much on my mind," she said. "I met the man who orchestrated the investment fund fraud and caused Phillip Gregory to kill himself. He was so uncaring that it has upset me. I've been trying to limit my involvement in the matter, but now I'm thinking that I might go much deeper into it."

"Could that be dangerous?"

"I doubt it. Most financial fraudsters believe they can outsmart everyone else and aren't typically violent," Ava said.

"Still, you'll be careful?"

"Of course. My risk-taking days are behind me."

"Excuse me—" Fai said abruptly, and the line went quiet.

What's happened? Ava thought.

"Ava, sorry about that," Fai said a few seconds later. "That was Andy Gao calling. He's downstairs waiting for me. He's going to take me to the set to meet the cast and crew."

"Then you'd better head downstairs. I'm going to go back to bed. Maybe I can sleep now," Ava said.

This time when she got into bed, she lay on her back, folded her hands across her chest, and began to breathe deeply. She sucked as much air into her lungs as she could and then slowly exhaled it through pursed lips, until her lungs were as empty as she could make them. After the fifth breath she started to feel light-headed. Sometime after the seventh breath, she fell asleep.

She dreamt most nights. When she was younger, her dreams had been strange, illogical, and frightening. Often they focused on futile attempts to connect with her father. But in recent years it was Uncle who visited her dreams, particularly when she was feeling indecisive or troubled. So she wasn't surprised to see him this night, although the fact that he was sitting on the patio of Trattoria Nervosa, her favourite Italian restaurant in Yorkville, was decidedly odd.

Ava stood on the sidewalk and stared at him. Uncle was drinking black coffee and had a lit cigarette dangling from his lower lip. No one else was visible, but she wondered how long it would take before he was told that smoking was not allowed on the patio.

Ava, come and join me, he said.

She skirted the wrought-iron fence that surrounded the patio and sat down at his table. *You can't smoke here*, she said.

I do not see any signs, he said.

Believe me, it's true.

He nodded, threw down the butt, and ground it under his heel. *You live in a world with too many rules.*

There are no rules in the world where you are?

The only world I inhabit is in your imagination.

And I'm so very happy that you're there.

Uncle smiled, and suddenly he looked as he had when she'd met him so many years before — a small, neat man dressed in a black suit with a white shirt buttoned to the collar, black hair flecked with grey, skin that looked ten to twenty years younger than he was, and dark, probing eyes. *I came because I sensed you needed me. Things have been going well for you, but there are challenges you are not sure you should embrace. The problem with Mimi's father, for one.*

What do you mean?

Well, you want to help the family but you cannot do it without taking on this man Malcolm Muir. Yet when you stood on his doorstep, you allowed him to dismiss you and close a door in your face. You need to send him a message that you are not a woman who accepts that. No one has the right to insult you. Anyone who does should know there will be consequences.

She took his remark as a criticism, and it stung. *That's the way I behaved when I was in the debt-collection business. When you left me, I let the business go, and the kind of behaviour associated with it*, she said.

This has nothing to do with collecting a debt. It is about righting a wrong and helping a friend. I know that is your intention, but you cannot forget the lessons I taught you, and that means you cannot go about it half-heartedly.

How have I been half-hearted? she asked, stung again by his words.

Perhaps it is more accurate to say that you have been distracted. I know this film business has been on your mind. If you are serious about pursuing Muir, then you need to put aside thoughts about the film and concentrate on the job at hand. I always admired your ability to shut out everything else and focus completely on the goal. If you do that with Muir, you will be successful. The film will not disappear. When you are finished with Muir, it will be there waiting for you, he said, lighting another cigarette and taking a deep drag. *One more thing, Ava. I know you will not charge your friends our normal fee, but if you collect more money than they lost, you should be compensated. This is not about the money. It is about what that kind of money can help you do.*

I don't understand, Ava said, and then she heard a phone ring. She looked at the trattoria's entrance, but no one was there. She turned back to Uncle, only to find him gone. The phone kept ringing. She tried to stand up so she could locate its origin, and then suddenly the daylight disappeared.

She found herself sitting up in bed in almost complete darkness, except for the glow coming from her phone. She reached for it. "Ava Lee," she said.

"This is Jacob. I apologize for calling so early, but I have part of what you wanted to know, and now I need further direction."

Ava glanced at the phone. It was ten minutes to seven, almost one o'clock in Amsterdam. Jacob hadn't wasted any time. "What did you find out?"

"I have the name attached to the account. I also found out where most of the money was sent and can make some assumptions about what it was used for."

"What's the name?" she asked, trying to contain her excitement.

"The account is registered to a Dutch numbered company doing business as Jewellery Circle."

"I'm not surprised it's numbered — Muir likes using numbered companies. But I haven't come across Jewellery Circle in any of my files."

"Who is Muir?"

"Malcolm Muir is the perpetrator of the fraud. Didn't I mention him to you?"

"Not until now."

"And you haven't come across his name in connection with Jewellery Circle?"

"No, the name that's on the incorporation papers in the bank's files is Jasmine Yip. That's Chinese, I think."

"It's most definitely Chinese," said Ava, surprised and immediately confused.

"She provided an Amsterdam address when she filed for incorporation. I checked it before calling you. It's a boutique hotel, and they know her. She's been a guest several times, but not for a while."

"Are foreign guests required to provide their passport when they check in?" Ava asked.

"They are, and this particular hotel also requests home and email addresses, both of which I was given and both of which I checked," he said. "The home address she provided is in The Hague; it turned out to be a library. I tried sending her an email and it bounced back."

"That's unfortunate. Any luck with the passport?"

"The hotel has a copy on file."

"Do you have it?"

"You're as impatient as ever," he said, laughing. "But no, I don't have it. They're sending me a copy this afternoon."

"And you're as clever as ever. How did you convince them to do that?"

"I told them I'm with the Dutch tax authority and she's a person of interest. That's something that businesses like theirs don't question. But I'm not so clever that I can handle the logical next step without some help and a bit of luck," he said.

"What do you want to do?"

"I need an entry into the Jain community in Antwerp. I had a contact, but I'm not sure he's still there."

"You've lost me," Ava said.

"Jasmine Yip has been wiring money to a company based in Antwerp. When I looked up the name in the Belgian companies register, I saw that it was in the diamond-trading business. But the owner's name — Fozdar — doesn't seem to be Jewish. I know from experience that the diamond business is overwhelmingly owned and run by Jains and Jews, so I'm assuming he's a Jain, and they're a small but powerful and close community."

"She's been buying diamonds from Jains?"

"It will take a bit of explanation —"

"You've captured my interest, Jacob," Ava said quickly. "But I need to take a short break to make some coffee. Can you call me back in fifteen minutes?"

"My time is your time," he said.

(11)

AVA HAD TOLD SMITS A LITTLE WHITE LIE. WHILE IT WAS true she wanted a coffee and had to go to the bathroom, her real reason for asking him to call back was that she needed a moment to gather herself. Her dream conversation with Uncle was still rattling around in her head, and she couldn't help thinking that the timing and content of Jacob's phone call was connected. Uncle had visited her because he already knew that she would go in pursuit of Muir, she thought, and his purpose was to remind her how it should be done. Except it wasn't just Malcolm Muir anymore; now there was a Jasmine Yip to deal with. *This is so weird. Who the hell is Jasmine Yip, and how did she get involved in this?* she thought as she got out of bed.

She needed to use the bathroom more than she needed coffee. Then, after throwing on a sweater and track pants, she went into the kitchen, put a large teaspoon of Nescafé into a mug, and filled it with hot water from the Thermos on the counter. She reached for her notebook and wrote *Jasmine Yip* across the top of a clean page, then sat back and waited for Smits. The phone rang before she had taken her fourth sip of coffee.

"Hello, Jacob. I'm ready to talk now," she said.

"Sorry for dropping that information on you the way I did, but I was a bit excited," he said.

"That's understandable. You've done great work."

"My contacts at the bank were quick to co-operate once they knew how much I'd pay. They're both mid-level, so they have access to a lot of information, but not so well paid that they can resist a healthy bribe," he said. "I decided to use both so I could ensure that the information I was getting is accurate."

"And they told you that Jasmine Yip is the ultimate account holder."

"They did."

"Do you have any idea where she's from?"

"I won't know anything until I see her passport. I didn't want to press the hotel manager over the phone."

"You aren't worried that he'll be suspicious about the passport copy being delivered to your office?"

"It isn't. I have a friend who still works for the tax authority who sometimes lets me use his office as a post office box. He'll bring it to me — for a small fee, of course."

"That should give us as a good starting point with Jasmine Yip, but what about the Jains? I've heard the name but I have no idea who they are."

"I didn't either until about three years ago, when I was working on a divorce case where the husband of my client was making their money disappear. I found out he was buying diamonds from a trading company in Antwerp. I contacted them by phone but they wouldn't talk to me. So I went to their office in Antwerp's Diamond Quarter, but I couldn't even get past the front door. Security is unbelievably tight in those places, and I didn't have an appointment. The security guard told me that if they didn't know me I would need a reference, and that ideally it should be from a Jain, since nearly all the traders were Jains. I did some research and eventually found a Jain in Amsterdam who had connections in Antwerp. A week later the doors were opened and I managed to meet the trader who was doing business with the husband. With his help I was able to prove that the husband was using diamonds to launder the couple's money."

"What did that cost you?" Ava asked.

"Absolutely nothing. The Jains are a highly ethical people."

"Where do they originate?"

"Those in Antwerp — where there are fewer than two thousand — are from a place called Gujarat in the western part of India, which is the diamond-cutting centre in that country. The first of them came to Antwerp in the nineteen-sixties. At the time Jews dominated the diamond trade, but the Jains slowly began to expand their role," Smits said. "The diamond business is run on trust rather than contracts, and, as I said earlier, the Jains are an incredibly tight-knit community. Many of the businesses are family-based. They brought together all their resources to undercut the Jewish traders and take over the majority of the market."

"I wasn't aware that Antwerp is a power centre for diamonds."

"Again, I didn't know either, but I learned that more than eighty percent of the world's diamonds are traded or cut there. The business exceeds fifty billion U.S. dollars a year."

"That's a staggering number," Ava said. "So Jasmine Yip or

Malcolm Muir spending five or six million a year wouldn't be extraordinary."

"I wouldn't think so."

Ava looked down at her notes. "What do you mean when you say the Jains were highly ethical?"

"Like I said, they've built a multi-billion-dollar business that depends on trust. The concept of theft is abhorrent to them, from both a business and a religious viewpoint, which is why the trader was prepared to help in the divorce case."

"What kind of religion is Jainism?"

"It's a sub-sect of Hinduism quite similar to Buddhism. They are non-violent in the extreme; I was told they won't deliberately harm any living creature, not even an insect."

"Do you still have your contact's information?"

"Yes, but I don't know if he's still active."

"If he is, he might be able to help."

"I'll call him when you and I finish."

Ava glanced at her notes again. "Jacob, if your contact is willing to help, how soon are you prepared to go to Antwerp?"

"I could go first thing tomorrow morning. It's a short train ride, just over an hour, and the central station in Antwerp is only a few minutes from the Diamond Quarter," he said. "But I won't go unless I'm certain doors will be open for me. It would be pointless otherwise."

"I understand. Once you know, call me either way. If they're willing to talk to you, I have some questions I'd like you to ask."

"Of course. And if they do talk to me, we should be able to confirm Jasmine Yip's identity beyond what her passport says."

"Why do you say that?"

"You don't get into those trading houses without having your photo taken and your fingerprints scanned. If she was there, they'll know just about everything about her."

"That's wonderful."

"They'll also have a record of whoever was with her. I'm assuming that's one of the questions you want me to ask."

"It is, but let's not get ahead of ourselves," Ava said. "Call me when you know where we stand."

Ava put down her phone. This was already going better than she'd hoped, but then her caution kicked in. These weren't stupid people she was dealing with. Muir had orchestrated a scam in Canada so complex that the RCMP, the OPP, and Todd Howell's law firm had washed their hands of it. Using diamonds as a way to launder that money was equally clever — what was more portable, more universally valuable, and more untraceable than diamonds? But who was Jasmine Yip? And why would Muir entrust his stolen money to her?

She finished her coffee, made a second, and sat at the kitchen table. How odd it was that Jacob Smits's phone call had come hard on the heels of her dream about Uncle, she thought again. Ava closed her eyes and tried to remember everything Uncle had said. She saw his face wreathed in smoke, listened to his advice again, and then reached for her phone.

"Has Mr. Howell arrived yet?" she asked when a woman answered.

"Just a minute, I'll try his line."

"This is Todd Howell. What can I do for you?" he said a moment later.

"This is Ava Lee."

"Ava Lee," he said, and paused. "I didn't expect to hear

from you so quickly. Is it foolishly optimistic of me to think this is a good-news call?"

"It's neither good nor bad. I simply have a few questions for you."

"Shoot."

"In the course of your investigation into Malcolm Muir, did you ever come across the name Jasmine Yip?"

"No," Howell said without hesitation.

"Are you sure? Please take your time and think about it for a few seconds."

"It isn't a name I would forget," Howell said. "Is she linked to Muir in some way?"

"She might be, but I have nothing definitive," Ava said, and then quickly changed subjects. "When I was in your office, you mentioned that Muir's wife was Marla Swift."

"That's right."

"I know the name is Western, but does she have any Chinese connections?"

"None that I'm aware of, and we did look into her background."

"I assume you looked even more closely into Muir's life."

"We did. I used a very good private investigator."

"Did the investigator uncover any girlfriends or mistresses?"

"No. You've already found something that we missed, haven't you," Howell said, his voice rising.

"Maybe, but I'm not ready to talk about it."

"Okay, but am I wrong to think that you've decided to go after Muir?"

"Before I commit to that," she said, ignoring his question, "I need a clear and binding agreement in place."

"What kind of agreement?"

"I'll send you a copy of the contract my partner and I had our clients sign. It gave us full authority to go after funds on behalf of our clients. We deducted a thirty percent collection fee for everything we reclaimed before remitting the balance," Ava said. "We looked after all our expenses whether we were successful or not. All that is identical to the agreement we had with Eddie Ng's Vietnamese friends. Do you have the authority to sign on behalf of your clients?"

"Yes, I still do."

"Then your firm's agreement will suffice. I'll scan and email a copy of the contract to you in the next half hour."

"Okay, but tell me, who is this Jasmine Yip you mentioned earlier?"

"I'm not sure who she is, but her name came up in association with Muir," Ava said.

"How?"

"I don't want to get into it."

"Please. You can't just throw a name at me and then stonewall."

"Okay, I'll tell you two things," she conceded. "Beyond that I won't elaborate, so please don't ask me any questions."

"I promise there will be no questions."

"First, I know where the money went when it left the Dutch bank. Second, Muir apparently wasn't working alone. Jasmine Yip was involved, but in what capacity I don't know."

"How in hell did you manage to learn that so fast?"

"That's a question," Ava said.

"So it is." Howell laughed. "I apologize."

"I have other things to attend to today, so I'm going to get started on them," said Ava. "Email me the contract after you've signed it."

"You can count on that," Howell said.

Have I done the right thing? Ava wondered as she ended the call, and then just as quickly answered her own question. Howell was correct that if she was going to try to recover money for June Gregory, she had to go after Malcolm Muir — and now, presumably, Jasmine Yip. And if she was going to do that, she knew from experience that it would take almost the same amount of effort to chase thirty million as for three million.

Ava checked the time and figured it wasn't too late to call Brenda Burgess in Hong Kong. Brenda was a partner in the law firm Burgess and Bowlby with her husband, Richard Bowlby, and had helped Three Sisters manage several challenging issues. Ava had faith in her judgement.

The phone was answered by Richard with a cheery "Hello."

"Richard, this is Ava Lee. I apologize for calling you at home."

"That's not necessary. We're always glad to hear from you — or maybe I should say that it's always interesting when we hear from you," he said. "Is it me you want to talk to, or am I right in thinking it's Brenda?"

"You're right, it is Brenda. Although that's not a reflection of my opinion of your legal skills," she said.

"You didn't have to say that, but it is appreciated," he said. "And I do understand that you two have developed your own relationship. Here she is."

"Hi, Ava. It's nice to hear from you, though I hope you aren't calling because you're in some kind of terrible trouble," Brenda said seconds later.

"I'm not in any trouble, but I need a plan if trouble arises."

"What kind of trouble?"

"It might take me a while to explain. How's your time?"

"You have all the time you need."

"Well, it started when I was in Beijing with Suki Chan to finalize purchase of the logistics company . . ." Ava began. Ten minutes later she had finished discussing the concerns both Fai and Chen had raised about the risks associated with financing Lau Lau's film *Tiananmen Square*. "We need to find a way to do it without being exposed. I'm hoping you might have some ideas," she said.

"Goodness me, Ava, I hardly know where to start," Brenda said. "What you've described is not exactly your run-of-the-mill legal problem. But before we talk about that, can I back up a bit?"

"Of course."

"Okay. For starters, do you fully understand how sensitive a subject the Tiananmen Square massacre is with the Chinese government?"

"That's been explained to me over and over again."

"Yet you still want to finance a film about it?"

"As I said, I made a commitment to Lau Lau. He's written a beautiful and compelling script, and maybe it's time the world understood what happened there," Ava said.

"You mean it's time the world saw Lau Lau's view of what happened there."

"From what I've read about the massacre, nothing he alludes to distorts the facts. What he does is take a period of political, cultural, and social turmoil in China and distill it down to its most basic human level — a mother searching for her lost son."

"But the backdrop is still the Chinese government sending

tanks into Tiananmen Square to disperse a protest, and in the process killing many of its own citizens."

"That's the fact of it."

"Except it's a fact the Chinese government totally rejects. Tiananmen is the most sensitive and widely censored topic in China. There is no official record of it. In the government's eyes, it never happened."

"Brenda, rather than debating the wisdom of shining a light on that piece of history, I would like to send you the script," Ava said. "After you've read it we can resume the debate, if you think that's necessary. For now, what I need you to tell me is whether or not you can help me create a solid wall between the money needed to finance the film and my own involvement."

Brenda went quiet. Ava waited patiently, knowing that the woman was as thoughtful as she was intelligent.

"Using someone else's money would be ideal. Could you arrange something like that?"

"Maybe."

"Because my strong advice is not to use your own."

"I hear you. But I'll cross that bridge when I come to it, and I won't do anything without discussing it with you first." Ava said. "But in the meantime, what kind of structure can we put together?"

"Would I be correct to say that films are usually financed by a production company?"

"That's what I've been told."

"Okay, then we could set up a production company owned by a numbered, or even several numbered, entities, in a jurisdiction where you and your partners have no presence," Brenda said. "The U.K. comes to mind. Richard has some very good legal contacts there."

"Would there be names attached to the numbered companies?"

"We could use a lawyer's name. It could be done by proxy, and that would be protected by lawyer-client privilege," Brenda said. "In fact, it might be possible to put two or more law firms between the money and its source. I know that may sound a bit excessive, but we would want to create as many roadblocks as possible between you and the film."

"Assuming Chen still wants to be the producer, would he be able to access the money he needs without any bother?"

"We can make that as easy as you want. Do you want to retain some control?"

"No. Once the money is in the bank, I don't want anything to do with it. Chen can give me an accounting sometime down the road, but I'm going to trust him to spend the money as it was intended."

"How much will he need?"

"I don't have a budget yet, but I can't imagine the film costing much more than seven or eight million."

"How soon will he need the money?"

"It isn't immediate, but I'd like to start building the groundwork. Could you please incorporate a company the way you suggested? I like the idea of the U.K. And when that's done, could you open a bank account for it?"

"I'll do both, and Richard can arrange for one of the U.K. firms to pay for the incorporation out of its own accounts."

"Thanks so much for this, Brenda. Who knows, none of it may be necessary, but I agree that we're far better off being safe than sorry."

"If the film is any good, I can almost guarantee that, given the subject matter, it will not go unnoticed in China," Brenda said. "And by the way, do send me the script. It would be irresponsible of me as your lawyer not to know what's motivating you to do this."

"It's in Chinese."

"We use a top-notch translation service. How long is the script?"

"A hundred and twenty pages."

"That won't take long. Please send it to me."

"Okay, I will. Have you seen any of Lau Lau's early films?"

"No, I'm woefully ignorant when it comes to Chinese cinema."

"Watch one or two with Fai in them. Lau Lau was amazing in his ability to dissect lives and capture emotion. I truly believe that he wasn't just China's greatest film director; he's one of the best the world has seen. Maybe with a little help he can reclaim that reputation," Ava said. "As for my motivation, when I think of him, I always remember the pleasure and inspiration I got from his films. This is my attempt to repay him for what he gave to me, and to so many others."

(12)

AVA SAT QUIETLY IN THE KITCHEN, STARING OUT THE window towards Avenue Road, for almost half an hour after speaking to Brenda Burgess. The lawyer's concerns — when added to those of Fai and Chen — had her wondering if she was being foolish in her determination to finance Lau Lau's film. Thoughts about the money brought one of Brenda's questions to mind, a question Ava hadn't been able to answer. She picked up the phone again and this time called Beijing.

"I'm talking to you more often than to any of my clients," Chen said after he answered.

"Sorry to be a nuisance, but I've been thinking about the money you'll need to make Lau Lau's film. Have you given any thought yet to the budget?"

"Actually I have. If we can restrict the bulk of the shooting to Beijing, and if Fai and Lau Lau work cheaply, then we should be able to bring it in for five or six million U.S."

"What might prevent you from shooting in Beijing?"

"We would need permits from the China Movie Syndicate and the city," Chen said. "We won't get them with the script as it reads now, so we would have to change it to get past them and then go back to the original script when we shoot. That's how we used to do it in the old days."

"But what if you can't get permits?"

"We could shoot some general exteriors in Beijing and then move the rest of the production to someplace like Taipei. It would cost a bit more, but we wouldn't be hassled."

"That sounds simpler, and the extra cost shouldn't be an issue," Ava said. "I would also want Lau Lau and Fai to be paid properly. I don't think a discounted rate is fair to them."

"That's good of you. I'll build those numbers into a budget over the next week or so and send it to you," Chen said. "Another decision that has to be made is who will talk to Lau Lau about the script and when will they do it. I'm sure he's anxious to hear our reactions. And the first question out of his mouth will be when he can start filming."

"Take me through the timing," Ava said. "Assuming there are no major impediments, when would we have a finished film?"

"Well, we have a script, a director, and a star, which is a great start. If we shoot in Taipei we'll have to do some location scouting, but that wouldn't be onerous," Chen said. "So, all in all, I think we could begin filming in four or five months. Lau Lau works quickly, but I'd still give him three months to finish. Then we have post-production and editing to complete. In total, I would expect to have the final product in about a year. Of course, we'd still have to figure out the marketing and publicity, and we'd have to be smart about planning the release."

"Okay. So if we hold off for a week or two before talking to Lau Lau, that won't be a big problem?"

"Not in terms of making the film, but he'll be getting more frantic with each passing day."

"I don't doubt that's true, but I have some very complicated issues to work through, and I need some time to do it. In fact, you probably won't hear much from me over the next week or so."

"How about I call him tomorrow," Chen said. "I'll start with an apology. I'll tell him I've been up to my armpits in problems and haven't had a chance to read the script yet. I'll promise to read it over the weekend and to forward it to Fai. That should appease him and buy you some time."

"Thanks for that, Chen," Ava said. Then she saw she had an incoming call with the country code 31. "I'm sorry, I have to hang up now. There's a call I need to take."

She switched lines. "Jacob, did you have any success?"

"I did," he said. "This has turned out to be one of those days that happen all too infrequently. You must be my good-luck charm."

"It's more likely that you're mine," she said. "What happened?"

"I managed to contact Mr. Jaswa, the diamond trader I dealt with before. He remembered me, and when I explained the reason for my call, he agreed to help. I gave him the name of the company that Jasmine Yip wired money to. He knows the owner very well and is going to arrange for me to visit."

"That sounds almost too easy."

"Truthfully, he was a bit reluctant to become involved in another company's business affairs, but when I told him about the size of the scam and Phillip Gregory's suicide, he came over to our side," Smits said. "He also made it clear that, while he will open the doors for me, it's up to me to convince the trader to share his information."

"Do you expect to hear back from him today?"

"I hope so."

"And if the result is positive?"

"I'll head to Antwerp tomorrow."

"Maybe I'll join you," Ava said suddenly. "KLM flies direct from Toronto to Amsterdam. Let me check the flight schedule."

Without waiting for his reply, she opened her computer, typed in "KLM Toronto Amsterdam," and within seconds saw there was a flight that evening at 5:15 that would get her into Amsterdam at 6:30 the next morning. She checked the availability in business class and saw that it was open. "I can be in Amsterdam first thing tomorrow morning," she told Smits.

"I didn't expect that," he said.

"Apologies. It just suddenly seemed the right thing to do. I don't know why I didn't think of it before."

"It isn't a problem. I'd like to have you with me, but what if I don't hear back from Mr. Jaswa today?"

"I don't mind spending a day or two in Amsterdam while we wait."

Smits laughed. "I'd forgotten how quickly you like to act."

"Holding these fraudsters to account has become increasingly important to me. Plus, I'm very curious about this Jasmine Yip. Talking with someone who did business with her might give me a better sense of who we're dealing with."

"Well, hopefully there'll be no need to wait in Amsterdam," Smits said. "Do you want me to meet you at the airport?"

"Have you finally bought a car?"

"No, I'm still riding my bicycle, but I can get a taxi."

"That's way too much trouble, and besides, I arrive at six-thirty," Ava said. "I'll book a room at the Dylan Hotel, where I stayed on my last trip. That will give me a chance to freshen up."

"I'll make every effort to get back to you before your flight," said Jacob.

Ava ended the call and, to her surprise, felt a surge of excitement. Despite all the negative things she'd said to Mimi and others about the debt-collection business, it had often provided a rush of adrenalin and an almost unbridled sense of satisfaction when she and Uncle were successful. Her conversation with Jacob had rekindled that feeling. *I guess I haven't completely lost my appetite for the hunt,* she thought. *I just hope I haven't lost my talent for it.*

She picked up the phone again and in rapid succession booked an airport limo; called her mother and left a message that Fai had gone to Taiwan for work and that she'd be out of town for a few days; and, after debating whether to phone or text, sent a text to Derek saying she was headed to Europe and would contact him when she could. She checked the time and thought that Fai might be sleeping, so Ava texted her to say she was heading to Amsterdam to pursue the money stolen from Mr. Gregory and that she'd contact her when she arrived. When she had finished, she went into the bedroom.

Many of the jobs she and Uncle had taken on had involved extensive and sometimes rapid travel. In fact, it hadn't been unusual for her to be in a different city or country every day for three or more successive days. Over the course of the first few years she had figured out how to pack to accommodate the sudden changes in her schedule. She had a Louis Vuitton bag that could hold her small laptop, a Moleskine notebook, and her passport, wallet, and phone. Her Shanghai Tang Double Happiness bag was large enough to hold one pair each of pumps and flat shoes, a pencil skirt, two pairs of slacks, three shirts, underwear, T-shirts, and a small toilet kit. If she didn't have an immediate appointment at her arrival destination, she often travelled in a T-shirt, running shoes, training pants, and an Adidas jacket. Given how early she'd be arriving in Amsterdam, she decided to go casual. She laid the clothes and shoes on the bed and headed for the bathroom to shower.

An hour later Ava was ready to leave for the airport. She carried her phone into the kitchen, made a coffee, and sat down while she checked her messages. There was a text from Derek wishing her good luck, but nothing from her mother, Fai, or Jacob. She checked her watch. There was still time for Jacob to call before the limo was slated to arrive.

No more than five seconds later, her phone rang and she saw his incoming number. "Jacob?" she answered.

"We have an appointment tomorrow at noon with the owner of the trading company in Antwerp that was Jasmine Yip's diamond supplier," he said quickly. "We are to meet Mr. Jaswa at his office. He'll take us to the meeting and make the introductions. After that we're on our own. In fact, Mr. Jaswa told me quite directly that meeting his contact wasn't a guarantee that he'd tell us what we want to know."

"It is a foot in the door."

"A foot that might be aided by the fact that we now know Jasmine Yip is from Singapore."

"You received the copy of her passport?"

"I did. I'll send it to you as soon as we finish talking."

Ava shook her head. "I can't stop asking myself why Malcolm Muir would send money to an account in Amsterdam controlled by a woman from Singapore who was using it to buy diamonds in Antwerp."

"It is quite out of the ordinary."

"Yes, it's definitely different," Ava said, and then checked her watch again. "My limo will be here soon. What time and where should we meet tomorrow morning?"

"The Dylan Hotel is close to the station. Why don't I meet you in the lobby at nine. There's a train around nine forty-five that will get us into Antwerp at eleven fifteen," he said. "I'll keep an eye on your flight. If it's any later, I'll reschedule."

"I'd appreciate that," Ava said. "Now please send me the copy of that passport."

While she waited, she turned to her computer and searched "Jasmine Yip Singapore." There were pages upon pages of links, but all of them concerned Singapore or jasmine flowers; there were a few Yips, but none of them named Jasmine. Ava then entered "Jewellery Circle" and again didn't find a match.

"After all our luck today, that was too much to expect," she muttered, and then saw there was an email from Jacob. She clicked on the attachment and saw the passport page with Jasmine Yip's photo. "At least I can put a face to you now," Ava said, looking at a middle-aged woman with a long, thin face, hair cut in a bob, a grim smile, and eyes that stared defiantly into the camera. The name on the passport was Yip Meili.

The word *meili* was Chinese for jasmine, leaving no doubt

about the origin of Yip's English name. *That's understandable, if lacking in imagination,* Ava thought as she typed the Chinese name into her laptop. A moment later she closed it in frustration.

(13)

THE KLM FLIGHT LANDED AT AMSTERDAM'S SCHIPHOL Airport on time, and thirty minutes later Ava walked out into a warm, humid morning. She had managed to sleep for several hours and hoped that would get her through the day without having to nap. For more than a decade she had crossed time zones so often that she had learned to adjust to the local time as quickly as possible. Going to bed at her regular hour was always the best strategy. So her plan when she got to the Dylan Hotel was to shower, change clothes, and have breakfast.

It was ten kilometres from the airport to central Amsterdam and the hotel. Inbound traffic was surprisingly light for that time of day; Ava saw as many buses as cars and far more bicycles than the two put together. At seven-thirty she reached the Dylan, which looked like something from another century with its stone façade and metal gateway crowned by high arches. In fact, it hadn't been conceived as a hotel; it comprised a number of three-storey brick and stone houses surrounding a courtyard and had been built in the 1600s. While there were only about forty rooms and suites, it had more amenities than most boutique hotels.

Ava had arranged for an early check in, and her room was ready when she arrived. She had requested the Kimono Room. It was entirely black and white, all ultra-modern Japanese minimalism with clean, hard lines. Even the bed's four posts were thin and reed-like, more for accent than function, more symbol than decoration.

She unpacked her bag and carried her toilet kit to the bathroom. Her room was on the top floor of the hotel, and the bathroom had been built loft-style, with black wooden beams crisscrossing from wall to wall and a glass ceiling open to a bright blue sky. As she stripped to shower, the light from above seemed to accentuate every pore in her body. Rarely had she felt so naked. Ava looked at herself in the mirror and was startled by how pale she looked, even more so when she turned sideways and saw the contrast made by a red scar on her thigh where she had been shot in Macau and the long scar on her arm where a machete had bitten into it during a fracas in Beijing. The arm scar was only a month old and hadn't reached its final definition, but it was definitely going to be permanent.

She had other scars on her back and shoulders, and, like the one on her thigh, they had been incurred during her days as a debt collector. Debt collection wasn't a business for the faint of heart. Over her years with Uncle, Ava had been punched, kicked, shot, hit with belts and a tire iron, and forced to fend off knives and machetes. She had always prevailed, but there had been a cost. Still, even in the harshness of the morning light, her body looked like that of a younger woman. A combination of genes, running, and bak mei had helped her maintain a physique that was beautifully proportioned, firm and muscular. Even the scars didn't detract; actually, as far as Fai was concerned, they added to Ava's sex appeal.

She turned from the mirror and looked around the bathroom. Like the rest of the suite, it was starkly minimalist, with the exception of an immense porcelain bathtub completely encased in black marble. Ava normally showered, but there was something about the tub that attracted her. She drew water, added bubble bath, and eased herself in.

As she soaked, she focused on two pots sitting on a ledge at the foot of the bath, white ceramic shot through with streaks of electric blue. They were Japanese, she guessed, but she had seen pots like them in Hong Kong. That thought triggered the realization that the last time she'd been in Amsterdam was when Uncle was dying in the Queen Elizabeth Hospital in Hong Kong. Had his suggestion that she hunt down Malcolm Muir brought her here again? Was it his way of closing a circle? *I have to stop reading so much into my dreams,* she thought as she climbed out of the tub.

Ava dried herself and went into the bedroom to dress. She had laid out her clothes on the bed before bathing and now put on the plain white cotton Brooks Brothers shirt, black linen slacks, and a pair of flat shoes. She normally wore mascara and a light touch of red lipstick, but given what Jacob had told her about the Jains, she'd decided to present an understated image. She did, though, brush her hair back and fix it with her ivory chignon pin. The pin was a Chinese antique that she'd bought in Tsim Sha Tsui after her first successful collection job. According to the dealer who'd sold it to her, the pin had belonged to a wife or mistress of a

Chinese emperor. Ava didn't know if that was true, but she did know it had always brought her good luck.

Ready for the day ahead, Ava checked the time and saw it was already 8:40. It was getting late for breakfast, so she decided to forego it. Instead she made a coffee, checked her phone, and saw she had a voice message from Fai.

"I'm getting ready to leave my hotel to go to the set for the first day of shooting. I'm very excited. Andy couldn't have been nicer yesterday, and I think the cast and crew are first-rate. Good luck in Amsterdam, stay in touch, and please don't take any unnecessary risks. I want you to come back to me in one piece. Love you," Fai said.

Ava smiled as she saved the message, and then she opened her laptop. Jennie Lee had sent an email: Ava, I'm worried about you. Is everything okay? You didn't mention anything about Fai going back to Asia to work, or about you going to Europe when we had dinner the other night. You know I don't like surprises, so if something is going on between you two, let me know. Love, Mummy.

Mummy, everything is just fine. Fai had a last-minute job offer that was too good to turn down, and I'm chasing the money that was stolen from Mr. Gregory, Ava wrote. I'll contact you again in a few days. Love, Ava.

She stood up, thought about making another coffee, and then realized it was almost nine o'clock. She grabbed her Louis Vuitton bag, which already contained her notebook, pens, wallet, and passport, and added the phone and her room card. She rode the elevator to the lobby and exited to find Jacob Smits waiting for her in his usual rumpled brown suit, white shirt, and orange tie. He grinned and stepped towards her.

Ava guessed Jacob was in his fifties; he was five foot seven or eight and had a prominent belly. His hair was sandy brown, thinning, and carefully combed to minimize the encroaching baldness. His face was round, with chubby cheeks, tiny ears with pink lobes, and deeply recessed bright blue eyes that almost sparkled. When Ava first met him, she had thought he had an extraordinarily kind face, and when he smiled that impression was even stronger.

"How was your journey?" he asked, extending a hand.

"Trouble-free," she said as she shook his hand. Then she pointed at the scruffy old black leather briefcase he held in the other. "That looks heavy."

"I printed two copies of all the paperwork you sent to me, one for us and one for Mr. Jaswa's colleague. I thought it would help validate our case with him."

"That's good thinking."

"I've also got a Thermos of black coffee and sandwiches. My wife is old-fashioned about spending money on food outside the house. She made a sandwich for you as well."

"I may take you up on the coffee," Ava said. "Now we should get going. How do you suggest we get to the train station?"

"We'll take the tram."

The tram stop was a block from the hotel. They reached the train station with fifteen minutes to spare. Jacob bought their tickets and moments later they left for Antwerp on schedule.

They sat in economy but were able to find two seats facing each other, separated by a table. Jacob took out the Thermos and placed it on the table with a plastic cup. "Are you ready for coffee?" he asked Ava.

"I only drink it black."

"So do I, and that's what we have."

"Then yes, please."

He poured coffee into the cup and then filled the lid for himself. Ava took a sip and was surprised by the smooth, rich flavour. "Your wife makes wonderful coffee," she said.

"She's also a very good cook. If you ever have time, I'd like you to come to our house to meet her and have dinner."

"That's the kind of thing I like to do when I'm on holiday."

"Have you ever been to Antwerp on holiday?" Jacob asked.

"No."

"It is an interesting old city, the largest in Flanders. The people speak Flemish, although, curiously, they refer to themselves as *sinjoren*, which is a bastardization of the Spanish word *señor*," he said.

"That is odd."

"The Spaniards occupied and ran the city in the sixteenth century. The other provinces that made up the territory were also occupied at various times, by the French, Dutch, and Germans. There was so much fighting on territorial soil that it became known as 'the cockpit of Europe.' Belgium as we know it today wasn't founded until 1830."

"In addition to your other talents, you're also a history buff?"

"I like to read, and I do have an interest in it, but I have to say my interest in Antwerp is more on a personal level," he said.

"Your wife is from there?"

"No, she's Dutch. My grandfather is the one who generated my interest. As a young man he was an exceptional athlete, good enough to qualify for the Dutch Olympic team that went to the summer games in 1920, which were held in Antwerp," Jacob said. He smiled and patted his belly. "As you can see, I don't exactly take after him."

"I'm sure you did when you were younger."

"No, this has always been my shape. Riding a bicycle around town is the most athletic thing I've done in my life," he said. "But my grandfather was different; he competed in the hardest event of all — the decathlon — and finished fourth, beaten out of a medal by only four points, by a Swede. I can't tell you how many times I heard him bemoan that he hadn't gone a tenth of a second faster in a race or a few inches higher in the high jump or a few inches farther in the broad jump. Being that close to a medal haunted him, and it burned the name of Antwerp into my memory."

"That's such a sad story."

"It shouldn't have been. He had fought in the First World War, and the fact that he survived and was able to compete at all should have been reason enough to make him happy. But being happy wasn't his natural state. I suspect that if he'd won that bronze medal, he would have been miserable because it wasn't silver."

"You don't take after him in that regard either."

"My mother was a jolly person. She thought that no matter how bad things were, they could always be worse, and she was grateful they weren't. Her attitude stuck with me."

"My mother is a bit like that," Ava said. "I'm not. I tend to be a worrier."

"You wouldn't have lasted too long in your profession otherwise. Taking things for granted is folly."

Ava looked across the table at Jacob, struck again by how astute he was. She started to say something, but, not wanting to delve any deeper into her old profession, she turned her head towards the window and lapsed into a silence that lasted until the train arrived in Antwerp.

They disembarked into a vast main hall with a huge dome towering over it. Ava was awestruck by the size and majesty of the station. She was still staring upwards when Jacob said loudly, "We'll exit over there. Mr. Jaswa's office is only a short distance away."

They walked out of the station into a day that had turned dreary and overcast. Ava stopped for a second to look back at the massive Gothic structure. As she did, a brisk gust of wind caused her to shiver. "It looks like it could rain," she said.

"I have an umbrella in my briefcase if we need it," Jacob said.

"That's a remarkable briefcase," Ava said. "I'm almost afraid to ask what else you have in there."

"I still have the sandwiches if you get hungry," he said.

"Maybe later," she said, having to hurry to keep alongside him. For a short, stout man he walked very quickly.

They hadn't gone more than a few hundred metres when Ava saw a sign on the side of a building that read DIAMANTKWARTIER. She followed Jacob as he entered a narrow street flanked by rows of nondescript three- and four-storey buildings. There were bollards at each end of the street, restricting access to just pedestrians and bicycles.

A steady stream of people were moving in both directions along the street and making their way in and out of the buildings. On the ground level of several buildings were jewellery stores or, more accurately, stores that specialized in diamonds. Ava had expected the security to be strong, but on the street it wasn't even visible. Jacob came to a stop at a frosted glass door and then checked his watch. "Good, we're right on time," he said, opening the door, and stood aside so Ava could pass.

She stepped into a lobby and was met immediately by a hulking security guard. He held out his arm. "Stop, please," he said.

"We are here to see Mr. Jaswa. We have an appointment. My name is Jacob Smits and my colleague is Ava Lee," Jacob said loudly from behind her.

Ava looked past the guard into the lobby. She and Jacob were no more than twenty metres from a set of elevators, but to get to them, their first challenge was to pass through a full-body screening device. It was impossible to avoid, because sheets of Plexiglas ran from it to the walls and from the floor to the ceiling.

"Their appointment is in the register," a guard sitting on the other side of the machine said.

"Okay, you can go on through. One at a time," the first guard said.

It took ten minutes to be screened, for Ava's bag and Jacob's briefcase to be emptied and the contents examined, for a retina scan, for their fingerprints to be taken, and for their passports to be copied.

"They didn't have the eye scan the last time I was here," Jacob said when they were finally permitted to make their way to the elevators.

Ava examined the building directory and did a quick count of the companies listed. If the list was accurate, there were about sixty company offices in a three-storey building that she wouldn't have thought could house twenty. She mentioned that to Jacob as they rode the elevator to the third floor.

"The entire diamond quarter is no more than a square mile, but, if my memory is accurate, I believe Mr. Jaswa told me there are more than a thousand trading companies operating within its boundaries," said Jacob.

They exited the elevator into a hallway that extended straight in both directions. It had a black linoleum floor, walls painted a drab brown, overhead lighting that was piercingly bright, and security cameras every three metres on both sides of the hallway. Jacob stopped in front of a grey steel door with a brass number six. He knocked and raised his head. Ava looked up and saw security cameras on either side of the lintel. She heard a loud click, and Jacob turned the handle and pushed the door open.

"Mr. Smits. I didn't expect to see you again so soon," said a tall, thin man wearing a crisp white shirt and creased black slacks.

"As I explained on the phone, my associate Ms. Lee represents some people who have been swindled in a most ungodly way by someone who purports to be a religious man," Jacob said. "It is regrettable that he chose to involve the diamond trading community in his scam, but the facts are what they are."

The man nodded and smiled at Ava. "You are Ms. Lee, I presume. My name is Nihir Jaswa."

"I can't thank you enough for agreeing to introduce us to your colleague," she said.

Jaswa smiled again, and Ava found herself admiring his perfect teeth. He was in his fifties or sixties, she thought, with a full head of shaggy white hair. His nose and chin were both long and pointed, and while the skin around his jaw was still firm, there were worry lines across his forehead and large bags under dark brown eyes. Trading diamonds, she thought, couldn't be a stress-free business.

"I didn't pass on to my colleague — whose name, by the way, is Ilesh Fozdar — everything that Jacob related to me. I thought I'd leave that up to you. All I told him was that one of his customers had been playing fast and loose with other people's money."

"Still, it was very kind of you to do that."

Jaswa shrugged. "I hope Ilesh is helpful, but I can't guarantee that he will be. He is among the most substantial traders in Antwerp. I know that he does due diligence on his more important customers, and I can guarantee that he would never knowingly do business with someone as unethical as your swindler," he said. "That's my way of advising you to tread carefully when you're speaking to him. For example, don't imply that he might have known what was going on and turned a blind eye to it."

"Jacob has explained to me the ethical underpinnings of your religion, so I have some understanding of your values," Ava said. "I will most certainly be conscious of them when I'm speaking to Mr. Fozdar."

"Then in that case, why don't I take you to meet him," Jaswa said.

"His office is nearby?" Ava asked.

"He is in this building, one floor down," he said.

"I read the company directory when I was in the lobby, and I couldn't help noticing that a lot of companies seem to be compressed into quite a small space," Ava said.

"Ilesh will trade two hundred million dollars in diamonds this year. I'll do a bit less," Jaswa said, motioning for them to exit the office. "Twenty years ago, when my father and Ilesh's uncle managed these businesses, the sales were smaller than that but our workspace and workforce were ten times larger. Can you guess why?"

"No," Ava said as they walked down the hall to the elevator.

Jaswa pushed the elevator button. "We had our own workshops. We bought rough diamonds and did all our own cutting and polishing. My father used to refer to it as buying in rupees and selling in dollars," he said. "Those days are gone. Wages and the cost of living in Antwerp are so high that most of the workshops have closed. Our trade is now almost exclusively in rough diamonds, and for that all we need is minimal office space, a few staff, a phone, and a computer."

"Where is the cutting and polishing done now?" Ava asked as the elevator arrived and they stepped into it.

"Some of it is done in China but the majority is done in India, in the city of Surat. That's in Gujarat state, where most of the Antwerp Jain families came from originally," Jaswa said. "We came here because Antwerp was the world centre of the diamond business and we wanted to stake our claim. Now, ironically, with so many workshops in Surat, business is shifting to India, and Mumbai has become a fierce trading competitor. I can envision a day when many of us will return to India."

They left the elevator and entered a hallway identical to the floor above. Jaswa led them towards double wooden doors with FOZDAR TRADING painted on them. He knocked and then looked up at the security cameras.

"Mr. Jaswa," a young woman said as she opened the door.

"My friends have an appointment with your father," he said.

"Yes, he's been expecting them," she said. "Will you be joining them?"

"No, I'm going back to my office, but please thank him again for his courtesy," Jaswa said.

"I'm quite certain that no thanks are necessary, but I'll pass along your best wishes," she said, and then turned to Ava and Jacob. "Please come with me."

The office was larger than Jaswa's, with ten occupied workstations as opposed to his four. Some private offices surrounded the common work area, and the woman led them to one that had its door closed. She knocked, waited a few seconds, then opened the door. Ilesh Fozdar sat behind an enormous wooden desk. He looked at them intently but didn't rise to meet them.

"You should sit in the chairs," his daughter said, pointing to two chairs that sat in front of the desk.

When she had left, Fozdar shifted in his chair and grimaced. "I apologize for not getting up to greet you. My back is particularly sore today, and I have difficulty standing."

Given that he was seated, Ava could only guess at his height, but his fleshy face, broad chest, and prominent belly were evidence that he was overweight. He put two chubby hands on the desk and leaned towards them. "Nihir told me that you believe one of my customers has been stealing from you and using your money to buy diamonds from me," he said abruptly. "I'd like to hear more."

Fozdar's manner was matter-of-fact, but Ava noticed that his hands were clenched and his eyes were more challenging than inquisitive.

"What Mr. Jaswa told you is essentially true, but there is a great deal that we didn't share with him," Ava said. "If you have no objections, we'd like to share it with you."

"I'm listening."

"We brought documents that detail the movement of money from Canada to a bank in Amsterdam and from there to your company," Ava said. "You can read them whenever you wish, but I wanted you to understand that we're here with facts and numbers, not spinning theories."

Jacob Smits opened his briefcase and slid a file across the desk to Fozdar.

"I'll read those when I have a chance. For now, explain to me what you think happened," Fozdar said.

"Well, a man named Malcolm Muir—" Ava began, only to be immediately interrupted.

"I know no one by that name."

"I believe you. It's a puzzle we still have to solve, and with your help maybe we can," Ava said. "But I am assuming you do know of Jasmine Yip and a company called Jewellery Circle."

Fozdar looked at her intently. Ava noticed his eyes narrow and his lips compress. "I know them both. I did business with Jasmine's father and his company, Jewellery Circle, for over ten years. She took over the business when he died, about six or seven years ago," he said finally. "Are you suggesting that Jasmine was involved in this theft? Because if you are, I have to tell you I'd find that hard to believe. I'm not sure now that I want to hear what you have to say."

"I don't know enough about Jasmine Yip to suggest she's a thief," Ava said. "But what I do know—and the paperwork verifies it—is that all the stolen money ended up in a numbered bank account in Amsterdam that was registered in her name."

Fozdar shook his head and looked down at the file. "Is that indisputable?"

"Absolutely."

"If that's the case, it would be irresponsible of me not to listen," he said deliberately. "Please go ahead. I am prepared to keep an open mind."

"Thank you," Ava said, leaning forward to close the distance between them. She spoke slowly and without hyperbole as she connected the dots between Harvest Table Bible Chapel, the Harvest Investment Fund, the web of companies Muir had created to steal and hide the money, the investigative work done by Todd Howell, and her and Jacob's involvement in finding the money in Amsterdam.

Fozdar tried to appear indifferent, but, as the details accumulated, his interest became more apparent. When Ava had finished, he immediately asked, "Are you convinced that your friend's father committed suicide because of this scheme?"

"There's no doubt, I'm afraid."

"How horrible."

"And it could be just the start. How many other lives, marriages, families will be ruined by this thievery?"

Fozdar closed his eyes. "This is very difficult, because even after everything you've told me, I still don't want to believe that Jasmine would knowingly have been part of this," he said. "But there are things you said that raise concerns."

"What things?"

He hesitated and then said carefully, "For the past ten years or so, any business I've done with Jewellery Circle has been in rough diamonds. With her father, I don't think it was ever more than a million dollars a year. Jasmine is more aggressive, but even so, until about four years ago she never spent more than two million with me. Then suddenly the business tripled, and tripled again. When I asked her about it, she told me she has contacts in China who are supporting her."

"You didn't question where that money was coming from in China? You didn't suspect that she could be laundering money?"

"I thought it might be possible but I had no way of knowing for sure. And even if she was, it could have been sanctioned by a government official."

"That last point is well taken," Ava said. "But the fact that she went from spending two million a year with you to what we figure was about ten million this past year . . ."

"Actually, it was almost double that amount."

(14)

IT WASN'T OFTEN THAT AVA WAS CAUGHT OFF GUARD, but Fozdar had managed to do it.

She looked at Jacob, who was examining a file from his briefcase. As he ran his index finger down a row of numbers, he frowned. "According to this, the past twelve months was the most active period for money transfers from Jasmine Yip's account in Amsterdam to Mr. Fozdar's company," he said to Ava. "The transfers amounted to approximately eleven million dollars, which leaves a significant discrepancy between the money she sent from Amsterdam and the twenty million Mr. Fozdar says he received from her."

"Perhaps you have a discrepancy, but I don't. I know we received about twenty million," Fozdar said.

"Does that mean nine million came from banks other than the one in Amsterdam?" Ava asked.

"Yes, and it was all done legally. I can assure you that everything we do is transparent and in compliance with international banking regulations and Belgian law."

"You misunderstood me. I wasn't suggesting the money came from illicit sources," Ava said quickly. "I was simply trying to confirm that banks other than the one in Amsterdam were used."

"They were."

"Can you tell me which ones?"

Fozdar looked uncomfortable, then finally shrugged and said, "I'm not sure that's an appropriate thing for me to do. Jasmine's business dealings with other banks have no bearing that I can see on your situation."

Ava sensed that his reluctance was real and knew they had reached a turning point in their conversation. Either Fozdar was going to be completely co-operative or he would stop answering questions altogether. "Mr. Fozdar, do you think I could have a glass of water?" she asked, trying to buy herself some time.

"Of course. I'll have my daughter bring it," he said, relaxing slightly as he reached for the phone. "How about you, Mr. Smits? Can we get something for you as well?"

"No, I'm fine, thank you," Jacob said, his focus still on the bank statements on his lap.

"What are you hoping to find?" Ava asked.

"I'm trying to figure out if it was possible for Jasmine Yip to make enough profit trading diamonds to account for the additional money."

The door opened and Fozdar's daughter appeared, holding a tray with a jug of water and three glasses. She put the tray on one side of the desk, poured three glasses of water, and asked, "Can I get anything else?"

"No, thank you. This is perfect," Ava said, picking up a glass. She sipped and then glanced at Jacob. "Mr. Fozdar, is it possible to make a profit of nine million dollars by trading eleven million dollars in rough diamonds over a twelve-month period?"

Fozdar hesitated. Then he said, "It's highly unlikely. When you're dealing with rough diamonds, the profit margins are too thin to return anywhere near that kind of profit."

"If that's the case, then logically Ms. Yip was — as you suggested — getting money from other sources," Jacob said.

"I have no knowledge of her other business arrangements," Fozdar said abruptly.

Ava detected his displeasure with Jacob's comment and knew she had to calm him down. "Mr. Fozdar, I understand that you are a man with ethical standards, and I respect that. But there is a balance to be weighed here. On the one hand, we have proof positive that money was stolen, sent to Ms. Yip's account in Amsterdam, and used to buy diamonds. On the other, we can only conjecture where her other money comes from. The two could be linked or not, but I'll have no way of knowing without your assistance. So, while I know I may be asking you to breach your code of conduct when it comes to managing your business, I sincerely believe there's a case to be made for the greater good. All we want is a chance for restitution. We have no interest in blaming you or any other company for doing business with her, but we do need the truth," Ava said. "That is why I feel compelled to ask you again if you'll tell me which other banks she was doing business with. And — fair warning — if you answer, I'll have other questions as well."

Fozdar rubbed his right index finger across his upper lip. "This is making me very uncomfortable," he said. "In all the years I've known the Yip family, I've never had reason to question their integrity."

"I apologize, but I'm sure you understand this is an exceptional circumstance. If you're concerned about us keeping your co-operation confidential, I'm prepared to give you our undertaking in writing," she said.

"That isn't what I'm thinking about," he said with a slight wave of his hand. "You mentioned you'd have other questions. What are they?"

Ava took a deep breath. "Well, in addition to the names of the banks she used, it would be useful to have account numbers, the names attached to the accounts, any bank contact information, and the records of all the transactions you conducted with the banks," she said. "I'd also appreciate any personal and business contact information you have for her."

Fozdar pursed his lips, looked at Ava and Jacob, leaned forward, and said, "It might take some time to pull everything together. May I suggest you go for a walk and come back in about an hour?"

(15)

AVA AND JACOB LEFT THE FOZDAR TRADING OFFICE without saying a word to each other. They were starting to walk in the general direction of the train station when Ava stopped in front of a coffee shop. "I feel like an espresso," she said. "How about you?"

"Yes, that would suit me. And I still have the sandwiches in my briefcase," Jacob said.

Ava smiled and continued into the shop. There was a small table for two in the window. Ava went to the counter and ordered two double espressos.

When she carried the coffees to the table, she saw that Jacob had set out the sandwiches. He looked up at her. "I've just decided that Fozdar is going to co-operate fully with us. If nothing else, he'll want to satisfy his curiosity about what Jasmine Yip has been up to."

"I agree. Now tell me, what do you think she has been up to?"

"I don't have a clue, though I am quite certain she didn't make all that money in the diamond trade," Jacob said. "It's more logical that she was using the diamonds to launder money."

"Money turned into diamonds and then diamonds turned back into money."

"Exactly. And then that money turned into something that generated enough profit to buy even more diamonds."

"It's either that or she had another pool of money to draw on," Ava said.

"How are you going to approach this?" he asked.

"You mean how are *we* going to approach this," Ava said. "If I need your assistance after today, are you free to keep on working with me?"

"I have a couple of small jobs on the go, but there's no urgency to them. Though, if I'm being honest, I'm not sure how much more I can do for you."

"For one thing, you might ask your contacts in Amsterdam if they can access banking information in Singapore."

"Do you think that's where we're heading?"

"Absolutely. A friend in one of the Canadian banks once did that for me, but he and his contacts were compromised, so I've been reluctant to use them," she said. "But it was remarkable how much information they could gather through bank-to-bank communication."

"But that still depends on Fozdar giving us the information about Jasmine Yip's banking."

They left the coffee shop an hour later, after devouring the sandwiches and two more coffees, and made their way back to the Diamantkwartier. Despite her confidence in front of Jacob, Ava wasn't completely sure that Fozdar would be co-operative, but she figured it was out of her control. Reassuringly, when they reached the building and entered the security-laden lobby, they were admitted without issue.

When they reached Fozdar Trading, the door opened as soon as they knocked. "My father is waiting for you," Fozdar's daughter said.

They entered his office. "How was your walk?" he asked from behind his desk.

"We didn't go far. We stopped for coffee."

Fozdar seemed distracted. As Ava and Jacob sat down, he tapped the file on his desk. "There don't seem to be any boundaries left in this world when it comes to business," he said. "For example, as we looked at the business Jasmine has done with us over the past five years, I was surprised to find she'd used four different banks to send us money. The one in Amsterdam that you know about and another in Chengdu, China, were the most frequently used, but a bank in Singapore wired money to us on two occasions, and one in Calgary, Canada, sent us money once. I had forgotten about the Canadian transfer until now, because it was several years ago and the amount wasn't substantial."

"When was that transaction?" Ava asked, leaning forward.

Fozdar opened the file. "Four years ago, and it was only for one hundred and twenty thousand."

"What was the name of the bank?"

"The Alberta Dominion Bank."

"Was there a name attached to the transaction?"

"I knew you'd be particularly interested in this transfer, so I had my daughter retrieve the paperwork," Fozdar said. "The wire came from a numbered company but included a purchase order that matched one that Jasmine had given us, so we assumed the money was from her."

"Do you have a copy of the wire?"

Fozdar smiled and handed Ava a slip of paper. She glanced at it and then gave it to Jacob. "Will you check to see if that bank and account number are on the list that Todd Howell gave me?" she asked.

As Jacob opened his briefcase, Ava refocused her attention on Fozdar. "What about the transfers from Singapore? How and when did they take place?"

"Both of them were made almost five years ago, and they were small. I don't think they'll be of much interest to you; they came from the Jewellery Circle bank account that her father had been using for years," Fozdar said. "What I don't understand is why Jasmine stopped using it and started sending us money from Amsterdam and Chengdu."

"That's a very interesting question," Ava said. "Do you have a theory?"

"Excuse me, Ava," Jacob said before Fozdar could reply. "The Calgary account number corresponds to one that Malcolm Muir established, but there isn't any record of the wire on the list of transactions Howell provided."

"It was a relatively small amount, it was four years ago, and the money went to Antwerp rather than Amsterdam, so it may not have seemed relevant. Still, we'll need to ask Howell about it," Ava said, and then looked at Fozdar. "Do you have any objections if I make a call to Canada?"

"Of course not. Feel free."

Ava found Howell's number in her phone and dialled. It would be ten in the morning in Toronto, and she hoped he'd be in the office. The receptionist said he was, and a moment later he came on the phone, sounding breathless. "You're the last person I expected to hear from today. Has something happened?" he asked.

"Yes, but nothing earth-shattering," Ava said. "I've discovered that Amsterdam wasn't the only destination for Harvest Investment money. Four years ago, a hundred and twenty thousand dollars was sent from its Calgary account at the Alberta Dominion Bank to the Fozdar Trading company in Antwerp. Did you know that?"

"Yes."

"Then why isn't it on the wire transfer list you gave me?"

"I told you I went through my files and extracted what I thought was most important," Howell said. "My focus was on Amsterdam. The Antwerp transfer was an outlier, a one-of-a-kind event."

"I can see why you might have thought that, but did you at least confirm the details of the transaction?"

"It was exactly as you described."

"Who authorized the transfer?"

"Muir."

"Do you have a copy of his request?" she asked.

"I have it somewhere in my files."

"And you're sure his signature is on it?"

"Absolutely. It was such an outlier that I remember every detail."

"Did you know that Fozdar Trading deals solely in diamonds?"

"I did," Howell said. "I contacted them to follow up on the transfer, but no one there would talk to me. They told me they never share information about their customers. At that point I gave up. I figured Muir had splurged on some expensive jewellery for his wife and left it at that."

"Todd, was it the only outlier you discovered? Could there

be other anomalies you didn't think were important enough to include in the file you gave me?"

"The wire sent to Antwerp is the only one."

"Thank you. That's very helpful."

"Ava, now that I've been so helpful, would you mind telling me how you found out about this?"

"It's too soon for that, but maybe later. Thanks again for the help," Ava said, abruptly ending the conversation and turning to Jacob. "Well, that confirms that the link between Muir and Yip goes back at least four years. And since it was Muir who sent the wire and a copy of Yip's purchase order to Mr. Fozdar, he also knew that the money was being used to purchase rough-cut diamonds."

"They had a long-term plan," Jacob said.

"That seems to be the case," Ava said, and then turned to Mr. Fozdar. "Excuse me for interrupting earlier. I think you were about to suggest a possible reason why Jasmine Yip stopped sending you money from Singapore and instead began remitting it from Chengdu and Amsterdam."

"If it was dirty money, I'm assuming she wanted to keep it separate from her regular business."

"If she was laundering money, the opposite would be more likely. She'd need a legitimate business to provide cover."

"That's a good point," Fozdar said, and then smiled wanly. "I'm not familiar with the ins and outs of money laundering."

"And I'm quite unfamiliar with China," Jacob said. "For one thing, I've never even heard of Chengdu."

"It's a city in western China, in Sichuan province," Ava said. "As I remember, it has a population of about ten million people."

"That's more than half the population of the Netherlands. I feel silly that I didn't know about it."

"There's no reason for that. It isn't even in the top five largest Chinese cities," Ava said.

"Why would Jasmine choose to do business there?" Jacob asked, and then looked at Fozdar. "Is it a diamond centre?"

"No, most of the diamond trade in China is in Guangzhou and Shenzhen," Fozdar said.

"Is all the information you have on the Chengdu bank in the file you've prepared?" Ava asked.

"It is, but you will find it very basic."

"How often were transfers made?"

"Every few months or so until about four months ago."

"What happened then?"

"Jasmine stopped making purchases."

"Over the past four years, how much did she spend on diamonds in total?"

Fozdar turned the page in front of him. "Approximately thirty-two million dollars."

"She stopped buying because she'd finished laundering all the money in the Amsterdam bank account," Ava said to Jacob.

"That's logical."

"Did you make copies of all the transfers for us?" she asked Fozdar.

"I did."

"And were the transfers tied to purchase orders like the one from Calgary?"

"Yes, and we've attached a copy of the purchase order relevant to each transfer."

"Thank you, that was very thoughtful of you," Ava said. "When can we get the file?"

"When you leave."

"Unless Jacob has some additional questions, I think we could leave now," Ava said.

"Not quite so fast. There's something I need to make clear," Fozdar said. "As I mentioned before, I don't want Jasmine — or anyone else for that matter — to know how you came by this information. My daughter wanted you to sign something to that effect, but I don't think we need to go to that extreme. Do we?"

"We don't. You have my word," said Ava.

Fozdar nodded, then pushed the file across the desk towards her. "When you conclude your investigation, I would like you to inform me of the result."

"You have my word on that as well."

"Hopefully it will turn out that this man Muir was the mastermind and Jasmine simply an innocent foil."

"However it ends, you will hear about it from me personally," said Ava.

They left the building a few minutes later with Fozdar's file tucked under Ava's arm. She was anxious to get into it but wanted to do it in a place where she could concentrate. "I'd like to get back to Amsterdam as soon as we can," she said to Jacob.

He checked his watch. "There's a train in twenty minutes. If we hurry, we should be able to catch it."

"Let's go," she said, picking up the pace.

They made the train with five minutes to spare. As they settled into their seats, Jacob pointed to the file. "What's your plan for that?"

"Let's go through it now. If it contains everything Fozdar said it does — and I don't doubt him — then there are two very obvious paths for us to follow immediately," she said. "First we need to find out everything we can about Jasmine Yip, and then get her to talk to us."

"Why would she agree to do that?"

"My former partner often said that people will do the right thing for the wrong reason," Ava said with a smile. "And sometimes you have to create that reason."

"I'll leave that to you," Jacob said, returning her smile. "But you mentioned two paths. What's the second?"

"We need information about the bank account in Chengdu. Who owns the account? Who controls it? Where did the money originate?" she said. "Do you think your bank contacts are capable of taking that on? They would have to be discreet. The last thing we want to happen is for the Chinese bank to suspect there's a problem and alert the account holder that foreigners are asking questions about their business."

"I might have to script an approach."

"Jacob, just so we're clear, they must not do anything that will raise an alarm. The only advantage we have right now is that no one knows we're coming after them."

(16)

IT WAS ALMOST SIX WHEN SHE ENTERED THE LOBBY OF the Dylan Hotel in Amsterdam, which meant it was close to midnight in Shanghai. Back in her room, she took out her phone, found Xu's number, and dialed.

Xu was her closest male friend and confidant. He was also the triad leader, or Mountain Master, in Shanghai, and had been mentored by Uncle. When Uncle died, Xu had entered her life and had been a fixture ever since. He was someone Ava trusted completely.

The phone rang four times, and Ava began to regret calling so late. Then she heard a lively "*Wei*" from Auntie Grace, Xu's housekeeper.

"Auntie, this is Ava. I'm sorry for calling at this hour, but if Xu is still awake, I'd like to speak to him."

"Is everything okay?" Auntie Grace asked, her voice instantly full of concern.

"Everything is fine. I do need help with something," she said, "but if Xu is sleeping it can wait until tomorrow."

"He would be angry with me if he knew you called and I

hadn't told him," Auntie Grace said. "Besides, I think he's still awake. Let me check."

Ava placed Fozdar's file and her notebook on the desk and waited. A moment later she heard Xu's distinctive voice. "*Mei mei*, it's good to hear from you. Are you and Fai still in Canada?"

Mei mei meant "little sister," and Ava responded with the term for "big brother." "No, *ge ge*, I'm in Amsterdam. A friend in Toronto has a problem that I'm helping with."

"Is Fai with you?"

"No, she's gone to Taiwan to make a film. It was a last-minute thing, but a tremendous opportunity for her."

"Is everything going well with you two?"

"It couldn't be better," Ava said. "The fact that I'm in Amsterdam and she's in Taipei is totally coincidental."

"That's good to hear. Auntie Grace and I think you're a terrific couple."

Ava paused, surprised by Xu's open support of her relationship with Fai. He knew about her sexuality, but it was something they hadn't discussed. "I've never been happier," she said. "How are you feeling?"

"I'm not pushing myself too hard. Quite honestly, I think I'm back to normal, though you wouldn't think so if you saw how Auntie treats me."

"You are her boy."

"I know, and I'm not really complaining, but being looked after so well is tiring in its way." He laughed. "I apologize for wandering off topic. You said you're in Amsterdam to help a friend?"

"Yes, my friend Mimi's family has run into some serious difficulties. Someone scammed them for all they were worth.

I've tracked the money this far, and now I could use some assistance."

"Tell me what you need, though I'm sure you know I have no influence in Toronto or Amsterdam."

"How about in Singapore?" she asked.

"I don't have much influence there either," he said.

"Really? The triads have no presence there?"

"No. During my father's time we had a loose affiliation with a gang called Ang Soon Tang, but the Secret Society Branch of the Singapore police wiped them out," Xu said. "Singapore is not a good place to run afoul of the law. Their Internal Security Act allows the government to detain people indefinitely without trial."

"Indefinitely?"

"The guy who headed up Ang Soon Tang died in prison after being held for twelve years, and that's not a record. There are people who have been held for longer than twenty years without a trial."

"I knew Singapore was almost fanatical about maintaining order, but I didn't know it went that far," Ava said. "That's rather discouraging."

"Well, there is another gang they didn't eradicate entirely. Most of the members operate independently, but they do assist one another from time to time. Depending on what you need, I might be able to find someone to help."

"Right now all I need is information."

"About what?"

"There's a woman named Jasmine Yip, or Yip Liling, who I'm told lives in Singapore. She runs a diamond business called Jewellery Circle. I would like to know as much as possible about her personal and professional life."

Xu hesitated, then said, "I think Tommy Tiu might be able to help you. He's in the money-lending business. Gathering information about clients is central to his work."

"Can he work quickly?"

"If I ask him to."

"And how much would he cost?"

"He owes me some favours. I'll call one in," Xu said.

"I couldn't ask you to do that."

"Ava, these favours go back years, and I have so little to do with Singapore that I've never had a chance to use them," said Xu.

"Then in that case, thank you. You know it's appreciated," Ava said. "Is there any chance you could call him tonight?"

"I expected that would be your next question, and the answer is yes. Once I've spoken to him, I'll get out of the way and let him communicate directly with you. I'll let him know, though, that supporting you is a priority for me, and that I expect him to do whatever you ask."

"Thanks again, *ge ge*."

"What's a big brother for?" he said. "Send me the information and I'll track down Tommy."

"Give Auntie Grace a hug for me," she said before she ended the call. Then she thought, *Thank goodness for* guanxi.

Despite being raised primarily in Toronto, Ava had been exposed to some key elements of Chinese culture. One of those was *guanxi* — the cultivation and utilization of personal relationships. Uncle had been a master of the craft, and she had learned from him. Anyone who wasn't an enemy was a potential friend, he taught, and even enemies could become friends through the judicious granting of favours.

"You always need to remember," Uncle had told Ava more than once, "a favour, however small, is always far more significant to the person getting it than to the one giving it. So never hesitate to give, but do it without asking for anything in return. The obligation will be there regardless, and by being selfless you make the person who owes you the favour all the more eager to repay. In my world those unspoken obligations, those favours exchanged, are more important and binding between two people than any contract."

Uncle's world was also Xu's, and as she opened her laptop, Ava couldn't help but wonder what favour Xu had granted Tommy Tiu. A few minutes later, everything she knew about Jasmine Yip had been sent to Xu. Now it was a matter of waiting.

Ava looked out the window that overlooked the courtyard. She checked her phone and saw that Fai had texted to tell her the day had gone well. Ava thought briefly about calling her but decided it was too late. Instead she texted, *Glad things are working out as you hoped. I had an interesting day here, but I expect I'll be on the move soon. I'll let you know where I'm headed as soon as I decide where I'm going.*

She heard a clap of thunder and looked outside again. Dark clouds had settled over Amsterdam and there wasn't much doubt that it was going to rain. Ava saw people scurrying along the sidewalk, trying to get where they were going before the storm began. She'd never had much luck with weather in Amsterdam, but at least this time she was dry and indoors.

A gaping yawn caught her by surprise. She had slept for maybe two hours on the plane the night before and knew if she lay down she'd be asleep in seconds. It was too early for that if she wanted to avoid jet lag, but she knew she couldn't stay in the room or the bed's attractions would get to her. She would have gone for a walk if the weather weren't so threatening, which left her the option of going downstairs to one of the Dylan's restaurants. She wasn't especially hungry, but this was about killing time.

The Dylan had two restaurants: Vinkeles, a Michelin-starred high-end eatery, and OCCO, a brasserie. Ava had eaten in OCCO before and decided it was worth another visit. It was long and narrow, with a floor inlaid with small red bricks and an exterior wall lined with twelve-panelled windows that on a sunny day infused the place with a sense of well-being. Even on a gloomy day the windows framed the outside world and made her feel less isolated.

The brasserie was half empty when she entered. She sat down in a round-backed black leather chair at a table next to a window, across from the bar. "Can I eat here or do I have to go into the dining area?" she asked a server.

"You can eat wherever you wish," the server said, putting a menu in front of her. "Can I get you something to drink in the meantime?"

"I'll have a glass of Chardonnay," Ava said.

When the server left, Ava opened the menu and made a quick decision. Then, hearing thunder once more, she turned her head and looked out the window, which was starting to streak with rain. *Thank goodness I didn't go outside,* she thought. As she did, the wind suddenly picked up and rain lashed across the courtyard. Ava watched a man outside struggling with an umbrella that had been blown inside out. She shuddered at his discomfort but felt all the more cozy and warm.

"Here is your wine," the server said, interrupting Ava's interest in the courtyard.

"Thank you," Ava said.

"Are you ready to order dinner?"

"I think so," Ava said, but then her phone rang. She looked at an incoming number she didn't recognize. "Hello?" she said tentatively.

"Is this Ava Lee?"

"Yes. Who is this?"

"I'm Tommy Tiu," he said. "I've just finished speaking to Xu. He told me you're looking for information about a Singapore woman named Jasmine Yip."

Ava was surprised by his abruptness but not by his accent, which was more English than Chinese. She knew from experience that the official language of education in Singapore was English. "That is correct. I didn't expect to hear from you so soon."

"The Jasmine Yip that you're interested in, was her father in the diamond business?"

"He was."

"This is remarkable—I haven't heard that name in years. I could hardly believe it when Xu mentioned her."

"So you know her?" Ava asked.

"Oh, I know Jasmine. Not as well as I knew her father, but well enough."

"I was told he's dead."

"Yes, he has been for quite a few years."

"How did you come to know him?"

"Like me, he was a member of Sah Lak Kau." Tiu said.

Ava waited for him to continue. When he didn't, she said, "I have no idea what Sah Lak Kau is."

"It is — or I should say it was — a Singapore-based gang made up mainly of Hokkien Chinese," Tiu said. "We were never that big, but the Singapore riot squad came after us like we were one of the huge Hong Kong triad gangs. The gang broke up. Some members were sent to jail, some left the city, and others like me and Simon Yip went underground."

"I take it that Simon Yip was Jasmine's father."

"He was."

"Then he did more than go underground. I was told he became a diamond merchant doing business with reputable firms in places like Antwerp."

"Calling him a diamond merchant is a stretch. Simon was a small-time hustler who was up for anything. He stole, he smuggled, and he laundered money for people like me. That's where the diamonds came in. I don't know how he came up with the idea of using diamonds to launder cash, but it sure as hell worked."

"How did it work?" Ava asked.

"When I had money that was a bit hot or I didn't want to declare to the tax man, I'd give it to Simon. He had a bunch of other guys doing the same thing. He'd wait until he had enough of a bankroll and then off he'd go to Antwerp to do a deal. When he came back, he would distribute the diamonds among us."

"And you'd sell them?"

"Sometimes I did, but not always. The good thing about diamonds is that they're easy to stash and really easy to sell when you decide to offload them."

"And Yip gave you good value? I mean, if you gave him a hundred thousand, the diamonds you got back were worth that?"

"Sometimes they were worth more, depending on the market and the kind of deal Simon struck. Remember, he was buying wholesale and in decent volumes," Tiu said. "One thing for certain, I never heard anyone complain about him shortchanging them."

"How did he make his money from the deal?"

"He charged a ten percent commission."

Ava tried to remember how much business Mr. Fozdar had said he'd done with Simon Yip, but she couldn't come up with a figure. "I was told Jasmine worked with him. Is that how you met her?"

"Yeah. Simon was really sick for a year or two before he died, and she ran errands for him — picking up money, dropping off diamonds. But everything went through Simon; he was still my main contact. I don't think I exchanged more than a few words with Jasmine during that whole time. And after Simon died I had no contact with her. I hadn't even heard her name since then until Xu mentioned it."

"She's still buying diamonds, and after what you've told me, she's probably using them to launder money also," Ava said. "Is it possible that some of your old colleagues could be doing business with her?"

"I don't think so," Tiu said. "I will make some phone calls, though."

"Can you think of anyone else who might be doing business with her?"

"How much business are you talking about?"

"A lot — more than twenty million American dollars last year."

Tiu became quiet and then laughed. "Holy shit! Simon would be proud of her."

"Except some of that money was stolen."

"That wouldn't have bothered Simon," Tiu said.

"It bothers me," Ava said, irked by that remark but equally aware that Tiu had no reason to care. "When you're talking to the old colleagues, you might ask them if they know of anyone else who's doing business with her."

"I'll do that. Xu said you also want some background information on her."

"I do, whatever you can dig up. Is she married? Does she have kids? Who are her best friends? Does she have business partners? How many relatives does she have and where do they live? What kind of lifestyle does she lead? Does she drink or do drugs? What hobbies does she have? Nothing is too trivial."

"I'll find out what I can."

"And you'll do it quickly, please?"

"As fast as I can, but you do know that I'm not getting paid for this? This is a favour for Xu."

"I know, he told me."

"He told you that, huh? You and he are close?"

There was the slightest insinuation in Tiu's voice. "I'm his *mei mei*," she said.

Tiu became quiet.

"Is that close enough for you?" Ava asked.

"I'll call you tomorrow," he said suddenly. "Is there a right time to call?"

"Whenever you have information for me is the right time. But I'm in the Netherlands and you're six hours ahead of me, so try not to call me in the middle of the night."

(17)

THE FIRST THING AVA THOUGHT WHEN SHE FINISHED her conversation with Tommy Tiu was that she should have brought her notebook. She stood up as the server arrived with her glass of Chardonnay.

"I have to go back to my room to collect something, but I'll be back," Ava said.

"Do you want to order food before you leave?" the server asked.

"I'll have the steak tartare as a starter, but I'm not ready to order a main course yet."

"There's no rush. With all this wind and rain, it will be a quiet evening here."

Nevertheless, Ava didn't dawdle. Within five minutes she was back at her table in OCCO with the notebook open in front of her. Between sips of wine she wrote down everything Tiu had told her about Simon and Jasmine Yip, and then she started on a list of questions. Before she'd finished the server brought the steak tartare. Ava thought of pushing it to one side, but it looked delicious.

She ate slowly, savouring the texture and trying to identify the ingredients. There were definitely Worcestershire sauce, a pepper sauce of some type, mustard, and capers. By the fourth bite she had discovered olives and parsley, but her taste buds didn't find the onion until she was almost finished.

Ava ordered another glass of Chardonnay when the server came to remove her plate. She reopened her notebook and read what she'd written earlier, underlined several points, added more questions, and then reached for her phone.

"*Hallo*," Mrs. Smits answered.

"This is Ava Lee calling. May I speak to Jacob, please," Ava said slowly.

Mrs. Smits didn't answer, but a few seconds later Jacob said, "I'm pleased to hear from you. I was actually thinking about calling you."

"Has something happened?"

"I think I've found the person we can use to contact the Chinese bank," he said. "The wife of one of the guys we used to get information on the Jewellery Circle account works in the foreign transactions department of the same bank. She has agreed to help."

"How much?"

"Five thousand."

"Is she already on board?"

"I wanted your approval."

"You have it," Ava said.

"Good. My plan is for her to send an inquiry tonight. With any luck we'll have some information tomorrow morning," he said. "Why were you calling me?"

"I found someone in Singapore who knows Jasmine Yip, or at least knew her a few years ago. He's going to collect as much current information about her as he can," Ava said.

She paused. "It turns out she's from a family with a history of using diamonds to launder money."

"But if she lives in Singapore, how did Muir connect with her?"

"That's one of the questions we need to answer," Ava said. "Another is, who in China was using her services, and is there any connection between them and Muir?"

"You don't think it's possible that Muir was recycling his cash through China?"

Ava looked at her notebook. "I agree with Mr. Fozdar that there wouldn't have been enough profit from selling diamonds to generate that amount of money. Besides, why would Muir open a Chinese bank account? It doesn't make any sense. As a Westerner, if he wanted to recycle his money it's far more likely he'd go to Panama or one of the Caribbean islands that offer private banking."

"So it's possible the Chinese bank may have absolutely no connection to Muir?"

"I think that's a strong possibility."

"Which means that we might have no money trail to follow."

"It's far too early to say, especially when I haven't had a chance to talk to Jasmine Yip," Ava said. "I've just been thinking that, given the amount of money involved, it wouldn't have been easy for someone unfamiliar with the diamond business to convert that many stones into cash. It makes sense that they would have needed help, and who could be more logical than Yip?"

"Are you sure you'll be able to find her?"

"If she's still living in Singapore, I'm confident we will."

"And what's your next step when you do?"

"That depends entirely on what my Singapore contact finds, and what you learn about Yip's Chinese banking arrangements."

"Speaking of arrangements, I should call the woman at the bank before it gets too late," Jacob said. "I'll call you tomorrow as soon as I have more information."

Ava ended the call and looked out the window at a night that was still wet and windy. *Perfect weather for sleeping*, she thought as a yawn overtook her. She checked the time and saw it was almost eight o'clock. If she showered when she got back to the room, it would be at least eight-thirty before she got into bed. It had been a long, tiring day, but considering what she knew now, it had been successful enough.

She looked at her notebook and at the questions she'd underlined. Too many of them were questions that only Yip could answer. "If Tiu confirms that you're still living in Singapore, I'm coming after you, Jasmine Yip," Ava muttered to herself.

(18)

UNCLE VISITED IN HER DREAMS AGAIN THAT NIGHT. HE sat in an easy chair in the corner of her hotel room, his face faintly illuminated by the glow of a cigarette.

I am proud of the way you carried yourself today, he said. *When I saw you in Toronto, I was worried you had lost some of your edge.*

Thank you, Uncle.

I was also pleased that you contacted the lawyer Burgess. She is capable. When I was Mountain Master in Fanling, I surrounded myself with capable men, but I have to say that with the women you have in your life, you have outdone me.

I don't just have women. There's Xu and Sonny and you.

Xu is a good man, like his father before him. I am glad you asked him to help you in Singapore. That can be a dangerous place. Be careful when you are there.

You told me many times that it's the most boring city in Asia.

That is why the slightest disorder attracts a disproportionate amount of attention. Hong Kong has law and order. Singapore values order above everything, including the law.

Xu has connected me with a man named Tommy Tiu.

I know Tommy. He can be lazy, and he is not very bright. Do not trust him with anything that requires real effort or intelligence.

Okay, Uncle.

Travel safely, he said, and then he was gone.

When she woke, Ava immediately felt clear-headed. She turned to look at the bedside clock and blinked when she saw it was seven o'clock. She had slept for almost ten hours, the longest she could remember. Ava felt a surge of energy, and then a touch of panic as she wondered if she'd slept through anything important. She reached for her phone and quickly scanned for texts, emails, and missed calls. There was a short text from Fai, but the rest of the world had ignored her while she slept.

She slid out of bed and headed for the bathroom. Ten minutes later she sat down at the room desk with a cup of coffee and opened the laptop. She found a travel site and searched for direct flights from Amsterdam to Singapore. As usual, the site ignored her request and listed the cheapest flights, all of which made several stops. Scrolling down, she found two airlines that flew direct — not surprisingly, Singapore Air and KLM. She preferred the service on Singapore, but the KLM flight worked better logistically; it left Amsterdam at nine in the evening and landed in Singapore at three-thirty the following afternoon.

It was premature to book, so Ava made a note of the flight numbers and times and then opened her email. She wrote to Fai, I got your text. The six-hour time difference is frustrating. I think I'll be heading to Singapore tomorrow. I'll let you know as soon as those plans are finalized. In the meantime, know that I miss you and am thinking about you. All my love, Ava.

She rose from the desk and went to the window that looked out onto the courtyard. The cobblestones were wet, and, although it wasn't raining, the sky was overcast and showed every sign of opening up again. She had thought to go out for breakfast but, like the night before, decided that OCCO was a safer choice. She had turned to go into the bathroom when her phone rang. She hurried back to the desk and picked it up. "Yes," she said.

"Good morning, this is Jacob."

"From the tone of your voice, it doesn't sound like it has been particularly good," Ava said as she returned to the desk.

"We had no luck getting information about the Chinese bank account."

"The bank hasn't responded?"

"Worse than that, it did respond but said it wouldn't release any of the information we requested."

"Did they give a reason?"

"No. Our young lady at the bank in Amsterdam was really surprised at the reaction. Normally a bank-to-bank request for basic information about a business account gets some measure of positive response."

"Shit," Ava said.

"So what do we do now?"

"I don't know. I need to think about it."

"I'm sorry, Ava," Jacob said after a slight hesitation.

"It isn't your fault, and not the young woman's either."

"By the way, she doesn't expect any payment for her efforts."

"I think we should give her something anyway. Would a thousand euros be enough?"

"That's generous. I'm sure she'll be pleased."

"I may try to use a Chinese bank to find a route into the Chengdu bank," she said. "I just need to figure out who to ask."

"Will you let me know how it goes?"

"Of course. As far as I'm concerned you're still working on this with me."

"That's kind of you to say."

"Besides, you haven't earned out your advance yet, have you."

"No," he said with a laugh.

"Well, until you do, we're partners."

"I am here and available."

"Thank you. I'll be in touch," she said.

Ava shook her head in disappointment as she ended the call. She hadn't anticipated that the Chengdu bank would give them everything they'd requested, but she had expected it would at least give them something. Who else could she use to make an approach? There was a bank in Kowloon that Uncle had partially owned, and Xu did business with several banks. May Ling dealt with a myriad of banks, and Three Sisters did as well. Ava was weighing the options when her phone rang again. She saw the Singapore country code, sixty-five.

"Is this Tommy Tiu?" she said.

"Yes, this is Tommy."

"What do you have for me?"

"I've confirmed that Jasmine Yip is still living in Singapore and is in the city right now."

"That's a very good start. How do you know she's there now?"

"I spoke to her." he said. "Don't worry, I was careful. I

told her I was talking to an old friend of her father's when her name came up and spiked my curiosity. I told her I had some money I needed to launder and asked if she's still in the business. She said no, so then I asked her what she's doing to make money these days. She said her father left the family in a comfortable situation and she's looking after her mother and her aunt. I asked if they're still living in the family home in Emerald Hill. She said they are, and that she's moved in with them."

"I take it that Emerald Hill is a neighbourhood in Singapore," Ava said.

"It is. That's where a lot of the Peranakan — the Straits Chinese — live," he said. "I told you that Simon was Hokkienese, but he married a Peranakan and moved to Emerald Hill to make her happy."

"I have never heard the name Peranakan."

"It is a mixture of Chinese and Malay. When the Chinese traders started coming here, they married local women. That's what their offspring have been called ever since."

"How would Jasmine regard herself, as Peranakan or Hokkienese?"

"Probably as a Singaporean. The new generation don't like the old terms."

"Well, whatever she calls herself, are you confident I'll find her at that address?"

"She had no reason to lie to me."

"Is the Emerald Hill address on the list I gave to you?"

"Yes."

"How about the other phone numbers and addresses I gave you to check? Are they still valid?"

"I tried her business line and got a recording. I went to the

Jewellery Circle office, but no one answered. When I called her personal line, she answered."

Ava made some notes. "I do wish you'd gone to the house in Emerald Hill."

"I didn't want to draw attention to myself. If you want I'll go later today, but I'm not sure it's the smartest move. Jasmine isn't stupid. A phone call and a visit from me on the same day after years of being out of touch would look suspicious."

"You're right," Ava said, realizing that Tommy was smarter than Uncle had intimated. "Can you at least check the housing records to see if her mother is actually a registered occupant?"

"I looked at the city directory, and the mother and aunt are both listed."

"Well, if Jasmine isn't there, perhaps they can direct me to her."

"I suggest you go carefully. When they were younger, the aunt was married to a loan shark and managed his accounts, and Jasmine's mother was the brains behind Simon Yip. I don't imagine either of them has slowed down that much."

"That's good advice. Do you have anything more on Jasmine?"

Tiu hesitated, then said, "I had trouble finding anyone who knew much about her. After her father died, there was no reason for us to stay in contact with her. I did manage to track down the wife of one of our guys who'd had coffee with her a few times."

"What did the wife say?"

"She said Jasmine has never been married, has no kids, and never mentioned a boyfriend or girlfriend," Tiu said.

"She said Jasmine talked mainly about her business. Evidently she was thinking about opening some jewellery stores, but the wife doesn't think anything came of it."

"So she has no personal attachments that you know of beside her mother and aunt."

"That's what I was told."

"Does she have business partners?"

"None that I could find, and the company listing for Jewellery Circle has only her name on it."

"What about friends?"

"I don't know, and neither did the wife. I'd be surprised if there were many. Jasmine was always close to her family. She didn't have time for much else."

"Does she have any brothers or sisters?"

"No."

"So the entire immediate family is Jasmine, her mother, and the aunt?"

"The aunt has two daughters. Jasmine was tight with them."

"What do you know about them?"

"I heard one of them married a Chinese guy. I don't know anything about the other."

"When you say a Chinese guy, do you mean he's Hokkien from Singapore or something else?"

"He's from China. That's all I know."

"Do you recall the girls' names?"

"The family name is Lam, and I remember one was called Essie, because it's a strange name."

Ava checked her notes again. "Did you run a credit check on Jasmine? I know you said her father left the family in a comfortable situation."

"I was saving that for last," Tiu said, his voice rising. "The house is in both her and her mother's names. It's worth at least ten million Singapore dollars — about seven million U.S. dollars. It has no mortgage and there's a credit line of five hundred thousand attached to it that's never been used. The taxes run to about fifteen thousand a year, and Jasmine has paid them for at least the past five years."

"That's quite an asset."

"Real estate values in Singapore are insane. Ten million isn't even that high," Tiu said. "I'm more impressed by her credit score and the car she drives. For someone with a reported income in the last two years of less than one hundred thousand, she's living a large life."

"Tell me about the car."

"Do you know anything about buying a car in Singapore?"

"No."

"Well, it isn't easy. The government wants to restrict the number of cars on the road, so it controls how many can be bought by issuing certificates of entitlement. You can't buy a car in Singapore without one, and even then it only lasts for ten years. The certificates are issued twice a month in varying numbers and auctioned off. I paid almost fifty thousand dollars for the one I bought last year," Tiu said.

"You mean you paid fifty thousand dollars just for the *right* to buy a car?"

"Yeah, and it doesn't end there. Once I buy the car, I'm obliged to pay an excise duty of twenty percent, a sales tax of seven percent, and an additional registration fee," he said, then paused for effect. "Jasmine bought a BMW 7 Series sedan six months ago. Its list price was close to two hundred thousand dollars, but by the time she'd paid for the certificate of entitlement and all the other duties, taxes, and fees, that car would have cost her almost half a million dollars. She paid it all in full."

"Which bank did she use?"

"I don't know, but it's unlikely it was the Jewellery Circle account. Its average balance hasn't been higher than fifty thousand for a few years."

"Did she buy the car from a dealer in Singapore? I know the government is unlikely to tell you how she paid, but maybe you could persuade the dealer."

"I thought of that. There are only two BMW dealerships in Singapore. I'll get to them when I can. I'm sorry, but it might not be today."

"When you can will be just fine, and I'll pay for the information, if that helps."

"There's no need for you to do that. I'll check it off as another favour repaid to Xu," Tiu said.

"Well, Tommy," Ava said as she looked at her notes, "what began as a rather discouraging report certainly picked up steam. Thank you for all this."

"I'll phone you in the next day or two after I finish with the car dealers."

"If you don't reach me right away, leave a message. I could be on a plane."

"A plane to Singapore?"

"I think that's possible, but it's not certain," she said, deciding to keep it vague.

"Well, if you do come, let me know."

"Will do."

Ava sat quietly at the desk for several minutes after talking to Tommy Tiu. He hadn't given her as much information as she would like, but his confirmation of Jasmine Yip's home address, and his assertion that she was currently in Singapore, were important first steps. There was also the potential that the car dealership could help identify a personal account attached to Yip.

The main question in her mind now was how fast she could get to Singapore. Despite her vagueness with Tiu, the instant he said that Jasmine Yip was there, Ava had made up her mind to go. She checked the time. She could try to catch that morning's Singapore Air flight or spend the day in Amsterdam and leave on the KLM evening flight.

Nothing will be gained by spending the day in Amsterdam. If I hustle I can get the Singapore Air flight, she thought, and headed to the bedroom to pack.

(19)

FOR THE SECOND TIME IN THREE DAYS, AVA ARRIVED in a foreign city just as the sun was coming up.

Over the years, she had been through Singapore many times, most often seeing only the airport as she caught a connecting flight. But she had stayed in the city a couple of times, and, although she couldn't claim to know it very well, her memories of it were vivid. Foremost was the weather. Singapore sat almost directly on the equator and had year-round summer, with daytime highs around twenty-seven degrees and lows that rarely went below twenty-four degrees. What's worse, it rained almost two hundred days a year in Singapore, which left the air perpetually heavy and humid. The weather contributed to the city's many lush and beautiful public gardens but made it uncomfortable for anyone who wanted to walk around in them.

Another thing she'd noticed on her trips to the city of six million was how clean and organized it was. There was none of the chaos and crowding that were common in cities such as Bangkok, Manila, Jakarta, and even Hong Kong. For more than fifty years Singapore had been run by politicians who were intent on keeping things orderly and open for business. Limiting the number of cars on the city's streets was only one example of the many regulations that in other places might be considered authoritarian. In Singapore they were simply practical steps taken by the People's Action Party to make the city the most modern in Asia. From what Ava had read recently, they might already have achieved that goal.

Despite its modernity — or maybe because of it — Uncle had hated the city. Ava had been surprised that he hadn't derided it more in her dream the night before. He had gone there three times that Ava knew of, once with her and twice on his own to meet colleagues. On all three occasions he was delighted to get back to Hong Kong. "That place has no soul," he had said whenever Singapore was mentioned. "It is a place contrived and constructed by bureaucrats. They want nothing old, nothing flawed. Everything has to be new and shiny."

Ava didn't completely share that view. While it was true the government seemed to overdo it at times, there was something to be said for a city in Asia of that size that actually functioned smoothly, absent the visible slums and poverty that were so conspicuous elsewhere.

"The Mandarin Oriental in Marina Square," she said as she got into a taxi at the airport. "How long will the drive take?"

"Fifteen minutes."

Ava had booked a suite at the Mandarin before leaving Amsterdam. The hotel was in the heart of the Central Business District, close to Marina Bay, and only fifteen minutes away from Jasmine Yip's house in Emerald Hill.

The twelve-hour flight from Amsterdam had been

uneventful. Singapore Air's service, as always, was impeccable, and Ava had taken advantage of the champagne and several fine white wines on offer. She'd tried to sleep and might have dozed off a couple of times, but she wasn't really tired, and her head kept replaying the conversation with Tommy Tiu. What she couldn't understand was how Jasmine Yip and Malcolm Muir had ever connected. And how had Yip generated so much profit from the Harvest Investment Fund money, and where did that profit eventually land? Was it flowing back to Muir? If so, where was the bank account?

Her phone rang and she saw Fai's number. "Hey, sweetheart," Ava said. "You're up very early."

"We start shooting at eight and the set is an hour's drive out of the city. My ride will be here in a few minutes, but I wanted to hear your voice," Fai said. "I was tracking your flight but I didn't know if you'd cleared Customs yet."

"Singapore might have the most efficient airport in Asia. I'm already in a taxi headed for the hotel. I was going to call you when I got there."

"You didn't tell me in your message how long you think you'll be there."

"That's because I have no idea. It could be a day or two, it could be longer. And depending on what I find, I could be off from here to some place like Chengdu."

"Why Chengdu?"

"The money that was stolen from Mr. Gregory and the other investors has made its way through several bank accounts. I think one might be there," Ava said. "When you start chasing money, you can't predict where it will finally land."

"So you're making progress?"

"Well, I know a lot more than I did a few days ago, but there's no clear end in sight yet," Ava said. "But tell me, how are you doing? How is the shoot? Is Andy Gao as good to work with as you expected?"

"Andy is a real professional, and the shoot couldn't be going any better," Fai said. "I can't imagine not finishing on schedule."

"Now that I'm in Asia, I'm only a few hours away from you. Do you get any time off?"

"We're shooting six days a week, and when we're not on set, Andy has us rehearsing scenes at the hotel for the next week's shoot," said Fai. "I'd love to see you, but I wouldn't have much time."

"And it sounds like I might be a distraction."

"Not to me."

"Anyway, it's premature for me to talk about visiting when I have no idea how much longer it will take to resolve this Harvest Investment Fund mess," Ava said. "But at least now we're in the same time zone."

"It's nice to hear your voice. I miss you terribly."

"Me too."

Fai paused and then said. "Ava, have you talked to Chen?"

"I have. Chen is going to stall Lau Lau until we can figure out how to proceed," Ava said. "I also spoke to my lawyer. She's trying to create a legal wall between the finance money and me. I've been persuaded it's the wise thing to do."

"I'm glad you're listening to the lawyer."

"Fai, I'm listening to all of you, and no one's opinion is more important to me than yours."

"I have something to confess," Fai said suddenly.

Ava felt an immediate sense of alarm.

"I gave Lau Lau's script to Andy. Chen and I may believe it's great, but I was wondering what a director with Andy's experience would think."

"And?"

"He thinks it's fantastic. He said that however good Lau Lau was as a director, his greatest strength is as a scriptwriter," Fai said. "I told him there isn't any contract in place but if the film is ever made, Lau Lau will direct. He asked if Lau Lau's health is sound enough for him to see a project like this through to the end. I told him I don't know but that he deserves the chance. Then he asked me which role I would play. When I said the mother, he told me that would be a mistake. He said it's typecasting, and he thinks I should take the role of the army general who opposes government intervention and becomes a secret witness to its horrors. He said it's a stronger role."

"He could be right. In fact, as I think about it now, it is a stronger role."

"Well, we'll see what Lau Lau thinks — assuming we get to a point where he'll be making that kind of decision," Fai said. "And Ava, in case you're concerned, I didn't tell Andy how the script came to be written or anything else about your involvement."

"I wasn't concerned, but you were right to be cautious, so thank you."

"Ah, my room phone just rang," Fai said abruptly. "I've got to get going or I'll miss my ride to the set."

"Love you. I'll talk to you tonight."

"Love you too."

Ava ended the call and looked out the cab window at the skyline of central Singapore. It had been several years since her last trip to the city. Then the most interesting sight had been the Singapore Flyer, a gigantic Ferris wheel that provided a bird's-eye view of Singapore's main island and some of the sixty-two smaller islets that comprised the city. Now the Flyer looked tiny in comparison with the Marina Bay Sands building complex. "The Sands looks spectacular," she said to the taxi driver.

He turned his head towards her and smiled. "People come from all over the world to see it."

The Sands consisted of three fifty-storey side-by-side buildings that housed an enormous casino, several theatres, famous gourmet restaurants, a museum, a convention centre, luxury shops, and an ice-skating rink. But what made it truly spectacular was the terrace that ran straight across the top of the three buildings for almost three hundred metres and then cantilevered into nothing but air for another seventy metres.

"The buildings were almost completed last time I was here, but the terrace hadn't been constructed. I wonder if the architect was inspired by Stonehenge in England, where large slabs of stone sit on top of pillars," she said to the driver.

"I've never been to England, so I don't know about Stonehenge," he said. "And we don't actually refer to it as a terrace. It's called SkyPark. It has gardens on it, a jogging trail, and restaurants, and at the very end of the overhang is the world's largest infinity pool. The park can accommodate almost four thousand people at one time."

"You could be a tour guide," she said, smiling.

"I'm proud of my city, and I'm always pleased to share information about it."

"What do you know about Emerald Hill?"

"That's the old Peranakan Chinese neighbourhood. It is quite central, near Orchard Road. I've taken tourists there to see the architecture. One of them called it Chinese baroque, though I'm not sure what that means. It's also a historic conservation area, and there aren't many of those in Singapore. Our normal operating style is to rip down anything remotely old and build anew."

"Like most cities in China."

"I wouldn't know. I've never been to China either."

"How much longer until we get to the Mandarin?"

"There it is, straight ahead," he said.

Ava had stayed at Mandarin Orientals all over the world, and her expectations in terms of quality and level of service were high. The Singapore hotel didn't disappoint. Within minutes of being greeted by a gorgeous young woman wearing a purple cheongsam, she was shown into a suite on the twelfth floor that offered a panoramic view of Marina Bay and the Sands complex. She unpacked and showered, then climbed into bed under a white duvet that was almost weightless.

She hadn't decided when she would confront Jasmine Yip, but when it happened, Ava wanted to be well-rested and alert. It would also be helpful if she had some hard information about the bank account in Chengdu, and for that she had decided that May Ling was best positioned to get access. It was seven-fifteen, still too early to call Wuhan, but she would do it as soon as she woke up.

Except sleep didn't come. Not even replaying bak mei exercises in her mind could calm an imagination that was full of questions about Jasmine Yip and Malcolm Muir. At eight she gave up and got out of bed, made a coffee, and called May Ling's office. When there was no answer, she tried her mobile.

"Ava, where are you?" May answered.

"Singapore."

"What the heck are you doing there?"

"It's a long story, but basically I'm chasing money that was stolen from my friend Mimi's father."

May Ling had first-hand knowledge of Uncle and Ava's debt-collection business, since she and her husband had employed them once. "How much?"

"It isn't an enormous amount but it's everything they had, and the loss caused Mimi's father to commit suicide. That's what motivated me to take this on."

"What a horrible thing to happen!" May said. "How can I help?"

"Money that might have a connection to the theft has been going through a bank in Chengdu. I tried getting some information on account activity through a bank in Amsterdam, but it didn't work. I thought that an approach from a Chinese bank, especially one associated with you, might be more successful."

"What do you want to know?" May asked without hesitation.

"The names that are attached to the account, who controls it, and the origins of the money that's been flowing into it," Ava said. "It would be ideal if I could also get a complete record of deposits and withdrawals, including the sources of the deposits and the beneficiaries of the withdrawals."

"What's the name of the bank?"

"The Mercantile Bank of Chengdu."

"Give me the account number."

Ava opened her notebook and read the number and the bank's address.

"I assume you want the information as quickly as possible."

"Please."

"I didn't expect any other answer," May Ling said, laughing. "Okay, I'll do what I can this morning. The president of one of the banks we use has lots of connections. He should be able to open the right doors. I'll call you as soon as I have something."

"Thanks so much, May."

"You know that thanks aren't necessary," May Ling said. "By the way, is Fai with you?"

"She's in Taipei making a film. It was a last-minute thing."

"Are you going to join her after you resolve this money issue?"

"I'd like to, but I think it's best to let her concentrate on her work right now."

"Then why don't you come to Wuhan for a few days or, better still, go to Hong Kong? I can meet you there and we could spend some time with Amanda. She's not a complainer, but every once in a while she lets me know that she'd like to see her partners a bit more."

"That's not a bad idea. Let me see where I am after I get this thing behind me."

"You'll solve it. You always do."

"May, I'm not going to solve anything without that bank information."

"Okay, I'm on it." May laughed again. "I'll call the president now."

(20)

UNTIL SHE HEARD BACK FROM MAY LING, THE DAY WAS going to drag. She contemplated calling Brenda Burgess to see what progress she was making in the U.K., but Ava knew that Brenda would call her if things were settled. She thought about calling Xu and then put that idea aside; neither of them was fond of aimless conversation.

She decided to call her mother. She got Jennie's voicemail, then remembered it was Thursday evening in Toronto and her mother would be at a regular mah-jong game. "Mum, this is Ava. I'm in Singapore looking for Mr. Gregory's money. Things have been going quite well, so there's no need to worry. I'm not sure how long I'll be here. I'll let you know if my plans change."

She made a fresh cup of coffee and sat by the window overlooking Marina Bay. *Be patient*, she thought to herself. *Sooner or later I'll hear from May Ling or Tommy Tiu. And as much as I want to meet Jasmine Yip, it's irresponsible to do so without knowing more.*

Ava finished the coffee and decided it would be wise to get something to eat. Ten minutes later she left the suite to go downstairs to the Melt Café. As a child, Ava had never enjoyed eating the bland rice porridge known as congee. Marian had the same distaste for it, so Jennie had stopped serving it to the girls unless Marcus was visiting — and then Ava and Marian were expected to pretend they liked it. Ava had thought she'd left congee behind her when she left home, but her involvement with Uncle brought it back into her life. He ate it every morning, adding a wide variety of ingredients such as sausage, soy sauce, pickled vegetables, hundred-year-old eggs, or spring onions, and he always ate it with fried bread that he could dip. During the final months of his cancer, Ava ate it with him every morning and developed her own appreciation for the dish.

The Melt had some variations she'd never experienced, including a seafood congee. She ordered it and coffee, then sat back and looked around the café. The Mandarin Oriental in Hong Kong was equally five-star, but its clientele were not quite so homogeneous. Every man sitting in the Melt was clean-shaven and wearing a suit, or at least a crisply ironed shirt. It was the same for the women, who were all beautifully dressed and coiffed. In the Hong Kong Mandarin she was accustomed to seeing at least some people who looked as if they hadn't slept in two days, and jeans were common wear for both men and women. In Singapore there was a formality, a sort of *we're better than you are* attitude that could either grate or engender admiration. It had grated on Uncle, but Ava couldn't decide.

One thing she was certain about was that the congee — laden with clams, scallops, shrimp, and tender slices of squid — was superb. She finished the bowl and was thinking of ordering another serving when her phone rang.

"Hi, Tommy. Can I assume you have some news for me?"

"Yeah, but it's bad news. I called the car dealership. A woman in the finance department confirmed that Jasmine bought her car there, but then it went downhill. I tried to spin a story about Jasmine applying for a loan from my company and using the dealership as a reference. I said I wanted to confirm her primary banking information and asked which bank she'd used when she bought her BMW."

"The woman obviously refused."

"She asked if I had Jasmine's permission to access that information. When I said yes, she immediately said that I shouldn't object if she put me on hold while she phoned Jasmine. I told her to go ahead, but when she put me on hold, I hung up."

"Does she have your name?"

"I gave her a phony one."

"Thank goodness for that," Ava said.

"I'm sorry, I did the best I could. Finessing information out of people isn't my strong suit."

"Never mind. I'll figure out another way of getting it," she said, already crossing the car dealership off the list in her head.

"I wish there was more I could have done."

"I'll still tell Xu that you were helpful."

"Thanks for that."

First Jacob and now Tommy Tiu, Ava thought as she ended the call. She wasn't accustomed to being disappointed so often, although to be fair, Jacob was a professional, while Tiu's approach to the car dealership sounded clumsy. Now it came down to what May Ling could conjure up. If she failed, Ava would be forced to confront Jasmine Yip with only limited information.

She returned to her room and opened her notebook, found Todd Howell's cellphone number, and dialed. His phone rang four times and she was about to give up when he said, "This is Todd Howell."

"And this is Ava Lee. Sorry for calling so late."

"You can call me any time. But tell me, what have I missed or done this time?"

"I apologize for being abrupt the other day. I was in a meeting and couldn't say too much. The information you gave me about the wire transfer from Calgary proved to be useful. It filled in part of the puzzle, but many pieces are still missing."

"You aren't going to tell me anything more specific, are you."

"There isn't much specific to tell. Things are still murky. I'm hoping you can help make them less so."

"Tell me what you want to know," he said.

Ava hesitated. "I didn't mention this earlier, but I went to Malcolm Muir's house in Toronto before I left the city."

"Why would you go there?"

"I wanted to put a face to the name. It was a spur-of-the-moment thing, quite unplanned. We had a short conversation before he slammed the door in my face. Curiously, he asked me if I'm Chinese and made a point of telling me he could tell Asians apart. He credited that ability—or whatever you want to call it—to the fact that he'd travelled extensively in Asia. I didn't see anything in your files about him travelling in Asia. And when I asked you if you'd heard of a woman named Jasmine Yip, you told me no and that you hadn't found anyone Chinese or Asian connected to Muir. I'm wondering if that was an oversight."

"I've thought about it since you asked me, and the only thing I can remember that's the least bit related to Asia is the humanitarian projects the fund purported to support."

"Did you check into them? Is it possible some of them really exist?"

"We had local lawyers in South Africa and the Ivory Coast investigate five projects. None of them existed. I didn't see any point in pursuing that line of inquiry any further."

"So you didn't check any in Asia?"

"No."

"Todd, how detailed are the fund's bank records?"

"We aren't missing anything that I know of."

"Then I'd like you to do something for me," she said. "I know Muir wasn't drawing a salary from the fund, but I assume there were expenses related to incorporation, legal bills, travelling across the country, et cetera, that were paid with fund money."

"There were."

"Could you have someone go through the records and pull out any payments made to a travel agent or an airline? I'll flag the ones that I want some additional research on."

"I'll put someone on it tomorrow morning."

"Thank you. And there's something else I'd like you to do," she said. "Would you humour me, please, and go back over your notes to look for any references to anyone Chinese in Muir's life or his wife's."

"Is this about Jasmine Yip again?"

"Yes, but also anyone else with ties to mainland China and maybe Singapore."

"Is there anything else specific you can tell me?"

Ava hesitated and then thought that being coy could only

lessen Howell's effectiveness. "Yes. I believe Yip is connected to Muir, though I don't know how. She lives in Singapore, which is where I am now. What I'd love to find out is how she knows him. Is it a personal relationship or are they connected through a third party?"

"Who is this Jasmine Yip?"

"She's a diamond trader," Ava said, deciding not to mention her talent for money laundering.

"That explains the wire transfer from Calgary to Antwerp."

"It's the smallest part of this puzzle, but it does connect Muir to Yip on at least one occasion, and it did bring diamonds into the equation."

"Ms. Lee, may I say that I'm very impressed with the work you've done so far."

"That's kind, but very premature. My former partner was extremely superstitious when it came to projecting success. All I've done is come up with some names. Unless I can locate the money that was stolen, no one is any better off than they were a week ago. So, please, let's not get complimentary until we make that happen."

"Message received."

"One more thing. I would appreciate it if you don't share our conversation with anyone else, including your office staff. We don't want anyone, accidentally or otherwise, to hear the name Jasmine Yip until I've had a chance to confront her."

"When do you think that might be?"

"I'm waiting on some information from a friend. I won't make a decision until I see what she's found. It could be today or it could be two days from now."

"But you're sure that Yip is in Singapore?"

"That's what I've been told. But Todd, before you get

excited, I have to make it clear that I don't know how deeply she's immersed in this scam. There is a connection, but she could be a bit player, an enabler of some sort, and nothing more. We can't afford to let our expectations get ahead of the facts."

"I understand. Tomorrow I'll do what I can with the bank records."

"Please email me whatever you come up with."

"Will do."

Did I do the right thing by telling him so much? was her first thought when she hung up. She didn't have Uncle to lean on, she knew she couldn't do it alone, and thus far Howell had provided information without asking for anything in return. *I trust Jacob, and now I guess I'm trusting Howell. I hope it doesn't come back to bite me.*

(21)

THE MORNING TURNED INTO EARLY AFTERNOON, EACH hour that passed seeming like three. Ava didn't let her phone out of her sight, twice taking it into the bathroom with her. By two o'clock her patience was wearing thin. She considered calling May Ling to get an update, but just as she was deciding to wait, her phone finally rang.

"Hey, I was getting antsy," she answered.

"Sorry. I had difficulty reaching my guy here, and then he had the same problem getting hold of his banker friend in Chengdu," May Ling said. "Ava, this is more complicated than I anticipated."

Complicated was a word Ava wasn't pleased to hear. "Can we start with the basics?"

"Sure. What's first on your list?"

"How many names are attached to the account?"

"Let me read from the banker's email: 'May Ling, the account in question is a U.S. dollar account doing business as Jewellery Circle. The signing authority for any action related to the account resides with Jasmine Yip and Su Na, either jointly or singly. On that last point, it appears that nearly all the activity was initiated and signed off on solely by Yip. My Chengdu associate told me that Yip provided two addresses when the account was created; one in Chengdu and the other in Singapore. Yip's Chengdu address is the same as Su's, and he suspects Yip may be using it for convenience. Without a local address, it is unlikely that the bank would have permitted her to open an account with them.'"

"Yip has two female cousins. One married a Chinese man," Ava said. "It's possible she changed her name to Su when she got married, and Na might be her original first name."

"Do you want me to check into this Su Na?"

"Please. I'm quite sure she was born in Singapore, but if she's now living in Chengdu I'd like to have the address she gave the bank."

"Will do," May said. "What else do you want to know?"

"Did the Chengdu banker provide the records of deposits and withdrawals?"

"Yes, he faxed everything to me — he still uses faxes for security reasons. I'll scan them and forward them to you as soon as we've finished speaking," May said.

"Before, you used the word 'complicated.' What did you mean by that?"

May hesitated, then said, "I may be reading too much into it, but for an account with significant sums of money going through it, I was surprised by how few actual transactions there were."

"I know Yip was buying rough diamonds in Antwerp from a company named Fozdar Trading. Those would have been large but sporadic deals."

"Fozdar is one of the two companies she was sending substantial amounts to, but that stopped a few months ago."

"What was the other?"

"Golden Emperor MicroLab in Chengdu, and that's been ongoing and very regular."

Ava drew a deep breath. "What kind of company is Golden Emperor?"

"According to the Chengdu banker, it's a drug manufacturer. Some of their production is pharmaceutical, but a lot of it is classified as industrial, which allows them to evade government inspection. He also said that the name MicroLab is misleading; it's one of the major manufacturers in Chengdu."

"Why would they want to evade inspection?"

"Golden Emperor is manufacturing fentanyl, for example, which has some medicinal value as a painkiller but is fifty times stronger than heroin and highly addictive. It also turns out large volumes of a synthetic opioid called carfentanil, and synthetic marijuana."

Ava felt a knot in her stomach. "Shit. Is he saying that Jasmine Yip is dealing in illegal drugs?"

"Some of them may be legal from a Chinese viewpoint, but in essence that is what he's saying."

"I thought she was simply laundering money."

"You might not be wrong. It might just be by a method you didn't anticipate."

Ava looked at her notes. "What about the money deposited into the Chengdu account? Where did it come from?"

"When Yip first opened the account, the majority of the money was transferred from a number of companies in Guangzhou."

"That's a major centre for diamond cutting and polishing. She could have been selling those companies the rough diamonds she bought in Antwerp."

"Judging by the names, I think that's probably the case," May said. "But then, a few years later, transfers started arriving from an account with the Evans Trust Company in Vanuatu, in increasingly large amounts."

"Vanuatu?"

"It's a group of small islands off Australia's east coast. It's also the new favourite offshore banking haven for many of our Chinese politicians, especially those who were named in the Panama Papers. No jurisdiction can guarantee complete secrecy, but from what I've heard Vanuatu comes very close."

"And what do you know about the Evans Trust Company?"

"Only what the Chengdu banker told me. He said it's a private bank, but nothing more than that."

"Where is it headquartered?"

"In Vanuatu. It was probably incorporated there, because it has no presence anywhere else he could discover."

Ava switched direction. "May, when Yip's account started receiving money from Evans Trust, was she already doing business with Golden Emperor?"

"Yes. It looks like Yip starting buying from Golden Emperor as soon as she opened the account, but Evans wasn't a player until a couple of years ago," May said. "My guess would be that the market for Golden Emperor's products expanded and Yip needed more working capital."

Ava circled the name *Evans* in her notebook and then drew connecting lines to *Yip*, *Fozdar*, *Golden Emperor*, and *Guangzhou*. "So the money initially goes from Amsterdam to Antwerp, where it's turned into rough diamonds. The diamonds go to Guangzhou, where they're turned into cash that's deposited in a Chengdu bank. The cash buys drugs that are sent . . . somewhere. At some point money is sent from Evans Trust to Yip's account in Chengdu to buy more drugs," she said, and then paused. "May, is there an address for Evans?"

"Only a PO box."

"Is there a number for the account in Vanuatu?"

"No, the transfers simply identify Evans as the sender."

"I need to know who controls that account," said Ava.

"I don't mean to be discouraging, but that isn't going to be easy."

"Maybe I can come at this from a different angle," Ava said. "I don't know if it's Yip or someone else who's buying the drugs, where the drugs are being sold, or where the proceeds from the sales are going. If I can find out those things, it might open other doors."

"Based on the Chengdu bank statements, I'd guess the proceeds are going to Evans. They send money to Yip's account just before she sends money to Golden Emperor."

"Which means the proceeds from the drug sales are being held and controlled in Vanuatu, not by Yip."

"I'm sure you'll make sense of it all when you see the bank documents."

"Could you send them to me now?" Ava asked. "I need to wrap my head around all this."

"Then what? Is meeting Jasmine Yip on your immediate radar?"

"She and I need to talk."

"Be careful, Ava. If she's dealing drugs, who knows what kind of people she's involved with."

(22)

HALF AN HOUR LATER, AVA WAS SITTING AT THE DESK with printouts of Jasmine Yip's Chengdu banking history in front of her. In another pile she had the records from the bank in Amsterdam, and in a third Todd Howell's summaries of Muir's Canadian banking activity. She turned to an empty page in her notebook and began to write down dates in an attempt to establish a chronology. She already had some idea of the timelines, but by putting them on paper she was hoping to find something — anything — that would help her to link Yip, Muir, the Dutch and Chinese bank accounts, a drug manufacturer, and a private bank in Vanuatu. When she was finished, she stared at the dates and the numbers and felt a wave of frustration. There was still so much she didn't know.

She turned to a new page and began to write.

What do I know?

Malcolm Muir established the fund in Canada, opened the Canadian bank accounts, and transferred the money to a bank account in Amsterdam that was under the control of Jasmine Yip — a woman he had to know well. But how did he know her, and why would he trust her with all that money?

Money went into the Dutch account only from the Canadian banks; there were no other depositors. And when the money was withdrawn, it was never replaced. The account was a one-way conduit between Muir and Yip.

Yip used the Canadian funds to buy rough diamonds in Antwerp, which she then sold to various diamond-processing companies in Guangzhou. The proceeds from those sales went directly into the bank account in Chengdu and were used to buy drugs from Golden Emperor MicroLab. How was Yip connected to Golden Emperor—or indeed, was she?

What happened to the drugs? Did she take direct possession and sell them or arrange for them to be sold? Did Golden Emperor handle distribution?

Finally, what happened to the money from the drug sales? Did it get sent to Vanuatu or was it kept at the point of sale?

Ava paused, underlined the last two questions, and reached for her phone.

"*Wei*," Auntie Grace answered.

"Hi, Auntie, it's Ava. Is Xu available?"

"Yes, darling. Hold on a second and I'll get him."

As she waited for Xu, Ava's mind returned to Jasmine Yip. Was it too soon to confront her? Perhaps, but the longer she put it off, the greater the risk that Yip would learn that people were poking around in her affairs. Once Yip knew something was up, she could go to ground. Ava had the advantage now, but it wouldn't last forever.

But how should she approach Yip? Maybe Tommy Tiu could persuade her to meet with him somewhere and Ava would be there instead. Except what reason could Tiu give? And, as he admitted, he didn't have much finesse. The best option was for Ava to go directly to the house in Emerald Hill and confront her.

"Ava, how are things in Singapore?" Xu asked, bringing her back to the present. "Tommy Tiu phoned this morning to tell me he'd done what he could for you."

"It's going okay, and Tommy did provide some help."

"He still owes me. If you need him again, just ask," he said. "Is that why you're calling?"

"No," she said. "I have another favour to ask."

"What is it?" Xu asked without hesitation.

"Do the triads have a presence in Chengdu?"

"Yes. They aren't as visible as they are in most cities that size, but they are well organized and well run. The Mountain Master is named Han."

"Do you know him well?"

"Well enough."

"I've been told that Chengdu is a major player in the production of synthetic drugs such as carfentanil," she said. "Is it possible that Han has some involvement in that trade?"

"I don't know, but I'll ask," he said, and then hesitated. "Ava, where is this leading?"

"I need information, that's all. If Han is involved in the trade or even knows people who are, he might be able to help me. I'm not on a crusade against the drug manufacturers or the people associated with them."

"What kind of information do you need?"

"I've traced the money that was stolen from my friend's family, and I believe some or all of it ended up in Chengdu, where it was used to buy drugs from a company called Golden Emperor MicroLab," she said. "The lab was getting money from a company doing business as Jewellery

Circle from an account at the Mercantile Bank of Chendgu, registered to the names Jasmine Yip and Su Na. I'd like to know who's actually conducting that business with Golden Emperor, what they bought, and where it was sent."

"You don't believe Yip and Su were doing the buying?"

"Jasmine Yip is the woman I had Tommy Tiu check on. But I'm beginning to think she was simply a facilitator. It seems to me that someone else is pulling the strings."

"What makes you think that?"

"From what Tommy told me, her father was a small-time money launderer in Singapore who used diamonds as the vehicle. He did it for a commission. Yip helped him with the business in his later years, which is how she met the diamond suppliers in Europe. She kept buying after he died, but always in small volumes until the past few years. She might have the connections to buy and sell diamonds, but that's the extent of her experience, and she sure as hell didn't have the kind of bankroll to finance anything in volume."

"So you're assuming that someone other than her set up the arrangement with the drug company in Chengdu."

"I have no proof, but it is logical."

"And you are forever logical," Xu said with a slight laugh. "Okay, I'll talk to Han. If he has no direct knowledge of Golden Emperor, I'm sure he'll know someone who does. You said the bank was the Mercantile Bank of Chengdu and the account was in the name of Jewellery Circle?"

"Yes, but you should also give him the names Jasmine Yip and Su Na."

"Any other names?"

"Malcolm Muir. He's the guy who operated the scam in Canada."

"I'll call Han now."

"Will you mention my name?"

"There's no need. I don't have to explain to him why I want the information."

"That's great. And you know I'm grateful that you're making the effort," Ava said. "I'm going to do what I can at this end to find out more, starting by dropping in on Jasmine Yip."

"Don't you think you should wait until I find out what Han knows?"

"I don't know how long that will take, and I don't want to risk her taking off on me," Ava said. "Besides, I think I know enough that I can squeeze some information from her."

"Good luck."

"I'm going unannounced. If she's at home, I'll find a way to get her to talk to me."

"And if she's not?"

"I'll improvise."

(23)

THE DOORMAN AT THE MANDARIN TOLD AVA THAT Emerald Hill was less than four kilometres away. "You could walk there if you choose. There's some pleasant sightseeing along the way," he said.

It was so humid outside that Ava was already feeling a bit sweaty just standing at the hotel entrance. "I'll take a taxi," she said.

The doorman hailed a cab and then turned to Ava. "What's your destination in Emerald Hill?"

"Emerald Hill Road."

"A lovely street," he said as he opened the back door of the cab.

Ava gave the street number to the driver as she slid into the car. As soon as it pulled away from the curb, she took the Moleskine notebook from her bag and started reviewing the questions she wanted to ask Jasmine Yip. Her strongest concern was that Yip wouldn't be at the house, but if she was there Ava had prepared a story that she hoped would get her past the door. If that didn't work she figured she'd become an unwelcome guest. It was all very iffy, but that had been the nature of the collection business and Ava had learned to be comfortable with uncertainty.

The taxi drove along Raffles Road, then made several turns before reaching Saunders Road and a final turn onto Emerald Hill. Ava wondered if that was what the doorman had meant when he mentioned sightseeing.

"Have you been to the Emerald Hill district before?" the taxi driver asked.

The question surprised her. "No, but I've heard nice things about it," she said finally.

"My wife and daughter go often. They like to browse the boutiques and sit on the café patios," he said. "And here we are."

He turned onto a brick-paved road, and Ava saw immediately what he was talking about. The street was lined with brightly coloured three-storey buildings that housed businesses at the ground level and apartments above. Tommy Tiu had mentioned that the mother and aunt lived in a house, and Ava wondered if he'd been correct. But as the taxi continued down Emerald Hill Road, she saw a row of white three-storey buildings that were more obviously houses.

The taxi stopped in front of an iron gate flanked by a two-metre-high white stone wall and crowned by a green tile roof. There were eight buildings in the row, each distinguished by its shrubbery and the colour of the wooden shutters attached to every window. Some shutters were coral, some gold, and others red, but the house that bore the number Ava was looking for had green ones.

She paid the driver and stood on the sidewalk taking in the environs. She couldn't see any security cameras and the gate didn't look like it was locked. Ava walked to the gate and pushed it open. She went up a red-brick path to a door that was painted the same dark green as the shutters. She took a deep breath and knocked.

Ava was wearing a white cotton shirt, black linen slacks, and flat shoes. It was the plainest and, she thought, the least threatening outfit she had brought with her. The slacks had become wrinkled during the cab ride, and she was running her hands down the front of them when the door opened.

"Can I help you?" a woman asked.

The woman was barely five feet tall. She wore a red silk blouse that hung loosely over baggy black pants, and her makeup seemed to have been layered on. Her hair was short, brushed back, and so slick that it looked like wet paint. When she spoke, Ava saw streaks of lipstick on her front teeth.

"My name is Ava Lee. I'm an American customer of Fozdar Trading in Antwerp. I was there a few days ago and mentioned to Mr. Fozdar that I was going to be in Singapore on a holiday. My family's company is looking for ways to expand our business in Asia, and since he knew I was going to be here, Mr. Fozdar recommended Ms. Jasmine Yip to me as someone who might assist us. He also gave me this address. I tried calling the numbers he gave me, but I couldn't reach her, so I decided to come here. I hope it isn't an inconvenience."

The woman eyed Ava suspiciously, then turned and said loudly, "Jasmine, someone is here for you."

Ava took a step forward but stopped when she saw the woman flinch.

A slightly taller woman appeared behind the older woman's shoulder. Ava recognized her long, thin face and bob haircut from the passport photo. She smiled and said, "You must be Jasmine."

"I am," she said curtly.

"My name is Ava Lee —"

"I heard what you told my aunt. There's no need to repeat it," Jasmine said.

"Excellent. I'm pleased I've been able to locate you. Mr. Fozdar wasn't sure you'd be in Singapore."

"Why not?"

"He said your business is quite international."

Jasmine stared down at Ava, her manner guarded. "That's strange. I don't remember discussing my business with him."

"Well, he said your family have been customers of his for many years. Perhaps he just made some assumptions based on that."

Jasmine pursed her lips and nodded. "What do you want with me?"

Ava shrugged. "Can I come inside to discuss it with you? It's rather awkward standing here on your doorstep."

Jasmine looked doubtful but then moved to one side. "Come on in."

Ava walked through a small hallway directly into a brightly carpeted living room. There was a large circular glass table in the middle surrounded by some heavily upholstered sofas. On one of them sat the aunt who had answered the door, her feet not touching the floor. On the other was a tiny grey-haired woman wearing black peasant pyjamas. Her face was long and drawn like Jasmine's, so Ava assumed it was her mother.

"Nice to meet you, Auntie," Ava said to the second woman.

The woman glared at her, and Ava felt a touch of trepidation.

"Wait here. I'll be right back," Jasmine said, and then disappeared through a door.

"So, you are American?" the aunt asked.

"Yes. I was born in Hong Kong but my family emigrated when I was very young. I think of Boston as home."

"My husband and I lived in Boston for three years. Where do you live?"

"My family lives in Weston but our business is in Back Bay, on Exeter Street."

"What is the business called?"

"We don't do retail," Ava said.

"But the business must have a name."

"Not one that is known to the IRS," Ava said with a smile. "My father doesn't believe in paying taxes."

"Hey!" Jasmine said loudly.

Ava turned towards the door. Yip stood there next to a large man who filled the frame. "We were warned about you. I was told you might be in Singapore," she said.

"I have no idea what you're talking about."

Jasmine shook her head and turned to the man. "Get rid of her."

He smiled and stepped forward, his upper body stretching a polo shirt to its limits.

"What's going on? Why are you acting like this?" Ava asked, not taking her eyes off the man.

"We're not stupid," Jasmine said. "I got a phone call from my car dealer saying that a man had rather clumsily tried to get information about where I bank."

"And then an old friend of mine phoned to say that Tommy Tiu was going around asking a lot of questions about Jasmine," the aunt said.

"I figured that Tommy and the caller were one and the same," Jasmine said. "I spoke to him an hour ago, and he told me about you."

"Loyalties run very deep here. Jasmine's father and my husband did business with Tommy for years. He couldn't lie to us when we confronted him — not that he's ever been a very good liar," the aunt said.

"Are you Mrs. Lam?" Ava asked.

"I am, but what's it to you?"

"Nothing," Ava said, turning back to Jasmine. "It is true I've been looking for you. Now that I've found you, why don't you give me ten or fifteen minutes of your time, and then I'll be on my way. There's no reason to get violent."

"Throw her out," Jasmine said.

The room was so crowded with people and furniture that Ava didn't have much room to manoeuvre. She began to back up towards the hallway, where there was some open space.

The man smiled as he walked towards her. Ava figured he was about six feet, but he looked taller in the cramped surroundings. He stopped just short of her and extended his hands with the palms up. "Why don't you just turn around and leave?" he said. "I really don't want to get rough with you."

"I'll leave after I've spoken to Jasmine."

"I hate stubborn women," he said as he reached for her.

Ava took a step back as his hand grabbed for her arm. He missed, and his foot slipped on a rug. He collected himself, his face turning an angry red. "The games are over," he said, balling up his right fist.

"Yes, they are," Ava said, as she lunged forward to drive a phoenix-eye fist into his belly. The phoenix eye was the most powerful strike in bak mei, and it had taken Ava years to perfect. It concentrated all the power her body could generate into the middle knuckle of the first finger of her right hand. It wreaked havoc on whatever it hit—in this case a cluster of nerves in the upper belly, at the base of the sternum.

The man collapsed on the floor, his knees pulled up in a fetal position as he gasped desperately for air. Ava checked him for weapons, and when she found none, she said loudly into his ear, "Stay down. The pain will start to ease in a few minutes. I don't want to hurt you again, but if you get up, I promise you that I will."

"That man is a goddamn useless idiot," a woman's voice said. "It takes a woman to handle a woman." Ava turned and saw Mrs. Lam advancing towards her with a long knife in her hand.

"You're joking, right?" Ava said.

"Leave before I cut you to ribbons," Mrs. Lam said. "I know how to use this thing."

"This is madness. I don't want to hurt you. Please put down the knife."

"Leave."

"Will you talk some sense into your aunt?" Ava said to Jasmine.

"She never listens to me," Jasmine said, a small smile on her face.

Ava looked at the way she was carrying the knife. *Will she try to stab me or slice me? Slice, I think.*

Mrs. Lam was now close enough that Ava could see beads of sweat glistening on top of her makeup. Then her top teeth bit into her lower lip, and she swung the knife in the direction of Ava's right arm. Ava spun, the knife flashed by, and before Mrs.

Lam could regroup, Ava had a grip on her elbow. She pressed two fingers into the soft flesh on the inside of the elbow until she found the nerve, then squeezed as hard as she could. The knife dropped, and then the screaming started. Ava held on, angry that the woman had dared to attack her; a paralyzed arm was the only way to ensure she wouldn't try again.

"Let her go," Jasmine's mother pleaded.

Jasmine and her mother were by the sofa. Ava stared at them as she continued to squeeze Mrs. Lam's arm. She counted to thirty for extra effect and then released her grip. The aunt stumbled backwards, tears coursing down her cheeks, her arm limp. Jasmine reached for her and pulled her down onto the sofa.

"None of this was necessary. All I wanted to do was talk," Ava said, picking up the knife from the floor.

"Except you want to talk about things that I've been told are not to be discussed."

"Told by whom?"

Jasmine glared at her.

"Let me make something very clear," Ava said. "The money you used to buy diamonds in Antwerp was stolen from friends of mine, and I'm determined to get it back. People are going to pay. And when I say pay, Jasmine, I don't simply mean that money is going to change hands. Ask Tommy Tiu about the kind of friends I have. Ask him about the ones in Shanghai. I don't care how afraid you are of the people you're conducting business with in Amsterdam and Chengdu. My friends are a whole lot scarier."

"Tommy told Auntie Nan that she has strong connections," Jasmine's mother said, and then looked at Ava. "You aren't a cop, are you?"

How far should I take this? she thought. *What the hell. These are people who'll understand who Xu is and what he can do to them.* "Tommy was referring to my *ge ge*. He's the Mountain Master, the head of the triads, in Shanghai. If you have any doubts about the truth of that, I suggest you call Tommy right now."

"That's not necessary," Jasmine's mother said, touching her daughter lightly on the arm. "Jasmine, I think you should talk to this woman. We don't want any trouble with triads."

Jasmine had lowered her head, and now she looked up. "You know about Chengdu?" she asked, her voice shaking.

"I know some. I need to know more."

"I can't help you."

"You won't know that until you hear my questions."

"I think you should listen to her," her mother said. "You haven't done anything wrong, and if she's right about it ending badly, then you should get out before you make new enemies."

Ava sat down, separated from the other women by the circular table. She place the knife in front of her. "Your mother makes a lot of sense. Do you want me to tell you what I think your role was in this?" she asked Jasmine.

"No, but I'm sure you'll do it anyway."

Ava ignored her sarcasm. "I believe you were hired to launder the money in Amsterdam. Someone knew about your father's business and knew that you had helped him. You had contacts in Antwerp and knew enough about the diamond trade to find buyers in Guangzhou. So cash turned into diamonds and then diamonds turned back into cash, which was deposited in Chengdu and used to buy drugs from Golden Emperor MicroLab. How am I doing so far?"

Jasmine mumbled, "I don't know anything about any drugs."

"Do you mean you weren't involved in buying drugs or you didn't know drugs were being bought?"

"No one told me anything."

"But you had dealings with Golden Emperor, yes?"

"I transferred money to them when I was told to, but I never asked what it was being used for," Jasmine said. "I thought it was the final step in the laundering process."

"I'll come back to those transfers," Ava said. "How much were you paid for laundering the money?"

"I worked for a commission. Five to ten percent, depending on the amount of money involved."

"That's odd. I didn't see any payments directed to you in the Chengdu bank statements."

"I took my commissions in diamonds."

"What about the money being transferred to Golden Emperor? You don't get paid for that?"

"I get a small set fee that's sent to my mother's account."

Ava nodded. "And the diamonds you took as commission, do you keep them here?" She saw Jasmine's hand tighten on her mother's and a fleeting look of panic cross her face.

"Don't worry. I'm not interested in them."

"My father never believed in keeping cash in a bank. He sold diamonds whenever he needed money. I've followed his example."

"Where do you sell them?"

"Sometimes in Shenzhen, other times in Mumbai. I put most of the cash into my mother's bank account."

"How did you pay for your BMW?"

"Out of my mother's account."

"Is that true?" Ava asked the mother.

The older woman nodded.

Ava leaned forward and asked as evenly as she could, "Who hired you to launder the money in the Amsterdam bank?"

Jasmine lowered her head again.

"Tell her," her mother said. "You have no reason to protect him."

"A man named Malcolm Muir," Jasmine said.

Ava's pulse quickened, but she said calmly, "How did Muir know what you could do, and how did he know how to contact you?"

Jasmine turned to her mother. "Mummy, are you sure you want me to get into this?"

"I don't see any harm in it."

"What will Auntie Nan think?"

"Right now Auntie Nan can't think about anything other than her arm," Yip's mother said, glancing at her sister. "Tell the woman what she wants to know."

Jasmine looked at Ava. "My cousin Essie called me to say she had a friend who had money that needed to find a safe home. She asked me if I was willing to help him do it in the way my father taught me. I said yes, and a few days later I heard from Malcolm Muir."

"How did your cousin know Muir?"

"Muir knows her husband."

Go slowly, Ava told herself. "Can I assume that Essie's husband also knows about your expertise?"

"He lived in Singapore for a few years — that's how he and Essie met. So he knew the family and what we did for a living," Jasmine said.

"Did Essie retain her family name when she married or did she take her husband's?"

"She took his."

"So what does she call herself now?"

"She's Essie Lam here but Esther Cunningham over there."

"Where is 'over there'?" Ava asked as blandly as she could manage.

"Canada."

"And what is her husband's first name?"

"Patrick."

(24)

AVA'S HEART LEAPT. THERE WERE SO MANY QUESTIONS bouncing around in her head that she longed for her notebook. But this wasn't the time to start writing, or to overreact to the mention of Patrick Cunningham.

"I'd like to go back to the man Malcolm Muir," Ava said calmly to Jasmine.

"What would you like to know?"

"Did he call all the shots?"

"He's a control freak. He told me what to do and when to do it. And he wanted copies of every transaction. I didn't do a thing without his say-so. "

"Did all the money from the diamond sales find its way to Chengdu?"

"Yes."

"Who decided it should go to Chengdu, and who established the bank account?"

"Muir chose the city and the bank and sent me there to open the account."

"Did you do it alone?"

"No. I needed a local reference, and he provided that as

well. Her name is Su Na. She came with me to the bank to provide local cover, and then I never heard from her again."

"Who is Su Na?"

"I guess someone Muir knows."

"Your family doesn't know her? She's not your cousin who married someone in China?"

"My other daughter is named Miriam," Mrs. Lam said weakly. "She's married to a Communist party official in Shenzhen."

"Thank you, Auntie," Ava said, then turned back to Jasmine. "The money in the Chengdu account is being used to buy drugs. But you say you weren't aware of that?"

"That's true. All I've done is transfer money to the Golden Emperor account."

"And you had no idea what the money was buying?"

"I never deal with the company directly. I arrange the transfers, and that's it."

"How do you know how much to send and when to send it?"

"Muir phones me."

"Does he ask for confirmation that the transfer has been made?"

"Yes. What's strange is that he doesn't want me to do it electronically, even though I could. He insists that I send written instructions to the bank under my company letterhead and that the bank confirms to me that they received them in writing," Jasmine said.

"It gives him a written record."

"He's only doing that to cover his ass. He has access to the account and can trace the transfers."

"He knows the account password?"

"Su Na set the account password and gave it to me. I assume she gave it to Muir as well."

"I already have the account number. Will you give me the password?" Ava asked.

Jasmine hesitated, then looked at her mother and aunt. Both women nodded. "Okay," she said.

"Will you also give me copies of the written transfer requests to the bank and the bank's confirmations?"

"Yes."

"Thank you," Ava said. "Now, when did money start arriving in the account from the Evans Trust Company in Vanuatu?"

"You know about Vanuatu too?"

"Obviously."

"It started a few years ago. Muir told me he had a new business partner and that money would be deposited into the Chengdu account on a regular basis. He didn't want me asking any questions about the account balance."

"Did you ever communicate with Evans Trust?"

"No."

"My understanding is that the amounts Evans deposits have increased substantially over time."

"They have."

"After a deposit is made by Evans, how long before it's transferred to Golden Emperor?"

"No more than a day or two."

"You're certain of that?"

"Yes. I never go more than a day or two without checking the account balance. I'm too paranoid."

"What's made you paranoid?"

"I don't trust Muir. If there were ever an issue with the

cops or the PLA, I know he'd dump everything on me. It wouldn't be hard, since my name is on every transaction."

"But I thought Muir was recommended to you by your cousin Essie."

"Essie was told what to do by her husband," Jasmine said.

"How do you know that?"

Jasmine looked at her aunt. "You should answer that question."

"My daughter isn't always her own person," Mrs. Lam said. "Since she met Patrick, she's forgotten her roots."

"Is he that controlling?" Ava asked.

"She doesn't fart without his permission," Mrs. Lam said. "There's no way she would have called Jasmine without Patrick telling her to do it."

"How did Essie meet him?"

"They worked at the same bank. They started dating, and, before we knew it, she was going to his church and spouting all their half-baked nonsense about sin and repentance," Mrs. Lam said. "When I told my daughter I was worried about her, she laughed. She said that Patrick was the most considerate man she'd ever dated. In fact, she bragged that he wouldn't sleep with her until they were married. I told her that was foolish of both of them. I mean, what woman in her right mind would marry a man without giving him a trial run in bed?"

Ava smiled. Despite the fact the woman had attacked her with a knife, she rather liked her. "But Essie did marry him."

"Yes, and then she had four kids in five years, one of them here and three in Canada. Patrick doesn't believe in birth control. Essie developed problems after the fourth pregnancy.

I think she miscarried three times before a doctor finally tied her tubes."

"Tell me, Mrs. Lam, when did Essie and Patrick move to Canada?"

"Seven or eight years ago. He got a well-paying job with a finance company but left after a year to work full-time for the church."

"Have you seen her since then?"

"I visited them once in Canada. I was supposed to stay three weeks but came home after two. I couldn't stand the way he treated her and the kids, and I knew if I stayed any longer I'd blow up at him. Everything had to be done his way. If it wasn't, he'd yell at Essie until she cried, and he'd spank the kids if they did something wrong," Mrs. Lam said. She pointed to Jasmine's mother. "My sister and I never raised a hand to any of our children, and there isn't a man alive who could make us cry."

"Our husbands wouldn't have dared yell at us or hit our girls," Mrs. Yip said. "Why are you so interested in Patrick?"

The question caught Ava by surprise. She had been so caught up with talking to Mrs. Lam that she'd almost forgotten the other woman was there. "There's a connection between Patrick and Muir that goes beyond Jasmine. They know each other from Harvest Table Bible Chapel."

"Are you saying that Patrick is in business with Muir?" Jasmine asked.

"It's a connection I need to explore."

"As much as I don't like Patrick, I don't think he'd ever get involved with drugs," Mrs. Lam said.

"I'm not suggesting that he is involved," Ava said, and then stood up. "I think I should get going now. You've been very generous with your time, and I thank you for that. Jasmine, can you give me the password for the Chengdu bank account and copies of the transfers?"

"The transfers are in a box in my bedroom," Jasmine replied.

"I'll wait."

"Do you need us to call a taxi?" Mrs. Lam asked after Jasmine left the room.

"No, I'll walk to the corner and catch something there," Ava said.

There was a loud groan, and all three women looked at the man on the floor.

"He's starting to recover," Ava said.

"So am I," Mrs. Lam said, shaking her arm. "That hurt like hell."

"Here you go," Jasmine said, re-entering with a sheaf of papers. "And this is my business card. I wrote the password on the back."

Ava took papers and the card. "Before I go, I have to make some things clear," she said. "I don't want a single word about what we discussed today to be shared with anyone. I don't want to see any of you get hurt, but if you disobey, I can't promise you'll be safe. "

"We get it," Jasmine said.

"We know how things work," Mrs. Lam said. "No word will leave this house."

"Also, I don't exist. My name won't enter any of your conversations."

The three women nodded.

"And for you, Jasmine, it should be business as usual. There's no reason for you to do anything different than what you've been doing — with one exception," Ava said. "I want you to contact me immediately the next time Muir asks you to transfer money to Golden Emperor. Will you do that?"

Jasmine nodded.

Ava took a card from her purse and handed it to Jasmine. "You can reach me at that email address or phone number," she said. "Now I'll be on my way."

"Before you go, I have a question for you," Mrs. Lam said.

"Yes?"

"Are you really from Boston?"

"I was there once," Ava said, and headed for the door.

(25)

AVA WALKED DOWN EMERALD HILL ROAD AND WITHIN a couple of minutes was in a taxi heading back to the Mandarin Oriental. She took out her notebook and began writing as soon as the car door was closed. When she had gone to meet Jasmine Yip, questions about the bank account in Chengdu and Golden Emperor MicroLab had been her main priorities. While they still mattered, Patrick Cunningham had now jumped to the top of her list.

Ava checked her watch. It was too early to call Toronto, but not Shanghai. She didn't want to start a conversation with Xu while she was in a cab, so she waited until she'd reached her room at the Mandarin.

"Auntie Grace, it's Ava. Can I speak to Xu, please?" she said when the housekeeper answered.

"Just a minute, darling," Auntie Grace said.

"I didn't expect to hear from you so soon. I spoke to Han about an hour ago," Xu said.

"Did he agree to help?"

"Eventually. He has no direct involvement with Golden

Emperor, but he knows who they are and says they know him. He'll see what he can find out."

"I'm sorry if that was difficult."

"I had to agree to trade, but it worked out well enough."

"Can you go back to him and ask for more information about Golden Emperor without upsetting the agreement?"

"I think so. I left it open-ended."

"Good. What I want to know is if the names Patrick Cunningham and Harvest Table Bible Chapel are familiar to the lab."

"And if they are familiar, you'll want to know why."

"Exactly."

"You do know this is getting a bit strange?"

"I'm just dealing with the facts. I have no idea where they'll lead me."

"Just be careful."

"I will," Ava said, and paused. "Speaking of being careful, Tommy Tiu ratted me out to the women I was tracking. It turned out all right in the end, but I don't think he's anyone you should trust in the future."

"That son of a bitch!"

"Like I said, it turned out all right. It might even have helped me indirectly."

"I still have to call him. He needs to know that I know. Then I'll let him stew for a few days before giving him a pass—and tacking on another IOU."

"Don't be too hard on him. He isn't overly bright."

"If being bright were a prerequisite to becoming a gangster, the world would be relatively crime-free," Xu said.

Ava laughed. "It's so nice to hear you sounding like your old self."

"I'm getting there," Xu said. "I'll call you as soon as I hear from Han."

Ava ended the call and opened her laptop. She found the website for the Mercantile Bank of Chengdu, entered the Jewellery Circle account number and password, and got immediate access. The balance was identical to the statement May Ling had sent her, and the list of past transactions matched the paperwork Jasmine had provided. If nothing else, she was now in a position to track the account's activity. If she knew when the next drug deal was imminent she might be able to turn that to her advantage.

She exited the bank site and entered the name Patrick Cunningham into a search engine. She got five pages of entries, but none of them fitted his profile. Frustrated, she got up from the desk and went over to the window. The Marina Bay Sands was lit up, and it looked just as spectacular at night. If the situation were different she would have considered visiting it, but right now Evans Trust, Cunningham, and the chapel were in her head, and she didn't need any distractions.

She checked her watch again. Derek would be out of bed by now, but it was unlikely that Todd Howell would be at the office. As soon as Jasmine Yip and Mrs. Lam had spoken about Cunningham, Derek and Howell had come to mind, but Ava hadn't decided whether to contact one or both of them. Derek was a top-notch researcher, but his talents were tied to his computer; no matter how skilled he was, the information Ava wanted wasn't going to be easy to access. She decided to call Howell first.

"Todd Howell," he answered.

Ava heard voices in the background. "This is Ava. I'm

pleased to catch you so early. Can you talk?"

"Just a minute," he said, and a moment later added, "Okay, I've closed my door. If you're calling about Jasmine Yip, I still haven't been able to find a connection to Muir."

"How about the trips he made to Asia?"

"Yes, I was going to email the details to you later this morning. We found travel charges of more than forty thousand dollars. Muir made four trips to Hong Kong and one each to Beijing and Shanghai."

"Was he travelling alone?"

"I don't know. We checked with the airline, and his was the only name attached to the reservations. But that doesn't mean someone else wasn't paying for their own ticket."

"Do you have a pen and paper handy?"

"Sure."

"Good. I think I may have found the final landing spot for the Harvest Investment Fund money."

"Are you serious?" Howell asked.

"Completely, and I believe Muir isn't the only Canadian connection."

"What!"

"Todd, before I get into this with you, I have to stress that I need speed from your end. I've involved more people here than I'd like, so the longer this drags on, the greater the chances word will get back to Muir and his pals."

"What is it you want me to do?"

"I need you to dig into the lives of Patrick Cunningham and his wife, Esther."

"Cunningham the CFO of Harvest Table?"

"More like the CEO, according to his mother-in-law. I met her today in Singapore, along with Jasmine Yip. Jasmine and

Esther Cunningham — also known as Essie Lam — are cousins. It was Esther who brought Jasmine and Muir together."

Howell didn't react at first, but then he blurted, "You've just unloaded one hell of a lot of names on me. How on earth did you find all this out?"

"That's not important. Now we know that Muir and Yip are linked and it was Esther Cunningham who brought them together."

"To do what, exactly?"

"Yip is a money launderer. She emptied the Amsterdam bank account and used the funds to buy diamonds in Antwerp. Then those diamonds were sold in China for cash, which was deposited in a bank account in Chengdu."

"Yip did all that herself?"

"Muir directed everything she did, but Yip was the front person."

"And Esther Cunningham knew her cousin was capable of doing this?"

"More important, Patrick Cunningham knew," Ava said. "If I remember correctly, it was Cunningham who positioned Muir to establish the finance committee, yes?"

"It was."

"It makes sense then that they knew each before that happened."

"Are you saying that Cunningham was involved in the scam?"

"Todd, at this point we have to stop thinking that Muir is our only villain. I'd be surprised if Cunningham isn't up to his ears in this as well."

"Holy Christ."

"So you need to find out everything you can about

Cunningham and his wife," said Ava. "And see if you can find anything that connects either of them financially to Muir."

"I can hardly believe what you just told me, but of course I'll look into it. We have some people in house who are good at this, and I have a friend who's a private detective."

"Use all of them, but there has to be a level of discretion."

"I understand that."

"And Todd, while they're looking at Cunningham, they might also want to examine how Bible Chapel is funded," she said. "Those two hundred acres it sits on must have cost a fortune, not to mention the building and the infrastructure that goes with it. Cunningham's mother-in-law told me about his role at the chapel, that he was the one who kept things running by keeping the bank happy."

"What about Pastor Rogers?" Howell asked. "Do you think this could go all the way up to him?"

"I can't discount the possibility. How close are he and Cunningham?"

"It seems like Rogers trusts him, and Cunningham comes across as someone who would do anything to please his boss."

"I don't know much about Rogers. Maybe it's time I learned more."

(26)

AVA PUT DOWN HER CELLPHONE WITH A SIGH. She checked the time again. She was desperate to hear from Xu but knew he'd phone the moment he heard anything. Almost absent-mindedly she hit Fai's number and then listened as her call went directly to voicemail.

"It's me. I'm in my room at the hotel and I'll be here for the rest of the evening. Call me whenever you can. Love you," she said.

As she hung up, she saw she had an incoming call.

"Ava, this is Brenda."

"Oh, hi," Ava said.

"You sound disappointed," Brenda said. "Am I taking you away from something?"

"Not at all. I'm just preoccupied with the money I'm trying to hunt down."

"How is that going?"

"Well enough, though it's more complicated than I had anticipated. But we'll get to the bottom of it."

"I'm calling to tell you that Richard and I are now silent

partners in a company called BB Productions. It has a London address — which is a law firm's — and a bank account with Barclay's that the lawyer will manage per our instructions. I figure if you can fund the account through a second party, that will put a bank, two law firms, and three people between you and the money."

"I'll buy the two of you dinner the next time I'm in Hong Kong."

"We'll take you up on that. Is there any chance that could be soon?"

"Possibly. I'm in Singapore now, and May Ling wants me to join her and Amanda in Hong Kong when I finish here."

"We'd love to see all of you," Brenda said, and paused. "Ava, I can't remember if May and Amanda know about the film project."

"They know some things but not all. They haven't read the script. Did you translate the copy I emailed to you?"

"I did, and I've read it and Richard read it," Brenda said. "Neither of us is qualified to pass judgement on how it will translate to the screen, but even in written form it's incredibly powerful."

"Can you understand now why I want to see it made?"

"Ava, I never said it shouldn't get made. My concern was always about protecting you from any political fallout. The banking arrangement in the U.K. is a good start to achieving that."

"Thank you again," Ava said, and then felt an adrenalin surge as Xu's phone number appeared on her screen. "I have to go, Brenda. I have an incoming call."

"Stay in touch."

"I will," Ava said, and switched lines. "Xu, I've been going quietly crazy waiting to hear from you. What do you have for me?"

"After I threw those extra names at Han, he decided it was getting too complicated. So rather than him talking to Golden Emperor on our behalf, he asked for a meeting and invited me to join him in Chengdu. I told him this concerns you, so I'd send you in my place."

"Was he okay with that?"

"Ava, Han has heard of you. In fact, there aren't many Mountain Masters who don't know your name. You have a reputation."

"So he was okay with me going," she said, not wanting to ask for details of that reputation. "And Golden Emperor agreed to a meeting?"

"They didn't even ask why he wanted one," Xu said. "Han is a man with a serious presence in Chengdu — he's someone people want to please. He wants to know when you can get to Chengdu."

"Let me check flights," she said, opening her laptop and quickly scanning her choices. "There's a SilkAir flight that leaves here around one tomorrow afternoon and gets to Chengdu at five-twenty."

"So you can be there by early evening. I'll call Han and tell him to set up the meeting. I want him to be there with you in person," Xu said. "I'll arrange for him to meet you at the airport."

"Both of which would be appreciated."

"And Ava, if you need him to lean on anyone, don't hesitate to ask. Han is an old-fashioned kind of triad and would be pleased to do it."

"I'll keep that in mind," she said, wondering what Xu

meant by “lean on” and hoping she would never have to find out.

After speaking to Xu, Ava phoned her mother to let her know she would be on the move again, and then she took a call from Fai that lasted almost an hour. Most of that was taken up by Fai talking about the film shoot. She was excited about how well it was going. Andy Gao was convinced the film would be a hit. He had told Fai she had a natural flair for romantic comedy and that he wanted to work with her again.

“After all those years doing the darkest kind of drama, it was strange to hear,” Fai said.

“You make me laugh.”

“That’s because you love me.”

“Everyone loves you,” Ava said.

Fai went silent and then said abruptly, “Oh god, I miss you. How is your project coming along? Is there a chance you could be finished soon and get over to Taiwan?”

“I’m going to Chengdu tomorrow morning. I don’t know how long I’ll be there, but with any luck it could be my last step towards getting Mr. Gregory’s money back,” Ava said.

“I pray that you’re lucky.”

When the conversation ended, Ava immediately became restless. She realized that for the first time in days there was nothing urgent for her to pursue. Howell and his people would be doing their thing in Toronto and didn’t need her to contribute. The meeting in Chengdu was set. She didn’t have all the details, but Han would share those with her when he met her at the airport. She tried to think of possible loose ends and came up with only one: Jasmine Yip. One phone call from Jasmine to Muir or Essie Cunningham and the whole thing could blow up. Had Ava's threat been strong enough? Or, to put it in its proper perspective, who was Jasmine more afraid of, Malcolm Muir or the triads? Ava remembered Mrs. Lam's reaction and felt a level of reassurance. The older woman understood the rules of behaviour within the structure of gangs, and after a lifetime of following them she wouldn't betray them so easily. Ava decided to leave well enough alone.

Her thoughts turned back to Howell. It was almost midmorning in Toronto. He could have unearthed something by now, but if he had he would have called. *Relax and let things unfold,* she told herself. Then Pastor Sammy Rogers entered her mind and she opened her laptop. On YouTube she found a plethora of videos and clicked on the most recent, posted six months ago, with the title "Pastor Sammy Rogers at Harvest Table Anniversary."

The quality of the video was very good. It started with a panning shot of what seemed to be a full-to-capacity worship centre and then cut to the stage, where a choir was finishing a song with a rousing "Amen, amen, amen." On the last "amen," Rogers walked onto the stage with his head bowed and a Bible hanging by his side. He stood directly in front of a large illuminated cross flanked by two smaller but equally bright ones.

Rogers raised his head and arms and shouted, "Welcome to the Harvest Table. Welcome to our house, where the Lord's will is done." As the congregation roared in response, he smiled and let the noise wash over him. Finally he opened the Bible and said, "This is the word of the Lord." He then read a long passage from the Old Testament book of Job in a slow, melodic manner. After about five minutes he stopped reading and lowered his head in prayer. Ava saw that most of the people in the congregation were following his example. Then Rogers closed the Bible, kissed it, and shouted, "I believe, I believe, I believe!" He began to pace back and forth across the stage.

He looked younger than Ava had imagined, but that image was created in part by the shoulder-length hair that he brushed back from his face as he walked. He was wearing jeans and a tight black shirt, a look that a man with his tall, rangy build could pull off. *He looks more like a rock 'n' roller than a pastor,* she thought.

When he started to speak, Rogers addressed the passage he'd just read. He began to dissect it, reciting lines from memory and imbuing them with meanings that Ava couldn't see, but the nodding congregation seemed to understand. The video was an hour long and she'd only watched ten minutes. How much longer would he actually talk?

She fast-forwarded to near the end. Rogers was still pacing and talking, but his tempo had increased and his voice soared whenever he wanted to emphasize a point. Ava saw that a large number of people were now standing with their arms extended and their palms facing forward. Some swayed back and forth. The pastor's combination of movement and timbre had obviously made an impact. Even though she thought the message mundane, his delivery was mesmerizing. But when he fell to his knees and raised the Bible above his head, all she saw was a man working at manipulating his audience. It became too much for her, and she turned off the video.

Enough of this, she thought as a yawn overtook her. The

day had been stressful. The following day promised more of the same, but she was making progress and the end might even be in sight.

Ava slept fitfully that night, expecting her phone to sound any moment with news from Todd Howell. When she woke for the last time, at seven, there was still no word from him. She started her day with coffee, followed by a trip to the hotel gym. Two hours later she was making her way downstairs to head for the airport.

SilkAir was a wholly owned subsidiary of Singapore Air and provided the same lounge privileges. Shortly after eleven Ava was in the SilverKris Lounge, settling into a leather easy chair with a double espresso and a plate of har gow and cha siu bao next to her on a table. She ate slowly, careful not to get any of the chili sauce she'd slathered on the dumplings on her shirt. When she'd finished, she went to get another espresso and carried it back to the chair with a copy of the *Wall Street Journal* and the *New York Times* international edition.

Both papers had headlines about the U.S. president feuding with his own intelligence experts over the reliability of the data they were providing him. Why he would doubt his own people and put more trust in what foreigners were telling him was a mystery to Ava. She wasn't political, at least not in any partisan way. She always voted and she donated to candidates whose character and general views she respected, regardless of their party affiliation. In Canada the differences among the various parties weren't that extreme, so she had actually supported candidates from three different political parties at various times. That would have been difficult to do in the United States, where visceral extremism had become the new normal.

The *Times* also had a story on the trade issues that were causing increasing tension between China and the U.S. Given the Three Sisters' investments in Shanghai and Beijing, this was something of keen interest to her. Chi-Tze Song, one of their senior executives who helped manage the PÖ fashion line, had been urging them for months to move their clothing production to Sri Lanka, where labour and overhead costs were much lower, leaving Shanghai as the design centre and headquarters. Amanda had discussed this informally with Ava and May Ling but wasn't ready to make a serious pitch.

Ava suspected that if a trade war erupted between the United States and China, the duties on finished goods going to the U.S. and on raw materials entering China would force them to relocate. She made a mental note to call Suki Chan, who managed their warehousing and logistics businesses in China. Any disruption in trade would affect those sectors as well, and Ava wanted to know if Suki was making contingency plans. As she contemplated the possibly tricky future for Three Sisters, her phone sounded. No incoming number showed on the screen.

She hesitated but finally answered, "Ava Lee."

"This is Todd Howell."

"Your number doesn't show."

"I'm using our home line. It's programmed as a private number," he said.

"Well, I'm glad I picked up."

"We've been trying to get some extra information, but it looks like it's going to be a challenge. So I thought I'd fill you in on what we have now. I figured you'd be anxious."

"I have been anxious. Thank you for being so considerate," Ava said. "What have you found?"

"Someone has been injecting a lot of money into the Harvest Table Chapel organization. It started four years ago but really picked up in the past two years. We have no idea where the money originates. That's what we're trying to nail down."

"The money is going to the organization? What about Cunningham and Rogers? What's their financial situation?"

"Cunningham has a salary of a hundred and fifty thousand dollars a year. He lives in a house that's worth well over a million and is mortgage-free. He has about four million dollars invested in stocks and Canada Savings Bonds. His wife has no income."

"So obviously he's doing something on the side."

"And in all likelihood so is Rogers. He has a lifestyle that goes well beyond his salary of two hundred and fifty thousand, and he has more money stashed away than Cunningham," Howell said. "But Ava, even combined, their net worth is peanuts compared to what's been going into the organization."

"How much are we talking about?"

Ava heard the rustling of paper, and then Howell said, "We followed up on your suggestion and looked into how much it cost to build the chapel and buy the land it stands on. They paid sixty million dollars for the two hundred acres, and it cost approximately another thirty-five million for the building and the infrastructure — driveways, parking, sewers — they needed to support it. They had a combined mortgage of eighty million on the land and the building."

"*Had* a mortgage?"

"Exactly. For the first two years of its existence the Chapel's income of weekly donations, some tithing, gifts, and a few bequests was sufficient to service the mortgage, cover the overheads, and leave a million or so in the bank," Howell said. "But then four years ago they paid down the mortgage by five million. The next year they put seven million against it. Then things really accelerated. Two years ago the mortgage shrank by twenty-two million, and last year it was paid down by thirty million. In four years an eighty-million-dollar mortgage has been whittled down to sixteen."

"But you don't know where the money came from."

"No. All we've been able to access is the mortgage records. We haven't been able to get into the chapel's bank account, and that's what we're working on."

"Which bank has the account?"

"Eastern Canadian Commerce."

"Do you have any contacts there?"

"Yes, but none who would breach their fiduciary duty and give me access to the account."

"Not even for a price?"

"Is that what you did in Amsterdam? Pay someone for access?" he asked.

"Yes, but I don't always do that. Sometimes I trade favours," Ava said. "In the game we're playing, everything is fair if the only people getting hurt are the thieves."

"Even if I agreed with you, my partners wouldn't. They get sticky when it comes to ethics."

"Are they sticky about ethics or reluctant to spend money?"

"A bit of both, actually," Howell said.

"So how do you plan to access the account?"

"We're trying to get in through the back door."

"You're trying to hack into it?"

"Yes."

"And your partners won't find that unethical?"

"I won't tell them, and the cost is minimal."

"Then good luck. If you need extra help with the hacking, Mr. Gregory's son-in-law, Derek, is quite talented."

"I'll keep him in mind if my regulars come up short," Howell said, then paused. "Can I ask what your immediate plans are?"

"I'm getting ready to board a plane to Chengdu."

"I can hardly believe the way you keep pushing forward. Was it always like that when you were on a job?"

"Always. There's no other way to do it. The moment I let up is the moment when I lose the advantage. I've got Muir and Cunningham in my sights, and I'm not going to give them a chance to evade me."

(27)

AVA WAS WONDERING HOW SHE WOULD CONNECT WITH Han as she entered the arrivals hall at Chengdu Shuangliu International Airport. Her question was immediately answered when she saw a sign with her name on it being waved over the heads of a wall of people waiting to meet passengers. She worked her way towards the sign, quickly realized she couldn't penetrate the human wall, and went around one end of it. The man holding the sign was peering straight ahead and didn't see her as she came at him from a different direction. He was startled when she said, "Hi, I'm Ava Lee."

"I'm Willie Lin," he said, recovering his composure. "The boss is waiting for you outside." Willie was still in his twenties, Ava figured. He wore jeans and a plain black T-shirt, was of medium height and build, and had no tattoos. His main distinguishing feature was an abbreviated mohawk haircut that was bleached blond.

"Then let's go," she said, expecting him to offer to carry her bag. He didn't. Instead he just turned and started walking away from the crowd.

Ava followed Willie across the arrivals hall to an exit door. Like every airport in a major Chinese city that she had visited in recent years, Chengdu's was new and had been built with the future in mind. The crowd at the arrivals gate aside, the rest of the hall was sparsely populated yet vast enough to accommodate thousands of people. Ava and Willie made rapid progress towards the door. He held it open for her and she emerged onto a sidewalk that faced six lanes of traffic.

In the lane closest to the terminal, a line of expensive cars was parked at the curb. "The boss's car is in that direction," Willie said, pointing to the right. They walked past several Mercedes-Benzes, a Land Rover, a Porsche, and a Jaguar to a white SUV, where a man with heavily tattooed arms leaned against the front fender. The SUV was a Haval H6, one of the top Chinese-made models. When the man saw them approaching, he straightened up and opened the rear passenger door for a man whom Ava assumed was Han. It was her turn to be startled.

Over the years she had encountered many big men. Suen, Xu's Red Pole, was six feet four of rippling muscle. Uncle's former bodyguard and driver, Sonny Kwok, was almost as large and had a temperament that made him even more fearsome. Ava had inherited Sonny when Uncle died, and although he lived in Hong Kong he was still part of her team, ready to do her bidding at a moment's notice. For a man his size Sonny was incredibly agile, and one of the few people Ava had ever met whom she wasn't sure she could best in a fight. The man standing on the sidewalk watching her walk towards him gave her that same impression.

Ava guessed he was about six feet eight inches tall. He was massive across the shoulders and chest and had a thick waist with no visible fat; his lightly tattooed arms looked like tree trunks. When he got out of the car, she noticed that he was nimble and light on his feet.

"Greetings, *xiao lao ban*," he said with a slight smile. "I'm Han."

Ava looked into a face that was full of contradictions. Han's smile and his eyes seemed welcoming, but the right side of his face was split by a scar that ran from the middle of his forehead, across his eye, and down the cheek to the bottom of his jaw. The scar was bright red; like the one on Ava's leg, it looked as if a very long worm had come to rest on his face.

She smiled. "I'm pleased to meet you, Mr. Han, though I'm a bit confused by your calling me *xiao lao ban*. I'm nobody's little boss."

"Just call me Han. It was our mutual friend Lam in Guangzhou who told me that's how Xu's men refer to you. He thinks it's complimentary. He also thinks it's fitting—he has a very high regard for you."

"Lam and I have done some business over the years, and I owe him a great deal. If he ever called in all his favours, I'm not sure I'd be able to meet them."

"That's like me and Xu. I'll never be able to repay him for what he's done for me. I'm hoping your business here will be successful so I can pay back a bit of that debt."

"If it is, it will be great for both of us," Ava said. "Now, when do we meet the people from Golden Emperor?"

"They're expecting us at their factory at six-thirty," Han said, looking at his watch. "Traffic is heavy now, but we should make it on time. Believe me, though, they won't leave if we're a bit late."

"Who are we meeting?"

"The Yang brothers, Fat and Smart. I don't know who gave them those nicknames, but Smart is almost as big as Fat, and neither of them is especially intelligent."

"It sounds like you know them well."

"I've known their family for years, but I suspect I'll know them even better after our meeting today," Han said, and then turned to Willie. "Put Ms. Lee's bag in the trunk."

Ava climbed into the back seat, where Han joined her. Although the SUV was spacious, she doubted they could have fitted a third person in the rear. The car moved away from the curb and joined the line of traffic leaving the airport.

Ava gazed up at a dull grey sky. "It looks like it's going to rain," she said.

"That's smog," Han said. "Chengdu has finally outdone Beijing and Shanghai in one area, and that's air quality. We have the worst pollution of any city in the country. My grandchildren aren't allowed to go outside at school. My daughter wants to move to the country, but her husband is my Red Pole. What's he going to do there, raise pigs?"

Ava looked at him again, surprised at the reference to grandchildren. To her eyes, Han looked to be in his early forties. "Who's to say that a triad couldn't raise magnificent pigs?" she said.

"Five hundred years of triad history."

"There is that," Ava admitted.

The car made its way onto the Airport Expressway going north. As Han had indicated, traffic was heavy, and the Haval couldn't go much faster than thirty kilometres an hour. As they crawled along, Ava looked out the side window at a familiar sight in large Chinese cities: row upon row of high-rise apartment buildings and, in the distance, skyscrapers in the centre of town. It was dusk and most of the buildings were brightly lit, making them seem more impressive than she expected she'd see in daylight.

"How far to downtown?" she asked Han.

"It's about fifteen kilometres north of here, but we're not going in that direction. We'll be heading east, away from the Qionglai Mountains. The Yangs' factory is in an industrial park that was one of the last developments approved for that area."

"Why was development stopped? That's unusual in the new China."

"The industrial park is close to a large primitive forest that's a giant panda habitat. There was an outcry when people thought the pandas might be endangered. It seems that the only two things you can't do these days in China are to criticize the Communist Party and threaten giant pandas."

A few minutes later the car left the expressway and started along a highway that was less congested.

"This is good. If it stays like this we'll be on time," Han said as he looked at his watch. He turned to Ava. "I don't mean to pry, but I heard rumours that Xu was having health problems, and I thought you might know something. He's an important man in our brotherhood, and we all want to see him continue on."

"Why didn't you ask him yourself when you were speaking to him?" she asked. "I'm sure he would have been truthful."

"It would have been awkward. I mean, my reason for wanting to know is that I care about him, but he might have thought I had an ulterior motive. Being suspicious is an essential trait in Mountain Masters who plan to survive for very long."

Ava lapsed into silence and looked out the window again as she calculated how many people knew about Xu's illness. Was this his way of testing her? Lam knew about Xu, of that she was certain, and if he and Han were close, the information could have been shared. And what was the harm if Han did know? Xu was functioning normally again, and now they knew the symptoms, any relapse could easily be identified and dealt with.

"He had meningitis," she said. "It was caught in time and he was treated. He's operating at one hundred percent again, and there's no reason to think he won't be doing that for many years to come."

"Thank you for telling me," Han said with a slight nod.

"Not many people know. I don't believe Xu would appreciate it if the information went beyond this car."

"I know how to respect a confidence," said Han.

Ava nodded and decided it was time to change the conversation. "Tell me what you know about the Yang brothers. How did they get into the pharmaceutical business?"

"It's the family business. It's been around for ever."

"The micro-lab?"

"No. Before it became Golden Emperor MicroLab, it was called Golden Emperor Herbal Remedies, and before that Golden Emperor Herbs. I know the two brothers are at least the third generation of Yangs in the business, because I remember my grandmother going to their grandmother to buy dried herbs. She sold herbs to treat every ailment under the sun."

"But how does one go from selling dried herbs to manufacturing synthetic opioids?"

"The brothers' father bridged the gap. He built a factory that put the herbs into pill and capsule form. I guess once you know how to make pills and capsules, the process is the same no matter what the ingredients are."

"I'm not sure that's true," Ava said.

"Me neither, but it's the only explanation I've got."

"Boss, we're getting close," Willie said from the front seat.

Outside, the scenery had shifted from apartment buildings to low-rise factories of various sizes. The car left the highway, took a left, and entered an industrial park. There was a dull sameness to the buildings until they reached the end of a street and turned right into a dead end. Straight ahead was a sheet metal fence and a steel gate topped by razor wire. Behind them loomed a windowless grey structure that was tall enough to have four or five levels inside. The name Golden Emperor in yellow metal letters at least a metre high was fixed across the front wall.

"This is a larger operation than I expected," Ava said.

"It's the biggest in Chengdu, and maybe in China, for all I know," Han said. "Is that a problem?"

"Of course not. In fact, it could be the opposite. If the guys I'm chasing were their biggest customer, then they might be more reluctant to be honest with me. From the size of this place, they must have a lot of customers."

"Don't worry about them being reluctant. If they are, it won't last long," Han said.

Ava glanced at him, saw his stony expression, and decided it was best to stay quiet.

When the car pulled up at the gate, Willie lowered his window and shouted at one of the armed guards who stood inside. "Mr. Han is here to see the Yang brothers."

The guard ran over to the security hut and spoke to someone inside. Seconds later, the gate swung open. As the car drove through, a man wearing a uniform with fringed epaulettes stepped out of the hut and came over. "If you go to the right, you'll see parking reserved for company executives. A space has been left vacant for you," he said to Han's driver.

As they drove into the courtyard and started around the building, Ava realized it was even larger than she'd initially thought. They drove for about a hundred metres before finding a row of luxury cars parked against the side of the building. One spot was vacant. When they had parked, a double glass door on the side of the building opened and a middle-aged woman wearing a powder-blue leisure suit stepped outside.

"You stay here," Han said to Willie and the driver. He opened the car door and slid out. Ava did the same from her side.

The woman stepped towards them. "Mr. Han, I am Mrs. Pan. I'm so pleased to greet you. And this young woman is?"

"Ava Lee," Ava said.

"I'm not sure we were expecting you, Ms. Lee."

"She's with me. Is that a problem?"

"Of course not," the woman said hurriedly. "Mr. Yang and Mr. Yang are waiting for you inside."

"Lead the way," Han said.

They walked through the door into a lobby with white marble floors and walls covered with prints of traditional Chinese waterfall scenes. Mrs. Pan led them to an elevator and pressed a button; the door opened at once. She stood to one side as Ava and Han entered. The elevator moved slowly but steadily for about a minute. Ava figured they were headed to the top of the building.

"How many levels are there in this building?" Ava asked.

"Six. The labs, production areas, and shipping and receiving occupy the first five. The top floor is reserved for marketing, purchasing, accounting, and our executive offices."

"You've been asked that question before," Ava said.

"Yes. Visitors are often confused by the lack of exterior windows clearly delineating the floors."

The elevator came to a halt. When the doors opened Ava saw a spacious reception area with a young man sitting behind a desk, flanked by security guards. As they approached the reception desk, the man looked questioningly at Mrs. Pan.

"These are special guests. They aren't required to sign in," she said to him.

They looped around the desk and came upon a double set of wooden doors. The woman turned an ornate brass handle on one of the doors and opened it. "There's water, tea, and coffee on the credenza to the right. Please help yourselves and make yourselves comfortable while I get Mr. Yang and Mr. Yang."

The boardroom was about thirty metres long and fifteen metres wide. A massive teak table sat in the centre, surrounded by thirty black leather chairs. The walls were covered in whiteboards and television screens. There were six credenzas; one held a pitcher of water, carafes, glasses, and cups and saucers, while the other five displayed an enormous number of jade sculptures and ceramic plates.

"Do you want something to drink?" Han asked.

"No thanks."

"Me neither," he said, taking a seat facing the door.

Ava sat next to him.

"The way we'll do this is I'll tell them you have questions you need them to answer," Han said. "Then I'll shut up and let you do your thing."

"That's fine," Ava said, as the door opened.

Mrs. Pan entered the room first, followed by two men in white lab coats who already looked uncomfortable. They were short and middle-aged, and each had a full head of black hair streaked with grey. One had a plump face and a pot belly that pressed against the lab coat; the other wasn't quite as rotund, and his face was pale. They wore white shirts and ties under their coats.

The Yang brothers crossed the floor with uncertain smiles on their faces and with hands extended. Han stood up. He towered over them, the men's heads barely reaching the middle of his chest. "Thanks for seeing us," he said.

"It has been a long time," the thinner brother said, and then looked at Ava. "Our families have known each other for many years, but I don't believe we've met you . . ."

"Ava is a special friend of a special friend of mine."

"Ah," the man said, offering her his hand. "My name is Jing, and my brother is Chao."

"I'm Ava Lee. Pleased to meet you both," she said, shaking their hands.

The brothers sat across the table from Ava and Han. Mrs. Pan sat several chairs away with a notebook open on the table in front of her.

"What's the notebook for?" Han asked.

"We maintain records of all our meetings. It helps clear up any misunderstandings that might emerge later," Jing said.

"Are you okay with that?" Han asked Ava.

"No."

Han looked at Jing. "No notebook."

Jing hesitated, then said, "Okay. But do you have any objections if our assistant stays?"

"She can stay," Ava said.

Han nodded, then put his forearms on the table and leaned forward. "Thanks for seeing us. I asked for this meeting as a favour to the special friend I mentioned earlier. Now I'm going to turn things over to Ava. She has some questions and I'd like you to answer them."

"We'll certainly do the best we can," Jing said.

"Tell me, do the names Jewellery Circle, Jasmine Yip, Malcolm Muir, or Patrick Cunningham mean anything to you?" Ava said.

Jing frowned then looked at his brother, who frowned in return. Chao looked at Han and said, "You have to understand that the business we're in demands a large amount of trust. We may not take an oath of secrecy like in your organization, but we still feel obliged to protect certain information that comes our way as we conduct business."

"I don't know why you're talking to me," Han said. "Ava asked the question. Answer her."

Chao turned his attention to Ava. "I'm sorry, we can't answer that question. And I say that to you not because of the specific names you mentioned. You could have asked about a hundred different names and our answer would be the same."

"*You little weasel!*" Han roared as he got to his feet. He raised his right hand and slapped it down so hard that Ava felt the table tremble. She looked up at him and saw that his face was contorted with rage. She started to say something but stopped when he reached across the table, grabbed Chao by the knot in his Burberry tie, and lifted him out of the chair. He held him aloft for a few seconds, which was long enough that Chao started gasping for air.

"*You will answer all her questions!*" Han shouted as he threw the man back into his chair. He remained standing, glaring at the brothers. The scar on his face had turned bright red and seemed to be pulsating.

Ava could see that Mrs. Pan was trying to hold back tears. Chao's eyes were blinking madly, and his hands were shaking. His brother had beads of sweat on his forehead.

Ava was stunned. The brothers looked terrified, and she actually felt a tinge of sympathy for them. "You know what, I think I will have a glass of water," she said softly.

(28)

YANG JING STUMBLED TOWARDS THE CREDENZA, poured water into a glass, and brought it back to Ava. "Thank you," she said.

"We are not trying to be difficult," he said to her, his eyes avoiding Han.

"I understand that you have a sense of loyalty to the people you do business with. I respect that, but at the same time you need to understand that not all of them may be doing business in an ethical manner."

"How would we know that?"

"Exactly, how would you know? The company and the people I mentioned, for example, may have presented themselves to you as law-abiding businesspeople. The problem is that they're not. I have every reason to believe that they stole millions of dollars from ordinary working-class citizens, and that ultimately they've been using that money to buy drugs from you."

"We know nothing about stolen money."

"I'm not accusing you of doing something improper," Ava

said, looking at each brother in turn. "Do you need me to repeat the names I mentioned earlier?"

"Please," Chao said.

Ava knew he was simply pretending he didn't remember but decided to go along with it. "Okay. Why don't I give you the names one by one so there's no confusion."

"Sure," Chao said.

"Let's start with Jewellery Circle. Do you do business with that company?"

"They are a customer."

"A good customer?"

"That depends on what you mean by good," Chao said.

Ava felt Han stiffen and spoke quickly to forestall another eruption. "Don't play word games with me, Mr. Yang. All you'll do is annoy Mr. Han and postpone the inevitable," she said. "But just so we're clear, is Jewellery Circle a regular customer? I'll define that as buying from you several times a year."

"Yes."

"And do their purchases involve the transfer of millions rather than thousands of dollars?"

"Yes."

"What kind of products do they buy?"

"A wide variety. Fentanyl, carfentanil, some other synthetic opioids, and synthetic marijuana in various forms."

"All of them legal?"

"All of them are legal for us to manufacture and sell here in Chengdu. After they leave our factory, we have no way of knowing where they go, who they are sold to, or how they are used," Chao said.

"Of course you don't," Ava said. "Now, do you know Jasmine Yip — or Yip Liling, as she might be known here?"

"My brother can answer that," Chao said, glancing at Jing.

Jing wiped his mouth with the back of his hand and then focused his attention on Ava. "We know the name. It's attached to transfers Jewellery Circle makes to us from the Mercantile Bank. But we've never met her."

"You were never curious about meeting the woman who transfers millions of dollars to you?" Ava said.

"We didn't need to know anything about her," Chao said. "She has nothing to do with the business except arrange for the transfer of money."

"She never discussed pricing with you or provided orders for product?"

"No."

"Who does negotiate prices and orders with you on behalf of Jewellery Circle?"

The brothers shuffled in their chairs, their discomfort painfully obvious. "Tell her," Han said, his voice level but menacing all the same.

"Malcolm Muir," Jing said.

"How did your relationship with Mr. Muir begin?"

"We were referred to him by another customer."

"Which customer?"

"SCM."

"What do the initials stand for?"

"I don't know," Jing said.

"Are you still doing business with them?"

"Yes. They have an office and warehouse here in Chengdu," Jing said, and then stopped abruptly as if he had realized he'd said more than he intended.

"Who is your contact at SCM?"

"A woman, Su Na."

"That makes some sense," Ava said. "Did you know she's a joint holder of the Jewellery Circle account at your bank?"

"No, I didn't," Jing said. "Her name was never attached to any transfers from that account."

"What else do you know about her?"

"What do you mean?"

"Don't start getting evasive with me again. We were just starting to get along," Ava said. "Where is she from? How long have you known her? What's the nature of your business relationship?"

"She's from Chengdu. We went to university together. She graduated with a chemistry degree the same year I did," Chao said, intervening on his brother's behalf. "She moved to Shanghai after graduation to work as a sales rep for a pharmaceutical company, but she came back here six or seven years ago with SCM. It's an American company. She told me she manages their Chinese operations."

"And those operations are buying and distributing pharmaceuticals?"

"I don't know what else they do, but that much I know for certain."

"Does SCM pay you out of the same account as Jewellery Circle?"

"No, they pay us separately. The money comes either from their account at the Mercantile Bank or from an account in Vanuatu."

"Which bank in Vanuatu?"

"Not a bank. The Evans Trust Company."

Ava felt the circle starting to close but thought it was too soon to pull it tighter. "I'd like to return to Malcolm Muir for a few minutes," she said. "When were you first contacted by him?"

"About five years ago. I don't have an exact date."

"How was the contact made?"

"Su Na phoned me. She said she had friends who wanted to do business with us. It was Muir and the other man you mentioned."

"Patrick Cunningham?"

"Yes. They were in Chengdu. She asked if she could bring them to the factory for a tour. We said okay, and one thing led to another," Chao said.

"The business started quite small," Jing added. "The orders were almost sample size. I figured they were testing our products in their market. But gradually their business picked up, and the last three years have been strong and getting stronger."

"And you had no idea where their market was?"

"We could guess but we never asked. Truthfully, we didn't want to know," Jing said.

"Everything we do is legal. We are in compliance with all the Chinese rules and regulations regarding the production and sale of our products," Chao said. "If someone else breaks a law, then it's on them, not on us."

"Again, I don't doubt the legality of your business, and I'm not here to cause you grief. My issue is with Malcolm Muir and Patrick Cunningham," Ava said. "How often do you hear from them?"

"We never saw or heard from Cunningham again, but every couple of months or so there's an order from Muir."

"How does he communicate with you?"

"He always phones first. We discuss products, quantities,

and prices. When he's ready to order, he sends an email," Jing said.

"Can I see the emails?"

"Yes, but they probably won't make much sense to you. He uses a code when he orders."

"Different names for the products?"

"No, he uses numbers, and he changes them every few orders."

"How do you know the codes?"

"He tells them to me over the phone."

"But when you get the emails, don't you transpose the codes into actual product names?"

"Of course."

"Then I want to see the emails, your transpositions, and the final shipping documents."

Jing raised an eyebrow at Chao. "We'll provide you with everything we have," Chao said.

"Excellent. Now, how often has Muir come to Chengdu?"

"Since the first trip he's been coming about once a year. In fact, he's scheduled to visit next month."

"Does he come just to see you?"

"No. He usually spends a morning with us reviewing new products and that kind of thing, and then later in his visit we'll have dinner with him."

"How long is his average visit?" Ava asked.

"A week or so."

"What does he do for the rest of the time?"

"I believe he spends most of it with Su Na."

"Why would he do that?"

"I thought I made it clear that Muir and SCM take possession of our product here in Chengdu," Jing said. "We ship everything they order to the SCM warehouse. They have their own business relationship, which we're not privy to."

"Muir's order is delivered to the SCM warehouse?"

"Yes."

"I apologize for not picking up on that earlier," Ava said. "This is a complicated affair."

"Not for us," Chao said, asserting himself ever so slightly. "We take orders, fill them, and run our business in a proper, legal manner."

"*Fuck* your sarcasm," Han said suddenly.

"It wasn't intended," Chao said, nervous again.

"And I'm not offended," Ava said. "Have you ever been to the SCM warehouse?"

"No."

"Where is it?"

"The address is in an industrial park on the eastern boundary of the city. I'll get you the address when we're done here."

"While you're at it, could you also provide me with all the contact information you have on Su Na?"

"We'll give you everything we have."

"Thank you. I appreciate the co-operation," Ava said. She hesitated as she searched her mind for questions that still needed answering. "How large was Muir's last order?"

"Close to four million dollars."

"That's a lot of pills."

"It was his largest order to date."

"When do you expect the next one?"

"He usually gives us an order when he visits, so I would expect a new one when he's here next month."

Ava sat back in her chair. "What do you know about the Evans Trust Company in Vanuatu?"

"Nothing."

"When you get wire transfers from Jewellery Circle, is Evans Trust ever party to them?"

"No."

"You're absolutely certain?"

"I'll give you copies of the transfers and you can see for yourself."

"Thanks," Ava said, and turned to Han. "After Mr. Yang gets me copies of the paperwork, I think we can leave."

Han reached across the table, his outstretched hand coming just short of the Yang brothers. "Listen to me, both of you. If Ava needs more information, you will provide it without question."

"We understand," Chao said.

"And you aren't to notify Muir, Su Na, or anyone connected with them that we had this conversation," Ava said.

"Of course not."

"If you do, neither of you will ever walk again," Han said. "Like I said, Ava is a special friend of my special friend. This is something that matters to me personally."

"Please, Han, we understand. You can trust us to stay quiet," Jing said.

"Good. Now go and get what she wants and we're done here."

(29)

HALF AN HOUR LATER, HAN AND AVA LEFT THE BUILD-ing. Jing and Chao Yang rode the elevator with them to ground level, all the while reassuring Han that they wouldn't discuss the meeting with anyone.

Willie greeted them in the parking lot and rushed to open the back doors.

"Thanks for everything you did in there," Ava said to Han after she'd climbed into the car. "I don't think I would have gotten very far without you."

"I enjoyed scaring those little shits," he said. "They know I mean what I say. I don't make idle threats."

"Well, whatever they thought, the end result was more than I expected. So thank you again," Ava said, wondering just how far he would have taken his threats.

Han shrugged. "What are we going to do next?"

"I should check into my hotel. I'm staying at the Ritz-Carlton in the city centre," Ava said.

"After that, do you want to pay a visit to the SCM warehouse?"

Ava checked her watch. "It's a little late. I would rather

go during the day, when there's a greater chance of catching Su Na. I'd also like a chance to review the paperwork the Yangs gave me."

"Well, would you mind if we scoped it out in advance?"

"No. I think that's a terrific idea."

"I'll have a crew check it tonight," Han said. "Where do you think those drugs are being sent?"

"It's logical that Muir is sending his to Canada. I have no idea about SCM."

"We've stayed out of that business. Some of my brothers in Chengdu believe I've been overly cautious, but I trust the judgement of men like Lam and Xu. They've always stressed that risky short-term gains — no matter how large — can't match long-term economic stability."

"They're astute businessmen."

"They are *business*men — that's the key word. Besides, I tell my men that our profit margins from selling Xu's knock-off perfumes and Lam's knock-off designer bags are almost as healthy as from selling drugs, without running the risk of the government really slamming us," Han said. "And that's what's going to happen to those drug manufacturers and peddlers. One day the government will feel the need to bring a stop to that business, and when they do it won't be a pretty ending."

"Let's hope that happens sooner rather than later."

"Will you join us for dinner tonight?" he asked suddenly. "I had planned to eat with my daughter Ru Shi and her husband, Lu, my Red Pole."

"I have work to do," Ava said, holding up the papers from her lap.

"The dinner doesn't have to be a long affair, and the

restaurant is close to your hotel," Han said. "And while Chengdu has China's worst air quality, it also has its best hotpot restaurants. The one I've booked tonight is famous. I had dinner there many years ago with someone you know, and he loved it."

"Lam?"

"Uncle."

"You took Uncle to dinner?"

"Not me, but I was there. Uncle came to Chengdu with Li, who was the Mountain Master in Guangzhou before Lam. My Mountain Master hosted them, and because both Uncle and Li had brought their deputies with them, I was invited as well."

"I know Lam was Li's deputy, but who was Uncle's at that time?"

"Fong."

"Uncle Fong . . . My god," Ava said with a smile. "I see him every time I'm in Hong Kong, and quite often we go to hotpot there."

"It can't be as good as ours," Han said. "Join us tonight. My daughter will be glad to have some female company."

"Okay, I'll do that. What time is the reservation?"

"Nine. We can meet you in front of your hotel ten minutes before."

"That's perfect. It will give me an hour to go through these papers and do a bit of research," Ava said.

Han nodded, took a phone from his pocket, and hit a contact number. A few seconds later he said, "Lu, phone Lao Ma Tou and tell them we're going to be four for dinner, not three. It shouldn't make a difference, but the place is so damn crowded you never know. Also, send some guys to check out a warehouse tonight at 77 Zhou Enlai Street in the Longquanyi District. They should do it quietly; I don't want anyone to know we're poking around. We might be making a visit there tomorrow, and I don't want any nasty surprises."

Ava saw they were nearing the downtown core and spotted the Ritz-Carlton logo at the top of a skyscraper. A few minutes later the Haval stopped in front of the hotel. Willie got out and opened Ava's door. As soon as she stepped out, he walked to the back to get her bags. Han rolled down his window. "I'll see you at ten to nine," he said.

The hotel lobby was busy, but no one else was checking in when Ava approached the grey marble reception desk. She handed the clerk her passport and credit card.

"You're in a Club Premier suite," the clerk said. "We have one available on the forty-first floor, which is the very top of the hotel."

"The hotel has forty-one floors?" Ava asked, surprised.

"No, we have thirteen floors, but they start at the twenty-eighth floor of the skyscraper that we're built over."

After getting her access card, Ava turned down an offer from a bellboy to carry her bags and made her way to the elevator. When she entered her suite, she was struck by its modernity. It was large — almost 900 square feet — and well furnished, and it had a tremendous view. She thought about freshening up and changing for dinner but didn't want to use up any part of the next hour on anything but work. Besides, if the hotpot restaurant was anything like those in Hong Kong, her hair and clothes would smell like oily chicken broth by the end of the night.

Ava sat at the desk and recorded the details of the meeting

with the Yang brothers in her notebook. Next she reviewed the papers and information they had provided. When she was finished, she opened her laptop and entered "SCM" into a search engine. When she didn't get a hit, she switched to "Su Na" but also found no references. Frustrated, she reached for her phone, hesitated for a few seconds as she wondered if she was doing the right thing, and then called Toronto. When Derek answered, she heard the baby crying in the background.

"Is this a bad time?" Ava asked.

"No, I've been anxious to hear from you," Derek said. "Give me a minute to pick up Amber. If I hold her in my arms she'll stop crying."

Ava waited as Derek made comforting noises to the baby. He had turned out to be a much better husband and father than she could ever have imagined.

"Okay, she's calm. We can talk."

"I'm in China, in Chengdu. Without getting into too much detail, I need you to do some research for me."

"Can you at least give me a clue as to what you're doing in Chengdu?"

His question surprised Ava. In the past, Derek had usually taken whatever she said at face value, but she realized he wasn't working for her now, and he and Mimi did have a lot at stake. "Some of the Harvest Investment Fund money has been circulating through here, although I'm not sure it's the final resting place, and that's what I need you to research. I know for certain that a company called Evans Trust is involved in whatever has been going on. Money is being redirected by them. That's all I know, because I haven't been able to find out a damn thing more about them."

"What else do you have for me to go on, other than the name?"

"The company is registered in and operates out of Vanuatu, which is a series of islands close to Australia that has become the flavour of the month for offshore banking. The local government doesn't acknowledge any financial laws or regulations except its own, and those laws support corporate secrecy to the utmost degree. I have an address, a phone number, a fax number, and an email address. I'll send them to you after I hang up."

"Well, that's a start."

"I also know they've been transferring funds to the Mercantile Bank of Chengdu, into an accounts registered to a company called Jewellery Circle and possibly another, called SCM. A woman named Jasmine Yip is attached to the Jewellery Circle account, and a woman named Su Na seems to control the SCM account. May Ling Wong helped me get banking information on the Jewellery Circle account, and she may be able to help with SCM. I'll call her later tonight on that."

"You have been busy," Derek said admiringly.

"Yes, but I can't help thinking it will all amount to nothing unless we can break into Evans Trust."

"What is it specifically that you want to know?"

Ava took a deep breath. "Okay, Derek, listen. What I'm about to say can't be repeated to anyone, including Mimi. I need you to promise to keep this strictly between you and me, at least for now."

"You have my word."

"I think there's a chance," she said slowly, "that money is going into Evans Trust from Malcolm Muir, Patrick and

Essie Cunningham, Pastor Sammy Rogers, and the Bible Chapel itself. It could be sent by any one of them, or by a combination. It could be sent from companies they control in Canada."

"That's a lot of connections to chase down."

"I know. Put your major focus on finding out who owns Evans Trust."

Derek was silent for a moment. "Ava, do you really believe that the Bible Chapel would do something like this?"

"The Bible Chapel might have nothing to do with any of it, but that doesn't mean everyone associated with it is so innocent."

"And if they aren't?"

"Then we know where to find them, and that's always a good starting point."

"Yeah, I remember from the old days how that worked," Derek said.

"Call me if you come up with anything. If you can't reach me, send me a text or email," she said. "I'll send you the Evans Trust information as soon as I hang up."

"I'm eager to get started," Derek said, and ended the conversation.

Have I ever involved so many people in a job? Ava thought as she began drafting the email for Derek. Deep down she knew she needed them if she was going to solve this puzzle.

When the email had been sent, she called May Ling.

"Ava, are you okay?" May said when she answered.

"Yes, I'm fine, and I apologize for calling so late in the day again."

"You know that's not a problem. What can I do for you?"

"It's the same bank in Chengdu but a different account. Could you ask your contact about a company called SCM and a woman named Su Na?"

"I don't think he'll be able to do anything tonight, but I'll reach out to him first thing in the morning."

"That will do. And thank you."

Next on Ava's list was Todd Howell. When she told him she wanted him to research whether Muir or Cunningham had set up companies of any kind, his response was, "I'll have my people on this within the hour."

She checked the time when she hung up from Howell, saw it was almost quarter to nine, and rose reluctantly from the desk. She could have made good use of another hour going through the paperwork. She almost wished she hadn't agreed to go to dinner with Han, but it was too late to back out now without causing offence.

The elevator stopped five times on the way to the ground floor, and when she exited she saw Han standing in the lobby by the hotel entrance. She waved and hurried towards him. "Sorry to be a little late. I got caught up in the information the Yang brothers gave us," she said when she reached him.

"*Meiwenti*," he said.

Ava smiled. *Meiwenti* was the Mandarin equivalent of *momentai* in Cantonese, and it meant "no problem." It was a phrase that Uncle had used repeatedly.

"Lu's Land Rover is directly outside," he said.

She followed him through revolving doors to be greeted by a striking young woman standing on the sidewalk next to a black Land Rover. "I'm Ru Shi," the woman said.

Even in flat shoes, Ru Shi towered over Ava. She was more

than six feet tall and slim, with long hair falling onto her shoulders.

"I'm Ava. Pleased to meet you."

"The man driving is my husband, Lu," Ru Shi said. Lu waved at Ava through an open window.

"We should get going," Han said. "They're holding a table for us at the restaurant, but that place is so busy that the owner gets upset if a table isn't being used."

Ava and Ru Shi got into the back seat of the car. As soon as Han closed his front door, they left the hotel and eased into heavy traffic.

"Have you been to Chengdu before?" Ru Shi asked.

"No."

"The city has a lot to offer if you have time to do some sightseeing. There are mountains, forests, and of course the panda bears."

"I don't think I'll be able to do much sightseeing," Ava said. "I'm here on business, and when that's finished I'll have to head home."

"Where is home?"

"Canada."

"I was there once. I went to Vancouver and then to Banff and Jasper. So beautiful, so many mountains and lakes, and the air was so clean and clear," Ru Shi said.

"But they didn't have hotpot like ours," Lu said, turning to smile at Ava.

He was in his mid-thirties, Ava guessed, and clean-shaven, with hair cropped short and no visible tattoos. He was wearing a shirt and jeans that looked as if they had been ironed. His appearance reminded her of Lop, one of Xu's senior men, a former officer in the Special Forces division of the People's Liberation Army.

"Excuse me for asking, but were you in the PLA?" she asked Lu.

"Yes, I was. Why do you ask?"

"You remind me of a friend named Lop. He works with Xu in Shanghai."

"I know Lop, but we didn't meet until both of us had left the service," Lu said. "He's a fine man."

"Yes, he is," Ava said, surprised one more time by the wheels within wheels that existed in the triad world.

They hadn't driven for more than ten minutes before the Land Rover stopped. Ava looked out at a neon sign flashing the name Lao Ma Tou Hotpot. Inside the restaurant she could see a group huddling near the door, and a line of people ran from the door for at least twenty metres along the sidewalk.

Their car was double-parked, but Lu and Han got out of the front seat anyway, and Ava followed Ru Shi out of the rear. A young man ran from the doorway towards them and Lu handed him the car keys. Han led them into the restaurant, where they were greeted by another man, who told them loudly that their table was ready and he'd take them to it.

Lao Ma Tou was packed and the noise level was almost deafening. They were seated at a table set against a wall near the back of the restaurant, which put them on the fringes of the noise rather than in the middle of it.

"Busy place," Ava said.

"It's like this seven days a week, fifty-two weeks a year," said Han.

Ava looked around. "Why do some tables have red pots and others have white?"

"The red pots are the more traditional. They contain chili oil and *hua jiao* peppercorns. The oil is very spicy, very hot, and the peppercorns help numb the mouth," Ru Shi said. "The white pots have chicken broth and sliced mushrooms. It isn't spicy at all."

"What will you have? Red, white, or shall we get both?" Han asked.

"I can't come to Sichuan province and not eat spicy food. I'll have the red," she said.

"My mother believed that our damp Sichuan weather is bad for the bones and circulation. The spicy food helps modify both and balances out the body temperature," Han said. "I don't know or care if that's true. I eat hotpot because I love it."

A server came to the table carrying a tray with bottles of Tsingtao beer and water. Without asking, he set the bottles on the table. Behind him, another server came with a red pot. He put it in an opening in the middle of the table and reached underneath to turn on a burner.

"We come here so often they know our tastes," Ru Shi said. "Is there something else you want to drink, or any special food you'd like to order?"

"I'll drink water, and I'll eat whatever you usually have."

A few minutes later the chili oil began to bubble, and right on cue the servers returned with trays of food that they set on small side tables. Ava recognized beef strips, cucumber, lotus root, bamboo shoots, and chicken kidneys, but two of the meats were foreign to her. She asked Ru Shi what they were.

"Pork liver and duck intestines," Ro Shi said, as she slid portions of everything into the oil.

Ava wasn't sure she wanted to eat duck intestines, but as the meat cooked it took on a rich brown colour that made it look appetizing enough to try. The food bobbed to the surface when it was cooked, and Ru Shi assumed the role of skimming it out with a small metal-mesh basket. She served Ava first, putting a variety of food on her plate. As Ava took a slice of beef in her chopsticks and placed in her mouth, she noticed that the others were watching to see her reaction to real Sichuan hotpot.

The meat was tender. Initially the flavour was mild, but then she felt a burning sensation on the insides of her lips. She waited for it to pass. Instead it lingered and began to expand over her tongue until she felt as if most of her mouth was on fire. She thought about reaching for a glass of water but was too proud to do that. The spiciness wasn't going to defeat her, she thought, and she plucked a piece of pork liver from the plate. As she chewed she started to sweat — not dramatically, but she was sure the beads were visible on her forehead.

"We can get a white pot if that would you suit you better," Han said with a sly smile.

"No, I'm fine with this. The flavour is exceptional," Ava said, quite sure that she wasn't the first visitor they had watched struggle with hotpot. She switched to vegetables and found them less intense. After finishing several bamboo shoots and some cucumber and lotus root, she went back to meat. The chicken kidneys were terrific, and she took more from the pot after she'd finished what was on her plate. She tried the beef again, and this time it wasn't such a shock because, she now realized, her lips were numb from the *hua jiao* peppercorns.

There had been little conversation and a lot of eating at the table. Ru Shi, Lu, and Han all had big appetites and made short work of the first round. When their plates were empty, Han raised an arm in the air.

"We'll be right there with more," a server shouted at him.

Ava took advantage of the break to drink some water. Both Han and Lu had two empty beer bottles in front of them, and Ru Shi had drunk several glasses of water. The restaurant was as busy as when they'd arrived, and Ava saw there were still lines at the door and outside on the street. She was about to comment on that when Lu's phone rang.

"*Wei*," he answered, listened for a few minutes, and then said, "That's good to know. Go back tomorrow morning at nine to see if they maintain that level of security."

"Was that Peng?" Han asked when Lu ended the call.

"Yes," Lu said, and then spoke directly to Ava. "My men went to the warehouse. It didn't seem to be open for business. Most of its lights were out, and the entry gate was locked. There were armed guards at the gate and scattered around the courtyard."

"Armed guards aren't that common in Chengdu," Han said to her.

"Will they be a problem?" Ava asked.

"We'll get you inside. Don't worry about that," Lu said with a quiet intensity that again reminded her of Lop.

Another wave of food arrived, and Ru Shi filled the pot. Ava noticed how calm she was. The prospect of her husband facing down armed guards didn't seem to concern her in the least. But then she was the daughter of a Mountain Master and married to a Red Pole. How much violence had she witnessed over the years?

"Ru Shi, do you have any siblings?" Ava asked.

"I'm an only child. My mother died shortly after giving birth to me."

"Ru Shi is a great daughter," Han said. "More children couldn't have made me happier and prouder than she has."

Ru Shi blushed and said to Ava, "Do you have siblings?"

"I have a sister in Canada, four half-brothers in Hong Kong, and a half-brother and half-sister in Australia," Ava said. "That sounds more complicated than it is. My father has three wives, and somehow he seems to make it work. I'm the younger daughter of the second wife."

"And Xu refers to her as his *mei mei*," Han said. "So it seems she's part of another family as well."

"I hope I can help my father and my husband half as much as you've helped Xu," Ru Shi said.

Ava looked uncomfortable.

"Lam has told me stories about you, and I related them to Lu and my daughter. There's no reason to be modest," Han said. "There's a lot to admire in a woman who can use a gun, think her way through any problem, and manage tough men."

"I don't manage any men, and I don't have a gun," Ava said, shaking her head. "So I hope you aren't expecting me to lead a charge into that warehouse. I'd rather depend on Lu's talents to get inside."

"My husband will get you into the warehouse, and you won't need a gun," Ru Shi said.

(30)

IT WAS WELL PAST ELEVEN WHEN AVA RETURNED TO THE Ritz-Carlton. There had been a third round of food, which she left mainly to the others, and two more bottles of beer for Han, each bottle making him more loquacious. As well as having met Uncle, Han had known Xu's father, and he regaled the table with stories he'd heard about their early lives as triads in Fanling, a town in Hong Kong's New Territories.

Lu said very little — another Lop trait — but Ru Shi shared her father's enjoyment of conversation, and all it took was one question from Ava about her children to unleash a torrent of tales. What pleased Ava was how attentive Han and Lu were when she spoke, and how proud they seemed of the children's exploits.

When they reached the hotel, Ava and Ru Shi shared a hug in the back seat. Han watched with a grin spread across his face. "What did you really think of our hotpot?" he asked Ava.

"It was wonderful, but my lips are still numb."

"It will wear off in an hour or so," he said, and then turned to Lu. "What time do you think will be best to pick up Ava tomorrow?"

"My men will scout the warehouse at nine. Once I know what we're dealing with, I'll formulate a plan and then call Ava to make arrangements."

"I'll stay in my room until I hear from you," she said.

"That's perfect."

Ava entered the lobby and rode the elevator to the forty-first floor. She didn't notice anything out of the ordinary until the elevator started its ascent and she saw the other passenger twitching his nose. It was then that the smell of chili oil penetrated her senses. She hadn't been aware of it in the car, but in the elevator's confined space it was unavoidably pungent. The man exited on the thirty-fifth floor, leaving Ava on her own. She smelled her shirt. It reeked of oil, and she was sure her hair and slacks were equally imbued.

She stripped as soon as she entered the suite and put everything in a laundry bag. A long, hot shower was the next thing on her to-do list, but before going into the bathroom she opened her laptop to see if there were any messages. Her phone had been quiet during dinner, which surprised her, because if nothing else she thought Fai would have called or texted. Instead she had emailed.

Andy has organized a dinner in the countryside for cast and crew. We're going by bus and I don't expect to be back at the hotel until very late. He has given us the day off tomorrow to compensate for what will be a boozy evening. I'll call you in the morning once I'm in shape. Love you, miss you. Fai

Ava replied. I just got back to my hotel after dinner at a famous hotpot restaurant. I feel like I've been dipped in chili oil so I'm just about to jump in the shower—although showers aren't close to being the same when you aren't having one with me. Talk to you in the morning. Love, Ava

Fifteen minutes later she emerged from the bathroom in a T-shirt and underpants, with her damp hair wrapped in a towel. The smell of chili oil was gone, replaced by the aroma of Asprey Purple Water shampoo, a Ritz-Carlton amenity. She had drunk only water during dinner and was in the mood for a nightcap. The mini-bar was well stocked; she took out a bottle of Chardonnay, poured a glass, and sat down at the desk. She opened her notebook at the first page, then slowly tracked her progress. It hadn't been a smooth journey, but she liked where she was. Even if May, Howell, and Derek didn't deliver, she had Su Na firmly in her sights, and with the assistance of Han and his gang Ava couldn't imagine that Su would be able to avoid dealing with her.

She also had the password for the Jewellery Circle account at the Mercantile Bank, which would give her access to the next large deposit when it was made. Jasmine had promised to call her when money was due to arrive, but Ava made a mental note to check the account herself every day in case Jasmine had a change of heart. That money wouldn't come close to covering what was stolen, but it might help make the Gregory family whole, and that, after all, had been her initial goal.

Ava closed the notebook, poured another glass of wine, and went into the bathroom to dry her hair. It had been a long day, and she suddenly felt tired. She turned off the hair dryer, drained her glass, and headed to the bedroom. After removing six pillows from the king-size bed, leaving her with two, she crawled under the white duvet. She was asleep in seconds.

For once she didn't dream, or at least she had no memory of dreaming when she woke at seven to go to the bathroom. As she was thinking about returning to bed, her phone rang. Still half asleep, she stared at it until the fourth ring brought her into the present. She looked at the screen and was suddenly alert.

"Hey," she said.

"I know it's early where you are, but you did tell me to call if I found anything," said Derek.

"Did you manage to hack into Evans Trust?"

"Not quite — they have a very strong security system. But I did manage to find a bug in their database that was open to exploitation. I wasn't able to get into their financial records, but I did find their articles of incorporation, and I thought that might be of interest," Derek said. "The CEO is a guy named Ronald Evans. He has an address in Tulsa, Oklahoma."

"Sammy Rogers went to a bible college in Oklahoma," Ava said quickly.

"I'm coming to that," Derek said.

"Sorry. Go on."

"I looked into Evans. He's a lawyer in Tulsa. The other two names in the articles of incorporation are employees of the same law firm. When I investigated the firm, what did I find?" Derek said, and paused dramatically. "It has two major clients: Blackstone Simmons and the Simmons Christian Ministry."

"SCM must be the initials of the Simmons Christian Ministry," Ava said.

"That's what it sure as hell looks like," Derek said.

"And the Simmons family and Sammy Rogers are tight."

"We know that's true."

Ava recalculated what she knew about the flow of money. "I bet Evans and his people are holding shares in trust. Like Jasmine Yip, they're just a front for the people who actually run the business. I'd give anything to find out who authorizes transfers from the Evans Trust account to Golden Emperor on behalf of SCM, and to the Jewellery Circle account at the Mercantile Bank."

"I'll try to get into the system again. But Ava, I'm not very confident I'll succeed," Derek said. "Do you think Simmons and Rogers are partners in this?"

"It seems obvious they're co-operating with each other at some level, but they also appear to be keeping their money separate. If they were partners, why would they each have their own bank account, and why would they be operating two different companies?"

"On that point, I noticed that Evans Trust was incorporated more than two years before Muir even started the Harvest Investment Fund."

"Which suggests that Blackstone Simmons found a way to make a lot of money that didn't involve fleecing his congregation, and either he or his son Randy told Rogers about it. Maybe Rogers is just piggybacking on their idea and using the system they established."

"You seem very confident that Rogers is involved."

"If he isn't, then it means Patrick Cunningham conceived and executed this operation himself. On the surface I don't think that's likely. And if we're right that SCM does stand for Simmons Christian Ministry, Rogers would have been their first point of contact, not Cunningham or Muir."

"This is all so unbelievable."

"It's strange and very complicated, but to me it's entirely believable," Ava said. "In any event, we'll know the truth soon enough."

Derek sighed. "I'm going to take the baby for a walk. It will help clear my head. When I get back, I'll start digging again."

"You've already been a huge help," she said. "Kiss Amber for me."

After Derek hung up, Ava remained seated on the edge of the bed. Her mind was so active she knew she wouldn't be able to sleep. If SCM was the Simmons Christian Ministry—and she didn't doubt that it was—that explained Evans Trust and the warehouse that Jewellery Circle shared with SCM. What it didn't prove was that they were partners in a business. From Ava's viewpoint, it was better that they weren't, because it would be easier to focus on Harvest Table. It was the money they'd stolen that she was after, not money that originated from God knows where in the United States.

She made an espresso, sat down at the desk, and opened her notebook to the chart she had started constructing to visually lay out the web of people, banks, and companies involved. She had Muir, the Amsterdam bank, Jasmine Yip, Fozdar, diamond cutters in Guangzhou, the Mercantile Bank, Su Na, Golden Emperor MicroLab, Patrick and Essie Cunningham, Evans Trust, and the SCM warehouse. Now she added *Sammy Rogers* with a question mark next to his name and contemplated whether she should include the Simmons family. She shook her head. As she looked at all the interconnecting lines she decided it was convoluted enough. Still, she couldn't ignore Simmons.

She opened the laptop, entered "Simmons Christian

Ministry," and accessed the ministry's website. She scanned the banner and then hit "Board of Directors." The board was charted like a pyramid, with a photo of Blackstone Simmons — looking like a distinguished and successful banker — at its peak. Beneath him were two former politicians whose names Ava recognized, plus Ronald Evans. On the lowest level were Randy Simmons, three people identified as heads of corporations, and two doctors of unidentified disciplines.

She closed that tab and switched to one titled "Corporate Team." It was a large group, with the senior Simmons again at the top of the heap as CEO, Randy listed as the COO, and Ronald Evans identified as corporate legal counsel. Ava didn't recognize any other name, although she noticed that a John Kelsey was vice-president of foreign missions. She made a note of his name, returned to the banner, and saw a tab for foreign missions. She opened it and read a statement of objectives that was eerily similar to the one included in the Harvest Investment Fund prospectus. Simmons Foreign Missions were committed to bringing education, better health, and the word of Jesus to those most in need around the world.

She scrolled down the page until she came to a list of missions. Two things surprised her. First, there were supposedly thirty-one missions at work; second, between Burundi and Djibouti in the alphabetical list was Chengdu, China. Ava searched the site for more specific information about the mission in Chengdu, but found nothing. Regardless, there was now a confirmed link between the Simmons ministry and Chengdu.

Ava made another espresso and stared down at the city

square, which was slowly welcoming the day. She contemplated what the morning might have in store for her. She hoped she would hear from Todd Howell and May Ling before going to the warehouse. She hoped even more strongly that Su Na would be at the warehouse when she got there.

Ava checked the time. If Lu was as efficient as Lop, he would scout the warehouse at nine as promised and be ready to act soon. She wanted to be ready to go when he called. If she showered and dressed quickly, she would still have time for breakfast. As she was deciding how to construct her morning, her phone rang. Thinking it would be May Ling or Todd Howell, she answered without looking at the incoming number.

"Good morning, this is Lu."

"I didn't expect to hear from you so soon," Ava said.

"I'm an early riser, and when there's a job to be done, I'm always anxious to get at it."

Yet another Lop trait, she thought, and then asked, "Have your men reported from the warehouse?"

"I decided to go myself. I'm sitting in front of it right now. The guards changed shifts half an hour ago. Ten new guards arrived in a minivan. Two of them are at the gate and there are eight in and around the building," Lu said. "Five minutes after the guards got here, a woman arrived in a Mercedes. The guards saluted her. I don't think it's a stretch to assume she's the woman you're looking for."

Ava tried to restrain a burst of excitement. "Will the guards be a problem?"

"That depends on their competence and commitment. I'll have ten of my men here within the next hour, and they'll be well armed. I'm also bringing a truck in case we have to crash the gate. Oh, and my *yuefu* wants to take part. Despite his age and position there's nothing he likes more than a fight."

"Han has already done so much for me. That isn't necessary," Ava said.

"When he says he's going to do something, there isn't much point in arguing. The best thing to do is simply say thank you. All that's left to decide is when you want us to get you into the warehouse."

"I can be ready to leave the hotel in half an hour."

"Fine. I'll call Han and let him know."

Ava smiled as she put down the phone. This Chengdu gang seemed to be as professional as Xu's, and that was saying a lot. But she wasn't going to take anything for granted when it came to her choice of clothes. If she was dragged into a scrap at the warehouse, she wanted to have as much freedom of movement as possible. That meant slacks and flat shoes.

Ava showered quickly, brushed her teeth and hair, dressed, and put on a touch of mascara and red lipstick. She slipped her notebook and phone into her bag. She tried to think if there was anything that might make an impression on Su Na and decided there wasn't. The information she had in her head and in the notebook was damning enough.

Ava left the room and hurried to the elevator. When she reached the lobby, she went directly to the hotel entrance. The Haval was already there with Han and the driver in front and the back door open and waiting for her.

"Good morning, Han," she said as she climbed in.

"Good morning to you. How are you feeling? Did the hotpot cause you any discomfort?"

"I'm fine, thank you."

"Good." Turning to Willie, who was driving, Han said, "Take us to the warehouse."

As the car pulled away from the curb, Han reached down to steady a large pistol that was sitting on top of the console. Ava was surprised to see it so brazenly left in the open. It looked like a SIG Sauer. Sonny had owned one for a few years before switching to a Cobray. When he did, he had offered the SIG Sauer to Ava, but it was far too large for her hand and she knew she'd never be able to handle it properly.

"Is that a SIG Sauer?" she asked Han.

"Yes. I was going to bring something bigger, but I thought that might be overkill. This should do the trick."

Ava blinked. She couldn't tell if Han was joking.

He looked back at her and smiled. "I don't expect I'll have to use it. This is the kind of gun that gets respect just by waving it in the air."

"Let's hope that's all you have to do."

"Either way, we'll have some fun."

(31)

THE MORNING RUSH-HOUR TRAFFIC WAS HEAVY AS they made their way across the city to Longquanyi. Han stayed in touch with Lu by phone, keeping him updated on their progress. At one point he gave his phone to Ava. "Lu wants to talk to you."

"I thought you'd like to know that for the past twenty minutes there's been a steady stream of people heading into the warehouse. I've seen fifty or more, and they're mainly women."

Ava looked at her watch. "They must start work at ten. Have you seen any other sign of the woman who arrived in the Mercedes?"

"No, but she was well dressed compared to the women who have been arriving recently."

"It has to be Su Na."

Lu paused. "The boss tells me you're only ten minutes from the warehouse, so you'll find out soon enough."

"We'll see you in ten," Ava said and handed the phone back to Han. "Lu is confident that Su Na is in the building. He's a first-rate Red Pole."

"He also has a good mind for numbers. I've been thinking of making him my White Paper Fan. He won't want to change, but I've got my daughter and grandchildren to think about. This isn't a city with a lot of gunplay, but however much there is, the Red Pole is usually in the middle of it. I don't want to risk losing him."

"Is that why you and the SIG Sauer are coming along with us this morning?"

Han looked at her in the rear-view mirror. "You bet your life it is. Though if things go well it might also help me sweeten my deal with Xu."

"If things go well, I'll make sure that happens —"

"We're almost at the warehouse," Willie interrupted. "I can see a couple of our guys ahead."

"Pull over and park. We'll walk from here," Han said. As they got out of the car, he tucked the gun into the front waistband of his jeans and covered it with his shirt.

Lu waved at them from his car. Han moved towards him with considerable agility and speed. Ava increased her pace to keep up.

When they reached Lu, he said, "We'll have to persuade them to unlock the gate."

Han nodded. "Follow me."

Ava walked between Han and Lu. Fanned out behind them were ten triads, all with guns in various modes of disguise.

There were three guards on the other side of the gate. They stared as Ava's group approached but didn't move, keeping their rifles across their chests. Past the gate was a courtyard, and behind it was a three-storey brick building with one metal entrance door in the middle and three loading docks on the right. The doors to the docks were closed. The ground floor had no windows, those on the second were boarded up, and there was a row of glass windows on the third level.

"Open this fucking gate!" Han shouted when he reached it.

The guards paled and glanced right and left, waiting for someone to respond.

"I said, open this fucking gate. We have an appointment with Su Na."

"We have to confirm that," the guard in the middle stuttered.

"Confirm this," Han said, pulling the SIG Sauer from his jeans and pointing it at him. As he did, the other triads pulled out their own weapons.

"Don't be foolish," Lu said. "You're angering our boss for no real reason. All we want is to talk to your boss. So open the gate and let us in. If you don't, then I expect my boss will lose his temper — and you do not want that to happen."

"*Open the fucking gate!*" Han roared.

The guard in the middle took a few hesitant steps forward, then turned and began to run towards the warehouse. "Follow me," he shouted to the others.

Han aimed his gun at him but didn't fire.

"We'll have to use the truck," Lu said. "We'll follow it through the gate and gather at the wall. We can figure out how to get into the building from there."

"Why don't you go back to my car until we get inside," Han said to Ava. "I'll send someone to get you."

"That's very considerate, but I'm going in with you."

Han looked ready to argue but said, "I guess I shouldn't be surprised."

Lu gave instructions to his men and a few minutes later

the truck arrived. It was a massive Volvo 800 rig with a reinforced front bumper that had a metal horn extending from it. Lu went to speak to the driver.

"That looks big enough," Han said.

The truck drove up to the gate and then reversed until it was fifty metres away. Lu and his men stood to one side and Han and Ava joined them. The truck revved its engine and then lurched forward. Ava had no idea what speed it reached in fifty metres, but it was enough to collapse the gate.

Lu and his men surged through, followed by Ava and Han. They congregated against the wall on both sides of the metal entrance door. Lu went to the door, turned the handle, and found it locked. "We can try the doors at the loading docks or go around the building and look for another entrance," he said.

"Who are you people?" a voice shouted from above.

"Who are you?" Han replied.

"My name is Zhong. I'm head of security here."

"I'm Han. Stop being so stupid. All we want is to talk to your boss. We told the guards that," Han said. "We know you're warehousing drugs, but we don't give a shit. We're not here to steal them."

There was a pause and Zhong said, "You look like Mr. Han the triad leader."

"That's who I am."

"What are you really doing here?"

"I told you. I have a friend with me. She wants to speak to Su Na. Send someone downstairs to unlock this door."

Zhong hesitated. "We don't want any trouble."

"Neither do we, which is why I didn't shoot your guards when I had the chance."

"Okay, I'm coming down. Please tell your men to put away their guns."

Han looked at Lu. "Move the men away from the door. Tell them there's to be no gunfire unless the other side starts it."

Ava stood by the door with Han, and Lu joined them after speaking to his men. A moment later they heard the sound of heavy boots hitting wooden steps. Then the door slowly opened and a solidly built man appeared. He was wearing the same uniform as the guards but with two gold stars on his epaulettes.

"I'm Zhong," he said.

"Where are your men?" Lu asked.

"They're all inside."

"Tell them to come out. They can stand with me until we're finished here."

"Where is Su Na?" asked Han.

"Upstairs in her office."

"Take us to her."

"She's quite upset by this. She wanted me to call in extra security. I talked her out of it when I realized it was Mr. Han himself paying us a visit."

"How do you know me?" Han asked.

"With all respect, sir, there aren't many people in my business who don't."

"Take us to her," Han repeated.

Zhong led them into the building. Ava looked around. "They don't use this floor?" she asked Zhong.

"Everyone works upstairs," he said, pointing to the left. "We'll take those stairs."

Zhong began to climb the flight of wooden stairs, with

Ava and Han trailing behind. When they reached the top, they were confronted by a heavy steel door with an access pad on the wall next to it. Zhong punched in a six-number code and pulled the door open. Ava immediately heard the animated voices of a large number of women.

The room was as big as the one on the ground floor, and it was fully occupied. Ava did a quick head count. There were twenty worktables on which sat white envelopes, computer printouts, and an assortment of small brown boxes. Two or three women sat at every station. Ava walked over to closest and watched one of the women address an envelope. She was writing in English, her handwriting impeccable.

"Ms. Su's office is on the upper floor," Zhong said, pointing to another set of stairs.

"Just a minute," Ava said, then spoke to the woman who was writing. "What goes into that envelope?"

The woman looked at Zhong. "Tell her," he said.

The woman reached into one of the brown boxes and took out a handful of small white pills. "It could be some of these or some of the others. The printout tells us what goes in."

"Where are you sending the pills?"

"These are going to the United States."

"Thank you for the information," said Ava.

"The women work in teams," Zhong said from behind her. "While one writes, the others prepare the order."

"Wouldn't it be more efficient to print the addresses on labels and stick them on the envelopes?" Ava asked.

"You'll have to ask Ms. Su about that," he said.

"Then let's go and see her," Ava said.

They climbed the second set of stairs and entered an open

office surrounded by a series of closed wooden doors with small brass plates that read ACCOUNTING, SHIPPING ND RECEIVING, SALES AND MARKETING, and SECURITY. Zhong approached a door that read SU NA, DIRECTOR, SIMMONS CHRISTIAN MISSION and knocked. "Ms. Su, it's Zhong. I believe it is safe for you to open the door."

Ava heard the sound of shoes clicking on tile, then the door swung open and a small middle-aged woman stood in its frame. Without heels, Ava guessed she would be about five foot three. She wasn't wearing makeup, which gave her a washed-out appearance that was accentuated by heavy black eyebrows. There were deep wrinkles at the corners of her eyes and along each side of her mouth. Her hair was short, fluffy, and carefully brushed towards the front to cover a bald spot. She had on a pink Chanel jacket and skirt with red trim. There was a white jade bracelet on one wrist and a thick gold bracelet on the other. The diamond studs in her ears looked large enough to be one carat each, and around her neck hung a platinum crucifix encrusted in what Ava assumed were rubies.

"Who are you?" Su asked.

"My name is Ava Lee."

"I wasn't speaking to you," Su said with a touch of defiance. "I was talking to the man."

"Who I am doesn't matter," Han said. "It's Ms. Lee who has business with you, so I suggest you listen to what she has to say."

Su looked up at Han, her eyes fixed on his scar. "Zhong told me you run the triads in Chengdu. Is that true?"

"Yes."

"Whatever this woman is paying you, I'm willing to pay

more if you leave my place of business at once and take her with you."

"That's not how this works," Han said, his voice taking on an edge. "Ava is a friend. We're here to support her."

"Support her how? I don't know her. I've never heard of her. I have no idea what she's doing here," Su said, and then looked at Zhong. "Isn't there anything you can do to stop this nonsense?"

"I don't want to start any trouble with Mr. Han. Truthfully, Ms. Su, I suggest you co-operate."

"All I want is to talk," Ava said, inserting herself into the conversation. "I have some questions about your business I need you to answer."

Su shook her head. "I have no interest in talking to you."

"I don't think it's wise to take that kind of attitude. I'm not going anywhere until we have spoken," Ava said. "My first preference is that you do so voluntarily, but if you want to be difficult, I am sure Mr. Han can persuade you to co-operate."

"I'm not frightened of you," Su snapped.

Ava felt Han move before she actually saw him slap Su across the side of the face. It didn't register until she saw Su crash backwards into the side of the door frame.

"I don't make a habit of hitting women, but in your case I'm making an exception," Han said. "You will talk to Ava and you will answer her questions. Tell me if that isn't clear enough."

Su held her hand against her cheek. Her eyes were watering and her mouth gaped open. She looked at Zhong as if she expected him to do something, but his head was turned away. "Are you going to let him to do that to me?" she said tearfully.

"I don't see what harm can come from speaking to the woman," Zhong said.

Su glared at him, then looked up at Han, whose face was impassive but menacing all the same. She wiped her eyes. "Okay, I'll talk to her, but I don't want to be beaten if I can't answer her questions."

First with the Yang brothers and now with Su, Han had brought his particular style of negotiating to bear. Ava would have preferred to get their co-operation her own way, but she couldn't deny that Han was effective.

"All I want is for you to be truthful. If you are, then you'll have nothing to fear," Ava said to Su. "Mr. Han, I think I can take things from here." She looked into the office. "We'll go in here. There's ample room."

"Do you want me to sit in with you?" he asked.

"Yes, I think that would be a good idea," Ava said, mindful of how helpful Han's physical presence was. "But we don't need Zhong."

"I'll go outside and join my men," he said, sounding pleased to get away.

Su turned and shuffled into the office with Ava and Han following. Su went behind a large grey metal desk and started to sit down, only to be interrupted by Ava. "I'll sit there. You sit next to Han," she said.

Su looked uncertain, but before she could say anything Ava took the seat behind the desk. As Su sat down, Ava took the notebook from her bag and turned to a page near the middle.

"The reason I'm here is that some friends of mine had money stolen from them. I won't get into the details of it, except to say that I'm trying to find out where that money ended up," Ava said.

"I have no idea what you're talking about," Su Na said.

"That's not important," Ava said. "Now, I'm going to start by simply reading some names. I want you to tell me if you have met or know of any of these people or organizations. A simple yes or no will be sufficient as an answer. Do you need this explained?"

"No," Su said, struggling to get comfortable on a chair that was a little high for her. She crossed and re-crossed her legs several times before just letting them dangle.

"Okay, let's get started," Ava said. "The first name on my list is Malcolm Muir. Do you know him?"

"No," Su said.

Ava closed her eyes and sighed. "That's a lie."

Han's massive right hand reached out and grabbed one of Su's legs just above the kneecap. He squeezed. She whimpered. He squeezed harder, and the whimper turned into a loud moan. "This isn't a good way to start," he said.

"Do you know Malcolm Muir?" Ava repeated.

"Yes," she blurted.

Han took his hand off her leg but left it hovering in the air above the knee.

"How about Patrick Cunningham, Sammy Rogers, Blackstone Simmons, Randy Simmons, and Ronald Evans?"

"I know them all, except for Evans."

Ava glanced down at her notebook. "Have you ever been to Vanuatu?"

"No. Why I would go there?"

"So you had no involvement in establishment of the Evans Trust Company?"

Su shook her head.

"But you know of it."

"Of course. They help finance us."

"We'll come back to Evans Trust later," Ava said, leaning across the desk. "First I want to talk about how you came to know the others."

(32)

AVA HAD GONE THROUGH THE NAMES IN THE ORDER she'd come across them. Now it was time to go back. "Who did you start doing business with first, the Simmons organization or Malcolm Muir?"

"Simmons."

"How did that relationship begin?" she asked.

"I'm a Christian," Su said. She bit her lower lip and looked at Ava. "It's a bit of a long story."

"I have lots of time."

"I'm from Chengdu. I went to university here then worked for a pharmaceutical company in Shanghai. One of the women I worked with was a devout Christian. We became friends, and I started to attend social events at her church. It was an Evangelical Baptist church. I was uncomfortable at first with the emotional intensity of the people there." Su paused. "Am I boring you yet?"

"No. Keep going."

"Apart from being uncomfortable with the emotions, there was also an element of danger attached to the church. It was an underground operation, frowned on by the government and a candidate to be raided at any time. Some of the members found that exhilarating, but it just scared me. I was thinking about ending the relationship with my friend when she asked me to join her at a religious event in a nearby town where the officials didn't hassle Christians," Su said. "I went with her, as much to get out of the city for a while as anything else. The event was part of a crusade that Blackstone Simmons was conducting in Asia. They held it in a small sports stadium and the atmosphere was electric. When Blackstone spoke, he touched my heart and my soul, and when he asked people to come forward and commit their lives to Christ, I did. I committed that night, and I have committed every day since."

"How did that get you into the Simmons organization?"

"The crusade was a week long. I went every night, and by the end of the week I had met Randy Simmons. The fact that I spoke English well and had a university education and some knowledge about pharmaceuticals interested him. Before he left, he asked me if I would consider working with them. They needed someone in China with business and management ability, someone they could communicate with. He asked me if I was willing to leave Shanghai."

"Why leave Shanghai?"

"They were running into government opposition there and wanted to operate where there was less prejudice. I told him I was from Chengdu and willing to go back."

"And when you did, you found yourself running a drug-dealing business."

"You have no idea what you're talking about," Su said loudly and then looked at Han as if expecting him to strike her.

"Then how do you explain what those women are doing on the floor below?" Ava asked.

"We're saving Christian souls from unnecessary pain and suffering. That is our one and only mission."

"Whose mission? The Simmons organization?"

"Randy explained to me how expensive the medical system is in the United States, how people who were ill and even dying don't have access to drugs to alleviate their suffering, because they can't afford them."

"So that's what you've been doing? Sending painkillers to people who can't afford to buy them otherwise?"

"Yes."

"Are you aware that several of those painkillers are highly addictive?"

"We can't be held responsible if people misuse their medicine."

"No, of course not," Ava said, knowing it was pointless to argue. "How soon after you returned to Chengdu did you start this business?"

"It was only a matter of weeks. Randy Simmons had already found a lab to supply the pills. We started very small, of course, and I was sending the pills in bulk at first. I worked out of my apartment. I did that for a year before we found a place and hired some staff. Even then it took a few more years before we had grown enough to move into the warehouse."

"Where were you sending the pills?"

"I sent some directly to Randy, but after a few months we had pharmacies, doctors, and pain clinics buying directly from us."

"Where were they located?"

"Mainly in the southern states at first, because that's where the Simmons organization is located, but we have expanded from there."

"How did you send the pills in bulk? Surely not in little white envelopes."

Su lowered her head, and Ava felt her discomfort.

"I don't care how you did it," Ava said. "I'm only after information. I'm not passing judgement."

"We hollowed out the insides of Bibles and filled them with pills. We wrapped the Bibles in plastic and put them in special large brown envelopes. The envelopes had Jesus on the cross embossed in red on the front, and 'A Gift of Thanks for Your Donation to the Christian Children's Foundation' printed underneath."

"Whose idea was that?"

"Randy's."

"You're still shipping them like that?"

"We do if the order is large enough, but most of our business now is smaller individual orders."

"You send those in the hand-addressed white envelopes I saw on the tables downstairs?"

"Yes. That business began about four years ago. It started slowly, but as our website traffic grew it became about half of our volume."

"You aren't worried about the U.S. Postal Service figuring out what you're doing?"

"We send the mail from different locations in China. The pills are wrapped so they can't be detected unless you're really searching for them," she said. "And all the painkillers we send are legal to use."

"And what is your website called?"

"It's called www.healthepain.com."

"That's appropriate," Ava said dryly. "Now let's talk about money for a moment. I know you're buying pills from Golden Emperor MicroLab —"

"How do you know that?" Su interrupted.

"Mr. Han and I met with the Yang brothers yesterday. They were quite forthcoming. I know that you're buying from them and they're being paid from an account at the Mercantile Bank of Chengdu that you control."

Su stared across the desk at her, and Ava saw her resistance fading.

"What I want to know," Ava continued, "is where the money you transfer to Golden Emperor originates."

"We get all our money from Evans Trust."

"You told me earlier that you don't know Ronald Evans. Is that still your position?"

"It is. I don't know the man at all, and I know nothing about the company except that our money comes from them. That's been the financial structure since the day I took this job."

"And you never asked Randy Simmons about Evans Trust?"

"I'm not particularly curious, and I always assumed that if Randy wanted me to know more about Evans he would tell me."

Ava made a note, then said, "How does the system work? Who decides when and how the money reaches your account?"

"We maintain an inventory of goods at the warehouse. When it needs to be replenished, I tell Randy what has to be bought. Normally the money is then sent to our Mercantile account from Evans within a day or two, although occasionally Evans will send it directly to Golden Emperor. I don't know why that is, and I haven't asked. But when the money comes to me, I place an order and transfer the money from our account to Golden Emperor when we receive our goods."

"You're the one who negotiates prices with the Yangs?"

"I went to school with one of the brothers, so there's a relationship. I also know quite a bit about pharmaceuticals."

"Do you negotiate pricing for Malcolm Muir as well?"

"No, they do that for themselves. In fact, they do everything for themselves except package and ship their orders."

"How are Muir and his people selling your products in Canada? Are you shipping pills in bibles or in white envelopes?"

"Both. I'd say it's about an even split."

Ava made another note and this time underlined it. "The Yangs told me that Muir often visits Chengdu. When he comes, do you see him?"

"Yes, he always visits the warehouse. We review the business and discuss fees. We also usually have dinner together."

"What kind of man is he?"

Su had been only glancing intermittently at Ava as she answered her questions, but now she looked directly at her. "He's the one who truly interests you, isn't he. The Canadian business is the reason you're here."

She's sharp, Ava thought as she calculated a response. "If it is, does that represent any particular difficulty for you?" she said.

"I work for the Simmons Ministry."

"Are you telling me you don't care about Muir?"

"Of course, I care, but he's only a customer," Su said. "If I knew for certain that's where your interest is and that you have no issue with the rest of our business, it would make for an easier conversation."

Ava hesitated, then said, "My primary interest is in Muir. Whatever else you're doing here is between you and the Simmons organization and between the Simmons family and God."

Su Na nodded. "Then ask your questions."

"What kind of man is Muir?"

"I don't like him," the woman said quickly.

"Why not?"

"He's rude and a bit of a bully. Whenever he's here he argues with me constantly about our fees. He always wants them reduced, and if I tell him they're going up, he gets very angry. If I refuse to back down — which I usually do — he threatens to go to Randy or Pastor Simmons and tell them I'm gouging him."

"Does he threaten to go directly to them?" Ava asked.

"Actually, he says he'll ask Patrick Cunningham or Pastor Rogers to deliver the message to Tulsa."

"When I asked you earlier if you knew the names Patrick Cunningham and Pastor Sammy Rogers, you said yes. Have you met them?"

"I've met Cunningham. He came here with the others."

"Which others?"

"Randy and Muir."

"When was that?"

"Just before we started doing business with Muir. Randy showed them our operation, and I explained how things worked. There were several dinners, a few more visits to the warehouse, and then Randy told me that Harvest Table

Bible Chapel was going to do in Canada what the Simmons Christian Ministry was doing in the U.S., and that our warehouse would be their supplier."

"Was Pastor Rogers with them?"

"No."

"Do you have any records from that visit?"

"I have pictures on my phone," she said. "I believe there's some with them standing next to our girls as they were putting pills in a Bible, and there's one with me that the floor manager took."

"Can I see those?"

"My phone is in my purse, in the lower right-hand drawer of the desk."

Ava opened the drawer, took out a Michael Kors bag, and passed it to Su, who tapped the screen, scrolled, and handed the phone back. "I don't take many pictures," she said. "I don't know why I decided to take these, except that it seemed like an important occasion."

"It's fortunate that you did," Ava said, looking at the first picture. It was of a smiling Malcolm Muir standing between Randy Simmons and a skinny, gaunt-faced man with a buzz cut who barely came to Simmons's shoulder. They were facing the camera with their backs to the women and the tables. What the women were doing was unclear.

"I've never seen Cunningham," Ava said, turning the phone towards Su. "Is that him to the right of Muir?"

"Yes."

"He looks a bit angry."

"I think it's his natural disposition," Su said.

Ava moved on to the next photo and smiled. Su Na, Cunningham, and Muir were standing directly over a box of white pills that a woman was funnelling into a Bible. The Bible's front cover wasn't visible, but in the next photo Muir held it in front of his chest. Ava didn't have to see any more. She put the phone down on the desk.

"Will you forward these photos to me?"

"I'm nervous about the ones that have Randy Simmons in them."

"I don't need those. Send me the rest. I'll give you my phone number and email address."

"I'll get them to you before you leave the warehouse."

"There's something else I want you to send me," Ava said. "I assume you have copies of your correspondence with Muir."

"I do."

"Are the shipping orders included?"

"Yes. There are hundreds of them."

"Could you send me representative samples for each year?"

"Who's going to see them?" Su asked after a slight hesitation. "I don't want any trouble with the government."

"They're for my personal use."

"I don't know what that means, but I guess it doesn't matter. I'll give the information to you," Su said. "Do you promise to keep our organization out of this?"

"I told you I would, and I will."

"Okay," Su said, and then pointed to a workstation in the corner. "If you want, I'll start sending you the information now."

"That would be wonderful. But before you start, I do have to say something unpleasant," Ava said. "You are not to discuss what happened here this morning with anyone at all. Not with Randy Simmons, certainly not with Muir, and not even with Zhong. Speak to no one."

"Listen to her and do what she wants," Han said. "I don't want to have to come back here."

"I won't say a word."

"Keep it business as usual."

"I will. But am I right in suspecting that it won't be business as usual with Canada for much longer?"

"That's a distinct possibility," Ava said.

(33)

AVA AND HAN LEFT SU'S OFFICE FIFTY MINUTES LATER. She had stood over Su's shoulder, choosing which emails she wanted her to forward. The first few years went quickly, but as they got more recent the number of shipping requests increased dramatically, a pattern that made sense, given the larger orders Muir had been sending to Golden Emperor.

When they were finished, Ava thanked Su and reminded her one more time that what had transpired in the office was to stay there. Su walked Ava and Han to her office door. Before her visitors could leave, she said, "Mr. Han, may I ask you something?"

"Go ahead," he said.

"I understand that you are here as a gesture of friendship for Ms. Lee. But in the future, would you consider helping me if the need arose?"

"That would depend on what you wanted me to do, but I would be willing to listen to any reasonable proposal."

"What if I wanted to replace the security company I'm using now with your organization?"

"You want us to provide you with security?"

"That's my general idea."

"I would have to discuss it with my executive committee. And we'd have to canvass the men to see if there was an appetite for that kind of work," Han said. "The money you'd be willing to pay would also matter."

"Why don't I put together a rough proposal and send it to you."

"Yeah, you do that," Han said, reaching into a jeans pocket. "Here's my business card."

"You'll hear from me in a few days."

Ava and Han started down the stairs. "That was a surprise," Ava said. "I guess you made a powerful impression."

Lu walked towards them. "How did it go?"

"It couldn't have gone much better," Ava said.

"What do you want to do now?"

"I want to go back to the hotel. I have some phone calls to make."

"How much longer do you think you'll be staying in Chengdu?" Han asked.

"If the flight schedules co-operate, I could be leaving as soon as tonight."

"You don't believe in sitting still, do you," Han said.

"If you don't keep moving, all you're doing is giving the person you're after more time to think up ways of avoiding you."

"My daughter is the same way. She hates procrastination," Han said, turning to Lu. "Isn't that right?"

"I know that only too well," Lu said.

"That makes me like her even more," Ava said as she climbed into the back of the Haval.

Willie made a U-turn and headed west. Ava rested her

head against the back seat. She knew she had enough hard information to go after Harvest Table; it was now a question of how and when to do it. Complicating things was the fact that she had told many different people in the past few days not to discuss her conversations with them. In her experience it was unrealistic to expect Jasmine Yip and her mother and aunt, the Yang brothers, and Su Na to keep quiet for long. Eventually one of them would talk to someone, and that would start a trail of gossip that would lead to a bad result for Ava. *I need to get back to Toronto,* she thought.

Han chatted with Willie about the events at the SCM warehouse as they made their way across the city to the Ritz-Carlton. He was pleased with himself, which she knew he deserved to be, but she couldn't help drawing comparisons with the far more reticent Xu. There was a reason why men like Xu and Uncle commanded so much respect. It had nothing to do with their physical stature and everything to do with the way they carried themselves. She had never heard either of them boast. They took on life as they found it, dealt with it as calmly as possible, and then moved on. She liked to think that she had some of those traits but believed that too often her emotions got in the way.

Before she could censure herself further, her phone rang and she saw Fai's number. "Hey, I was going to call you earlier but I thought you might be hungover," she answered.

"It was a late night, but I went easy on the wine," Fai said.

"Was it a good party?"

"It was terrific, mainly because everyone was so welcoming. It makes me realize there could be a bigger life for me, in the film industry outside China. I think I might start getting serious again about learning English."

"Andy has made some films in English."

"I know, and he told me he'd cast me if I wanted to give it a go. But then he started talking about *Tiananmen Square* again. Ava, I think he really hopes Lau Lau won't be fit to direct it."

"Chen said Lau Lau is doing well in rehab."

"He told me the same thing yesterday," Fai said.

"Then there's no reason to think he won't be fit to direct."

"I wish I had your confidence."

"And I wish I had your talent."

"Put those two things together and you have a great team," Fai said.

"Which is what we are."

Fai groaned. "I miss you."

"Me too, and I'm afraid we'll be missing each other for at least another week or so. I'm finishing up in Chengdu but I have to head back to Toronto. I have unfinished business there."

"Have you recovered the money stolen from Mimi's father?"

"I know what happened to it. All I have to do now is get it back."

"How hard will that be?"

"I don't know. It depends on the other parties."

"And if they aren't reasonable?"

"It could be a mess," Ava said. "I just hope they have the sense to realize there can only be chaos if they decide not to give in."

"You'll succeed. You always do."

"That's not true, but I have won more times than I've lost."

"You'll let me know your schedule?"

"Of course. I'll call you once it's set." Ava saw the Ritz-Carlton come into view. "Fai, I'd better go. I'm getting close to the hotel. Love you, and I'll talk to you later."

"Love you too."

Han turned to look at Ava after she ended the call. "Call me too once your schedule is set. I'll send my driver to take you to the airport."

"That isn't necessary."

"I know, but I want to do it all the same."

A moment later the car pulled up in front of the hotel. "I'll be in touch," Ava said to Han as she got out.

She walked briskly through the lobby, mentally prioritizing the calls she was going to make. It was late in Toronto, so those would be first, and then Jasmine Yip, May, and finally Xu. In between calls she would need to eat, and there were still flights she had to book. It was going to be a busy few hours, which was how she liked it when the end was in sight.

Ava went directly to the desk when she entered the suite. She found the room service menu, phoned downstairs, and ordered an Australian wagyu beef burger with bacon, cheese, and a fried egg. When that was done, she opened her notebook, reviewed the notes she'd made while Su was speaking, and added some comments and questions. There were still several loose ends to tie up, but at least she could identify them, and that was the first step towards resolving them.

She took her phone from her bag and found Todd Howell's mobile number. It rang five times before going to voicemail. "This is Ava. Call me as soon as you can," she said.

She was starting to dial Derek's number when her phone rang and she saw it was Howell. "Hey," she said.

"I was in bed and couldn't get to the phone quick enough," he said.

"I apologize for calling so late."

"There's no need for that. I'm glad to hear from you. I thought about phoning you earlier this evening, but I had nothing to report. The entire day was an exercise in frustration. We couldn't find any companies attached to Rogers or Cunningham."

"Well, let's try a different approach," she said. "Muir and the Harvest Table crew are selling painkillers online, opioids that include fentanyl and carfentanil. I'm told they operate multiple sales websites, which probably feed into a master server."

"I still find this shocking. Have you actually confirmed it?"

"I have. I've met with the company manufacturing the pharmaceuticals and with the outfit that's handling distribution from China. The distribution is all done by mail, using lists of customers provided by Malcolm Muir. He also personally negotiates pricing and orders the products from the factory. I have a complete paper trail connecting him to the distributor and the factory," she said. "I'd like you to locate all the Canadian websites that sell these products and find out who operates them. I'll be surprised if some familiar names don't appear on the registrations."

"Yes, that makes sense. I'll put my people on it first thing tomorrow morning," Howell said.

"I'd like to know what they're selling, how they're pricing it, and how people are expected to pay."

"Okay. I'll call you as soon as I have some information."

Ava hesitated, thinking about her schedule. "It's better for me to contact you. I'm not sure where I'll be during the next twenty-four to thirty-six hours. There's still more digging to be done on this end."

"However you want to handle it."

"Thanks. Oh, there's one more thing I meant to ask," Ava said. "Did your hackers have any luck getting into the Harvest Table bank account at Eastern Canadian Commerce?"

"No, sorry," he said.

"I may have someone who can help. I didn't want to ask him, but he may be our only option," Ava said. She ended the call, waited for a few seconds, and then hit Derek's number. It rang only twice before she heard his familiar voice.

"I'm still working on Evans Trust," he said.

"Any progress?"

"Not yet."

"Then let's change direction," she said.

"In what way?"

"There's a website in the U.S. called www.healthepain.com. It's selling painkillers online, and it may operate as the master server for similar websites. Who registered the website? Who owns it? Who operates it? What are they charging for pills? What kind of payments is it set up to receive — credit cards, electronic transfers, cryptocurrency? No matter how the payments are made, I believe all the money eventually ends up in an Evans Trust account in Vanuatu, but I don't know how it gets there. Is it automatically redirected through the master website, or does it have to go through an American financial institution of some kind?"

"I am not saying I won't jump right on this, but why are we focusing on an American website?"

"One, it might give us a back door into Evans Trust, and two, there's a good chance that Muir set up a similar structure in Canada. I've asked Todd Howell to investigate Canadian websites selling painkillers. I would have asked you to do it, but I figure you'll have enough on your plate figuring out what's going on in the States."

"I get it," Derek said. He paused. "I can hear some excitement in your voice. This is like the old days."

Ava's doorbell rang. "My lunch is here," she said. "I don't need this information right away, so get some sleep. If you come up with something and can't reach me by phone, send me a text or an email."

"Where are you headed next?"

It was Ava's turn to hesitate. "Toronto," she said. "I'm leaving tonight, and I'll be home within the next twenty-four hours."

"Ah," Derek said, excitement in his own voice. "You've already locked your sights on those sons of bitches."

(34)

THE WAGYU BURGER WAS GOOD, ALTHOUGH AVA wasn't focused on the flavour. She ate at a coffee table in the sitting room before returning to the desk and opening her laptop. She started searching for flights and quickly realized that, if she didn't want to spend another entire day in Chengdu, she would have to move fast. Her best option was a late afternoon Air China flight to Beijing that connected to an early evening Air Canada flight to Toronto. If all went smoothly, she could be home by around seven o'clock the following night.

With that arranged, she reached for the phone again.

"*Wei*?" a woman's voice answered tentatively.

"Jasmine, is that you? This is Ava Lee."

"It's me."

"I'm glad I reached you. How are things going? Have you heard from Muir?"

"No. He never calls unless it's to tell me to transfer money."

"I guess I can assume he hasn't put any money into your Mercantile account."

"You have my password. You can check."

"I just want to confirm that things are okay and that the password hasn't been changed."

"The password is the same."

"I'm pleased to hear that. Contact me at once if anything changes."

Ava ticked Jasmine's name off her mental list and moved on to the next.

"*Wei*," May answered.

"It's Ava. Are you free to talk?"

"Yes, but I haven't heard back from the banker about the SCM account in the Mercantile Bank."

"There's no need to pursue that now. I found what I needed through another source. Please thank your banker for me, and tell him I apologize for putting him through the unnecessary bother."

"He won't mind. He was happy to do me a favour," May said. "But if you got the information you want, does that mean you're getting your hands on the stolen money?"

"Close enough that I'm heading to Toronto tonight. Hopefully I'll have more leverage by the time I land."

"I'm pleased it's gone well, but Amanda is going to be disappointed. I told her there was a chance we might get together in Hong Kong while you're here."

"If I can wrap this up quickly, I'll be coming back to visit Fai in Taiwan. I could stop in Hong Kong on the way back."

"We'd both like that. I take it Fai's film shoot is going well."

"It sure sounds that way," Ava said.

"What about Lau Lau's film? Are you still having second thoughts?"

"Not as much as I was," Ava said. "Brenda Burgess has set up a company in England called BB Productions and opened a bank account with Barclays. Several law firms are layered between them and the company so there's a level of anonymity. Now, when it comes to the money to finance the film, let's put any discussion about that on hold for now."

"Hey, we're partners. Amanda and I talked this over, and we're both prepared to put in our fair share. She was wondering when that might be."

"There's no rush, and my point is that it may not be necessary. There might be other options."

"Have you told Amanda about this?"

"No. You know I always speak to you first."

"Do you want me to tell her?"

"If you want to."

"We have a call planned for later this afternoon to go over some expansion plans she intends to propose after the numbers are finalized," May said.

"Thanks, May," Ava said. "You know, I don't think I've ever thought about doing something that's caused me this much worry. Truthfully, there are times when I ask myself if I did the right thing by making that commitment to Lau Lau."

"Is it too late to back out?"

"The time for that was when Lau Lau called me to say he was prepared to go to rehab and described the film he wanted to make. Then I didn't quite grasp all the complexities and sensitivities surrounding Tiananmen. If I had, I might not have committed," Ava said.

"We'll deal with whatever happens," May said.

Ava sighed. "Well, first things first. I've got to settle things in Toronto. I'll call you from there."

"Travel safely."

"Thanks, and I love you, May."

"Love you too."

Ava immediately hit the speed dial button for Shanghai. Xu's house phone rang six times and wasn't answered. That was odd; it was rare for Auntie Grace not to pick up. She switched to Xu's cellphone.

"Ava, your ears must be burning," Xu answered.

"Why do you say that?'

"I just got off a call from Han telling me how impressed he was with you, and of course to make it clear that he'd greatly contributed to your success in Chengdu."

"Actually he was tremendously helpful. Without him, I don't know what I would have accomplished. He deserves a bonus."

"To set up the meeting with the lab, I promised him an allocation of iPhones. He says he set up two meetings, not one, and that the allocation should be doubled."

"He did set up two, but the allocation is for you and him to work out — although he isn't a man I'd choose to annoy," she said.

"He does have a style that's all his own. Suen and Sonny remind me a bit of him, except, as big as they are, they don't have his ability to frighten people just by looking at them."

"He did more than look. He screamed at people. He picked a man up by the neck. He slapped a middle-aged woman. He terrified them all," Ava said. "That's not a criticism. I needed them to co-operate, and he made sure they did."

"Maybe I will send him those extra iPhones."

"Speaking of phones, I called the house first and Auntie Grace didn't answer."

"She's gone for a walk to the French bakery."

"Where are you?" Ava asked.

"I'm sitting by the fish pond having a smoke."

"And I'm getting ready to leave Chengdu. I'm flying back to Toronto tonight."

"You've solved the problem you were chasing down?"

"I can't solve it until I'm back in Toronto, but I think the end is in sight."

"Keep me up to date on it."

"I will," Ava said, pleased that he cared enough to want to know.

"Auntie Grace will be sorry she missed you. She'll ask me when you plan to visit Shanghai again. What should I tell her?"

"After this case is over, I intend to see Fai in Taiwan. I've also promised May and Amanda that I'll fit in a side trip to Hong Kong. I'll try to spend a few days in Shanghai as well."

"That will make both of us happy."

"Give her a hug for me. I'll call you in a few days."

Ava checked the time as she put down the phone. She needed to go to the business centre to print the emails from Muir that Su Na had forwarded. When those orders were tabulated, she could match them with the purchase orders Muir had issued to Golden Emperor. That was her work project for at least part of the flight home. But while she would know what Muir was paying for the opioids and the volume he was moving, she still wouldn't know the selling prices or the profits being made. There were also the huge question marks that were the Evans Trust account in Vanuatu and the Harvest Table bank account in Toronto. Evans Trust was in Derek's hands, but she had to decide what to do about the Harvest Table account. She scrolled through her contacts and found Johnny Yan's cell number. It would be rude to call him at this hour; she'd phone him from Beijing, she decided. She just hoped he'd take her call.

Johnny had been Ava's classmate at York University and then went to work at one of the major Canadian banks. While at York, he and Ava were part of a support network that consisted of Chinese and Chinese Canadian students. Ava thought of it as Canadian-style *guanxi*. The network continued after school, the members trading favours and assisting each other to advance in their careers. Ava had directed a lot of business to Johnny and in turn had gone to him several times for help, which included unlocking bank accounts. But the last time he helped her had involved the governor of Nanjing, and Johnny's assistance had drawn unwarranted attention and became a problem for him. He wasn't asked to leave his position, but he sensed that his career was at least temporarily dead-ended, so he moved to another bank. Ava hadn't spoken to him since the change and wasn't sure how he would react to her approach. All she knew was that it was worth making the effort. What was the worst that could happen? Johnny telling her he couldn't help?

Time to do some printing, she thought. She got up from the desk, collected the room service tray, and left it outside her door before going to the elevator. Half an hour later she returned with copies of the documents. There were more than she'd realized, but it was a long flight from Beijing to Canada. *Two more things to do before I pack,* she thought as she called Han.

"Ava, what can I do for you?" he answered.

"You offered me a ride to the airport. My flight is at four."

"Then Willie will pick you up at two. I won't be with him, though."

"I didn't expect you to be. Thank you for sending Willie, and for everything else you did for me."

"No, thank *you*. Xu has just increased my supply of iPhones, and I'm sure you had something to do with that."

"Perhaps I did," Ava said, not reluctant to earn a favour. "I told him you were wonderfully supportive."

"*Wonderful* is a word I haven't often heard attributed to me."

"Perhaps you're spending too much time with people who don't appreciate you."

Han chuckled. "Now I know why Xu prizes you so much."

"That's a nice thing to say, even though it is an exaggeration," Ava said. "Anyway, I enjoyed meeting you and the rest of your family. Say goodbye to them for me."

Ava checked the time. She still had to change her clothes and pack, and she wanted to call Fai with her schedule. She went into the bedroom and put on a clean black T-shirt, ankle socks, Adidas training pants, her running shoes, and an Adidas jacket. Her mother chided her for dressing so casually when travelling, but Ava had learned that on long flights, comfortable clothing took precedence over fashion. She packed quickly then went into the sitting room to call Fai.

Until she met Fai, Ava had never enjoyed long phone conversations. Her style was to keep calls short and to the point. But when they were separated, the phone was the way they kept connected. They had tried Skype, but Ava never felt comfortable with it. They had used WeChat, a popular multipurpose Chinese app, for about a week, until Ava discovered that the Chinese government was using it for surveillance. So they talked on the phone, and, given that Fai loved to chat, they sometimes talked for hours. Ava had about an hour to kill before Willie got to the hotel. She could devote that time to tabulating numbers or talking to Fai. *Not a hard decision to make,* she thought, as she called Taiwan.

(35)

THE AIR CHINA FLIGHT ARRIVED IN BEIJING ON TIME. Ava didn't have to change terminals for her connection to Air Canada, and she arrived at the Air China business-class lounge with an hour to spare. It was packed with travellers, and Ava had to circle twice before she found a seat that provided some measure of privacy. She checked her phone for messages, saw none, and pulled up Johnny Yan's cell number.

"Ava Lee?" he answered almost immediately.

"Hi, Johnny. Thanks for taking my call. I hope my timing isn't inconvenient."

"I was just about to leave the house for work."

"Can you talk?"

"Of course. But maybe the question should be not if I *can* talk to you, but if I *should* talk to you."

"I'm really sorry that last project caused you so much trouble," Ava said.

"I'm teasing you," Johnny said. "I was on a slow track to nowhere at that bank, and you motivated me — intentionally or not — to get off my butt and look elsewhere. Now I'm in a job that I really love and I'm making almost double the money."

"That's great to hear. But it also makes me hesitant to ask if you could do me another favour," she said. "Just say no if you don't want me to continue."

"I'll listen, but that's all I'll promise," he said.

"That's entirely enough," she said, gathering her thoughts. "Have you heard of Harvest Table Bible Chapel?"

"Is that the megachurch up around Aurora?"

"That's the one."

"What could you possibly be doing with them?"

"I don't believe I should get into a lot of detail with you. It's best if I keep it simple," Ava said. "I just promise you, Johnny, that I'm not doing anything illegal."

"Okay, keep it simple."

"To begin with, this doesn't involve your bank. The chapel banks at Eastern Canadian Commerce. I'm hoping that you have some contacts there."

"And if I do?"

"I need to know about some activity in the chapel's account," she said. "Specifically, over the past couple of years it's been able to pay down its mortgage by sixty-four million dollars. That amount of money didn't trickle its way into the account by way of the weekly collection plate. I suspect there have been several large deposits from another source. I'd really like to know what that source is."

"What do you suspect?"

"I have a hunch the money is coming from an offshore account, possibly located in Vanuatu."

Johnny became quiet, and Ava wondered if her request went beyond what he thought he could deliver.

"If you don't have any contacts that can help, I understand," she said.

"I have a relatively senior contact, but she's not Chinese. We've traded favours in the past, but I don't want to owe her one on your behalf. I'd rather be able to offer her something concrete."

"I'll pay her," Ava said quickly.

"She'd be insulted if I made that kind of offer," Johnny said. "I'm thinking more along the lines of throwing some business her way. She's trying to build a wealth management division at the bank, and I know it's been a bit of a struggle. Would you consider putting some of your money under her management?"

"Is she capable?"

"Very. She's also discreet, and she could be a useful contact for you."

"How much money would I have to put up?"

"Twenty million would be a good start," he said.

"Fine. I'll meet with her when I'm back in Toronto, and we'll make some arrangements. In the meantime, I'd love to get my hands on that information."

"I'll call her as soon we hang up."

"What's her name?"

"Susan Kennedy."

"Please stress to her that there's some urgency to this."

"To be clear, we're talking about large deposits totalling sixty-four million dollars going into the Harvest Table Chapel account over the past couple of years?"

"Yes. And to be clearer, I'd like to know the sizes of the deposits, when they were made, and, of course, where they originated," Ava said. "And if she looks into the account and sees other transactions — in or out — that look odd, I'd like to hear about those as well. The sixty-four million might be only part of what's been going on."

"I think it's best that I act as an intermediary," he said after a slight pause.

"That's fine by me. I'm going to be in transit for the next thirteen hours or so, but I'm flying on Air Canada, so I should have access to Wi-Fi for part of the flight."

"If I get something I'll send it to you. Otherwise we can talk when you land," Johnny said. "I'm dying to ask what all this is about, but experience tells me I'm better off not knowing."

"Then it's better not to ask," Ava said.

She ended the call and walked over to the lounge bar to get a glass of Chardonnay. She took out her notebook and wrote Susan Kennedy's name next to the entry for the Eastern Canadian Commerce Bank. Ava had a lot of balls in the air. Sipping the wine with gusto, she thought about the flight ahead of her. On the flight from Chengdu to Beijing she had gone through the emails, purchase orders, and other documents that Su Na and the Yang brothers had given her. She thought she had a firm grasp on what they contained and didn't see any real value in reviewing them again. *I should take this opportunity to relax,* she thought. *A few more glasses of wine on the plane and maybe the distraction offered by a good film might do the trick.* As she finished her glass and was contemplating getting another, she heard the first boarding announcement for her flight. Ava liked to board early and get settled, so she got up and headed for the gate.

Half of the Signature Class pods were occupied by the time Ava boarded. When she first started flying to Asia on a regular basis, business class had offered a wider, deeper seat, good wine and food, and not much else. Now with the pods there was a measure of privacy and, importantly, lie-flat beds. She had always been able to sleep during flights, but the bed was a definite plus.

After the flight attendant served her a glass of Prosecco, Ava purchased the Wi-Fi service. She knew it didn't work perfectly and that there would be blackouts en route, but it still gave her a feeling of being in control of what was happening on the ground.

The Prosecco was replaced by champagne after takeoff. As Ava sipped she searched the entertainment system for a film to watch. There was nothing new that appealed to her, but under the classics she was drawn to *Key Largo* with Bogart and Bacall, and then in the foreign section she found *In the Mood for Love*. She had seen it at least three times before, and on every occasion it had been just after a romance ended. The film's melancholy atmosphere and the sadness of the unrequited love story were like rubbing salt into an open wound; the extreme emotions it generated had helped Ava move on. How would the film affect her now that she was happily in love?

Ava's mother adored the female lead, Maggie Cheung, partly because she had been told countless times that she resembled her. There was some truth in the comparison, but Ava's appreciation of Cheung emanated from her talent. She was a marvellous actress, definitely on a par with Gong Li and only — in Ava's biased eyes — a bit short of matching Fai. The male lead was Tony Chiu-wai Leung, a versatile actor who starred in comedy, gangster, and drama films with equal success. Ava selected the film.

Twenty minutes later she was so absorbed that she hardly

heard the flight attendant asking what she wanted for dinner. She chose beef medallions and a Cabernet Sauvignon. She ate slowly, finished one glass of wine, and started another as the characters' lives kept intersecting but never connecting. When they finally realized they had feelings for each other, they began a platonic relationship that led nowhere because their opportunities to commit always ended up unfulfilled. It was this failure to commit that had gripped Ava when she saw the film previously, because that had been her role in the relationships that had ended. Now all she saw was the loneliness it left in its wake, and she felt a twinge of guilt for the way she had treated some of her lovers. She had thought from time to time about reaching out to them to see how they were doing, but she'd always decided it was best to let bygones be bygones.

When the film ended Ava's first thought was to email a love note to Fai. She tried to open the Wi-Fi, but without success. *What the hell,* she thought as she drained her second glass of Cabernet. She looked around the cabin for the flight attendant and saw that many of the cabin's lights were dimmed. Almost reflexively she adjusted her seat to flat bed mode, covered herself with a blanket, and moments later, savouring memories of her and Fai naked and intertwined, fell asleep.

She found herself sitting in an old-style business-class seat with Uncle next to her.

I hope I am not being a nuisance, he said.

I'm always happy when you visit me, though it's never been in a plane before, she said. *In fact, in all those years we worked together I can remember only a handful of times we flew together.*

One time was auspicious — when we flew to Wuhan to meet May Ling and Changxing. Who would have thought that would turn out the way it did.

The only reason May and I are friends is because you forced me towards her. Without your counsel I'd still be thinking of her as an enemy, not one of my very best friends.

May loves and she trusts you completely, he said. *I noticed that again when you were speaking to her about financing the Tiananmen film. When you mentioned wanting to put off discussing financing because there might be other options, she did not ask you what those options might be. She trusts that you will tell her when you think the time is right.*

Except I don't have any other options, Ava said. *I was stalling.*

I have been thinking about it, and I believe there is a way that the money you need to finance the film can be captured and put in place without any of your businesses ever being associated with it.

How?

You are going to close this case, I know you are. Your fee will be ten million dollars. Do not collect it directly. Have the money deposited into Todd Howell's bank account and have his law firm send it to the BB Productions account at Barclays Bank. You will be invisible.

Howell would have to agree to that, she said, but she sensed immediately that Uncle had found the answer to her dilemma.

He will do it, Uncle said.

(36)

AVA AWOKE TO FIND HERSELF IN THE POD WITHOUT Uncle beside her. She was somewhere over the Pacific Ocean and had a desperate need to go to the bathroom. With their conversation still resonating in her head, she grabbed her toilet kit and hurried down the aisle. She had slept for more than six hours, which meant only four hours to go; they were already flying over Canadian territory.

Ten minutes later she left the bathroom feeling refreshed. She asked a flight attendant for coffee, turned down the offer of breakfast, and opened her computer. Accessing the Wi-Fi, Ava smiled when she saw she was connected and went to her email. There were nine unanswered messages, but the one that captured her immediate interest was from Johnny Yan. "Please be good news," she murmured as she opened it.

She scanned it quickly then reached for her notebook and pen. Rereading the message, she was amazed once more by Johnny's ability to get the information she needed. Canadian banks prided themselves on the security they provided their customers, but even if they'd built the most complicated security systems in the world, there was nothing to prevent someone who had authorized access sharing what they found with someone who didn't. Johnny's talent lay in winning the trust of many kindred spirits in the banking community who could help provide that access.

She hit the Reply button and typed, I can't thank you enough for this. Please tell Susan that I will most definitely put twenty million into the wealth management division. The only other question I have is: what can I do for you?

Ava sat back in her seat and started calculating how the information could be put to the best use. "Ms. Lee, here is your coffee," a voice interrupted.

"Thank you," Ava said, and quickly added, "I would appreciate a refill in a few minutes."

When the flight attendant had left, she wrote to Derek: I don't know what you've found in the U.S., but I think I already have enough information to proceed against Harvest Table. I am on an Air Canada flight direct from Beijing to Toronto, and I obviously have access to email. I should be arriving in Toronto around 10 a.m. Can you meet me at the airport? I also think a meeting with Todd Howell is necessary. Are you available if I can set one up for this afternoon?

The coffee was lukewarm. Ava drank it anyway, emptying her cup and pushing it to one side. She was about to start a message to Howell when she saw she had just received one from Jasmine Yip. She opened it and read: I thought you should know $3.2 million was put in the Chengdu account a few hours ago. Muir always calls with instructions soon after, so I expect to hear from him.

Ava replied: Thanks for the update. Please let me know the moment he calls and what he has to say. Emailing is best.

Under no circumstances do I want you to transfer the money from that account to Golden Emperor, or to anyone else, until I tell you it's okay. If Muir insists that you do, find a way to put him off for about twenty-four hours. Tell him the bank is closed for a Chinese holiday or something like that.

Three million dollars was a start, she thought, and given that she had the password, she could move it out of the account herself. But the timing wasn't right. The last thing she wanted was to alert Muir that they were on his trail. Assuming that the people she'd threatened into secrecy kept their mouths closed, she still had the element of surprise. That surprise, properly leveraged, could be a powerful weapon.

The flight attendant came down the aisle with a pot of coffee. "Do you still want a refill?" she asked, interrupting Ava's thought process.

"Sure," Ava said, and was immediately distracted by an email arriving from Derek. She waited for the attendant to leave before opening it.

He wrote: Good to hear from you, and even happier you're arriving today. Sounds like you're still making progress. I made a little headway. I found the website and talked a friend in New York into registering. The site sells a wide range of drugs. I have a list of the products, selling prices, and payment options if you need them. I bought some synthetic marijuana, and when I chose to pay by wire transfer I was directed to a bank in Charlotte, North Carolina. That's where I dead-ended. I couldn't get into the bank's system or the website's. I'll keep trying if you want.

I just checked your arrival time and the flight is on schedule. I'll meet you at the airport. Do you want me to call Howell and ask him to be on standby for this afternoon? As for me going to a meeting, I'm available 24 hours a day until this thing is resolved.

Ava replied: Too bad about the U.S. bank, but don't sweat it. It was a long shot, and we don't actually need that information to make our move in Canada. And yes, I think calling Howell is a good idea. When you reach him, tell him we'll definitely be meeting and I expect him to put everything else aside. You should also say that I'm in the air but have access to email. I'd like to know what he's managed to uncover. Does that sound too bossy?

Seconds later, Derek wrote: No more bossy than usual. He'll get used to it—like I did.

Ava smiled. She had almost forgotten how humorous Derek could be, and he was often at his drollest when events were most dire. Even when they were about to take on armed men, he'd found a way to make it seem like a game that the poor suckers on the other side had no chance of winning.

Sipping her coffee, which was fresher and hotter than before, she contemplated the options she had for dealing with Harvest Table. None of them were particularly brilliant, and one of the reasons she wanted to meet with Howell was her hope that he'd help refine them. She hadn't misspoken when she told Derek that the U.S. information wasn't necessary. Susan Kennedy's information had almost closed the circle around the Canadian operation; all that was missing was the name of the bank where the money used to buy drugs in Canada was being sent. Maybe Howell's people had been able to burrow deeper than Derek, she thought as she returned to her laptop.

Good morning, Todd. I'm inbound to Toronto and will arrive

this morning. I want us to meet this afternoon. Derek will be calling you to emphasize how important it is that we do. In the meantime, could you let me know what your tech team managed to uncover? Best regards, Ava.

She opened her notebook, riffed through the pages, and stopped at the one where she had diagrammed the route the Harvest Investment Fund's money had taken. There was a large question mark over *Evans Trust*. Who controlled the flow of money from Evans Trust to the Jewellery Circle bank account in Chengdu? That question was still unanswered. She could make an intelligent guess, but knowing for certain would help determine which strategy they chose. Was it Muir? Cunningham? Rogers? Some combination of the three? The Harvest Table account at Eastern Canadian Commerce listed Cunningham and Rogers as co-signees, but that was normal enough; it would have been a surprise if they weren't.

Ava checked again for new emails and realized she was getting impatient. She had a couple of hours before they would land, and there wasn't much more she could do from the air. *I need to relax,* she told herself. She opened the entertainment centre, found the HBO series *Gentleman Jack* — about an early nineteenth-century English lesbian — and began to watch the first episode, glancing frequently at the laptop. An hour later she had just started the second episode when a message appeared.

Hi, Ava. I just spoke to Derek. I've cancelled all my appointments this afternoon, so whenever you get here, I'll be available, Howell wrote. As for my tech team, I've had Mark Wilson, my lead techie here, and two outside colleagues working around the clock since yesterday. Mark will be briefing me at

11 a.m., so by the time you get here I'll have some information to pass along.

Ava shook her head, her impatience returning. Why did Howell have to wait for a briefing? Why would she have to wait to find out what his people had learned? She considered firing off a response that echoed those sentiments, then paused. Nothing was going to happen until they met. Anything they found out in the interim would contribute to the meeting and nothing more than that. She was so close to success she could almost feel it. There was no reason to upset people she needed.

She returned to *Gentleman Jack*.

(37)

AVA WALKED THROUGH THE GLASS DOORS AT PEARSON International's Terminal 1 arrivals hall to find Derek waiting for her. He gave her a tiny smile, and Ava could feel the tension in his body as they hugged.

"I spoke to Todd Howell. He can meet us any time after one o'clock," Derek said as he took the Shanghai Tang bag from her.

"Yes, I know. I emailed him just in case you couldn't reach him."

"He told me you did and asked me if I knew why you seemed so eager to get together," Derek said. "I told him I have no idea but that you aren't someone who wastes other people's time."

"I think we're getting close to getting the money back," she said.

"I guessed as much. What's still missing?"

"I want to be able to draw a direct line between the outfit selling drugs in Canada and a bank account in Vanuatu. Right now I can't, though that doesn't mean I don't have enough information to go after them," she said. "I'm also struggling to decide which strategy has the best chance of success. A key part of any strategy includes ending this as quickly as possible."

Ava had been speaking as they walked towards the parking garage. They came to a stop behind a line of people at the machines where parking fees were paid.

"Are you going to discuss strategy with Todd Howell?" Derek asked.

"That's my plan, and of course you'll be included as well."

"What if Howell wants to involve the police?"

"The only time I'll agree to that is after we've gotten all the money back."

"Will he be okay with that?"

"From the discussions I've had with him, I think so. He wants to resolve this almost as badly as we do, and as long as we don't go completely outside the law, I expect he'll go along with us."

"What do you mean by 'completely outside'?"

"Well, I have no plans to use a machete."

Derek smiled. "Do you really believe things could get physical?"

Ava shrugged. "Who knows how the other side might respond when they know we're coming after them."

It was Derek's turn to pay, and he stepped in front of the machine. A moment later they walked into the short-term parking area, where Derek's white Honda CR-V was only a few spots from the door. He put Ava's bags in the back next to Amber's car seat.

Ava was still struck sometimes by Derek's transformation from Ferrari-driving, hard-drinking party boy to an SUV-driving doting father and husband. "Whatever happened to that red Ferrari you had?" she asked as she climbed into the front passenger seat.

"I sold it to Max Tung. I got enough money for this car and half the down payment on our house."

"Do you still see him?"

"Not often. He hasn't changed his lifestyle, so he's out most nights and sleeping most days."

"Do you ever miss that?"

"Truthfully, it was hard for the first six months, when it was just Mimi and me. She was working, and during the day I didn't have much outside of bak mei training and video games to occupy myself. But from the second Amber was born, she became the most important thing in my life. During Mimi's maternity leave I looked after both of them, and I enjoyed it, but I was kind of pleased when Mimi went back to work and it was just me and the baby," Derek said.

"Have you told Mimi that?"

"Oh yes — and she laughed. She said she'd been a bit worried when the baby was born that fatherhood might be too much for me to handle. Instead she has to put up with the fact that, where the girls of the house are concerned, she's playing second fiddle."

"Are you planning to have more kids?"

"We're working on it," Derek said as he exited the airport and headed down Highway 427 towards the Gardiner Expressway. He looked at the time on the dash. "I'm assuming you want to go to your condo first to freshen up."

"You know me well."

It was late enough in the morning that traffic was moving steadily. "We should be there by eleven-thirty and leave for Howell's office by twelve-thirty."

"That's fine. It should give you time to do some copying for me. I have a raft of papers in my Vuitton bag," she said, reaching into it. "The Four Seasons Hotel on Yorkville has a decent business centre you can use. I'd like four copies of everything."

"What papers are those?"

"Purchase orders from Muir to the drug manufacturing company, emails from him to the company handling distribution, and all sorts of banking information."

"Does Howell know you have all this?"

"I didn't go into detail with him, but he has a broad idea of what I've got," she said. "I'm more anxious to know what he's got. He's had a team of technicians trying to find Canadian websites selling the Chengdu meds. I'm hoping to learn where the money is being sent."

"The missing link."

"Exactly."

The SUV turned east onto the Gardiner. Straight ahead Ava could see the CN Tower and a skyline that had been expanding ever since she could remember. Toronto didn't have quite the heft of New York, and the condo towers that ran along Lake Ontario, the city's southern edge, lacked the design originality and soaring presence of the Hong Kong and Shanghai waterfronts, but it was home, and she loved it.

Ava leafed through the papers as Derek made his way to the Spadina Avenue exit. She saw no reason for him to copy every document. A representative sample detailing the steps that turned stolen money into diamonds, diamonds into drugs, and drugs back into money that paid down the chapel's mortgage and lined pockets would be good enough to make her case. She selected the necessary papers and fixed them together with a large clip.

She had been so focused on the paperwork that she hadn't noticed that they drove past old Chinatown. When she finally looked up, they were almost at Bloor Street. "That was quick," she said.

"We were lucky. Let's hope it's an omen."

Derek turned right onto Bloor and drove past the Bata Shoe Museum and the Royal Ontario Museum to Avenue Road. In rapid succession a left, followed by a right onto Cumberland, and a left into a public parking garage brought them to a stop, and they walked through the lot to its Yorkville Avenue exit. Ava's condo building was almost directly across the street, while the Four Seasons was a couple of blocks to the east.

Ava gave Derek the papers she'd taken from her Vuitton bag. "I'll see you at twelve-thirty at this exit," she said.

The building's concierge acknowledged her as she entered the condo lobby. "Welcome back, Ms. Lee. Another successful trip?"

"Not yet, but I'm hopeful."

She had purchased the condo at a time when her mother could boast to her friends, "My daughter has bought a condo in Yorkville," and get some jealous reactions. Ten years later the neighbourhood had become even more trendy and expensive. The fact that she owned a condo on the top floor of a building on Yorkville Avenue usually generated begrudging admiration, but admiration all the same.

Ava entered her unit, went directly to the kitchen, and checked her home phone for messages. There were two, one supposedly from the Canada Revenue Agency saying they were ready to lay charges against her and she should call them to avoid any further action, and the second from someone selling duct cleaning. For the tenth time in as many months, Ava resolved to get rid of her landline.

She quickly checked emails and found nothing new. She emailed Fai: I'm home. The flight was uneventful. I'll call you when I can. Love you, miss you. Ava

Fifty minutes later she was standing by Derek's SUV in a black A-line skirt, a white Brooks Brothers shirt, black pumps, and a tasteful application of red lipstick and mascara. He wasn't there yet, and after waiting five minutes she was beginning to wonder what had happened to him. He finally appeared with five large manila envelopes.

"What took you so long?" she asked, taking the envelopes from him.

"That was a lot of paper."

They climbed into the car, turned left at Avenue Road, and headed downtown to Howell's office in the Toronto Commonwealth Bank Building.

"I read some of the documents. It made everything you've been talking about so much more real. I don't mean it didn't seem real before, but seeing it in black and white really hit me hard," Derek said as they reached Queen's Park Circle. "It's hard to believe the nerve and hypocrisy of these guys. How did they think they'd get away with this? They obviously don't give a fuck about the people they're killing with the junk they're selling. So much for Christian values."

"Well, they have been getting away with it, and from what I know, the Simmons organization in the States has been getting away with it for much longer," Ava said. "As for Christian values, they're easy to preach as long as your self-interest isn't affected. The moment it is, those values tend to become flexible. Look at what's going on in the U.S. with their president. He's the compete antithesis of moral, but the evangelicals find a way to twist their value system to accommodate him because he's anti-abortion and homophobic."

"Ava, these chapel guys are selling drugs that kill people. How can that be accommodated by their value system?"

"I was told they believe that what they're doing is an act of kindness. They claim they're bringing relief to people in pain who otherwise can't afford the medication," she said. "And I'm sure Rogers and Cunningham believe the profits from the business are enabling the chapel to grow, and in their eyes that's a good thing and ample justification."

"That is such bullshit! I bet they've even found a way to rationalize stealing money from their own congregation — and Phil Gregory's death!" Derek shouted.

Ava saw he was on the verge of losing control. "I don't want to talk about this anymore," she said. "I find it upsetting, and I need to get my thoughts together for the meeting."

"Sorry, I didn't mean to let go like that. Around Mimi I've been keeping my feelings pent up."

"You're a good man, Derek. Mimi is lucky to have you."

Derek nodded and kept his eyes locked on the road.

They hit heavy traffic a few blocks from King Street and had to inch forward one car length at a time. Ava said, "This will take forever. Why don't you turn right up there and find a parking lot. We'll walk the rest of the way."

They found a parking lot on Richmond Street a block west of University Avenue, which meant they had to walk six blocks to Howell's office. "I hate being late," Ava said, looking at her watch. "Let's hustle."

They reached the building with a few minutes to spare, and it was only a minute past one when they walked into the offices of Howell, Barker, and Mason.

"Mr. Howell is waiting for you in the main boardroom," the receptionist said. "It's there on the left. The door is open."

Ava and Derek walked over to the door. She stuck her head into the room and saw Howell sitting at the far end of a long teak table. A man in a suit was on his right, and a young man with a blond ponytail and black T-shirt that read STAY CALM. EVERYTHING IS HACKABLE sat on his left.

"Come in, come in," Howell said as he stood up. "Ava, this is your fan Eddie Ng, and this is Mark Wilson, our tech wizard, who I mentioned in my email."

After a round of handshakes, Ava and Derek sat down.

"I know you asked for this meeting, Ava, but before we get to your agenda I thought you'd like to hear what Mark and his team have found," Howell said. "He briefed me this morning, and I asked him to stay so you can hear it directly from him. I think you'll find it interesting."

She looked across the table at Wilson. "I hope that message on your T-shirt was fulfilled when you worked on our project," she said.

The techie glanced at Howell, who smiled. Wilson opened the laptop on the table in front of him and hit several keys. A screen on the wall behind Howell came to life. "As you can see, we found four websites promoting the sale of a multitude of synthetic drugs in Canada," he said

Ava looked at the list on the screen.

"The content of the websites is rather low-key, with a focus on pain management."

"Tell Ava about the domains," Howell said.

"Two of the sites are registered in the Isle of Man and two in Malta. All of them are owned by a numbered company with a post office box in the Isle of Man. The numbered company has one registered owner —"

"Patrick Cunningham," Howell interrupted, a broad smile splitting his face.

"This is great work," Ava said to Wilson, trying to contain her excitement. "What else did you and the team find?"

"What interests you the most?" Wilson asked.

"The money that flows in and out of those websites."

"Todd predicted that you'd say that," Wilson said. He hit another key on the laptop.

Ava looked at the chart Wilson had put up on the screen, and this time her face burst into a huge smile.

"The four websites only accept credit card payments. The money goes directly to an online payment processing company called LockBox. They act as a middleman, charging 3.5 percent plus forty cents on every transaction."

"I've never heard of LockBox," Derek said.

"They're a lot smaller than Stripe or PayPal, but they're also more flexible — which is a roundabout way of saying that they'll do business with companies the other two would avoid," Wilson said. "Their transaction fees are also higher than what most processing companies charge. I imagine they're charging a premium because of the nature of the transactions."

"And, for the same reason, the companies are only too happy to pay a premium," Ava said, and pointed to the chart. "It appears that the money from all four sites goes into a single account at LockBox."

"That is how it's structured."

"Who opened that account?"

"Patrick Cunningham."

Ava looked at Howell, who was smiling even more broadly than before. "What happens to the money when it leaves LockBox?" she asked Wilson.

"Once a day that account is emptied when LockBox transfers the money to the account of a numbered company."

"You don't have that on the chart. Is it the same numbered company that's headquartered in the Isle of Man?"

"No, it's a different company, registered in Vanuatu."

"So the money is being sent to Vanuatu?"

"Yes."

Ava bit back the question that was immediately front of mind and instead asked, "Did you find out who owns the company in Vanuatu?"

"Not yet. That kind of information is restricted, and Vanuatu has the most impenetrable network any of us have encountered."

"So I keep being told," she said, and then looked across the table at Wilson. "I assume this numbered company in Vanuatu uses a bank."

"The money is sent to a company called Evans Trust," Wilson said. "We tried to break into their system as well, but failed."

"You've given us more than enough, thank you," Ava said.

"What do we do now?" asked Howell.

"It's time to get even."

(38)

AVA WAITED UNTIL MARK WILSON HAD LEFT THE BOARD-room before passing out the envelopes. As Howell, Derek, and Eddie Ng opened them, she walked over to a whiteboard and wrote *People Trail* across the top of the board. Under it she wrote *Malcolm Muir* and connected that name to Jasmine Yip's, then Jasmine to Essie Lam, Essie to Patrick Cunningham, Cunningham to Sammy Rogers, Rogers to the Simmons family, Randy Simmons to Su Na, and so on, until the board was a spider's web of interconnecting lines.

"What I don't know," Ava said when she'd finished, "is how Cunningham and Muir first came together. But there's zero doubt in my mind that Cunningham recruited Muir to set up the fund and run the drug operation. Jasmine Yip was used to front some of the business and is a common link. I have some photos, so there's no denying there's a relationship, but how far back does it go?"

"Before he joined the chapel, Cunningham ran the collections department at a finance company in Toronto. He hired Muir from time to time," Eddie Ng said.

"How do you know that?" Ava asked abruptly.

"I saw the company's name a few days ago when I was researching Cunningham's business connections for Todd, and I remembered that it was one of the companies that Muir had worked for."

"Why didn't you mention that to me?" Howell asked.

"You wanted me to look into companies Cunningham had ownership in. He was only an employee at the finance company. I didn't think it was relevant."

"Jesus, Eddie," said Howell.

"It doesn't matter when he found out, as long as we finally know it," Ava said as she drew a line between Cunningham and Muir. "Now everyone connects."

The room fell silent as the group contemplated the board. Ava was the first to speak. "Derek, would you please take a picture of the board," she said as she moved over to another one. She wrote *Money Trail* across its top and *Harvest Investment Fund* underneath, then began to connect Amsterdam, Antwerp, Guangzhou, Chengdu, Toronto, and Vanuatu.

"They used the money that originated with the fund to buy diamonds in Antwerp through Jasmine Yip. Jasmine then sold them in Guangzhou and that money went into the Mercantile Bank of Chengdu, where it was used to purchase drugs through an account in the name of Jewellery Circle," she said. "Eventually they finished recycling the fund money; there was no more need to buy diamonds and no need to keep anything but a minimum balance in the Mercantile Bank account. From then on they funded the drug buys on an order-by-order basis, using money wired from the Evans Trust Company account in Vanuatu to Mercantile. That money, as we now know — thanks to

Mark — was directed to Evans Trust from online sales through LockBox. The money is clean. It took five years to get it to that point, but they were building a business that is now self-sustaining."

"How did you manage to discover all this?" Eddie Ng asked.

"The key piece of information was provided by Todd. Once I knew the fund money had been sent to a bank in Amsterdam, the rest of it fell into place," Ava said. She turned to Derek again. "Take a picture of this too, please. Todd, why don't you and Eddie read what's in the envelopes."

Howell and Ng had been so caught up in Ava's whiteboard scrawls that they hadn't read anything. "What's in them?" Howell asked.

"Proof of everything I've put on this board," she said, pointing to the one headed *Money Trail*. "We have bank statements, copies of wire transfers, purchase orders for diamonds and drugs, emails from Muir detailing the online orders for the distributor in Chengdu, and so on."

"A moment ago you mentioned something about photos," Howell said.

"Yes," Ava said, returning to the table. She took her phone from her bag and handed it to Howell. "Patrick Cunningham and Muir at the drug distribution centre in Chengdu. You can see the ladies behind them putting pills into envelopes. This was taken during their first trip there, before they got into the business."

"How did they know where to go?" Eddie Ng asked.

"Rogers is close to the Simmons Christian Ministry in the U.S. He worked for them before he came north to start his own church. I'm told he and Randy Simmons are especially close. It was the Simmons family that started this business. In fact, the distribution centre in Chengdu operates as a Simmons Christian Mission."

"You're joking, right?" Howell said.

"I wish I were, but it's true. I think Randy Simmons convinced his friend Rogers that this was a good way to make money and they had a blueprint that worked. Rogers copied it in almost every detail. We know Harvest Table had a heavy debt load at the time, so it's safe to assume they lacked the working capital to make it happen. The fund provided that capital and more."

Howell passed the phone back to Ava and said, "I'm very sure you've got it well papered, so I don't have to read these documents. What I don't know is what we should do with all this."

"We have more than thirty million dollars to recover," Ava said.

"How do you think we'll accomplish that?"

Ava pointed to the whiteboards. "We have to use this information to leverage the chapel. One way or another they're going to give us back the money."

"I understand that's our goal. What I don't know is how you plan to achieve it," said Howell.

"We need to get in front of Rogers, Cunningham, and Muir so we can persuade them that co-operating with us is their only available option. I want a meeting with them, and I want it by tomorrow. I don't care where it's held, as long as Rogers, Cunningham, and Muir all attend."

"What are you going to say to them?"

"I'm still working on that," she said. "Now, who do you think you should call to set up the meeting?"

"I doubt that Muir would talk to me, and I hardly know Rogers. That leaves Cunningham."

"Then please call him now. You can do it from your office if you don't want an audience."

"He'll ask me why we want to meet."

"Tell him you've come into possession of some information concerning the chapel that is, on the surface, alarming. Tell him you've considered going directly to the police, but, to be fair, you think the chapel should have an opportunity to explain first. Emphasize that there's an urgency involved," Ava said. "And Todd, keep me, Derek, and Eddie out of the conversation. Let him think you'll be going alone. We'll be a pleasant surprise."

"He'll want to know what I have."

"Of course he will. And you'll tell him it's something you won't discuss over the phone."

Howell nodded. "Okay, I'll go call him now."

Eddie Ng stood up as Howell left. He walked over to the whiteboards. "I can't tell you how impressed I am with this."

"It's what I was trained to do," Ava said.

Derek pushed back his chair and put his hands behind his head. "There's something that's bothering me," he said.

"What's that?"

"I can't help wondering why they completely emptied the fund. They were making good money selling drugs. Why didn't they put some of it back?"

"I've asked myself the same question," Ava said. "They've paid down the mortgage on the chapel and the land by more than sixty million dollars in the past few years. That could have been their priority, and maybe they were initially planning to replenish the fund when the mortgage was totally paid off. But something happens to people's good intentions when money enters the mix. Uncle and I saw it many times. Once they've stolen ten dollars and not gotten caught, the temptation to steal again, and more, is hard to resist. Maybe they tell themselves they're only borrowing it and will pay it back, but after a while they start to believe the money is actually theirs . . . But that's a long answer without much substance, because the truth is, I really don't know. Maybe we'll find out when we meet with them tomorrow, although I'm not interested enough to ask. All I care about is getting the money back."

"He wouldn't take my call," Howell said as he entered the boardroom.

Ava turned towards him. "He wouldn't or couldn't?"

"I don't know. I told the receptionist I was phoning for Mr. Cunningham. She asked me who was calling. I told her, and she put me on hold for about a minute. When she came back on, she said he was unavailable and asked if I wished to leave a message. I told her it was a very urgent matter and I needed him to call me back today."

"Wait fifteen minutes and call again."

"That's fine. If I can't get through, I'll try Rogers," Howell said. "Is it possible that someone has warned them that you've been on their trail?"

"It's possible, but I think it's highly unlikely," Ava said. "While we wait, could you give me your firm's banking information?"

"Are you that optimistic?"

"This has nothing to do with optimism. I'm considering transferring three million dollars into your account later today, from the chapel's account at the Mercantile Bank in

Chengdu. You should let whoever handles your banking internally know it might be coming," Ava said. "That money is my contingency plan for the Gregory family. If everything else fails, I'll have recovered that much for them at least."

"Is there any point in my asking how you'll be able to transfer three million dollars from their account?" Howell asked.

"No."

(39)

AT THREE-THIRTY AVA AND THE THREE MEN WERE STILL sitting in the boardroom at Howell, Barker, and Mason. There had been two more futile attempts by Howell to connect with Cunningham.

"He's deliberately avoiding me," Howell said.

"I agree."

"He must have been warned," Howell suggested again.

"Not necessarily. The fact that you represent members of the congregation is reason enough for him to be cautious. Perhaps he wants to talk with his lawyer before speaking to you," Ava said. "By the way, who does represent them?"

"When this first began, they were using a small local firm in Aurora, but when I met with Cunningham he had Hugh Campbell with him. Campbell is a founding partner of one of the big King Street firms."

"Is he good?"

"Very good. We're small potatoes compared to them," Howell said.

"What are we going to do if Cunningham keeps refusing to talk to Todd?" Derek asked.

"I have a backup plan. I didn't want to have to use it, but if it comes down to it, I will."

"Can you share the details?" Howell asked.

"No, it's too soon for that," Ava said as she stood up. "I think we'll head out now, but I would appreciate if you could keep calling. Make a nuisance of yourself. Maybe Cunningham will finally talk to you in order to get some peace. If he does, let me know right away. If I don't hear from you tonight, I'll reconnect with you in the morning and we'll figure out how to take it from there. The one thing we can't do is let them drag this thing out."

Ava and Derek left the office and retraced their steps to the car. Derek was quiet until they were inching around Queen's Park Circle. "Were you serious about transferring three million dollars from the chapel's bank account?" he asked.

"Technically the account is Jasmine Yip's, but Muir controls what goes in and out of it. Deciding to transfer the money is a balancing act, a judgement call."

"Why is it a judgment call?"

"You've heard the old saying that a bird in the hand is worth two in the bush?"

"Of course."

"The bird in hand is the three million in the Chengdu account. I have the password for the account and can trigger the transfer any time. The problem is that the money has been put there for a drug buy. Muir usually instructs Jasmine Yip to pay the money to Golden Emperor MicroLab a day or two after it hits the account. If she doesn't do it, he'll figure something odd is going on and he'll react," Ava said. "I have no idea what he'll do — which is a problem — but he'll do something. Jasmine made it clear that he's perpetually suspicious and distrustful.

"The two birds in the bush is the thirty-plus million that could be sitting in the Evans Trust account in Vanuatu or is now part of the equity the chapel accrued by paying down its mortgage. Getting our hands on that is the priority, but what if we can't? I got involved in this to help Mimi and her mother, and the three million will set things right for them, but I can't ignore the fact that other people were also hurt. The problem is timing. If Jasmine pays Golden Emperor, that buys us more time to go after the big money. But there's no guarantee we'll be successful, and the three million will be lost. If I tell her not to pay and I transfer the money to Canada, then we could be putting the bigger play at risk."

"Do you really believe there's that much risk of failure?"

"I don't know these people," she said. "Uncle taught me not to make assumptions and to never underplay how difficult it is to separate thieves from the money they've stolen. These are smart people and they have the advantage, since most of the money is in a secure place."

"When do you have to make a decision about the three million?"

"I'm going to call Jasmine in a couple of hours to see if she's heard from Muir. If she hasn't, then I'd guess we have about twenty-four hours to get something done. If she has, we only have until the close of banking hours in Chengdu, which would be four o'clock tomorrow morning here."

"Either way it's very tight."

"I know," Ava said with resignation in her voice.

The car came to a stop in heavy traffic well short of Bloor Street. Derek tapped his fingers impatiently on the steering wheel and glanced several times at Ava. "Can I ask you a question you might find misplaced?" he said finally.

"Sure."

"Were you asking what I thought you should do — about the birds in the hand and the bush?"

"In a roundabout way I suppose I was."

"And that question is, do we grab the sure thing, the three million, or do we gamble that you'll be able to leverage the thirty million out of the chapel?"

"That's correct. Although, to be clear, I told Howell at the outset that the first three million of anything we get goes to Mrs. Gregory."

"That's only fair, considering she's the reason why you're doing all this work."

"One more thing — which you may not think is fair — is that I also negotiated my usual collection fee. I'm not taking it for the money I get for Mrs. Gregory, but I will for the balance. I have a reason for doing that, which I still think is valid."

"I'm sure it is, and I don't need to know what it is," Derek said. He paused briefly. "Look, I believe I'm speaking for Mimi when I say that we'll support whatever decision you make. The money is important to Mrs. Gregory, but she can survive without three million dollars. And personally, I'd hate to see all the work you've done to expose these creeps go to waste."

"Me neither, but I can't stop being practical, and I know the three million is a sure thing," she said. "Still, we have all of tonight ahead of us. Maybe Howell will get through to Cunningham. Maybe Muir will hold off telling Jasmine to pay Golden Emperor. All we need is one break."

Derek finally reached Bloor and came to a stop at a red light.

"Just go straight and let me off at Yorkville Avenue," Ava said.

"Okay."

"And thank you for this conversation. When Uncle was alive, he was my touchstone. I could tell him anything without worrying about how he'd react, because his reaction was always constant support. I'll never replace him, but I'm blessed to have friends like Mimi and you."

The light changed, and Derek drove through the intersection, stopping just short of Yorkville Avenue. Ava opened the door and leapt out.

"Call me if you hear anything tonight," Derek said.

"Count on it," she said.

(40)

AVA'S BODY CLOCK WAS STILL ON CHENGDU TIME, AND as she walked into the condo she felt a sudden urge to sleep. She knew she couldn't, for fear of throwing off her sleep pattern, so she needed to do something that would re-energize her. Going for a run was more demanding than she might be able to handle, but a long, brisk walk would fit the bill. She went into the bedroom and changed back into her travel clothes.

As she was about to leave the apartment, Jasmine Yip came to mind. It was still the middle of the night in Chengdu and under normal circumstances far too early to call someone, but there was nothing normal about this situation. She found Jasmine's cell number and hit it. The phone rang three times before she heard a sleepy voice say, "*Wei.*"

"Jasmine, this is Ava. I apologize for calling so early. I've just returned to Canada and want to know if you've heard from Muir."

"He called me three hours ago," Jasmine said. "I was going to email you when I got out of bed."

"Did he instruct you to pay Golden Emperor?"

"Yes."

"Can you delay doing it?"

"Not for very long. He'll expect me to do it as soon as I'm up," she said.

"So that means I have only three or four hours."

"Three or four hours to do what?"

"Nothing. I was just talking to myself," Ava said.

Jasmine hesitated and then said. "Ava, I know you wanted me to stall Muir, but he's very domineering and I find it hard to say no to him."

"I know you're in a difficult situation. Just don't forget that you and I have an understanding that can't be broken, or there will be consequences."

"You didn't have to say that."

"Sorry. I felt a need to counterbalance the fear Muir seems to generate in you."

"Consider that done," Jasmine said.

"Okay, just hold on as long as you can, and call me before you actually send money to Golden Emperor."

"I will."

Ava put down the phone. It was time for that walk.

It was still rush hour in Toronto, which meant Avenue Road and Bloor Street were basically parking lots. Ava didn't drive much when she was at home, so she hadn't often suffered the stress of driving in what was becoming one of the worst cities in North America for commuting. She stood at the corner of Yorkville and Avenue Road and debated going north or south. North was a better walking route because it was a straight line with fewer stoplights. South was more scenic and more stop-and-go.

She went south, past the Royal Ontario Museum and

its former planetarium. The Ontario Legislature sat in the middle of Queen's Park Circle, surrounded by the expansive campus of the University of Toronto. Ava had explored parts of the campus but not all of it, and when she reached Wellesley Street she decided to take a right. Walking past unfamiliar buildings, she reached Hart House Circle. She knew of Hart House. It had an indoor running track that a former girlfriend had used and had promised to take Ava to. The relationship had ended before she could. *Let's have a look*, Ava thought.

The two-storey stone university buildings on Hart House Circle were built in the Gothic Revival style. Ava was admiring them when she noticed a large metal relief sculpture on a wall that was almost entirely covered by some sort of ivy. She might have missed it if it hadn't looked so out of place and been so distinctive. She stood transfixed. The sculpture depicted a bicycle that was bent and twisted, and near the bike were several loose shoes. Running across the bicycle were tread marks like those made by a tank. Beneath the relief was a plaque on a stone cairn that read: IN MEMORY OF THOSE WHO GAVE THEIR LIVES FOR DEMOCRACY ON JUNE 4, 1989, TIANANMEN SQUARE, BEIJING. A GIFT FROM THE STUDENTS OF THE UNIVERSITY OF TORONTO TO THE STUDENTS AND CITIZENS OF CHINA Below that were the same sentiments in Chinese.

As she stared at the sculpture, Ava thought it was a wonderful thing — so simple, but so precise and powerful all the same. She closed her eyes, and a scene from Lau Lau's script leapt into her mind. It was the first meeting between the mother searching for her son and the female army officer who had witnessed the events in the Square. The officer talked about the tanks rolling forward, never hesitating, never stopping, as if they were being driven by robots programmed to follow a path from which they couldn't deviate. It didn't matter what was in their path, she said, the tanks crushed without discrimination.

Ava's eyes were full of tears when she opened them. She reached up and touched a handlebar of the twisted bike. Could this actual bike have been in the Square? She doubted it, but she had no doubts that its distorted frame was representative of what might have been left after the tanks had done their work. How was it that she had known so little about the horrors of Tiananmen Square? The Chinese Communists were good at burying history that didn't buttress their ideology, and most of the rest of the world didn't care enough to remember it. But thank goodness there were people like Lau Lau, who not only remembered the tragedy but was determined to shine a bright and very public light on it.

"We have to make that film," Ava said aloud. She touched the bike again. "We'll make sure Lau Lau helps the world remember you."

She turned away from the wall and began to walk back towards Yorkville. The image of the memorial was fixed in her mind, mingling with thoughts about Lau Lau and the money he'd need to make his film. Whatever uncertainty she'd felt in the car with Derek began to disappear; as she walked, it was replaced by determination. She wasn't going to wait for Cunningham to respond to Howell. She needed a new plan.

When she reached her condo, Ava went directly to her laptop and accessed the Jewellery Circle account at the

Mercantile Bank. The balance was $3,210,774.56. She hesitated for a second, trying to decide how much to transfer, and then muttered, "To hell with it, I'm taking it all." When the transfer was completed, she reached for her phone and called Todd Howell.

"I'm still at the office trying to reach Cunningham," he answered, his frustration evident. "I'm being stonewalled."

"I've been rethinking our strategy," Ava said. "It's too passive."

"It wasn't passive a few hours ago. Has something happened to change your mind?"

"Yes. I moved all the money from their Mercantile Bank account into your law firm's."

Howell grunted. Ava didn't know if it was in disapproval or surprise. "You actually did that?"

"I told you I might."

"I thought that was hyperbole."

"I don't engage in hyperbole," Ava said.

"Evidently not. It also appears that you don't hesitate to change strategies without consulting your partner."

"Todd, I don't mean for this to sound insulting, but I don't have partners. I have people who I'm working with to resolve a problem. There is a difference."

Howell went quiet, and Ava knew he felt insulted. "I understand the distinction," he said finally.

"Thank you. And anyway, the deed is done, so let's talk about the ramifications."

"How will taking that money help us get to a positive resolution?"

"I wanted you to set up a meeting with Cunningham, Rogers, and Muir because I thought we might be able to surprise them. Now I think that's the wrong approach. This way is more impactful; it shows them that we have some strength and is more certain to get their attention — especially when I show up on Muir's doorstep to tell him the money is gone and that I took it."

"Why would you tell him?"

"I want them to understand that we're onto them, that we have a measure of control. And given that they won't know what else we're capable of doing, meeting with us becomes a necessity."

"Okay, I can see all that, but why do you want to go to Muir's house?"

"He's a ten-minute walk from my apartment. And I want to see his face when I tell him."

"What if he reacts badly?"

"My only worry is that he'll refuse to speak to me," Ava said. "But once he knows about the three million, I can't imagine he'll be able to resist."

(41)

NOW THAT SHE HAD MADE HER DECISION, AVA WAS anxious to get on with things. She called Jasmine Yip in Singapore.

"I didn't expect to hear from you so soon," Jasmine said.

"Has Muir called?"

"No."

"Good. I suggest you turn off your phone and tell your mother and aunt to do the same, in case Muir tries to call them."

"What's happened?"

"Change of plan. I emptied the bank account at Mercantile."

"Muir will find out. When he sees the money is gone, he'll think I took it. He'll go crazy."

"Don't worry. I'm on my way to tell him I took the money."

"He'll still think I gave you the password."

"I'm going to tell him Su Na gave it to me," Ava said. "You have nothing to worry about. Just keep your phone off for the next day or two. Everything should be resolved by then."

"I guess I'm out of a job now."

"Go back to laundering money for the small-timers in Singapore. It may not be as profitable, but it's definitely safer," said Ava, ending the conversation.

Han was her next call. "Who is this?" he answered.

"This is Ava Lee. I apologize for calling so early."

"Are you in Canada?"

"I am, but the situation in Chengdu is still on my mind."

"What's up?"

"I'm very close to resolving my problem. I hope to meet with the other parties tomorrow morning and bring it to a close. The thing is, they may need a concrete reason to settle with us. We could threaten to go public with our information or go to the police, but neither action would have an immediate impact — or a predictable outcome. I need to be able to hurt them quickly and decisively."

"You have something in mind?"

"Yes. I think shutting down Su Na's distribution business would do the trick."

"Shutting it down entirely?"

"Yes, for as long as it takes to get the people I'm dealing with to agree to a settlement."

"And you're calling me because you think this is a job we can do for you?"

"Yes. In return, I'll pay you or ask Xu to extend another favour."

"How about you do both?" Han said.

"How much money do you think is adequate?" Ava asked, pleased by Han's tacit agreement to do the job.

"Fifty thousand yuan to close it and twenty-five thousand a day to keep it closed."

Ava was surprised at how rapidly Han had come up with

the numbers. "That's a deal. How do you want to receive the money?"

"We'll work that out when the job is finished, and you can let Xu know about the favour the next time you talk to him. There's no rush."

"Thank you for that level of trust."

"We're like family," Han said. "Ru Shi was quite taken with you. You're the only woman she's ever met who can match the men in her life."

"Please tell her it was a real pleasure to meet her."

"I'll do that. Now, when and how do you want the job done?"

"My meeting should be tomorrow morning at ten — that's ten in the evening in Chengdu. It will be helpful if SCM is shut down in the late afternoon and if you can hold Su Na in her office, in case I have to put her on the phone to verify what you've done."

"Lu will make the arrangements this morning."

"Can you phone me when you get there? I'd like to be able to explain to Su why she's being shut down and what the people here have to do before she can reopen."

"I'll do that," Han said.

Ava smiled as she ended the call. She had no doubt that Han and Lu would conduct themselves with the same level of competence she'd seen in Chengdu.

Ten minutes later, Ava made her way over to Elgin Avenue. When she saw Muir's Mercedes in the driveway, she knew he was at home. As she got closer, though, she saw that he wasn't in his office. Without a second thought she walked along the pathway and up the steps to the front door and pressed the buzzer. She heard a dog bark, and then the sound of high heels clicking on tile. A slim middle-aged woman with auburn hair, wearing a red silk blouse and jeans, opened the door.

"Good evening, Mrs. Swift. Is Mr. Muir at home?" Ava said.

Marla Swift squinted at her. "Do I know you?"

"No."

"Then how do you know me?"

Ava shrugged, then heard Muir's voice calling, "Who's at the door?"

"Some woman asking for you."

"What the hell?" Muir said.

The woman moved to one side, and now it was Muir who stood in the doorway. He stared down at Ava.

"Not you again," he said. "You're becoming a nuisance." His hand moved towards the door, and Ava knew he was about to close it in her face.

"I have a message for you. I have emptied your account at the Mercantile Bank in Chengdu. There was just over three million in it. I took it all."

She thought she saw a fleeting look of panic cross his face before the door slammed shut.

Ava descended the front steps and waited. A moment later she saw Muir walk into his office. She moved onto the front lawn so she could get a better view.

Without looking out the window, Muir went directly to his desk, sat down at the computer, and began to type. She figured he was accessing the Mercantile account, and watched for a reaction. She could tell he was trying to control himself, but his furrowed brow and tightly set mouth showed that he was worried. Then he stopped typing and stared at the screen. His mouth slackened, and he seemed confused. Then he lifted his head and looked over the top of the screen at Ava. She waved. He glared at her, and she saw him clench his teeth.

We need to talk about this, she mouthed slowly.

Muir slapped his hands onto the arms of his chair and propelled himself to his feet. He left the office more quickly than he'd entered it, and seconds later the front door flew open. Ava walked across the grass towards him. As she stepped over a low hedge onto the pathway, he shouted, "I don't know what kind of fucking game you think you're playing, but this isn't going to end well for you!"

"It isn't a game. Three million dollars makes this a serious business. And it's only the beginning of what you and your partners are going to repay," Ava said.

"Who the fuck are you? I remember the face, but not the name."

"My name is Ava Lee, and I'm working with Todd Howell on behalf of the Harvest Fund investors."

Muir stepped out of the house. Ava was standing at the bottom of the steps, and he towered over her. "I have no idea what you're talking about. What I do know is that you're going to return that money or you can spend the next few days looking over your shoulder."

"The money stays where it is."

"You goddamn bitch," he said, taking a step forward.

"You don't seem to be thinking this through," Ava said. "At the very least I thought you'd be interested in knowing how I managed to get the password to the account."

"I don't have to ask. Jasmine fucking Yip gave it to you," he said.

"Who? I've never heard of her."

"Bullshit."

"I'll make you a promise," Ava said. "When we have our meeting tomorrow morning, I'll tell you who provided me with the password."

"We're not having any fucking meeting."

"Yes, we are. At ten o'clock in the boardroom of Howell, Barker, and Mason. I want you, Patrick Cunningham, and Pastor Rogers there. You can bring anyone else you want, but for the three of you, this is a command performance," Ava said. "We'll outline all the information we've gathered about your drug-peddling business, and then the three of you can decide how you're going to respond." She had kept her eyes locked on Muir's face, and she saw him flinch when she said "drug-peddling."

"You fucking bitch! Who do you think you are?"

"Just so it's clear, I expect to see the three of you at ten o'clock tomorrow in Todd Howell's boardroom."

He shook his head and smirked. "If we aren't there, start without us."

"That wouldn't be wise. If I were you, I'd talk this over with my partners before making a decision that could prove to be disastrous," Ava said. "Because if you don't come, we'll shut down your business — and we'll shut down the Simmons family business. And something else you can tell Pastor Rogers is that if we shut down the Simmons business, we'll lay the blame squarely at your feet. I don't know how much value for Rogers his relationship with the Simmonses has, but it will go up in smoke. You can choose to believe me or not, but if you aren't there by ten you'll be out of business by the end of the day, and the information we have will be turned over to the police."

Muir moved down the steps and Ava saw him make a fist with his right hand. He took another step and then lunged awkwardly towards her, his left hand reaching for her arm. It wasn't a swing, but it was enough for Ava. She moved to one side as she drove the first knuckle of her right hand into his ear. His head shot to one side and then he wobbled and fell into the hedge.

Ava leaned over him. "Ten o'clock. All three of you. Todd Howell's boardroom. Be there," she said. "You know, I wanted to break your nose just now. I could have splattered it across your face. Do you know why I didn't?"

He didn't answer.

"Because I don't want you to spend the night in a hospital. I want you to be fit enough to talk to Rogers and Cunningham tonight, and I want you fit enough to be at that meeting."

"Fuck off," he groaned.

"Ten o'clock," she said.

(42)

THERE WAS A SPRING IN AVA'S STEP AS SHE WALKED back to the condo. It hadn't gone entirely smoothly with Muir, but she'd delivered the message, and he had to realize that not showing up carried far more risk than going to the meeting. If nothing else, they would be wanting to learn what Ava and Howell knew about their operation.

Ava's appetite was starting to kick in. She weighed her dining options and decided to go to Trattoria Nervosa. As always, the restaurant was busy, but after a short wait she was seated on the patio. She ordered sparkling water, carpaccio with truffled cannellini beans, and a risotto with braised beef short ribs and porcini mushrooms. When the server had left the table, Ava reached for her phone to call Todd Howell.

"Hey," he answered instantly.

"It's done," she said.

"Did you talk to him?"

"I did. He was abusive and uncooperative, but he certainly got my message. I'm confident that Muir and the others will be at your office tomorrow morning."

"How can you be so sure?" Howell asked.

"These people may be vile, but they aren't stupid. They must realize that ignoring us would be risky."

"I wish I felt as certain . . ." Howell said, then drifted into silence.

"Is something bothering you?" Ava asked. "If it is, say so. We need to speak with one voice tomorrow morning."

"Nothing is bothering me. I would just like to set the game plan."

"I agree. Who will be attending from your firm?"

"Eddie and myself."

"I'm bringing Derek. Why don't we meet at your office around eight-thirty. That should give us ample time to get prepared."

"That's fine."

"Good. So we'll see you then," she said, ending the conversation.

The server brought the carpaccio to the table. Ava had been about to call Derek, but the translucent slices of beef looked so appetizing that she couldn't resist taking a bite. It was melting in her mouth as she phoned him.

"What's going on, Ava? Did Todd get hold of Cunningham?" he answered.

"No, but I spoke to Muir."

"How did you reach him?"

"I went to his house."

"Are you kidding?"

"No, but it was no big deal. I explained the situation and he listened — not well, but well enough that I'm sure they'll come to Todd's office tomorrow morning," Ava said. "You and I should be there by eight-thirty to get organized. Does that work for you?"

"Do you want me to pick you up?"

"I'd appreciate it."

"Mimi will have to stay home from work, but that won't be a problem."

"Speaking of Mimi, I transferred all the money from the Chengdu account to Howell's law firm. It was a bit more than three million dollars. You can tell Mimi if you want, but you might want to wait until Todd confirms it's in the account."

"That's fantastic," Derek said. "I was hoping you'd do it, but not at the expense of everyone else."

"I haven't given up on everyone else, but the meeting tomorrow is crucial."

"If anyone can pull this off, you can," Derek said. "I'll be at your condo by eight. I'll wait outside."

Ava put down her phone, picked up the glass of water, and drank half of it. Then she stood up and stretched as she tried to shake her lethargy. Half an hour later she left Nervosa with her appetite sated but the jet lag deepening. It was almost eight o'clock when she got back to the condo. She planned to kill half an hour showering and getting ready for bed, but the first thing she did was call Fai in Taiwan.

"Hi, babe," Fai said.

"Hi yourself. I'm glad I caught you. I've missed hearing your voice."

"I'm in a van with Andy and some of the cast. I can't talk for long," Fai said.

"Then I'll talk fast. I'm going to wrap up this case in the next few days. When it's over, I want to come to Taiwan. Are you still good with that?"

"I'd love it."

"And I sort of promised May that on the way back we'd

spend a few days in Hong Kong, and Xu wants us to go to Shanghai. What do you think?"

"Why don't we do both?"

Ava sat on the side of the bed. "Terrific. I'll let them know."

"That's crazy!" Fai said suddenly as a horn blared in the background.

"What happened?"

"We were almost sideswiped by a bus," Fai said. "Ava, I'd better go. Things are bit hectic in the van right now."

"Love you, and talk to you soon," Ava said as a huge yawn captured her. She put down the phone and flopped backwards onto the bed. *I'll shower in a few minutes,* she thought.

When she woke up, it was quarter to six.

(43)

AVA COULDN'T REMEMBER THE LAST TIME SHE HAD slept in her clothes. But it had been a terrific sleep, and she felt refreshed and bursting with energy. After a quick trip to the bathroom, she went into the kitchen to make coffee and check her laptop for messages.

There was an email from Fai that read: Sorry I had to cut short our conversation, but there was bit of an uproar about the bus. Good luck today. Anxious to see you. Love, Fai

We have a meeting at ten that will decide how the case ends. I'll email you after it's over to let you know how it went. Love, Ava

There was nothing from Han, which didn't surprise her. Like Xu, he was more comfortable using a phone than email. She riffled through the pages of her notebook, reconstructing the events that had led her to this point. Every journey was somehow both different and the same. The characters involved obviously changed from case to case, as did the locales and the scams that were perpetrated. But her methodology didn't. She went methodically from A to B to C until she reached the end. Now it would come down to a confrontation, to a test of wills.

Uncle's style in meetings of this kind was to lead with news the other party didn't want to hear, with no tiptoeing or easing into the meat of the subject. Ava wasn't sure that was the best approach in this instance. The information on the whiteboards and the documents that supported it eliminated any doubt about what had happened. Should she use them to construct a spider web before offering Rogers and the others a way to escape it? Should she let them imagine outcomes that might be worse than what she would demand? *No,* she thought. *It will be more effective to use Uncle's strategy.*

Ava thought about calling Han and decided to wait. He had told her what he'd do. There was no reason to think he hadn't done it and no sense in rushing into the morning. She made another coffee and then headed for the bathroom.

She took a leisurely shower, washed and dried her hair, and laid out the clothes she'd wear to the meeting. She went into the kitchen to get a third coffee, saw it was just past seven, and decided it was time to call Han.

"This is Han," he said.

"And this is Ava. How are things in Chengdu?"

"Things are as you wanted them to be. Lu closed the warehouse today around four. The workers were sent home and told not to come back," Han said.

"Was there any resistance?"

"Not from security, but Su Na kicked up a bit of a fuss until Lu explained everything to her."

"Are you at the warehouse now?"

"I'm sitting in Su Na's office. Do you want a word with her?"

"Please."

There was a pause, and then Ava heard Su Na's angry voice. "This is going too far. You won't get away with this."

"Ms. Su, I'm going to be meeting with Pastor Rogers, Patrick Cunningham, and Malcolm Muir in a few hours. If they are reasonable, the warehouse will be allowed to reopen," Ava said calmly. "Now, there is a way you can contribute to your business's well-being. During the meeting I'm going to call you. I'll put you on speakerphone so you can confirm that the warehouse is closed and that Han is capable of keeping it closed for as long as necessary."

"Listen, I know you have an issue with the Canadians, but why are you penalizing the Simmons operation? We've done nothing to you," Su said. "If you let me reopen, I promise that I'll ship only to the United States. In fact, I don't care if I never ship to Canada again."

"That doesn't work for me — I can't separate them. The only reason the Canadians are there in the first place is that Simmons sponsored them."

"You're going to make an enemy of the Simmons family."

"I couldn't care less."

"How long am I going to be held here against my will?" Su Na asked.

"If things go as I hope, you should be home by midnight," Ava said. "But that doesn't mean the warehouse can open tomorrow. Even if I get what I want, there will be loose ends to tie up, and that might take a day or two. Han will keep his men at the warehouse until everything is finalized."

"What if things don't go as you hope?"

"You'll be out of business," Ava said. "Now give the phone back to Han."

"Yes, Ava," he said, seconds later.

"My meeting is at ten. I'm going to call you after it starts so Su can confirm that the warehouse is closed. I told her she could leave around midnight, but you can let her go any time after the phone call," Ava said.

"We'll wait until midnight in case you need her again," Han said. "Lu will drive her home. It won't hurt to see where she lives, in case we have to pay her a visit in the future."

Ava imagined Su's reaction to that last remark. "It's your call; I trust your judgement," Ava said. "I'll be in touch later."

She returned to the bedroom to dress. She had laid out black linen slacks, a snugly fitting white silk shirt, and a pair of black alligator pumps she'd bought in Hong Kong. When she was dressed, Ava applied lipstick, mascara, and her favourite Annick Goutal perfume, then pulled her hair back and fixed it with the ivory chignon pin. She examined herself in the mirror and thought she looked suitably dressed for battle. The only thing missing was her Tank Française watch, which she now slipped on.

Ava gathered her papers and headed downstairs to meet Derek. She was five minutes early, but his Honda was already sitting at the curb.

"How did you sleep?" he asked.

"I fell asleep in my clothes, but I got a solid ten hours," Ava said. "Did Mimi mind staying home from work this morning?"

"Not when I told her we have a meeting that might result in her mother getting her money back," Derek said as he drove towards Avenue Road. "I was tempted to tell her about the three million, but caution kicked in—I followed my own advice and didn't. I was afraid I'd jinx us."

"You know I believe in jinxes."

"Oh, I know, though I don't remember you having that much bad luck."

"That's because I do everything I can to avoid jinxing myself," Ava said with a smile.

The traffic heading downtown was heavy. Derek had the radio tuned to an all-news station that gave traffic reports every ten minutes. It was barely audible, so Ava reached for the screen on the dashboard and turned it up. The traffic volume they were experiencing was normal enough that it didn't warrant a mention.

Ava took out her notebook and began to leaf through it. Derek didn't interrupt her, so they drove in silence to the parking lot he had used the day before. Fifteen minutes later they walked into the lobby of the Toronto Commonwealth Bank Building, and at eight-forty they were entering the offices of Howell, Barker, and Mason.

Eddie Ng hurried to greet them. "Todd is in the boardroom. I've never seen him so revved up."

When they entered the boardroom, they saw Howell hunched over a pile of files. He smiled and said, "There's coffee in the Thermos. Help yourselves."

"I've had enough coffee," Ava said.

"I'm fine," said Derek.

Ava and Derek sat next to each other across the table from Howell. She looked at the whiteboards and saw that sheets of paper had been rather raggedly taped over them. "Are the document packages ready?"

"They are, but we're only going to need one."

"Why?"

"For starters, there won't be any lawyers from the other side attending."

"I like that," Ava said.

"And only Cunningham is coming."

"I don't like that."

"He phoned me late last night. Muir contacted him after your visit and reported what you had to say. Cunningham found your comments alarming, but there was no admission of guilt. In fact, he said he thought many of your remarks were libellous, and that Muir has grounds to charge you with assault. He said he was calling me because he assumed that you're my client."

"Assault?" Eddie Ng said.

"Muir claims that Ava knocked him out," Howell said.

"I knocked him to the ground when he tried to grab my arm."

"Believe me, if Ava had wanted to knock him out, he wouldn't have been fit to talk to anyone last night," Derek said.

"That notwithstanding, what I'm trying to explain is that Cunningham didn't sound the least bit worried. He was completely adversarial," Howell said.

"So why is he coming?" Ava asked.

"He said he's concerned about the reputation of the chapel, that he can't sit idly by and allow someone to make wild accusations."

"He's coming on a fishing expedition," Ava said.

"I agree. He was putting on an act. When I asked him if he'd bring legal counsel, he said he didn't need a lawyer. I expect he's coming to find out what we know. Once he does, their lawyers will emerge out of the woodwork."

"Why isn't Muir coming?" Ava asked.

"Cunningham said Muir has absolutely nothing to do with the chapel. He emphasized that after what he called 'the regrettable series of events involving the Harvest Investment Fund,' Harvest Table cut all ties with Muir."

"And why no Rogers?" asked Ava.

"He said he didn't want to cause the pastor any unnecessary alarm."

Ava looked at the covered whiteboards. "It seems we have a decision to make. Do we meet with Cunningham alone, or do we insist that all three of them attend?"

"Cunningham reminded me that he's the chief operating officer of the organization and has the authority to speak for it," Howell said.

"His is also the only name linked to LockBox through the companies he registered in the Isle of Man," Eddie Ng said.

"It's true that we don't have Rogers's name attached to anything, and what we have on Muir is purchase orders and shipping instructions," Ava said. "Maybe Cunningham is the money man."

"Then we should meet with him, don't you think?" Howell asked.

"Yes, but let's not show him the whiteboards too soon. I'd like to hear what kind of lies he spins before we drop the hammer on him."

"Who's going to question him?" Howell asked.

"I will, as long as you don't have any objections," Ava said. "But I think you could start, by explaining that my involvement is related to the Harvest Investment Fund, that you've shared the information you have with me, and that we've been working together to identify where the money went."

"I have no objections, and I'll be pleased to provide the background," Howell said.

Ava nodded, then turned to see a grey-haired man standing in the boardroom's doorway.

"Todd, can I speak to you for a minute?" he said.

"This is Matt Mason, one of my partners," Howell said to Ava as he rose from his chair and left the room.

Howell rejoined them quickly.

"Bad news?" asked Ava.

"The opposite. The money you transferred from the bank in China has arrived in our company account."

Ava looked at Derek. "If you want to call Mimi now, I don't mind."

"I think I'll wait to tell her in person," he said.

"Congratulations," Eddie Ng said.

"I told Eddie what you'd done," Howell said to Ava.

"It's a start," she said. "But I want the rest of it."

A woman stepped into the room. "Mr. Howell, a Mr. Cunningham is here to see you."

Howell checked his watch. "He's early."

(44)

PATRICK CUNNINGHAM WAS SHORT — NO MORE THAN five foot seven or eight — and skinny, and he had a buzz cut that made him look almost skeletal. His dark brown eyes were deeply recessed and even from a distance seemed intense. He wore jeans that looked expensive and a floral shirt that Ava guessed had been bought at Tommy Bahama. The casual clothes didn't match his general demeanour.

"Thank you for coming, Patrick," Howell said, "It was good of you to travel all this way."

"I apologize for being early, but you never know how traffic is going to be in this city. I was lucky this morning," he said in a voice that Ava found tinny but self-assured.

"Let me introduce my colleagues," Howell said.

"If she's Ava Lee, there's no need," Cunningham said as he pointed at Ava.

"She is Ava Lee, so please take a seat," Howell said. "Can we offer you something to drink?"

"No, let's get started," Cunningham said.

Howell started to speak, but Cunningham, leaning forward, cut him off. "You owe us an apology," he barked at Ava.

"I owe you what?" Ava asked, surprised by his sudden aggression.

"You owe Pastor Sammy Rogers and Harvest Table Bible Chapel an apology," he said. "I only hope the lies you told Malcolm Muir last night haven't gone any further."

"Just one minute —" Howell said, only to be interrupted by Ava.

"If this meeting is going to be contentious, let's have at it," she said to Cunningham.

"By all means," he said.

"Fine. I think that for the past four or five years you've been partners with Malcolm Muir in thievery and drug dealing."

Cunningham looked at Howell. "You're a witness to this libel."

"Technically it's slander, but if it's the truth, it's not even that."

"I won't sit here and listen to this nonsense," Cunningham said loudly. "If she has proof of any of it, why hasn't she gone to the authorities? Why is this meeting necessary?"

"I'll answer those questions. If you want details, it will take longer," Ava said.

"Keep it short."

"Good. Eddie, could you uncover the first whiteboard, please," Ava said.

Ava saw that Cunningham was trying not to stare at Eddie as he peeled the paper from the board. When it was visible, she said, "The people named on that board conspired to steal more than thirty million dollars from members of your congregation by using the Harvest Investment Fund as a front. The money was converted into diamonds and then back into cash, which was used to buy synthetic drugs from a lab in Chengdu, China. Those drugs were made available to people in this country through a number of websites and distributed through a warehouse in Chengdu. The stolen money and the profits it accrued were then used to pay down the mortgage on the Harvest Table Bible Chapel buildings and land — and to line several pockets, of which one was yours. There, Mr. Cunningham, you have your summary."

His face had paled during her recital, and the fingers of his right hand were drumming the table. But when he spoke he sounded under control. "What I see is a bunch of names on a board with lines connecting them," he said.

"Unveil the next board please, Eddie," Ava said, and tapped the folder she had in front of her. "We have transaction records from all the banks noted on this board. We've met with Jasmine Yip, Su Na, and the Yang brothers at Golden Emperor MicroLab. They were all co-operative. We have copies of purchase orders issued to the lab by Malcolm Muir and copies of shipping orders he sent to the warehouse. What else do you want to know?"

She watched Cunningham's face as she listed the facts. His attention was partly on her, but he couldn't resist looking at the second whiteboard.

Cunningham looked at Howell and her, then shook his head. "As I told Mr. Howell last night, Malcolm Muir has nothing to do with the chapel. We've severed all ties with him. It's true he may have orchestrated the theft of the money you mentioned, but Mr. Howell pursued that and came to a dead end. I also know that Mr. Howell approached the authorities and couldn't convince them to take up the case.

So as far as I'm concerned, what you're doing here is trying to revive a dead horse."

"Two of the websites selling drugs are registered to a numbered company that's in your name," Howell said.

"Muir is a devious fellow," Cunningham said. "I wouldn't put anything past him, including using my name."

"Where did the money come from that paid down the chapel's mortgage by more than sixty million dollars over the past few years?" asked Howell.

"Pastor Rogers has a passionate following. We were fortunate to be blessed by substantial endowments from some devoted Christians who prefer to remain anonymous."

As Ava listened to Cunningham, it occurred to her that, though her visit to Muir had brought Cunningham to the boardroom, it had also given them a heads-up. Cunningham had his answers ready.

"When was the last time you saw Malcolm Muir?" she asked.

"Why is that relevant?" he said. "I spoke to him last night when he called to report your unwelcome visit to his home. Before that I hadn't seen him since he left the chapel."

"Has the pastor spoken to him since he left?"

"Of course not. In fact, I can't remember Pastor Rogers speaking to him even when he was still attending the chapel."

"I see. Now, if you will look at the whiteboard, Mr. Cunningham, you will see the name Su Na. I mentioned her earlier in conjunction with Jasmine Yip. Do you know Su Na?"

"The name isn't familiar to me."

"What about Jasmine Yip?"

Cunningham pursed his thin lips and then smiled at Ava.

"You are clever, aren't you. Jasmine is my wife's cousin — but of course you already know that. What you might not know is that they've been estranged since my wife moved to Canada with me eight years ago," he said. "Jasmine still lives in Singapore and engages in any number of illegal activities. It wouldn't surprise me if she had some minor involvement with Muir."

"How would she and Muir have met?"

"You'll have to ask them that question."

"I did ask Jasmine. She told me your wife asked her to help Muir launder money."

"That is a blatant untruth!" Cunningham said, showing signs of agitation. "My wife would never do such a thing."

"Then I guess Jasmine lied to me."

"She certainly did."

"Just like you've lied to me," Ava said.

Cunningham looked at Howell. "This conversation is over," he said.

"Before you run off, take a look at this photo," Ava said, pushing her phone across the table.

He hesitated, then, with a show of reluctance, picked it up. He stared at the screen.

"That's a photo of you, Malcolm Muir, and Su Na in the Simmons Christian Mission warehouse in Chengdu," Ava said. "If you scroll right, you'll see several more. The women behind you in the photo are putting pills into envelopes and Bibles. The more salient point, though, is that you and Muir are both there with Su Na and, as you'll see from the date at the bottom, you were there long after you claim you cut ties with Muir."

Cunningham slid the phone forcefully towards Ava,

who stopped it before it fell to the floor. "You can do all the fancy gymnastics you want trying to explain away Muir and Jasmine and the money you've been raking in, but these photos speak for themselves," she said. "And what they're telling me is that you're lying through your teeth."

"I'm leaving," Cunningham said abruptly as he rose to his feet.

"No, you're not. Not just yet, anyway. If you try to leave, my friend Derek here will prevent it. You're going to stay here until I finish what I have to say."

Cunningham looked at Derek, who stared back at him grim faced, and then turned his attention to Howell. "Do you actually condone this behaviour?"

"I haven't seen anything that causes me concern," Howell said. "All Ava has asked is for you to sit down and listen."

Cunningham slowly lowered himself back onto the chair. "I'm listening, but when you finish talking, I'm gone. And I don't care what your thug tries to do about it."

"My *thug*, as you so nicely put it, is married to the daughter of one of the people who put his life's earnings into the Harvest Investment Fund. When that money was stolen, he went into the shed in his garden and blew his brains out."

"I know nothing about that," Cunningham said. "Where are you going with this?"

"I'll keep it simple. You are going to transfer . . ." She paused to open her notebook. "I was going to say $31,554,629, because that was the amount taken from the Harvest Fund account, but I think we'll round it off to thirty-five million dollars. What do you think, Todd? Does thirty-five million work for you?"

"It does."

Cunningham smirked. "Even if I thought your request was sane, where would we get thirty-five million dollars?"

"You can take some from your account with Evans Trust in Vanuatu. You, Muir, and the pastor can kick in a few million each from your personal accounts. You can remortgage the chapel property. You can ask the pastor to borrow some money from his good friends the Simmons family."

"I've never heard of Evans Trust," Cunningham said, but without the conviction of his earlier denials. "We're not going to give you thirty-five million dollars — or even thirty-five dollars."

Ava shrugged, picked up her phone, and hit Han's number.

"*Wei*," he answered right away.

"I want you to put Su Na on the phone," Ava said in Mandarin. "Tell her to speak English."

A few seconds later, Ava heard Su's tentative "Yes?"

"Ms. Su, this is Ava Lee. I'm going to put you on speakerphone so everyone can hear you. Please speak clearly and be completely honest with us," she said. "I'm here with an old friend of yours, Patrick Cunningham. You do remember Patrick, don't you?"

"I remember him very well."

"I'm sure he's pleased to hear that," Ava said. "Now, can you explain the nature of your business in Chengdu?"

"I am the director of the Simmons Christian Mission in Chengdu. I am employed directly by the Simmons family. We operate a distribution centre that ships medicinal products to the United States. And under a separate contract, we've been shipping the same products to Canada."

"The contract to ship product to Canada is between which parties?"

"The initial contract was between the Simmons Christian Ministry in Oklahoma and Harvest Table Bible Chapel in Canada."

"Whose signatures are on the contract?"

"I don't have a copy of the original contract; all I have are the pages relating to the fees we'd charge. But I did see it at some point and remember that Blackstone Simmons and Pastor Sammy Rogers were the signatories, and Randy Simmons and Mr. Cunningham signed as witnesses."

"Did you deal with any of those gentlemen after that?"

"Randy is my boss. I deal with him all the time when it comes to the U.S. business."

"Who is your contact for Canada?"

"Malcolm Muir," Su said.

"And how often do you and he communicate?"

"Several times a week by email, sometimes by phone, and he makes an annual visit to the warehouse."

"Thank you, Ms. Su, that's very useful information," Ava said, glancing across the table at Cunningham, who was trying to look stoic. "Now tell us, what is the state of your business at this very moment?"

"We've been forced to shut down by your friend Han and his gang."

"I apologize that I had to ask Han to do that, but I need Mr. Cunningham to understand the gravity of the situation, and I thought it best if it came from you."

"I'll tell him all right," Su said, her voice rising. "We're closed. Han and his men came here this afternoon, sent all the workers home, and told them they weren't to come back. This is your fault, Mr. Cunningham. I told Ms. Lee that it isn't fair, that it isn't right to shut down the Simmons business because of Canada. She won't listen to me. Maybe you can persuade her."

"Is there anything you'd like to ask Ms. Su?" Ava said to Cunningham.

"What those men are doing is illegal. Can't you go to the police?" Cunningham asked.

"The last thing anyone would want is to have the police coming to the warehouse," she said. "Besides, even if I did call them, once they knew that it's Han who's here, they wouldn't interfere."

"Who is this Han?" asked Cunningham.

"He's the head of the major triad organization in Chengdu. My so-called security team at the warehouse is terrified of him."

Cunningham looked at Todd Howell. "This woman is hiring gangsters. How can you approve?"

"This is the first I've heard of it," Howell said, and then turned to Ava. "Is it true?"

"No, they're just friends who are doing me a favour," Ava said, which brought smiles from Eddie and Derek. "But they'll stay in the warehouse for as long as I want. And without an agreement with Mr. Cunningham, I'm afraid that could be weeks or months or actually become a permanent closure. Ms. Su, did you hear what I just said about the possibility of permanent closure?"

"I heard."

"And in case you think you can find another location, I would ask Han to pay a visit to the various labs in the city to make sure none of them sell anything to you without his permission."

Su didn't respond immediately, then blurted, "Mr.

Cunningham, you need to resolve this. Randy will be angry beyond belief when I tell him what's going on."

"Speaking of Randy," Ava said, "I'm going to ask Han to take you home in a few minutes. When you get there, the first thing I want you to do is call Randy. Tell him exactly what's happened and what it will take to resolve it. Han can give you my cellphone number, and if Randy wants to speak directly to me, we can make that possible."

"You can count on me doing that."

"Then we're finished. Thank you for your honesty," Ava said.

The four men sitting at the table said nothing when Ava ended the call, and for the first time Cunningham seemed to be decidedly uncomfortable.

"I know that Pastor Rogers and the Simmons family are close, but the thing is, the Simmonses are running a business in Chengdu that has to be taking in hundreds of millions of dollars," Ava said to him. "It's easy to be partners in Christ when there's no money on the line. I'm not sure the Simmonses will want to be partners with your pastor in anything if their business falls apart."

"You don't know anything about the strength of their friendship," Cunningham said.

"You're right, I don't. But I think I'm going to find out, once Randy Simmons learns what's happened in Chengdu."

"You could be disappointed."

"Perhaps, but the Simmons family isn't our only leverage. If we can't reach an agreement, I'm going to call some friends I have in the RCMP and turn over all the information I have. With all due respect to the efforts Todd made in the past, I don't think the Mounties will pass on it again. We'll also ensure that the news media are briefed."

Cunningham glared at her.

"I'm giving you a chance to avoid all that unpleasantness," Ava said. "All you have to do is send thirty-five million dollars to Mr. Howell's law firm."

"This is blackmail."

"No, this is justice. Any impartial person would think we're being fair. If we had calculated the damage you caused to people who trusted you, we could have asked for fifty million."

Cunningham lowered his head, and she knew she had gotten to him. "If it was up to me, I would tell you to go ahead and do your worst," he snapped. "But obviously I have an obligation to speak to the pastor, and he may need to speak to some board members."

"You can call the pastor from here if you want. We'll leave you alone in the room while you do."

"This isn't something I would discuss with him on the phone, and most certainly never from here."

"Well, if you're going to meet with him, you'd better do it fast. I have a deadline that we haven't talked about yet."

"What do you mean you have a deadline? We won't be rushed. The charges you're tossing around have ramifications that must be thoroughly discussed," he said. "And that's not an admission of any wrongdoing, only my acknowledgement that your slanders could damage the chapel and the pastor's reputation."

"Did the pastor know you were coming here for a meeting?" Ava asked, ignoring his last comment.

"Why does that matter?"

"Because I'm assuming you told him about the call from Muir," Ava said. "If you did, then I'm sure he's waiting for a report. So when we're finished here, you can scurry up to Aurora and give him one. My deadline for an answer is midnight tonight."

"Are you serious?"

Ava stared at him and sighed. "I am entirely serious. I want thirty-five million dollars deposited into this firm's bank account. We'll give you until midnight to tell us if you're going to do it or not. You should call Mr. Howell with your decision. If he doesn't hear from you, we'll assume you aren't going to pay. If the answer is no, we will go to the RCMP and the news media, and we'll keep the Simmons distribution centre in Chengdu closed permanently," Ava said. "If you do decide to pay, it will be a single full payment — we don't do installment plans. Once we have the money, the distribution centre can reopen."

"And if we decide to pay this blackmail, I suppose you'll want the money by tomorrow," Cunningham said sarcastically.

"We're not that unreasonable," Ava said. "We'll give you a few days."

Cunningham stood up.

"Before you go, there's something you should take with you," Ava said, reaching for a file folder. "Earlier I mentioned that we have copies of bank transactions, purchase orders, and shipping orders. A representative sample is in this folder. If you want more, we'll supply them, but review what I'm giving you with the pastor. It might help you reach a decision."

Cunningham glared at Ava as he took the folder. He tucked it under his arm and left the boardroom, slamming the door behind him.

"I don't think that went quite the way he expected," Ava said.

(45)

CUNNINGHAM'S DEPARTURE LEFT A THOUGHTFUL silence in its wake. No one spoke for a minute, until Derek finally said, "That was one angry little man."

"No shit," said Eddie.

"Did you notice that he didn't mention the three million you transferred out of the Chengdu bank account? I thought when you asked for thirty-five million it might have come up," Howell said.

"He didn't want to acknowledge it because it would mean he knew about the bank account, and that would tie him to Muir. He'll try to blame all this on Muir and Jasmine Yip," Ava said.

"How can he deny his involvement after that conversation with Su Na?" Howell said.

"We caught him off guard. By the time he gets to Aurora he'll have figured out some excuse."

Howell pointed to the whiteboards. "But how can he plausibly deny the chapel's involvement when we have all this information?"

"I didn't say he was going to be plausible. I just meant he would pretend," Ava said.

"What do you think they'll do?" Derek asked.

"They won't concede, at least not at first," she said. "I expect they'll try to find out how firm we are about the money and the deadline."

Howell mulled over Ava's words and then said, "What do you want to do now? You can stay here for as long as you want. We have a couple of empty offices you can use."

"I think I'll go back to my apartment. You can reach me by cellphone if anything happens."

"And if we don't hear from them by the deadline?"

"Then we'll reconvene in the morning, figure out an approach to the RCMP, and decide which journalists we should contact."

"You were serious about that?" Howell asked.

"Completely," she said as she stood up. "I think the meeting went well. Frankly, I can't think of anything else we could have said. We made our position clear, so now it's up to them."

She said goodbye to Howell at the door, then walked to the elevator with Derek. They rode it in silence to the ground floor, but when they reached the street, he said, "That was really good, Ava. You haven't lost your edge from the old days."

"I'm glad you think that, because it didn't come as naturally as it used to. That's why I kept looking at my notebook."

They drove north on University Avenue, making small talk as they went.

"I'll get out here," Ava said when the car stopped at a red light at the intersection of Bloor and Avenue Road. She leaned over and kissed Derek on the cheek. “Thanks for your support these past few days. Now you can go home and tell Mimi about the three million.”

“I think I’ll wait until things are completely settled,” he said as Ava opened the car door. “You will call me if you hear anything from Todd?”

“You will most definitely hear from me,” she said, and sighed. “But I suspect this is going to be a very long day.”

Ava stood on the corner for a moment after Derek drove off. She was on her own, with time to kill. What to do? She thought about going for a run, but if Howell called and needed to see her, she might be kilometres from the condo and would need time to change back into her business attire. Within minutes of where she stood were three outstanding museums: the sprawling Royal Ontario Museum, the Gardiner Museum of Ceramic Art, and the Bata Shoe Museum. It had been some time since she’d been to the Gardiner, she thought. The museum was only a hundred metres south of where she was standing. Ava turned and started walking towards it.

The Gardiner was set back from the road. Ava admired its minimalist exterior, which featured an immense screen promoting current exhibits. As she climbed the steps leading to the entrance, however, she realized that the exterior reminded her almost eerily of the front of Malcolm Muir’s house, with its modern brickwork and dominant front window. The thought had no sooner entered her mind when her phone rang.

She looked at the screen and saw a Singapore number. “This is Ava,” she said, coming to a stop.

“This is Jasmine. What have you done?” she said angrily.

"I assume you're referring to my meeting with Patrick Cunningham this morning."

"What else? Essie just called her mother and went on a rant about me betraying the family by telling lies about Patrick."

"I thought I asked you not to have your phones on."

"My aunt doesn't always listen to me, and it was her daughter who was calling, not Muir."

"Did you talk to Essie?"

"She kept insisting that my aunt put me on the phone. I refused, because I didn't know what to say to her," Jasmine said. "You promised to keep me out of this, and now you've thrown me into the middle of it."

"Essie was probably calling to confirm what you told me. I said I would shield you, but there's no way I could disguise the fact that you're a key player in what's been going on," Ava said. "And I swear, the only time I mentioned Essie was to tell Cunningham she called you to ask if you could help Muir launder some money. Besides, we're going to resolve this entire matter today. One way or another it will be over, and I will make sure that you and everyone else who helped me is protected."

"How can you do that?"

"Cunningham knows we used triads to shut down the distribution warehouse in Chengdu. Su Na told him over the phone, and she emphasized that she was terrified of the men we used. So he and the others know I have connections with people who don't always play nice. I will threaten to unleash those same people on them if they try to harm you."

"Okay . . . I guess."

"Listen, Jasmine, this thing with Essie will blow over."

Jasmine paused. "Is Essie in trouble?"

"No, but Cunningham could be. We'll know soon enough. He and his colleagues have a big decision to make. This will be resolved today," Ava repeated.

"You're sure of that?'

"Absolutely."

"Can you let me know which way it goes?"

"Sure."

"Thanks. I hope you get what you want."

"Me too," Ava said, and ended the call.

Cunningham hadn't wasted any time contacting his wife, and she had been just as quick to reach out to Singapore. It appeared that he was trying to confirm what Ava actually knew and how she had come to know it.

Ava climbed the final steps to the museum, paid her admission fee, and was quickly immersed in the delicate world of ceramics. She spent over an hour in the Japanese and Chinese sections. As someone who could barely draw stick people, Ava was awed by the artistic ability and craftsmanship on display. After the Asian galleries, she made her way to a special exhibit called *Savour: Food Culture in the Age of Enlightenment*. As she was slowly taking it in, she checked the time and saw that the day was drifting by. She had left her phone on vibrate, and as she was leaving the exhibit, it buzzed.

"This is Todd. How soon can you get back to my office?" he said.

"What's happened?"

"I just got a phone call from the chapel's lawyer. He wants to meet."

"That was fast."

"Hugh Campbell, the lead lawyer, has been in

communication with the pastor. He said something uncomplimentary to me about your deadline and added that rushed law makes for bad law."

"Will the pastor be at the meeting?"

"No, it will just be the lawyers — Campbell and two of his associates. Your attendance was specifically requested. I have to let Campbell know when you can get here."

"I'm two minutes from the Museum subway station. I can be in your office in about twenty minutes."

"Ava, I have to tell you that Campbell is quite formidable. He's a top-notch lawyer, smart and tough," Howell said. "If he has a weakness, it's that he likes to lecture."

"I'm good at listening to lectures."

"Just don't overreact if he starts to run on."

"I'll behave," she said. "See you in about twenty."

She called Derek while she was walking to the subway station. "Hey," he answered.

"The chapel lawyers want to meet. I'm heading to Howell's office."

"Shit, I can't leave the house right now. Mimi went out to run a few errands and I'm alone with Amber."

"Well, come when you can. We'll probably start without you, but I'll try to stall so you don't miss too much."

"I'll head downtown as soon as Mimi gets here."

"See you soon."

(46)

EDDIE NG WAS WAITING FOR HER AT RECEPTION WHEN she arrived at Howell, Barker, and Mason. "Todd will be here in a minute, but he wants to know if you want me to cover the whiteboards again," he said.

"Leave them as they are, and make sure we have three sets of the documents to hand out," she said.

"Everything is set."

She and Eddie went into the boardroom and took the same seats they'd used that morning.

"Hey," Howell said from the doorway.

Ava saw that he'd changed into a crisp white shirt. "You've dressed for the occasion," she said.

"Campbell is always immaculately dressed. He thinks it gives him a psychological advantage," Howell said, joining them at the table.

"I looked up Campbell on the way here," Ava said. "I wouldn't have thought someone that senior would be involved in day-to-day operations. Is there a reason why he's handling this personally?"

"Money," Howell said.

There was a knock at the door and the office assistant said, "Your visitors are here, Mr. Howell."

"Show them in," he said.

Both Howell and Eddie Ng stood up. Ava did the same.

The tall, thin man who led the trio of visitors into the boardroom had a striking appearance. Campbell was six feet two inches tall, Ava guessed, with thinning ginger hair tinged with grey and a neatly trimmed beard. Bright blue eyes were set over a long, narrow nose. He wore a charcoal-grey suit that looked tailored, a white shirt, and a tartan tie of blue and green squares with thin lines of red and white.

"Thanks for seeing us on such short notice, Todd," he said in a plummy voice. "These are my associates, Greg Berry and Lisa Tran."

Howell extended his hand. "It's my pleasure, Hugh. And these are my associates, Eddie Ng and Ava Lee."

"Hi, Lisa," Eddie said. "Good to see you again."

"Same here, Eddie," she said, and looked at Campbell. "Eddie and I graduated in the same class."

Campbell shook Howell's hand and then turned to Ava. "I've been looking forward to meeting you," he said.

"I can't imagine why," Ava said, her eyes on his tie. "Is that the Campbell tartan?"

"This is Campbell of Cawdor," he said. "There are four official Campbell tartans. This is the most colourful; it brightens up what I'm told is a somewhat dour personality."

"Let's sit," Howell said. "Does anyone want coffee or tea before we start?"

"I think we should get right down to business," Campbell said. "But before we start, Todd, do you have any objections if this meeting is off the record? This is complicated subject matter, and I think candour from both sides would be beneficial."

"I have no problem with that," Howell said.

"Do you speak for Ms. Lee as well?"

"On that subject he does," Ava said.

"Excellent," Campbell said. He sat across from them, with Tran and Berry on either side. Berry looked to be in his thirties. His hair was dishevelled, his face was haggard, and he seemed tired. Lisa Tran was petite and wore a black pantsuit and no makeup, which made her look pale; her silky black hair was tied back like Ava's. She and Berry had notepads in front of them and pens in hand.

"I would like to start, if you have no objections," Campbell said. Before Howell could answer he nodded at Ava. "I would like to know more about you, young lady. You appear out of nowhere, reinvigorate my friend Howell and that tiresome Harvest Investment Fund situation he chased so unsuccessfully, and then you put the fear of God into Patrick Cunningham. So tell me, who are you? What's your stake in this?"

"Hugh, I don't think this is —" Howell began.

"No, Todd, I don't mind answering those questions," Ava interrupted. "I am a Toronto resident, Mr. Campbell. I'm a trained forensic accountant with degrees from York University and Babson College in Wellesley, Massachusetts. I worked for more than ten years with a partner in Hong Kong in the debt-collection business."

"You're a debt collector?" Campbell said, managing to combine surprise and disappointment.

"I *was* a debt collector, but we didn't work for Visa or American Express. The debts we pursued were in the millions.

Tommy Ordonez, the wealthiest man in the Philippines, was twice a client and is now a friend, and so was Changxing Wong, one of the wealthiest men in China. But not all our clients were situated in Asia. We represented, for example, a group of Canadian citizens of Vietnamese origin who lost more than thirty million dollars in a bank scam. We recovered it all," she said, and noticed Lisa Tran glance at Eddie.

"When my partner died, I closed the agency and started an investment company with two friends. We are majority shareholders in various companies in Asia."

"What kind of companies?"

"Logistics, warehousing, a furniture manufacturer, and a trading company. And we control PÖ, a fashion house in Shanghai that sells worldwide."

"Have you heard of PÖ?" Campbell asked Lisa Tran.

"I have. It's a very trendy brand," she said.

"That's enough about your personal affairs, I think," Campbell said. "Now, why are you involved in this business?"

"My best friend's family was torn apart when her father committed suicide in a shed in the family's garden. He had lost his entire life's savings to the crooked Harvest Investment Fund. My friend reached out for help getting the money back, and I said I would try. That's when I met Todd. He shared what he had with me, and I took it from there."

"To where?" Campbell asked.

"Todd had traced the money to Amsterdam. I tracked it from there to Antwerp, then to Guangzhou, and then to Chengdu, where it's being used to purchase synthetic drugs that are distributed in Canada." Ava pointed to the whiteboards. "If you wish, I'll take you through what happened in detail. And we can provide you with a paper trail of bank documents, emails, company registrations, purchase orders for drugs, and customer orders for the same. I gave a copy of those papers to Patrick Cunningham, but I doubt he had time to share them with you. We also have some photos if you want to see them."

"I am interested in your presentation, and we will also examine the paperwork, but to put it all in a proper context, perhaps you could tell me what kind of result you're expecting after all this effort."

"I'm expecting that by midnight today the people responsible for this scam will agree to put thirty-five million dollars into this firm's bank account and then conclude the transaction within a few days."

"Mr. Cunningham explained that to us. I was hoping he hadn't heard correctly," Campbell said. "He also mentioned various actions you threatened to undertake if your financial demands aren't met. I have to tell you, Ms. Lee, threats like those carry absolutely no weight with me."

"I hope Cunningham also explained Harvest Table's involvement in the drug business I mentioned a moment ago."

Campbell smiled. "Mr. Cunningham told us what information you claim to have, but I want to hear your reiteration. Given the time constraints, could you stick to the main points? "

"Certainly," Ava said. She spoke for more than thirty minutes, using the whiteboards to cover the major points and tying them neatly together. No one else said a word, but Campbell's attention never left her, and Berry and Tran made copious notes. When she had finished, she pointed to the document packages in front of Todd Howell. "As I said earlier, we also have a paper trail. Eddie, could you pass everyone a documentation package?"

Eddie walked to the other side of the table and put a file in front of each of the Campbell lawyers. "Why don't we give you an hour to review the documents, and then we can reconvene," Ava said.

"You seem inordinately fond of setting deadlines, Ms. Lee," Campbell said with a slight smile. "We'll advise you when we're done."

Ava stood up. "We'll leave you to it then." She left the boardroom, with Eddie and Howell trailing behind.

"We'll go to my office," Howell said.

When they got there, Howell held the door open for Ava and Eddie and then closed it behind them. He sat down behind his desk, shook his head, and said, "Your presentation was terrific. I kept waiting for Campbell to interrupt you with questions or comments, but you had him transfixed."

"I wanted him to realize that we're dealing in facts."

"I have no doubt he got that message, and it will be hammered home even more forcibly when he sees that the paperwork supports everything you said."

"I hope you're right," Ava said, looking past Howell at the view out his window. "Now we're back to waiting. I think I'll go downstairs and get some fresh air."

"Don't wander too far," said Howell.

Ava took the elevator to the ground floor and walked out onto King Street. The building had benches set along its front wall, and she sat down on one that was in the shade.

Her phone rang and she leapt at it, thinking it might be Howell telling her to come back to the office.

"Is this Ava Lee I'm talking to?" a man asked with faintly Southern twang.

"It is. And who is this?"

"I'm Randy Simmons. I believe you know of me."

"I do. I assume you're calling me because Su Na asked you to."

"She did."

"Good."

"That doesn't make this any better in my eyes."

"It is a complicated situation."

"Not from where I sit," Simmons said. "What I've got is a woman I don't know closing my business for no reason I can understand. I'm not taking kindly to it."

"Have you spoken to Sammy Rogers yet?"

"My business has nothing to do with Sammy Rogers."

"Unfortunately it does, since he's using your facility in Chengdu to distribute his drugs," Ava said.

"He pays us for a service, that's all. Su Na says she made a commitment to you not to fill any more Canadian orders. You can leave some of your men there to make sure she keeps her word."

"It's more complex than that. I think of you and Sammy Rogers as partners — maybe not in a formal way, but your businesses are certainly intertwined. You market your products the same way. You have the same supplier. You share the same warehouse. You use the same distribution method. I know you even bank at the same places, and Rogers's websites bear an uncanny resemblance to yours."

Simmons paused, and Ava knew he was evaluating what he'd just heard. "I repeat, we are paid for providing a service. We will cancel the service. We will sever all ties with the Harvest Table organization until whatever problem you have with them is resolved. I don't know why that wouldn't satisfy you."

"I'm sorry, but I'm keeping the warehouse closed until the issues with Rogers are resolved."

"What issues? I have no idea what this is about. Su Na said it was something to do with money. If it is, it has nothing to do with me. Sammy operates independently from us."

"Sammy and his partners stole a substantial amount of money from the people I'm representing. He used that money to fund the drug business. My intention is to get that money back."

"You want me to pressure him to pay you? Is that what this is about?" Simmons said.

"It is," Ava said.

"Well, that makes things clear. But even if I agreed, why would Sammy listen to me? He's his own man."

"That's for you to figure out. You know him better than I do. Pressure him, persuade him, or threaten him — whatever you think will work — but find a way to convince him he has to settle with us. As long as he doesn't, the warehouse in Chengdu will stay closed."

Simmons became quiet and then said harshly, "What you're doing is breaking the law."

"Coming from someone who's illegally selling painkillers, I find that comment more than a little hypocritical."

"We're providing relief to people whose lives would otherwise be full of suffering," he said.

"Whatever you choose to believe."

"I can't tell you how much I hate this conversation and how distasteful I find you," Simmons said. "This sticks in my craw, and every fibre in my body wants to tell you to go fuck yourself."

"This situation calls for you to be logical, not emotional."

Simmons became quiet, and Ava wondered if she had lost him.

"I'll call Sammy and I'll give it my best shot, but only because I have to," he said finally. "But what if I can't get him to come to your party? Is there any room for us to work out something else?"

"We need to see results. The distribution centre will stay closed until Rogers pays us."

"You are a real bitch," he said.

"I've been called worse."

The line went dead. *That didn't go so badly*, Ava thought. She hadn't set out to make Simmons angry, but given that she had, her hope was that his anger would be transferred to Rogers.

"Ava, what are you doing out here?"

She turned to see Derek standing only a few feet away. "We've finished round one of the meeting. The lawyers are going over our documentation now. When they're done, we'll resume."

"How did it go?"

"They listened to what I had to say, but their lead lawyer isn't happy with our deadline. I suspect that won't be the only thing he doesn't like."

"Speaking of intense, I called out to you a couple of times, but you seemed really involved in that phone conversation."

"Sorry. I was speaking to Randy Simmons, and I guess I didn't hear you," she said.

"How did it go with Simmons?"

"He's not very happy with me."

"Is that a good thing?"

"Most definitely," Ava said.

Her phone rang again. "Ave Lee," she answered.

"This is Eddie," he said. "They're ready to resume the meeting."

"Derek has just joined me. We'll be right there," she said.

(47)

TODD HOWELL WAS WAITING AT THE RECEPTION DESK when they returned to the tenth floor.

"How is the mood in the boardroom?" Ava asked.

"Serious, but I wouldn't call it grim. They left the door partially open, and my assistant kept an eye on them. Greg and Lisa went through the paperwork, and Campbell spent a lot of his time on the phone, likely with Cunningham or Rogers. Campbell sent Greg to tell us they're ready to talk, and he seemed calm enough."

"They didn't take a lot of time."

"The paperwork was well organized and self-explanatory," Howell said, and then he smiled at Derek. "Glad you could make it."

They entered the boardroom to find Campbell standing with his back to them and talking on his cellphone. "Shall we come back when he's finished?" Howell asked.

"That won't be necessary. I'm done," Campbell said, returning to the table.

"Let me introduce Derek Liang," Ava said. "He's a friend who has been helping with this case."

Campbell nodded to Derek. "Patrick Cunningham mentioned you. Is it true your father-in-law committed suicide?"

"He did. He was one of the victims of the Harvest Investment Fund theft."

"How tragic. You have our condolences," Campbell said to him. "But tell me, when Ms. Lee says you helped her with the case, does that mean you're familiar with all the details?"

"It does."

Campbell looked at Howell. "This could be a complication."

"What do you mean?" Howell asked.

"Sorry, I'm leaping ahead of myself," Campbell said. "Do you still represent the investors in the fund?"

"I never stopped representing them, though the case was no longer being actively pursued."

"As I understand it, Ms. Lee approached you and you shared your files and your opinions with her, at which point she undertook an independent investigation."

"That's correct," Howell said.

"Do your clients know that she was involved?"

"No. I had the authority to contract with Ava on their behalf. I didn't consult with them."

"What kind of contract was that?"

"I gave her full authority to represent our interests as they related to recovery of the stolen money."

"So she was working for you?" Campbell asked.

"And on behalf of the clients I represent, including Mr. Liang's wife and mother-in-law."

"Do you have a financial arrangement with Ms. Lee?"

"I do, but I'm not going to share the details."

"I don't need them. It's enough to know that you two are contractually bound."

"Hugh, where are you going with this?" Howell asked.

"I just want to be clear about who knows what."

"The people at this table are the only ones from our side who know anything."

Campbell pursed his lips. "Under those circumstances," he said slowly, "my clients are prepared to attempt to reach a settlement."

"Who exactly are your clients? You haven't been clear about that," Ava said.

"Harvest Table Bible Chapel and its senior officers," Campbell said, apparently surprised by the question.

"And what are the circumstances that could lead to a settlement?" she asked.

"You are unrelentingly straightforward," Campbell replied.

"That's the second time I've been told that in the past hour," she said.

"And Ava's question is to the point," Howell added.

"I was commenting on her style, not objecting to the question," Campbell said.

"Then please answer it," Howell said.

"Of prime importance, my clients insist that whatever settlement we reach must be maintained in the strictest confidence."

"You want a non-disclosure agreement?" Howell said.

"Yes, and one that is strict about penalties if it is broken."

"What can't be disclosed?"

"All that information," Campbell said, pointing to the whiteboards. "And all of this," he said, touching the file folder. "And anything else you know about this nasty piece of business. None of it can ever see the light of day."

"Would this settlement include admission of guilt or wrongdoing?" asked Howell.

"It most definitely would not. My clients have no guilt, although the pastor does rue the day he met Malcolm Muir."

"So they are laying the entire responsibility at the feet of Muir?" Ava said.

"Not entirely. The woman Jasmine Yip, whom you identified as managing various bank accounts, has some accountability," he said. "And I'm told that the local Chengdu woman, Su Na, who manages the warehouse, is another of Muir's associates."

"Yip only did what Muir told her to do, and she didn't know Muir until Patrick Cunningham's wife introduced them," Ava said. "Su Na distributed drugs for the chapel under conditions of a contract signed by Pastor Rogers."

"I didn't see a copy of any such contract in the paperwork you gave us."

"We don't have a copy, but Su Na saw it."

"Does she have a copy?"

"No."

"Of course she doesn't. It doesn't exist."

"This is getting absurd," Ava said.

Campbell smiled. "It's certainly becoming counterproductive, and I think we're wasting time with these suppositions. Let's go back to square one. You've been given the basis for a settlement. Do you want to pursue it or take another path? Frankly, I don't see another way forward. And I have to add that, if I had my way, there wouldn't be an offer of a settlement at all. You have shown me nothing that connects the pastor to this business, while Muir's name and activities are all over it."

"If you believe that, why are you offering a settlement?" she asked.

"Harvest Table is Pastor Rogers's life's work, and he doesn't want to risk having its reputation sullied."

"Excuse me, Hugh," Berry said softly, and then whispered something to Campbell.

"Apologies. Greg has just reminded me that our clients also want a statement attesting that none of the signatories of the non-disclosure agreement assigns one iota of guilt to the chapel or its senior officers."

"That's going a bit far, isn't it?" said Howell.

"That's what my clients want. They won't pay you ten cents without it."

"Who would be party to the non-disclosure?" Ava asked.

"All of you."

"And in return the chapel pays thirty-five million dollars?" Ava asked.

Campbell shifted in his chair and leaned forward. "In truth, we think your demand is wildly excessive," he said to Ava. He turned to Howell. "We're asking you to be reasonable. We can pay less money immediately as payment in full, or we can pay more over an extended period of time."

"What is less money?" Ava asked.

"My clients can't raise more than five million dollars right now, and that's with tapping every resource available."

Howell interrupted before Ava could speak. "And what do you have in mind as a larger payment over more time?"

"Ten million over three years," Campbell said.

Ava put her hands on the table and started to rise. Howell touched her lightly on the wrist. "Ava, before you say anything, I think we should take some time to talk."

"That's very good advice, Todd," Campbell said. "And I want to stress, Ms. Lee, that I don't doubt you are a woman of your word and that your demands are sincere. But we are in the business of determining a middle ground between what one party wants and what the other is prepared to give. I advised Pastor Rogers not to give you anything. For the reasons I've mentioned, he decided an offer should be made, and I think it is a generous one. There's a saying about a bird in the hand being worth two in the bush, and I think this is one of those occasions."

"Jesus," Derek said, looking at Ava.

"I know," she said to him.

"You know what?" Campbell asked.

"It isn't important," Ava said, and turned to Todd. "Okay, let's talk."

A cellphone buzzed. Campbell took his from his pocket and looked at the screen. "Excuse me, I have to take this. It's the pastor, and who knows — he may have decided to listen to me and take his offer off the table."

"Go ahead," Howell said.

Campbell walked to the far corner of the boardroom and turned his back on them. The conversation lasted several minutes. When it ended, he returned looking slightly uncomfortable. "He hasn't changed his mind, but there's one more thing to factor into your deliberations," he said. "This is a request and not a demand, but if we can reach a verbal agreement today, as a show of good faith my client would appreciate it if you would remove the people you have employed from the premises of the Simmons Christian Mission in Chengdu."

"We'll talk about that as well," Ava said.

"Excellent. my colleagues and I will leave you to it," Campbell. "Call me when you are ready to resume our talks. We've set aside the rest of the day and the evening for this, so we can be here in a jiffy."

(48)

NO ONE SPOKE UNTIL THE CAMPBELL LAWYERS HAD left the boardroom, and then it was Howell who said to Ava, "I know you don't want to hear this, but I have to congratulate you."

"Are you serious?"

"Campbell wasn't as overbearing as I've seen him before. But he was certainly trying to provoke you, and I thought your calm in the face of it was wonderful."

"I hardly deserve a compliment for containing my temper," Ava said.

"Perhaps not, but you do for getting a settlement offer from these people," Howell said. "I spent months chasing after that money with no results. I would have been thrilled to get five million dollars to split among the investors, and five million in this case may not be the final figure."

"Do you think there's room for negotiation on the amount?" Derek asked.

"It was an opening offer. I'm sure he's expecting us to counter."

"What should we counter with?" asked Eddie.

Howell looked towards Ava. "I think that's up to Ava to decide."

She sighed and looked at each of them in turn. "You know I hate having to back down," she said.

"What are our options?" Howell asked.

"We could tell them to go fuck themselves and move to Plan B," Derek said.

"After listening to Campbell, he might like it if we did," Howell said. "I believed him when he said he didn't want to settle. He's normally combative, but even more so when he senses weakness in the opposition's position."

"What's our weakness?" Ava asked.

"Can I hypothesize without offending you?"

"We're in this together. Be blunt."

"Well, Campbell did make a good point in that you haven't actually connected Rogers to the operation in Chengdu, or to the money in any way," Howell said.

"The chapel's debt was paid down by sixty million dollars. Where else did that money came from?" Eddie asked.

"Even if we can disprove Cunningham's story that the money came from wealthy donors, they can still claim that Rogers knew nothing about the chapel's finances," Howell said. "Cunningham is the chief financial officer as well as the chief operations officer. They could say he has complete control of all the chapel's money and that Rogers has only vague knowledge of their financial situation."

"Wouldn't that mean throwing Cunningham overboard?" asked Eddie.

"Maybe they're prepared to do that to protect Rogers and the chapel," Howell said. "But I can envision a nudge-nudge, wink-wink kind of deal, where Cunningham takes some of the blame but his involvement is characterized as a sin of omission rather than commission."

Ava nodded at Howell. "In other words, his only failure was to be too trusting."

"Exactly. He believed his old friend Muir and his wife's cousin when they told him the business was legal, and he had no idea what was actually going on."

"But Cunningham knew Muir stole from the fund," Derek said.

"He knows we claim it was stolen. What if he says Muir told him it was lost through bad investments and offered up his bankruptcies as proof? Who's to say Cunningham wouldn't buy a story like that? Moreover, what if he thought his old friend was genuinely contrite and deserved a second chance?"

"I'm glad you aren't representing the other side," Ava said.

"All I'm doing is getting into Hugh Campbell's head," said Howell. "I can hear him making all these arguments."

"They're fiction," Derek said.

"I know, but that doesn't prevent them from being peddled by two brilliant communicators — Rogers and Campbell."

"But we have the facts," said Derek.

"Facts only matter if someone is willing to listen," Ava said. "Todd is right. If nothing else, the other side can sow doubt and confusion."

"The RCMP would listen," said Derek.

"Probably, but then we'd be into a legal process that would take years, with an uncertain outcome. The investors still might not get any money back," she said. "Cunningham blamed Muir this morning. If Muir picks up and leaves the country, who's left to say that Cunningham's version of events isn't wrong? The only other person with direct knowledge is Jasmine Yip, a woman who lives in Singapore, and outside Canada's legal jurisdiction."

"How about the media?" he asked.

"I guarantee that every major news outlet you approach will go to the chapel for confirmation. At that point Hugh Campbell and his team will issue denials and threaten to sue anyone who runs a story," Howell said. "That's one of the things I meant earlier when I said Campbell might like us to try Plan B. His number of billable hours could skyrocket."

"Ava still has leverage if she keeps the distribution centre in Chengdu closed," Derek said.

"Can you do that indefinitely?" Howell asked her.

"For a while at least, but obviously it isn't a permanent solution. They'd eventually find someone else in China to supply them with pills, and they'd find another warehouse somewhere."

"I'm not trying to be negative with all this, and everything we've discussed is hypothetical, of course, but it had to be said out loud," Howell said. "What we need to do now, I believe, is find out how much Campbell and Rogers are really prepared to pay. Which brings me back to the subject of a counter-offer."

"I still don't like it, but you've made some good points. So yes, let's find out where we stand," Ava said.

"What would be an acceptable number for you?"

"Let's ask for twenty million. That's meeting them not quite halfway."

"Considering he started at five, I think that's a bit rich," Howell said.

"Then he'll say no."

Howell signalled his discomfort with a heavy sigh. "Why don't we try fifteen?"

Ava pursed her lips and slowly moved her head from side to side, as if struggling with the number. "Okay, fifteen. But we want all of it in one payment," she said finally.

"Do you have an issue with the non-disclosure agreement and the statement that we don't attach any guilt to Rogers or the chapel?"

"If they give us fifteen million, I don't care about those things."

Howell reached for the phone on the table. "I'll tell them we're ready to meet."

"Why bother? Let's do it by phone," Ava said.

"All right," Howell said.

Derek smiled encouragingly at Ava. "Fifteen million is a good number if we can get it," he said.

Howell put the phone on speaker mode as he called Campbell.

"Todd, are you ready to sit down again?" Campbell asked when he answered.

"We thought we'd do it by phone. We're all here on speaker."

"That's not a problem. Give me a minute to round up Greg and Lisa."

"Do you want to handle this?" Howell asked Ava.

"You do it."

Ava stared out the window as they waited for Campbell to return. All her instincts told her it wasn't going to end well. Was she just following Uncle's advice to expect the worst and be grateful for anything better than that?

"You have our full attention," Campbell said finally.

"Well, Hugh, we want to settle this, but we don't think the offer on the table is sufficient," Howell said.

"What do you think would be sufficient?" Campbell asked.

"A one-time payment of fifteen million," said Howell.

"That's ludicrous," Campbell said quickly. "How did you come up with that sum?"

"Our initial request was for thirty-five million. This is meeting you more than halfway."

"It's meeting us more than halfway only if we'd accepted that your initial demand had any merit — which we most decidedly did not," Campbell said. "So as not to waste time, let me be frank with you. Our absolute upper ceiling is ten million, and we've already offered you that."

"Over three years."

"Yes, and we will never pay that amount on a one-time basis, so don't bother asking."

"You have no flexibility at all?"

Campbell didn't respond right away, but Ava could hear background conversation and assumed he was speaking with Berry and Tran. *He's playing with us*, she whispered to Howell.

Howell frowned, and she knew he wasn't pleased with the way the conversation was going.

"I'll tell you what," Campbell said after a full minute of silence, "since ten is our ceiling, we're prepared to offer you six million as a one-time payment. That's us meeting you more than halfway."

"Hugh —" Howell started to say.

"That's our final offer," Campbell interrupted. "If you need time to discuss it, please take all that you need. We'll be here for another few hours and then back in the morning. Unlike

Ms. Lee, I don't believe in setting arbitrary deadlines."

Howell looked at Ava. *What do you want me to do?* he mouthed.

She leaned closer to the phone. "Mr. Campbell, we'll take the six million," she said, and tried to ignore the shocked reaction from Derek, Eddie, and Howell.

"Is this Ms. Lee speaking?"

"Yes."

"Excellent. Let me thank you for being reasonable. One of the things I like about accountants is their practicality," Campbell said. "But I still have to ask Todd if you're speaking for him as well."

"She is," Howell said, after the briefest of pauses.

"That's good to hear. And can I assume that the non-disclosure agreement and a statement asserting that Pastor Rogers and the chapel are innocent of any wrongdoing are agreeable to you as well?"

"They are," Ava said.

"What about the request to allow the Simmons Mission to resume its business?"

"No."

"I beg your pardon?"

"We're keeping the warehouse closed," she said.

"That wasn't my understanding."

"Mr. Campbell, you framed your request that we let it reopen as a show of good faith, not a condition," said Ava. "I've decided that I'm not interested in extending good faith."

"But you'll be paid as soon as the non-disclosure agreement is finalized. Unless I'm misjudging the competence of Todd's firm, we can have that done within forty-eight hours. What's forty-eight hours?"

"Who said anything about forty-eight hours?"

"What are you implying?"

"I'm not implying anything. I am stating quite clearly that the warehouse will remain closed."

"For how long?"

"Until I say it isn't."

"And when will that be?"

"I have no idea."

"The business operating there will suffer considerable losses."

"Why should I care? In fact, why should you care?" Ava said. "The Simmons family means nothing to me, and according to you, Pastor Rogers has no involvement in either business."

"Don't pretend you don't know this will be a problem."

"And don't *you* pretend that Rogers knows nothing about what's been going on in Chengdu," Ava said. "I was feeling guilty the moment I was prepared to accept thirty-five million dollars to ignore that fact, but my primary concern was for the investors."

"The pastor insists he knew nothing about those businesses."

"Then keeping the warehouse closed shouldn't be an impediment to closing the deal."

"For our part, we have no vested interest in keeping it open or closed," Campbell said. "All the pastor is doing is trying to help a friend. Given that we're prepared to pay you six million dollars and that closing the business the way you did is an illegal act, I don't think letting it resume its normal activity is too much to ask. You'll have to do it sooner or later."

"Then it will be later."

"I have to tell you, the pastor will not be happy to hear this. I hope it doesn't jeopardize our agreement."

"I'm sure you can explain the difference between a condition and a favour. In my world, favours come at no monetary cost. Conditions don't."

Campbell became quiet. "I'll have to get back to you," he said finally.

"That doesn't surprise me," Ava said. "We'll stay here until you do."

She pushed the END CALL button on the phone.

"What just happened?" Howell said.

"I decided to go with Plan C."

"I didn't know there was a Plan C."

"There wasn't until now," said Ava.

(49)

HOWELL PUSHED BACK HIS CHAIR BACK AND ROSE TO his feet. Ava thought her unilateral decision might have irked him, and for a few seconds she thought he was going to leave the boardroom. Instead he went to the credenza, poured a coffee, and came back to the table.

Ava waited until he sat down before saying, "As you and Campbell were talking, I was processing what you said to us earlier," she said. "I believe they think we're bluffing, which is why they're being so hard-nosed. They don't believe we'll go to the Mounties or the news media and risk getting nothing. And I'm sure that, in the back of their minds, they know they have Muir, Jasmine, Su Na, and maybe even Cunningham to use as scapegoats if they have to. If I had managed to connect Rogers to the operation in Chengdu or any of the bank accounts, we'd be in a different bargaining position. But I didn't, and they're taking advantage of that."

"Is that why you agreed to take the six million?"

"I want more than six million. As far as I'm concerned, we're still negotiating. Keeping the warehouse in Chengdu closed is our leverage."

"What if they make the six million conditional on your reopening it? What if they threaten to take the money off the table?" Howell asked.

"Then our deal will go up in smoke and we'll get nothing, because I'm not reopening the warehouse unless we get paid to do it."

"Then what do we do if we have no deal?"

"Show them we're not bluffing by reverting to Plan A."

"I can't imagine Campbell will cancel the agreement because of the warehouse," Eddie said. "If he cared about it, he would already have made it a condition."

"I think that's an accurate assessment. I believe Campbell was being truthful when he said they have no vested interest in the warehouse. If I'm reading between the lines correctly, I believe the chapel has decided to get out of the drug business — at least for now and at least in Chengdu. That's why they didn't include reopening the warehouse as a condition. And I have to say that, from an ethical viewpoint, it makes this negotiation a lot easier for me. The idea of taking their money and letting them continue to import opioids was troubling me," she said.

"Do you really think they want out?" Howell asked.

"They're smart enough to realize that carrying on could be dangerous. If we could figure out what they've been up to, why can't someone else? Right now they're still safe, so it's the perfect time to cut and run. We're their only threat, so they're prepared to pay us to go away. If we do, the business becomes a memory. The only fly in the ointment is Rogers's relationship with the Simmons family. If they're tight as I hope they are, Rogers won't want to leave them in such a difficult position."

"So this is all about using the Simmons family to bring pressure to bear on Rogers?" Howell asked.

"That's exactly what it is," Ava said.

"Did the other collection jobs you did get this complicated?"

"Some of them," Ava said. "Now, Todd, you'll have to excuse me. I should be making a call to Randy Simmons. Is there an office I can use?"

"You can use mine," Howell said.

"If Campbell calls while I'm gone, tell him we'll phone him back."

Ava left the boardroom and made her way to Howell's office. She didn't feel comfortable with the idea of sitting behind his desk, so after closing the office door she sat in one of the visitor's chairs. She found Simmons's number on her phone but sat still for a while and gathered her thoughts before dialling.

"This is Randy," he answered.

"And this is Ava Lee. Have you heard from Sammy Rogers in the past few minutes?"

"No."

"I expect you will, unless he decides to keep you in the dark," she said. "They've made us an offer that's wholly inadequate, but for reasons I don't want to get into we've told them we'll accept it."

"I'm glad you've come to your senses," Simmons said.

"You won't be so glad when you hear that I am keeping the warehouse closed."

"Is that until you're paid?"

"No. Reopening the warehouse isn't a condition of the settlement. All they care about is a non-disclosure agreement and a statement that they have no connection to whatever was going on in Chengdu."

"Sammy told me he'd make reopening the warehouse a priority," Simmons snapped.

"Maybe his lawyer didn't hear him properly, because all he asked of us was to consider reopening it as a sign of good faith," Ava said. "Truthfully, Randy, I believe Sammy's people have no interest right now in returning to the business, so they aren't going to need a warehouse. And if they aren't, why should they care if it reopens?"

"This is beginning to sound like a shakedown."

"The last time we spoke you asked me if there's room for you and me to work something out. I'm calling to tell you there is room. I don't think that qualifies as a shakedown."

"What do you want?"

Ava hesitated. One of the things Hugh Campbell had said during their negotiations was that somewhere between what someone wanted and what the other party was prepared to give was a number they both could live with. She had decided on a number and wasn't prepared to budge from it. "I told you before that my clients lost more than thirty million dollars in an investment fund scam that Harvest Table Bible Chapel was involved in," she said deliberately.

"How much of that did Sammy offer you?"

"Six million."

"Do you expect me to pay the difference?"

"I accept that it may be unrealistic to expect full repayment, but six million isn't close to being enough."

"How much more do you want?"

"I can live with twenty million. So if you want the warehouse reopened, someone has to pay us another fourteen."

"I'm not going to give you fourteen million dollars."

"I'm not asking you to. I want you to talk to Sammy. He owes you. However much money he made in Chengdu was because you made it possible. This is his opportunity to pay you back," she said. "You need to go back to him, and the two of you have to make an arrangement. I don't need to know the details."

"You're assuming that Sammy and I are close enough that he'll make an accommodation."

"I am."

"And if we aren't?"

"Then I'll get six million, and you'll get a massive loss of revenue," Ava said. "I know you're probably thinking you can set up another distribution centre, but I promise you that if you do, we'll find it and shut it down."

"Threat upon threat."

"No, promise upon promise."

Simmons went silent. "You'll hear from someone," he said, and he ended the conversation.

(50)

AVA SAT IN HOWELL'S OFFICE FOR SEVERAL MINUTES, going over her conversation with Randy Simmons. She had rarely felt so conflicted. Part of her wanted the twenty million while part of her wanted revenge on Simmons and Rogers. How could she get both? She left the office with that question bouncing around in her mind.

"How did it go with Simmons?" Howell asked as she entered the boardroom.

"He heard me out, and I have no doubt that he's calling Rogers," she said. "Beyond that, I have no idea what the outcome will be."

"How much did you ask for?" asked Howell.

"Twenty million. And if Campbell comes back to us with less, I'm inclined to say no to them."

"And do what?" Derek asked.

"Go to the Mounties and to the news media with the information we have. I couldn't link Rogers to anything, but maybe they can," she said. "And I think Todd should simultaneously launch a civil suit against the chapel for the full thirty million, plus costs and interest and whatever else he can think of. Given that Cunningham is both COO and CFO and we've connected him to Muir, who's connected to the money, the chapel has a level of fiduciary responsibility for what transpired."

"Ava is right about Cunningham," Eddie said. "They can try to pin it on him, they can say he went rogue, but all that would prove is that there wasn't proper oversight within the organization."

"But only about an hour ago we were discussing how going to the Mounties and the media is problematic," Howell said to Ava.

"What we had were questions about its effectiveness. If all we're offered is six million or thereabouts, then I'm prepared to gamble that it can be highly effective," she said.

Howell looked at Eddie. "What do you think?"

"I'm with her."

"I don't know why I bothered asking," he said with a smile, and then looked at his watch. "It's almost eight, and that's my dinnertime. Since we can't leave, why don't we bring in some food. There's a first-rate sandwich shop on the concourse level."

"That sounds fine. Order what you want — I eat everything," said Ava. "While you're doing that, I need to pay a visit to the ladies' room."

"You'll have to go out of the office and turn right."

"I won't be long," she said as she stood up.

Ava left the boardroom and crossed the office floor. She was almost at the door when Matt Mason, Howell's partner, opened it to come in. She nodded at him.

"How's it going?" he asked.

"We don't know yet," she said, not sure how much Howell had told him.

"I hope you get it resolved in your favour. It's really been eating at Todd."

"He seems to be holding up well enough."

"Don't let his demeanour fool you. I've never seen him so on edge."

"Well, we'll know where we stand by the end of the night."

"Good luck," Mason said.

"Thanks," Ava said, and then moved past him.

After using the toilet, Ava washed her hands and splashed cold water over her face. It had been a long, stressful day. She thought she had handled herself well enough, but she felt that her reaction time was slower than it had been when she was collecting debts full-time. Still, they had ended up in a good place.

"Ms. Lee," a woman's voice said. Ava turned and saw Howell's assistant standing at the washroom entrance. "Mr. Howell wanted me to tell you that Mr. Campbell is on the line," she said.

"I'll be right there," Ava said.

She dried her face and followed the woman back into the office. The boardroom door was open, and she could see Howell, Derek, and Eddie hovering over the phone. When Howell saw her, he pressed the speaker button. "Hugh, we can start now. Ava has arrived."

"I'm here at our office with Lisa and Greg, and Pastor Rogers has joined us via conference."

Howell cocked an eyebrow at Ava. "Hello, everyone. Thank you for getting back to us so promptly," he said.

"Before we discuss our revised offer, the pastor wishes to speak to you," Campbell said. "I trust that this can still be off the record."

"Absolutely," Howell said.

There was a stretch of silence, and then Rogers said. "This is rather awkward, and more than a little embarrassing." His voice had the same rich timbre Ava had noticed in the YouTube video, but there was a touch of hesitation to it, as if he was carefully selecting his words. "I don't want to get into the role Patrick Cunningham played in this, or discuss the relationship he had with Malcolm Muir," Rogers said. "The board and I will deal with Patrick appropriately, and whatever was going on in China will come to an immediate halt."

"Are you saying you knew nothing about it?" Ava asked gently.

"I am —" Rogers began.

"And that's all we're going to say about that," Campbell interrupted. "I don't intend to let you interrogate the pastor."

"Then let's move on," Howell said quickly. "I'm keen to hear the revised offer."

Ava could hear the shuffling of paper and some whispering from the other end of the line. When Campbell spoke, he sounded as if he was reading. "We are prepared to offer twenty million dollars to settle this matter if we are satisfied with the non-disclosure agreement and your affirmation that the pastor and the chapel are guilt-free and played no role — directly or indirectly — in any matter relating to the investment fund and the operation that was being run in China," he said.

Howell looked at Ava. "That is acceptable to us," she said.

"Excellent. I'll have Lisa and Greg hammer out a first draft of the agreement tonight, and we'll get it to you by lunchtime tomorrow," Campbell said. He paused and then continued.

"All that leaves is the matter of the Simmons warehouse in Chengdu."

"I will instruct my people to allow Su Na to resume operations," Ava said.

"When can they go back to work?" Campbell asked.

"I have a few questions I'd like to ask before I answer," Ava said.

"Go ahead," said Campbell.

"Do we have the pastor's word that no more pills of any kind will be shipped to Canada?"

"I don't think—" Campbell began.

"You have my word on that," Rogers said.

"Will the websites that have been selling the pills be taken down?"

"They will be taken down as soon as possible."

"Then, as a sign of good faith on our side, I will let Su Na and her team go back into the warehouse tomorrow."

"Thank you," Campbell said. "Hopefully that brings an end to what has been a remarkable day. You know I thought Ms. Lee's deadlines were ridiculous, but I have to admit that they did hurry us along."

"We still need to stay on schedule," Ava said. "The cheque should be in Todd's firm's bank account within seventy-two hours."

"We can make that work," Campbell said. "Todd, we should talk again tomorrow after you've seen our first draft."

"I'll be here," Howell said.

The line went dead. They stared at the phone, no one speaking, until Howell raised his arms above his head in a victory salute and shouted, "Yeah, yeah, yeah!"

"Holy shit, we did it," Eddie said.

Derek looked at Ava, and his smile quickly disappeared. "What's the matter? You look as if we lost," he said to her.

"I should have asked for the entire thirty million," she said. "Rogers was ready to pay anything to get out from under Randy Simmons."

(51)

HOWELL LEFT THE BOARDROOM TO TELL HIS PARTNERS about their success. When he returned, the sandwiches had arrived, and right behind them came Matt Mason carrying two bottles of champagne. For the next hour the boardroom was abuzz as lawyers and staff came to offer their congratulations to Howell and Eddie Ng. Howell made a point of deflecting the praise in Ava's direction, but she waved it off. "This is your moment. Goodness knows, you've worked long and hard enough to earn it."

When things finally settled down, and it was just the four of them again, Derek asked, "Do you really think Sammy Rogers didn't know what Cunningham was doing?"

"I'm not sure," Howell said.

"I'm convinced he knew," Ava said. "But what does it matter? We can all pretend otherwise in return for twenty million dollars and bringing a stop to that business."

"How much of the twenty do you think Simmons paid?" Eddie asked.

"I'd guess not very much, if anything."

"And you're still going to turn them in to the American feds?"

"That's my intention once things are finalized here, but first I have a friend I need to ask for advice. I'll listen to what he has to say," she said. "Now, I don't want to seem rude, but do you think you and Derek could leave Todd and me alone for a few minutes?"

"Sure," Eddie said, getting to his feet.

"Do you want me to drive you home?" Derek asked.

"Sure. This won't take long."

Howell waited until the two men had left the boardroom before asking, "What's this about?"

"Money."

"Ah."

"I've been doing some rough calculations," she said. "My usual fee is thirty percent. I think I'll take only twenty-five this time, because I want your clients to get back more than half of what was stolen. I've recovered all of Mr. Gregory's money separately, so Mrs. Gregory doesn't need part of the twenty million."

"That's quite considerate of you."

"There is a catch."

"Of course."

Ava smiled. "It's nothing outrageous. You will get an email from the law firm of Burgess and Bowlby in Hong Kong instructing you to transfer my share to a bank account in the U.K. I don't want my name attached to the transfer, and as far as anyone is concerned, those were never my funds."

"Tax evasion?"

"No, it's a bit more complex than that."

"So I shouldn't ask?"

"You can ask, but I won't answer," Ava said. "I do assure you, with all the solemnity that Pastor Rogers can muster, there's nothing illegal involved."

"Burgess and Bowlby?"

"You will hear directly from Brenda Burgess."

"I'll look out for her instructions."

"And with that, I think we can call it a day."

"And what a day it was."

Eddie and Derek were sitting at a desk near the boardroom when Ava and Howell exited. "I have rarely been so ready to go home," she said to Derek. "Between the jet lag and the massive drop in adrenalin, I'm completely whacked."

"I'll touch base in the morning when I get the draft from Campbell," Howell said.

"Don't bother unless there's been a change," Ava said. She looked at Eddie. "It's been nice working with you. Say hello to my Vietnamese friends."

"I'll do that."

She looked at Howell. "I think I should give you a hug."

"I'd welcome one," he said, extending his arms.

A moment later, Ava and Derek walked silently to the elevator and rode to the ground floor without saying a word.

"Where's your car?" she asked as they climbed down the steps to King Street.

"In the same lot I've been using."

"I was hoping it was closer," she said, looping her arm through his. "If I fall over, pick me up."

(52)

ON THE RIDE BACK TO HER CONDO AVA KEPT MAKING mental lists of the things she wanted to do, but fatigue had taken over to the point that when Derek stopped in front of her building, he had to remind her they had arrived. She climbed out of the car. "You can tell Mimi and Mrs. Gregory about the money now, and make sure you send June's bank information to Todd."

"They were on my list."

"Am I repeating myself?"

"Not yet, but I sense you're getting close."

"I am very tired."

"Go to bed. You've earned a good night's sleep and more," he said. "We love you so much, you know. I don't know how we'll ever be able to repay you for this."

"I love you too, but I hate any mention of repayment. You know there's no need."

When she entered the condo, Ava fought off the urge to go directly to bed and instead went into the kitchen. She opened her notebook and made a list of people she needed to call. Brenda Burgess and Chen were near the top of it. She opened her laptop and started writing an email to Brenda, then stopped, realizing that some other things took priority. She shook her head, trying to get rid of the fuzziness, and reached for her phone.

"*Wei*," Han answered.

"There's been a change in plans. Let Su Na know that the warehouse can reopen for business today. You can tell your men to leave."

"You've resolved your problem?"

"I have, and I couldn't have done it without you. Many, many thanks. When I talk to Xu, I'll be sure to tell him what a great help you were."

"I appreciate your putting in a good word. As for the job, it was a nice change for us, something different. Don't hesitate to call if you ever need anything else."

"Please give my best to Lu and Ru Shi," she said.

Her next call was to Singapore, and it went directly to Jasmine Yip's voicemail. "Jasmine, this is Ava. We've reached an accommodation with Harvest Table Bible Chapel. You should not hear from Muir again. I don't know how Cunningham will react, but if he gives you any problems, let me know, and I'll deal with it," she said.

She looked at the notebook. May Ling or Xu? Auntie Grace answered the phone in Shanghai and, after a few pleasantries, turned it over to Xu.

"How's it going?" he asked.

"It's done. We didn't get everything we wanted, but we've made some people a lot happier than they were," she said. "Han and his people were indispensable. I promised him I'd ask you to send him more iPhones."

"It's the least I can do to thank him for looking after you so well," Xu said. "What's next on your schedule?"

"I have to spend a few more days here until matters are completely finalized, and then I'm going to Taipei to be with Fai. When her shoot ends, we'll come to Shanghai and then move on to Hong Kong. I'll let you know as soon as the dates become firm."

"Auntie Grace will be thrilled."

"Give her a hug for me," Ava said. "I'll call you again in a few days."

She tried May Ling's office number next, but it went to voicemail, as did the call to her cellphone. Ava repeated what she'd said to Xu about Taipei, Shanghai, and Hong Kong and then promised to call again the next day.

She returned to the email to Brenda Burgess. Brenda, sometime in the next few days, please forward the U.K. banking information for BB Productions to Todd Howell, a lawyer here in Toronto. I have cc'd him on this email so you have his address. Todd's firm will be transferring five million Canadian dollars to the BB account in about a week. Hope this finds you and Richard well. Best, Ava

She started another email, and then decided that, given the subject matter, it made more sense to phone Chen.

"This is Ava Lee. Could you put me through to Mr. Chen, please," she said when his receptionist answered.

"Ava, where are you?" he asked a moment later. "When I talked to Fai a few days ago, she mentioned something about Chengdu. For the life of me I couldn't figure out what would take you there."

"I was helping a friend with a problem. It's solved now, and

I'm back in Toronto, but I'm going to Taipei in a few days to spend some time with Fai," she said. "I'll try not to be too much of a distraction."

"Were you calling to tell me that?"

"No, I want to know if you've worked up a budget yet for *Tiananmen Square*."

"I've done a rough pass. As long as we can avoid going overboard with tanks and the like, and if Lau Lau can stick to a tight shooting schedule, I think we can bring it in under sixty million yuan."

"Eight million U.S. dollars?"

"Yes, that's about right."

"In a few days there'll be five million sitting in the U.K. bank account of a company called BB Productions. You will have sole signing authority for that account. I'll have to arrange for my Hong Kong lawyer, Brenda Burgess, to send you the necessary paperwork to make that happen, but we can do that after the money is in place. When you need more, we'll find a way to get it into BB."

"You're giving me sole signing authority? What kind of system do you want in place for budget control?"

"You're my budget control. Why would I need to get involved?"

"I really appreciate that level of trust. I'll make sure it isn't misplaced," Chen said. "Can I tell Lau Lau we're going ahead? He's been quietly harassing me for news."

"Sure, tell Lau Lau," she said, thinking that she couldn't jinx herself any more than she already had.

"And would you mind if I join you in Taipei for a few days? We might have to do some shooting there, and I'd like to scout some potential locations."

"I'd love to see you, and with Fai on set all day, I'll have time on my hands."

"Perfect. Email me your schedule when it's set."

"I'll do that," Ava said, and ended the conversation.

She went to the fridge, took out a bottle of Chardonnay, and poured herself a glass. That simple act reminded her of Fai's absence. Ava thought about calling her but knew she'd be on set. Instead she sat at the laptop and wrote: It was a good day. We managed to get Mrs. Gregory's money back and a substantial amount for the other investors. It will take two or three days to wrap things up here, but once that's done, I'm heading to Taipei. Chen may join me for a few days to scout locations for *Tiananmen Square*. He's also going to tell Lau Lau we're going ahead with the film. So that's it—I'm in. I can't say I'm not feeling a little apprehensive about the outcome, but I'm convinced it's the right thing to do. Love you! I'll call you in the morning my time.

Ava yawned. Her bed was beckoning, but she had one more phone call to make.

Alasdair Dulles was a CIA agent. He and Ava had worked together in the Philippines solving a mystery involving the mass murder of potential jihadists. The murders had been orchestrated by a rogue agent who was financed by an American billionaire with strong evangelical ties. Dulles had made it clear that he didn't share the billionaire's religious beliefs, which made Ava comfortable with the idea of calling him. In truth, he was also the only senior American official she knew well enough to feel comfortable sharing confidences with.

The phone rang four times. Disappointment was settling in when she heard a familiar voice. "Goodness me, is this really Ava Lee?"

"Alasdair, how are you doing?"

"Same old, same old," he said. "How about you?"

"Things are fairly normal."

"Except that your idea of normal is far different from anything I've ever encountered." He laughed. "And I don't imagine this is just a social call. Are you in Manila?"

"I'm in Toronto, and no, it isn't a social call. Although even if you can't help, it's good to get in touch with you again. We worked very well together."

"Yes, we did, and it's still being talked about," he said.

"As I remember, neither it nor I was being talked about kindly."

"That depended on who was talking. You did have some detractors, but I assure you, you have at least as many admirers, including me and Brad Harrison."

"What's your position these days?"

"I have been rehabilitated. I'm now station head."

"Congratulations. And how about Brad, is he still working?" Ava asked, referring to Dulles's boss in Washington.

"He just keeps rolling along. He could have retired last year, but given the political atmosphere in Washington, he's decided that leaving would be irresponsible." He paused, then continued. "Now are you going to tell me why you're calling?"

"I need your help with something."

"That's a rarity."

"No, seriously," she said. "I have a problem that involves an American evangelical organization and the illegal sale of drugs into the U.S. from China."

ACKNOWLEDGEMENTS

THE IDEA FOR THIS BOOK CAME TO ME FOUR OR FIVE years ago, and I actually started a first draft before abandoning it after fifty or sixty pages. The story never left me, but it did begin to morph and develop in different directions. Actually, maybe too many directions, because the manuscript I submitted was 560 pages long. Doug Richmond, my editor, must have cursed a few times as he tried to winnow it down to an acceptable size. Now that you've read the final version, I hope you agree he's done a great job.

Thanks are also owed to Maria Golikova, the managing editor at House of Anansi, and my team of first readers. Thanks aren't actually sufficient for the readers. They make contributions large and small that strengthen every book. They are — in no particular order — Catherine Rosebrugh, John Kruithof, Carol Shetler, Ashok Ramchandani, Kristine Wookey, Robin Spano, Christina Sit, Carleena Chiang, and Lam Lau.

No book is written in my world without the active support of my wife, Lorraine, and no book is sold without my agent, Bruce Westwood. They know how much I appreciate their support.

IAN HAMILTON is the author of fourteen novels in the Ava Lee series and two in the Lost Decades of Uncle Chow Tung series. His books have been shortlisted for numerous prizes, including the Arthur Ellis Award, the Barry Award, and the Lambda Literary Prize, and are national bestsellers. BBC Culture named Hamilton one of the ten mystery/crime writers from the past thirty years that should be on your bookshelf. The Ava Lee series is being adapted for television.

NOW AVAILABLE
from House of Anansi Press

The Ava Lee series

Prequel and Book 1

Book 2

Book 3

Book 4

Book 5

Book 6

Book 7

Book 8

Book 9

Book 10

Book 11

Book 12

www.houseofanansi.com • www.facebook.com/avaleenovels
www.ianhamiltonbooks.com • www.twitter.com/avaleebooks

ALSO AVAILABLE
from House of Anansi Press

Uncle returns in...

The Lost Decades of Uncle Chow Tung

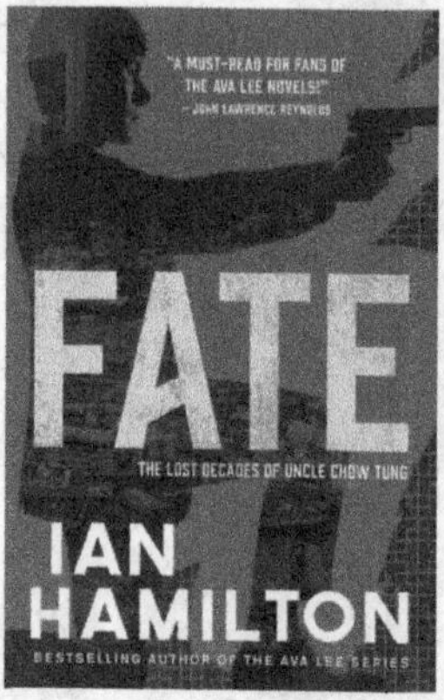

COMING SOON

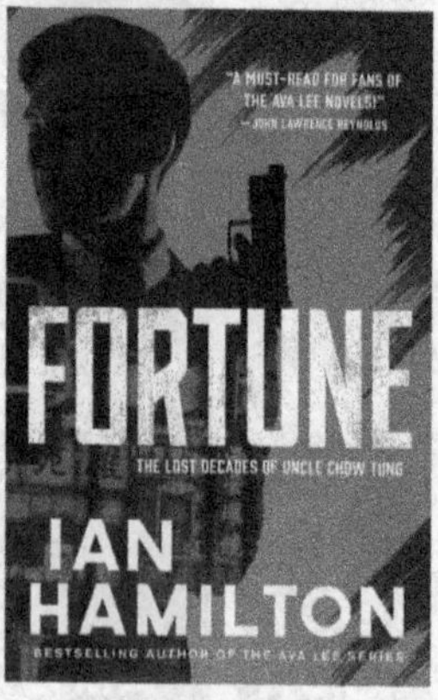

January 2021

WWW.HOUSEOFANANSI.COM